"I haven't thanked you for rescuing me."

Vivian smiled at Billy, determined not to reveal any of her trepidation at his size and her vulnerability. "Thank you. You were an answer to a prayer."

He nodded solemnly. "You're welcome. I'm sure 'twas God that led me there. No other reason I should be where I could hear you." He tipped his head toward the baby. "I guess rightly speaking, it was this wee thing I heard."

Suddenly, the windows rattled as the door behind her opened. A cold breeze blasted across the room. She cuddled Joshua to her chest, protecting him from the icy invasion.

An older woman walked into the room, scrubbing her hands over her hair until it was a tangled mess. Vivian's jaw dropped. She suddenly realized who they were.

Mad Mrs. Black.

And her son Big Billy.

Everyone was terrified of the pair. Rumors said they'd turned wild after being captives of Natives for years. But despite the talk, could he be anything but a good man if he acknowledged God's hand in rescuing her?

Linda Ford

Dakota Child
&
Dakota Father

HARLEQUIN® LOVE INSPIRED®CLASSICS

LOVE INSPIRED BOOKS

ISBN-13: 978-1-335-47361-5

Dakota Child & Dakota Father

Copyright © 2019 by Harlequin Books S.A.

The publisher acknowledges the copyright holder of the individual works as follows:

Dakota Child
Copyright © 2009 by Linda Ford

Dakota Father
Copyright © 2011 by Linda Ford

Recycling programs for this product may not exist in your area.

www.Harlequin.com

Printed in U.S.A.

CONTENTS

DAKOTA CHILD 7

DAKOTA FATHER 231

Linda Ford lives on a ranch in Alberta, Canada, near enough to the Rocky Mountains that she can enjoy them on a daily basis. She and her husband raised fourteen children—four homemade, ten adopted. She currently shares her home and life with her husband, a grown son, a live-in paraplegic client and a continual (and welcome) stream of kids, kids-in-law, grandkids and assorted friends and relatives.

Books by Linda Ford

Love Inspired Historical

Big Sky Country

Montana Cowboy Daddy
Montana Cowboy Family
Montana Cowboy's Baby
Montana Bride by Christmas
Montana Groom of Convenience
Montana Lawman Rescuer

Montana Cowboys

The Cowboy's Ready-Made Family
The Cowboy's Baby Bond
The Cowboy's City Girl

Christmas in Eden Valley

A Daddy for Christmas
A Baby for Christmas
A Home for Christmas

Visit the Author Profile page
at Harlequin.com for more titles.

DAKOTA CHILD

I have loved thee with an everlasting love;
therefore with loving kindness have I drawn thee.
—*Jeremiah* 31:3

To my grandson, Tyson.
I've watched you grow and mature and my heart
is filled with pride and joy. I love you and pray
God will bless you all the days of your life.

Chapter One

Quinten, North Dakota, 1890

She was lost. The world had disappeared into swirling, biting snow. The rough ground beneath her feet convinced her she'd veered off the road. Her toe caught a lump and she staggered to keep her balance.

Nineteen-year-old Vivian Halliday's thoughts filled with a fury of denials. She couldn't be lost. No one would realize her predicament. No one would look for her. No one knew where she was. *Lord, God, help me.*

The same prayer she'd uttered so many times. Not for herself. She knew she didn't deserve it. There were times she hadn't listened to God or followed His voice as she ought. There were times she'd totally ignored Him and done her own thing. But she prayed for another and, lately, her prayer had grown more urgent. Today, however, her need was solid and desperate. The cold had already tightened her ribs to the point she could barely breathe, but thinking about how much she had to lose gave icy spears to the cold as it clawed into her lungs.

Snow coated her cheeks and iced her lashes. The wind tore at her cloak. She pulled the heavy woolen material tighter, then bent her head low and turned her back to the storm, letting it push her. It mattered not where she went. One direction was the same as another in this white wilderness.

"God, help me," she called, but the wind whipped her words into silence. She stumbled. Righted herself. Swayed.

A mewling sound came from inside her cloak.

The tiny cry filled her with fresh determination and she lifted her head and peered into the white nothingness.

She must escape this storm. She just had to keep moving and find shelter. Nothing must defeat her—not man, not beast, not beastly weather. *Lord, God, in You I trust. Save me.*

Snow blasted around her. Dizziness swept over her until she felt like she rode the circling wind. She could no longer tell up from down and melted into the cold, snow-shrouded ground.

The thin sound, from close to her heart, came again. All her pulses crashed against her skin like thunder. She would give her life to save the tiny life she sheltered.

She shook the basket cradled beneath the meager protection of the cape, trying unsuccessfully to still the protesting sound. Was her precious bundle suffering from the cold? She dare not look and allow even a hint of the cold to enter the shelter under her cape.

Suddenly, a huge shape darkened the snow to her left. She shrank back, her limbs brittle with fear. Was it a bear? A wandering, angry bull? She rocked harder. *Hush. Hush.*

"Someone there?" the massive shape bellowed.

Vivian sank back, trying to disappear into the snow. She crushed the basket closer and patted the sides.

The bulky figure swept trunk-sized arms about,

searching for the source of the sound that wouldn't stop despite all Vivian's desperate measures. The cold bit at her throat. The wind howled louder. She prayed it would drown the sound coming from beneath her cape.

The creature—be it man or otherwise—encountered her shoulder with his great paw.

She stiffened. Perhaps he'd think her a bush and move on.

Fingers probed gently down her arm then up and across her back.

She held her breath. *Lord, God, save us.* She wanted to be left alone to find her way to town and safety. Instead, she was swept into strong arms, the cloak tucked around her, her face pressed into a broad shoulder. Then with great strides the huge creature plowed into the storm.

Protests formed but her lips refused to work, frozen with both cold and fear. One solitary thought remained in sharp focus—being captured by a wild man did not fit into her plans.

The wind held less bite. The cold's sting moderated. Must be the bulk of the man protecting her.

The last remnant of warm blood jolted through her veins. She would not find protection in the arms of a stranger. She struggled to escape.

"Settle down. I'll get you to a warm, safe place."

The thought of warmth enticed. But safety? She might be safer in the storm. She opened her mouth to protest but the cold grabbed her throat. She couldn't speak and her ineffectual efforts to escape allowed the snow to sneak under her cloak, robbing her of the bit of warmth his arms provided. She resisted for the space of another heartbeat, but the safety of his chest proved too alluring and she burrowed deeper into the bulky protection.

"That's better," he murmured, as he continued his hurried journey. His footsteps thudded hollowly as if his boots encountered wood, then he bent forward and took another step.

The wind ceased. A golden light washed over Vivian's eyelids. Loath to face reality, fearing it might be unkind, she kept her eyes shut.

Her rescuer shifted and lowered her into a chair. "Let's see what you have here." His huge hands brushed her arm as he spread open her cape. Strong fingers began to unwrap her grip on the basket.

"No." She jerked her eyes open as alarm returned so fierce and overpowering that her heart thudded against her chest. She stared into a square face, half buried in a thick fur hat. Eyes as blue as a spring sky regarded her with what she could almost describe as amusement. His mouth tipped to one side in a wry expression. The man was huge, towering over her, blocking everything except bright flames from the fireplace at her side. For a moment, she ignored her fears and her need to protect all that was hers and darted a longing look at the promise of heat.

"I'll just have me a little look." He again sought to open the basket.

The cold tormenting Vivian's skin and bones balled up inside her heart and froze there. She clutched the basket more tightly to her chest and hunched her shoulders protectively as if she could defend herself against this giant. "Just let me sit here a minute until I'm warm," she choked out.

His eyes narrowed. His mouth drew into a thin line. "I ain't about to hurt you none." He waited.

Did he expect her to believe him? She darted a look at his mitt-sized fist on the handle of the basket. He could crush her with one hand. The damage he could do to a smaller body, an infant, was beyond imagination.

She shivered, and not from cold.

The mewling sound came again, louder, more demanding. Was everything all right? She ached to be able to check but instead clutched the basket closer and prayed he would leave her alone.

"Let's have a look," the giant said, and lifted her hand easily from the handle even though she squeezed as hard as she could.

She sprang forward, ready to defend. Realizing how futile her efforts would be, she frantically tried to think what she could do. Seemed the best she could hope for was that she could move faster than he. She tried to force her muscles to coil into readiness despite their numb coldness and found them stiffly uncooperative.

He put the basket on a stool before the fireplace. The warmth of the yellow-and-orange flames made her ache to hunker down and extend her hands. But she didn't dare move. Who knew what would trigger this man into action? And she wasn't about to hazard a guess as to what sort of action he might take. Instead she waited, alert and ready to protect what was hers.

He bent over and eagerly folded back the blanket to reveal the contents, then jumped back as if someone shot him. "It's a baby," he muttered. The look he fired her accused her of some sort of trickery. "I thought you had a cat."

His eagerness at thinking cat and his shock at seeing baby were such a marked contrast to what she expected, she almost laughed with relief. Fearing her amusement would spark anger in the man, she changed her mind before the feeling reached either her lips or her eyes.

He fixed her with a probing stare. "What you doing out in a storm with a baby?"

"I got lost." Did he really think she planned to be

out with this precious infant? The man who gave her a ride toward Quinten, her hometown and destination, had dropped her off with an apology that he must take the other road, and assurances she was only a few miles from town and could easily walk the distance.

He obviously hadn't expected it to storm and if there'd been signs of its approach, she hadn't noticed. The storm caught her in the face as unexpectedly as if she'd fallen. In the driving wind she must have gotten turned around. Once the snow engulfed her, all that mattered was protecting the baby.

The man leaned forward and peered cautiously into the basket. "A boy or girl?" The huge man shifted his gaze to her, his eyes curious.

Vivian smiled. "A boy." The sweetest, fairest, most precious little boy in the whole world. She would never allow anyone to take him from her again. And she'd fight this giant of a man with everything at her disposal if she must.

"How old is he?"

"Almost two months." Seven weeks, four days and—at last reckoning of the time—six hours.

The baby's thin cry continued.

"I think he's hungry. Maybe you should feed him." The man nodded at her chest.

Vivian's cheeks thawed instantly. He expected her to nurse the baby. "There's a bottle in the basket." She'd have to find a source of milk as soon as possible. She stilled the panic twisting her heart. Where would she find milk in this place? She suddenly had a hundred different details to consider. She knew nothing about caring for a baby despite the few lessons Marie had given her. Marie had always been the one to gravitate toward the infants in the orphanage, while Vivian sought sanctuary in the kitchen. And when she'd been sent out to work for the Weimers, there had been no babies. How would she manage?

The man tossed his hat to one side. His dusty-yellow hair tangled in a mess of curls. Something stirred at the back of Vivian's mind. He seemed vaguely familiar. She tried to think where she'd seen him, but before she could figure it out he leaned over, scooped the baby from the basket and offered the bundle to Vivian.

She looked into a wrinkled and squalling face. Suddenly, an incredible ache filled her and she cradled her son to her chest, stilling a sob but unable to stop her eyes from growing moist. She might not know about caring for this little one but she knew about loving him and wanting him. The rest would follow.

"He got a proper name?"

She had not been allowed to name him legally but had, in her thoughts, given him her father's name. "Joshua. After my father."

"Big name for such a little bitty thing."

"He'll grow—" She slid an amused glance at the big man. "Some."

He looked startled and then his eyes crinkled with understanding. "Ain't too many get to my size, but his name will suit, I 'spect."

Vivian smiled at the baby. "It suits him just fine." For some reason it did. "Can you hand me the bottle?"

He pulled it from the basket, hesitated. "You want I should warm it?"

"Oh, of course." She knew that. Just hadn't thought of it. Again, doubts grabbed at her resolve. Someone else should be caring for this tiny scrap of humanity. Someone who knew how to tend a baby. Remembering the seven weeks, four days and six hours when someone else did, she forced away her uncertainty. No one else should care for this baby but her. She would learn how just like every first-time mother did.

As the man moved to plop the bottle in the open kettle hanging over the flames, cats sprang from every corner of the room, meowing and clamoring around him.

"Now, you all just settle down. Ma will be in with your milk soon 'nough. This here is for that noisy fellow over there." He rubbed the heads of several of the animals.

Ma? The man was married. That boded well for Vivian and Joshua. And they milked a cow. She relaxed fractionally and jiggled the crying baby as she waited for the man to take the bottle from the hot water, and let some of the contents drip into his mouth.

"Seems about right." He handed it to her.

She'd only fed the baby a couple of times before and always with the help and supervision of someone who knew how to do it with ease and comfort. Even on her ride today, the farmer's wife had begged to give him his bottle. She took a deep breath, prayed the baby would know more about what to do than she, and popped the nipple into the open mouth. The baby stopped crying and gagged.

Vivian jerked the bottle away and stilled her panic. What if she drowned the poor little thing? Maybe they were right in thinking she wasn't fit to raise him. Again she yanked her thoughts back from heading in that direction. She'd endured almost eight weeks of aching arms and a weeping heart. Never again would she go through that.

Praying she wouldn't harm him, she nudged the bottle into the baby's mouth again. He pushed at the nipple with his tongue, swallowed back a mouthful of milk, looked startled then settled into sucking.

She slowly let her lungs relax. This wasn't so bad.

She glanced about the room. The brick fireplace filled most of the wall to her right. A recessed area beside it held split logs. Braided rugs lay on the polished wood floor in front of the chair where she sat, and before the wooden rocking chair facing her. On the far side of the room was a kitchen table in rich brown wood and the normal kitchen things—chairs, stove, cupboards. A straw broom leaned in the corner next to the stove, along with a bucketful of kindling. At the corner opposite the fireplace a basket of raw wool and some carders sat beside a low chair. To one side, a quilt in muted grays and browns lay half rolled on a frame. Two narrow windows revealed nothing but white. The storm continued. How long would she be stranded here waiting for it to end? Stuck with a man who could easily harm them. But the room showed all the signs of ordinary farm life. She almost breathed scents of a happy, contented home and this squelched her fears. Surely she and the baby would be safe even with this huge man until such time as she could complete her journey. All she had to do was be as quiet and unobtrusive as possible. The chair she sat in had stuffed arms and she let herself sink into the deep cushions.

Joshua sucked at a leisurely pace as if he hadn't been demanding food for the last half hour. Then he stopped. She jiggled the bottle. He'd only taken half an inch. Surely he needed more. Didn't he? She truly had no idea.

"Little guy needs a burp, maybe."

Vivian nodded. Marie had told her that. She'd seen it done. How hard could it be? Gingerly, she lifted the baby to her shoulder and patted his tiny back. Warm and cuddly, he made snuffling sounds against her neck and she smiled.

He let out a noisy burp and she laughed. Such a large sound from such a tiny body.

She resumed feeding him. The next time he stalled, she knew enough to burp him. This wasn't so hard after all, even with that big man watching her. She darted a glance at him. His gaze lingered on the baby with a look of amusement. She tried to place the twinge of recognition. Where had she seen him? She scoured her memory but came up empty.

Only a bit of milk remained in the bottle. Joshua curled in her arms, already asleep. So this is what they meant by sleeping like a baby. So peaceful, so relaxed and content. Her love for her son warmed and sweetened her insides.

She shifted, thinking to put Joshua back in the basket, but changed her mind. She liked the comfort of his little body, the way he settled against her as if welcoming her care.

"You got clean nappies?" the man asked.

Vivian kept her attention on the baby. Change wet pants? She could handle that. She wished she'd paid more attention to Marie's instructions but at the time she'd been far more concerned with making her escape before Matron or some of her helpers prevented it.

No doubt everything she needed was in the shopping basket, which served nicely for carrying baby supplies. Marie had prepared it for her saying no one who saw her would suspect the basket held a baby.

She pulled the basket closer. Yes, a wad of white nappies, a tiny blue sweater set and several white nighties lay in the bottom. She pulled out a nappy and looked from it to the baby. Where? How? Could she really do it?

The man pushed the stool closer. "You could lay him here."

"Thanks." She sucked in a deep breath and carefully

transferred the baby. She unwrapped him from the bundle of blankets until he lay exposed in his nightie. His tiny fists curled against his chest. She rolled back the skirt to expose thin legs and amazingly small feet in blue booties. Her heart pushed up in her throat as a wave of tenderness washed through her. Her baby. Her son. So little. So perfect.

And wearing a dampish nappy fixed with big pins.

Undoing the pins posed no problem. Nor did removing the wet nappy. But what to do with it? She settled for dropping it on the floor. The clean nappy was folded to fit. Vivian did her best to fix it back in place the way the other had been. *There you go.* She resisted the urge to say the words aloud as she pulled Joshua's nightie down and wrapped him up again, quietly smug with her success. 'Course, she shouldn't take all the credit. God helps fools and children. He certainly had taken care of her this day. She could well be frozen to death—Joshua, too—if not for this man, who was no doubt guided by God's divine hand....

"I haven't thanked you for rescuing me." She smiled, determined not to reveal any of her trepidation at his size and her vulnerability. "Thank you. You were an answer to a prayer."

He nodded solemnly. "You're welcome. I'm sure 'twas God that led me there. No other reason I should be where I could hear you." He tipped his head toward the baby. "I guess rightly speaking, it was this wee thing I heard."

She met his eyes squarely. Despite his size, could he be anything but a good man if he acknowledged God's hand in rescuing her?

The windows rattled as the door behind her opened. A cold breeze, straight from the jaws of the storm, blasted across the room. She cuddled Joshua to her chest, protecting him from the icy invasion.

The man at her side, who had been hunkered down on a sturdy wooden stool, bolted to his feet. "Ma's back. Ma, Ma…"

But whatever he meant to say was drowned by an ear-splitting scream.

Vivian jerked to her feet and spun around.

A woman swaddled in a bulky woolen coat and hat faced her, a bucket of frothy milk in one hand. The woman put the pail on the floor, yanked her hat off and rubbed her pale hair into wild disarray, all the time making the sound of a cat with its tail slammed in the door.

Bony fingers of fear dug into Vivian's scalp. She tried to back up but ran into the stool she'd used a few minutes earlier for changing the baby. The fireplace blocked her retreat to her left; the big man blocked her right.

The screeching woman stopped to suck in air.

"Ma, I found them in the storm. I couldn't leave them to freeze."

The woman scrubbed her hands over her hair again until it was a cloud of faded blond tangles. "Nobody comes here. Nobody." Her voice shivered along Vivian's nerves.

Vivian's jaw dropped. Although she hadn't seen this woman or her son in eight years, she knew who they were.

Mad Mrs. Black.

And her son, Big Billy.

Everyone was terrified of the pair. Rumors said they turned wild after being captives of Indians for years. Vivian scrambled to remember what she knew or heard. But it was just before her own disaster. Seems she'd misplaced bits of her memory along with losing her parents and home. About all she knew was she couldn't have landed in a worse situation.

She clutched the baby to her chest and prayed to be able to save him from this savage pair.

Chapter Two

He saw the way she jolted. Knew she'd figured out who they were. Knew, too, what direction her thoughts took. He'd heard the comments often enough, seen hands raised to mouths to unsuccessfully hide a whisper. Everyone thought the Blacks were mad and dangerous. He'd long ago given up trying to prove otherwise, no longer cared what people thought so long as they left him and Ma alone. Though, if he could convince just one person it wasn't true, it would be the woman standing wide-eyed with fear not inches from his elbow.

But he didn't have time to deal with that right now. Ma was about to explode before his very eyes. She didn't handle strangers well, never let anyone in her house.

Ma choked off another screech, sent Vivian another fear-filled look, then glared at Billy. "Why'd you bring her?" She poked her mittened hand toward the woman as if she could drive her away. "Get out."

"Ma, it's okay. It's only until the storm lets up."

He couldn't remember a time when she didn't go from an ordinary housewife to this raving creature when anything upset her routine, though he guessed before she'd been captured by Indians, she'd been perfectly normal. However, he was too young at the time to remember.

Ma cranked around.

Sensing her intention, Billy strode for the door. Only the fact she struggled with the latch allowed him to get there before she opened it. He took her hands. "Ma, what are you doing?"

"Let me go." Her voice was thin and high-pitched.

"Ma, you can't go out. It's storming." He took her restless hands, guided her to the kitchen area and pulled out a chair. He tried to ease her down, persisting until she gave in and sat. As soon as he released her, she jerked the chair around so she gave her back to the woman.

Ma hadn't even glanced at the baby. Maybe if she did… For some unknown reason, he wanted Ma and Vivian to be friends. A little jeering finger jabbed inside his thoughts. In a mocking voice, it insisted Billy knew the reason. But Billy had grown very good at ignoring things he couldn't do anything about, and he shut out the voice.

"Ma, there's a tiny baby. You want to see him?"

For answer, she started to rock.

He took that for no. For himself, he could barely take his eyes off the little critter. He'd nursed every kind of baby animal—kittens, puppies, a fawn, several kinds of birds, the usual calves and colts. But he'd never seen a bitty-sized human. Tiny little fingers and toes, a kiss of a mouth, ears that folded like spring buds, legs no bigger than his little finger. New life was such a miracle of God's powerful love and creative power. But this replica of humanity took his breath away. Everything in perfect tiny detail. He knew a protectiveness stronger than he'd ever known before. He thought of the few minutes when he'd held Vivian in his arms, plowing through the storm toward home. He hadn't known it was her until he dropped her in the chair but he remembered the almost nothing-ness weight of her, the way she had fought so bravely and then the sweetness of her head pressed to the hollow of his shoulder as she huddled against the cold. He curled his fists. He was being fanciful and tried to remember how to push his thoughts beyond acknowledgment.

It took a few seconds for him to succeed, then he shifted his attention to Vivian. He liked the way she cradled the baby to her, though perhaps as much out of fear as any other reason. Everyone was afraid of the Blacks.

However, good or bad, she was stuck here until the storm ended. Just as Ma was stuck with the uninvited pair.

"I guess you figured out who we are." Seeing her again made him wish for a heartbeat his life was different. Only half a heartbeat, really.

The woman nodded. "I remember you from school."

"Didn't know if you'd recall." He'd gone to school less than two weeks before he figured out he wasn't exactly welcome. He recalled only one person who had treated him kindly. He'd almost decided to continue to face his tormentors in order to see her—Vivian Halliday. Looks to be she was now other than Halliday. Married with a baby. With a practiced hand, he pushed aside any hint of regret. He only hoped she was happy.

"You're Billy Black."

"Huh." He was surprised she didn't call him Big Billy Black. It was the only way he'd ever heard his name said in town.

"You probably don't remember me. I was barely twelve last time I was in Quinten. Vivian Halliday."

She'd called herself Halliday. Perhaps an unconscious slip of the tongue.

"I remember." He'd recognized her the instant her eyelids snapped open and he looked into coffee-brown eyes revealing fear, and lots more besides. He saw flickers of the determination and gentleness he remembered from school. How often he'd thought of her and wondered how she fared.

He hadn't even realized she was gone at first, though he wondered that he never managed to glimpse her. 'Course, he avoided town as carefully as he avoided crossing paths with a skunk. Only necessity drove him to venture in by way of alleys.

It was Lucas, the man at the general store, who served him at the back door, who told him of the Halliday's misfortune.

"Mr. and Mrs. Halliday were among those who died in the flu epidemic. Their daughter went to an orphanage."

Remembering what happened to Vivian, Billy's fists still clenched. He would have given her a home. A curl of amusement lifted one corner of his mouth. Yeah, he could see anyone agreeing to that.

Best he face the situation head-on. "I guess you know what everyone else knows. That I'm too big to be trusted and Ma is crazy."

Vivian shifted her gaze from Ma to him. He saw the same compassion tucked beneath her fear that he'd seen eight years ago and had never been able to forget. Somewhere beyond the reach of his control, long-denied yearnings tossed rebellious heads reminding him of all the things he couldn't have—and somehow they all centered in this particular woman. He did his best to ignore the treacherous thoughts. She had always been out of reach and now even more so as a married woman. He had only one concern—keeping her safe until she could get back to her home.

As if aware no one watched her, Ma bolted to her feet and made a break for the door.

Billy didn't need to hurry to beat her to it. He leaned against the wooden barrier and crossed his arms over his chest. It about killed him to see her this way. What people didn't know was she didn't act crazy all the time. Only when something upset her bad, and nothing upset her like having a stranger close by. Couldn't get much closer than in her own house. She must be knotted up inside like an old hunk of neglected rope. He hated opposing her but he had to make sure Ma wouldn't hurt herself.

"Let me go." Ma's words were breathless as if forced from forgetful lungs.

"You ain't going into the storm."

Ma darted a glance out of the corner of her eye, indicating the stranger in their midst. "Can't stay here. You know what they say."

He knew. Had heard more'n he cared to. "Crazy Indian woman." "Unnatural giant." Neither was true. No one, not even he, knew what Ma had suffered in captivity but she had been a good and affectionate mother since her return. And Billy didn't figure he was that big. He'd met a couple of muleskinners even bigger.

"She's got to stay until the storm ends. She and the little one. They'd die outside."

Ma nodded. "I know. But I can't stay. I can't stay."

He led her back to the chair. "I'll make sure she doesn't bother you." He waited until his mother settled before he threw a length of wood into the iron staples on either side of the door, effectively barring it. He knew from experience Ma couldn't lift the heavy piece out of place.

She keened like a woman bereft of her baby. The sound drove nails to Billy's heart. It was not like he had any choice. Vivian and her baby had to stay until the storm ended. And he had to keep Ma from running out into the cold.

He faced Vivian, her brown eyes wide in what he took for fear. The hood of her cloak fell back to reveal damp brown hair in a soft roll. The cloak slipped down her shoulders. From the little he could see, it appeared she wore a plain gray dress. She must have married a man of simple means. The idea caused him to swallow hard. She deserved to wear fine things like lace and velvet.

"Ma won't hurt you."

With a flick of her eyelids, without uttering a word, she effectively expressed her doubt.

"Your husband will be out looking for you." Would he have another stranger in their midst before nightfall? Ma would have a really hard time with another person stranded in her house, especially a man.

"I don't expect so." She shifted her eyes toward the fire, as if fascinated with the bright flames.

"But…" 'Twere none of his business, but if he had a wife and wee son he would not rest unless he was certain they were safe. Perhaps they'd argued and she wondered if her husband would let angry words keep him from action. But love quickly forgave. "He'll want to be sure you've found shelter—especially with the baby so small."

She shifted, darted a look at him. In the brief glimpse of her wide brown eyes, Billy saw something that set his mouth into a hard line. He'd seen fear. "Are you running from your husband? Afraid of him for some reason?" She need not fear a cruel man so long as Billy was around.

"No. Not at all." Her fingers moved restlessly against her son's blanket.

Billy wasn't much for beating around the bush. "Then what were you doing out in the storm when you should be safe in your home?"

She dragged her gaze toward him, shifted to study Ma's back, then back to stare at Billy.

Again he saw fear, accompanied by uncertainty. He tried to be indifferent to it. After all, she was another man's wife. Up to that man to protect and comfort her. But he wasn't here to provide it at the moment, and Billy took half a step toward her then caught himself. "He'll be worried over the little one." He held her gaze in an invisible grip, inviting the truth. Silently assuring her she was safe with him in every way.

"He doesn't know."

He heard the words but they made not a lick of sense. "Doesn't know you're out, lost in the storm 'cept for God leading me to you?"

She worked her lips back and forth. Swallowed hard. "About the baby."

"Vivian, you ain't making a lick of sense." Had the cold affected her brain? "Of course your husband knows about the baby."

"I am not married." The whispered words seemed to escape against her will and as soon as she spoke them, she clamped her lips together. All expression disappeared from her face as if she'd wiped it away with a corner of the baby blanket. Though if he looked real hard he could see just a bit of something hurt and defensive, like the look in the eyes of the puppy he'd ripped from the hands of the man he found trying to shake it to death.

Knowing she expected some cruel word or gesture, he took care to reveal none of his shock, but, despite having lived with censure most of his twenty-two years, knowing she had a baby out of wedlock brought a sudden narrowing of his thoughts. Just as quickly, he let the criticism vanish. Everyone deserved a chance to prove himself. He'd offer this woman as much. On the heels of the realization she was unmarried came a flare of relief that he pointedly denied.

Her eyes narrowed as if she'd read something in his face—something he had meant to hide.

"He's mine." She splayed her hands over the baby. Her lips tightened.

Well, he never expected that. Had kind of thought she might see how relieved he was to know she wasn't married. Why, all of a sudden, was she insisting the baby was hers? He hadn't even considered otherwise, but her quick insistence and the defensive tone of her voice triggered misgivings in his mind. He carefully added up the things he noticed without heeding.

She didn't know enough to warm the milk.

Nor remember to change the wet pants without his reminder.

She was out in a storm. What could be bad enough to drive her out in this weather?

It all added up to suspicious. Was she in danger? If so, he would protect her. Or had she done something that would bring a posse down about the rafters? Even then, he would see she was treated fairly.

"I'm going to town to find Joshua's father. We'll make things right. You'll see."

He nodded, then turned to peer out the window. Snow plastered against the glass as if painted there by an unseen hand. His insides churned like he'd guzzled a gallon of sour milk. Why had this storm dumped her into his life, upsetting the peace his ma needed…triggering thoughts and desires he thought he'd successfully buried years ago?

He stilled the impatience in his heart knowing he could do nothing to change the weather except pray. He leaned against the wall, staring at the whitewashed window. *Lord, with one word You stopped the storm when You were on earth. Maybe You could see fit to say a word or two today to stop this storm.*

As soon as he could see to find his way, he'd take Vivian and her baby to town. Before Ma came apart at the seams. Aware of a faint call from some distant part of his heart, he added, before his carefully constrained life exploded out of control.

In the meantime, they needed shelter.

And the cats clamored to be fed. He rescued the bucket from the floor where Ma abandoned it and poured the milk through the clean cloth saved for that purpose. He filled the half-dozen pans under the table and the cats happily lapped at their dinner. He set jugs of strained milk to cool. Good thing Ma insisted on keeping the cow producing. Otherwise, how would they feed the baby?

Funny, Vivian didn't nurse her baby. He mentally added it to the list of things causing suspicion.

Vivian sank into the rocking chair where she could keep her gaze on Ma's back. The air quivered with tension from both women.

Billy stood at the cupboard, wondering how one entertained a pretty, young guest. He could think of nothing to talk about.

Cat and Fluffy crawled into Ma's lap and she stroked them. Maybe that would calm her.

Billy eased back to the fireplace and hunkered down on the stool he'd built specially for his weight. His insides settled into claylike heaviness at the way Vivian's arms tightened, and how she blinked as if startled. She might be kind but she still feared him.

"Got to be hard—on your own with a new baby."

She chuckled softly. He liked the sound of her amusement—soft and calming, reminding him of the wind through the top branches of the trees along the creek.

"Much harder than I dreamed." She ducked her head but not before he saw a flash of stubbornness.

He allowed a one-cornered smile to tip his mouth. He admired a person with lots of grit when it came to facing life's challenges. And he suspected Vivian had more than her share of difficulties tossed her way and yet she'd come back to Quinten as if to defy those circumstances. His smile fled, replaced with wariness that tightened his mouth. A stubborn woman could mean trouble for him and Ma. And no, he wouldn't welcome a bit of trouble for the enjoyment of some time spent with Miss Vivian.

The wind howled around the house, rattled the windows and sent shafts of cold across the floor. He didn't need to stir himself to know the storm worsened rather than let up. The room seemed overcrowded with Vivian and the baby in one corner, and Ma shivering in the other, and he went to the window and stared out. He longed to be able to trot out to the barn and check on the animals. But he didn't dare leave Ma alone.

Vivian's kindness had been so easily given when they were both at school. Truth was, he placed her on kind of a pedestal. Yet every instinct in him said she was going to turn his life inside out and upside down if he wasn't careful.

If only the storm would end.

Lord, why have You put me in this situation?

Was God expecting him to see no harm came to that little baby?

It was the only thing that made sense.

As if to confirm his thinking, the baby started to cry.

Ma let out an echoing protest and covered her ears. "Don't like baby crying."

Billy sighed. Life would not settle back to normal as long as this woman and the little one remained. He gave one more imploring look at the window, sent up one more imploring prayer for the storm to stop, then turned to face the room.

Ma rocked Cat and Vivian rocked the baby as it continued to wail.

Billy looked from one to the other. Seemed they both wore similar frantic expressions, each one scared and upset by the other.

Vivian pressed the baby against her neck and rocked harder and harder as the cries grew louder and louder.

Billy scrubbed his fist across his chin. Oh, for the peace of the outdoors.

"What's wrong with the little guy?"

Vivian shook her head. "I don't know. I suppose I could try feeding him again." She reached into the basket for the bottle.

That was another thing. The basket looked like something a woman would carry shopping in. Or store sewing materials. Not hardly big enough for the little critter. Was a wonder it hadn't suffocated. He squeezed at his thoughts, not wanting to shed one whiff of criticism on Vivian but it seemed she was running. From what? Was she in danger? His insides pushed at his bones. No one would hurt her while he was around.

Vivian found the bottle and examined its contents— an inch of old milk. She tipped the baby into the crook of her arm and hesitated.

Surely, she wouldn't give the baby that. When he saw she intended to do so, Billy reached for the bottle. "I'll get some fresh milk." He scrubbed the bottle in hot water before filling it. While it warmed, he studied Vivian.

She must have felt his eyes on her for she gave him a hard look. "What?"

"Nothing." He handed her the bottle. "Except, how come you know nothing about caring for a baby?"

She turned her attention to the infant. "Haven't had much experience. Have I, Joshua?"

"You said he's almost two months old." He let his words convey his doubt.

She didn't answer as she tried to persuade the little guy to take the bottle. But the baby screamed and gagged. "Come on, Joshua. Eat something. You'll feel better." She struggled to no avail. "Please, take the bottle." Her voice grew sharp, edged with desperation.

Ma rocked harder and moaned. Cat decided he'd had enough and scrambled from Ma's arms. Ma tried to grab the cat but it meant uncovering her ears and she quickly returned her hands to the sides of her head.

"Ma, pick up Fluffy. He'll let you hold him."

When Ma made no effort to do so, Billy strode over and scooped the cat into her lap. Ma shot him an accusing look as she wrapped the cat into her arms and returned her hands to her ears. At the sight of tears washing her face, Billy closed his eyes and prayed for patience and wisdom. The weather better change real quick before things went downhill any further.

The baby's protests turned to screaming. Milk ran down his cheeks and pooled in the folds of his neck.

Billy stated the obvious. "I guess he ain't hungry."

Vivian set the bottle aside, wiped the squalling face, and cleaned the baby's neck. The screaming continued, assaulting Billy's eardrums.

Fluffy squirmed in Ma's tight grasp. Tom and Tiger edged toward the sound, ears tipped in curiosity. The rest of the cats shrank back under the stove.

"Can't you make him stop?" Billy demanded.

"I would, if I knew what to do." She looked annoyed and frustrated at the same time.

"Why don't you know?" He waited as she scowled at him. "He ain't yours, is he?"

She snorted. "You wanting him? Right now, you could have him. Real cheap. Free, in fact."

Billy blinked. His mouth pulled down at the corners. "You can't give a baby away just because he's crying."

"No?" She pushed to her feet, took three steps and thrust the squalling bundle into Billy's arms. "You make him stop." She dropped back to the chair as if exhausted.

Billy couldn't move. He'd never felt anything like this little bitty human. He had to remind himself to breathe.

The baby weighed next to nothing, yet had the lungs of a cattle drover. The little bundle of noise drew in a breath, pulling his mouth into a pout.

The poor thing.

Billy lifted the baby to his chest and patted gently. The wails continued. Billy walked toward the door, turned and walked back. Were the screams less intense? He hummed the tune, "Fairest Lord Jesus, ruler of all nature."

The baby snuffled a bit, then grew quiet.

Billy let the sweetness of success, the incredible pleasure of holding this baby, fill his thoughts.

Ma stopped moaning, stopped rocking.

He kept humming, fearing the baby would begin his caterwauling again if he quit. He sank to the chair across from Vivian and continued the song.

Vivian sighed and tipped her head back.

Convinced there was something not right about this whole situation—a woman who admitted she wasn't married and obviously knew little about caring for the infant she claimed was hers—he tried to figure out a way to get the truth from her. But she could answer questions any way she chose. Truth or lie.

"You hiding from someone?" He kept his voice the same timbre as his hum, relieved the baby didn't protest and Ma seemed content murmuring comforting noises to Fluffy. A fragile peace settled about his taut nerves.

Vivian studied him intently.

He thought for a moment she intended to ignore his question.

"What concern is that of yours?"

The baby whimpered and Billy hummed for a few minutes before he answered. "I think it's my concern if someone is looking for a missing baby. Last thing I need is trouble with the law."

She gave a tight smile. "It seems to me you can handle most any trouble."

"You mean my size."

"I think it would be a good deterrent to any nosy parkers."

"I ain't talking about snoops. I'm meaning angry citizens or lawmen. I make a mighty big target for a bullet."

Again that look of defiance. "I'm not planning to stay." She glanced at Ma and gave the barest shiver.

Billy guessed she wasn't aware of it any more than she realized the fear in her eyes.

Tom and Tiger, the most curious of his cats, jumped to his lap and nosed around the baby, sniffing and meowing. Tom, the more aggressive one, laid his ears back as if to say he didn't approve of sharing his space with this strange creature. "Tom, you be nice." Tom meowed innocently then edged under Billy's arm, making Billy chuckle. "You always got to be first, don't you?"

He felt a little foolish talking to his cats in front of this woman, and shut up.

"I'll be gone as soon as the storm lets up," Vivian assured him.

"It shows no sign of doing that." And suppertime approached. His stomach began squeezing his backbone. He didn't care to miss a meal. Nor delay it even a few minutes, but Ma didn't look about to make anything.

Vivian was a guest. She could hardly be called on to prepare food. Besides, she might expect him to eat like she did. In which case he'd leave the table as hungry as he was now.

That left him—with a sleeping infant in his arms. He shifted the tiny bundle and handed it back to Vivian.

The baby protested at the change of arms but didn't waken.

"I'll make us something to eat." He hated cooking. Seemed to take forever to prepare enough food to satisfy his appetite.

They had a good supply of venison; potatoes and turnips from the garden; eggs, milk, cheese and a storeroom with beans, flour and cornmeal. His mouth watered at the thought of fresh-from-the-oven corn bread drowned in molasses, but that took too long.

He pulled out three big fry pans and dropped a dollop of bacon drippings into each. As soon as it sizzled, he put venison chops in one pan and browned them. He cut leftover potatoes into the second and broke two dozen eggs into the third pan. He sliced a roll of Ma's bread and wished for some fresh green vegetables, but garden season was a long way off.

"It's ready. Come and get it." He filled a plate for Ma, filled another with an equal amount for Vivian and set them on the table. The rest he scooped to a platter for himself.

When Vivian rose, Ma jerked to her feet. "Don't come any closer."

Vivian stopped so fast she teetered.

Billy stared from one woman to the other, feeling as if he were caught in the middle of two storms, not knowing which one would intensify first, nor what damage each would inflict.

"Ma, we got to feed the woman. It's uncharitable not to."

"I'll leave," Ma said, and before Billy could think what she meant to do, she dropped Fluffy to the floor, grabbed her plate and retreated past the stove into the doorless pantry. She pressed into the farthest corner, out of sight.

"Ma."

"I'll eat here," she mumbled.

"I can eat here," Vivian said at the same time.

Billy wanted nothing more than to sit down and fill the hollowness some people called hunger. Instead, he had these two people—three, if you counted the baby—to contend with.

And a storm in his head as violent as the one raging outdoors.

Chapter Three

A shiver raced across Vivian's shoulders and reached down her throat to grab her heart in a cruel grip. She was hungry, yet she hesitated. Mrs. Black scared every last bit of courage from her heart.

"Ma won't be changing her mind. You might as well pull up to the table."

Vivian ducked her head to hide the sudden sting of tears. She longed to be safe. Until this morning, she had always chosen the easy route, doing what was expected of her. Her fear switched to anger. Look where that had landed her.

"I'm getting mighty hungry and when I'm hungry I get cranky." Billy sounded as if he'd already crossed the line into that state.

Realizing her precarious position, Vivian jerked as if lassoed unexpectedly from behind. She did not want to see Billy upset in any way. She remembered him from school. How he'd stood with fists curled as the boys taunted him. She'd wondered how they had the nerve to test Billy's mettle. Even back then he was big enough to do serious harm to several of them before they could stop him by the sheer weight of their numbers. As she'd watched, her heart tight with distress at their taunts, tears raced to her eyes. Then Billy looked directly at her. She'd seen the pain in his gaze and knew how much this tormenting hurt him. Then his anger exploded. Only he didn't turn on the boys responsible. He started pounding on the walls of the barn on the school property. She'd almost been ill at how he'd thrust his fists again and again into the unyielding wood until his knuckles were torn and bleeding.

She did not want to trigger such a violent reaction because of something she did or failed to do, so she slowly made her way to the table hoping he would think her shivers came from moving away from the fireplace.

To think she'd handed the baby to Big Billy. Certainly, his crying made her feel helpless and frustrated, but as soon as she shoved the bundle into his hands she knew she'd made a mistake. Billy had only to curl his big fists to squeeze the life out of the infant.

She'd held her breath, praying he would choose not to. God mercifully answered her prayers. The big man cradled the baby gently and the little bit of squalling intractability settled down.

Suddenly, her fears subsided and her heart calmed. Somehow, and she couldn't explain it, she knew Billy would not harm a living soul. Perhaps it was seeing how gentle he was with the numerous cats, or watching his patient concern over his mother or realizing that even in his anger almost eight years ago, he had not turned against those responsible.

She straightened her shoulders, shifted the baby and walked to the table. There were three chairs. She avoided the one vacated by his mother.

Billy waited until she sat, the baby cradled in her left arm. "I'll pray for the food."

Startled by his announcement, expecting him to care little about godly things, she darted a look at him, caught him watching her and quickly bowed her head.

"I ain't a bad man," he muttered.

She wanted to tell him she didn't think so, but when she stole another glance he had closed his eyes. Just as well. She wasn't sure what she thought of this big man. She, too, bowed her head.

"Lord, some have hunger, but no meat; some have meat, but no hunger; I have both. God be praised! Amen."

Vivian coughed to hide her sudden desire to laugh. She kept her head down, glad of the need to concentrate on her meal. She doubted Big Billy would share her amusement at the grace he'd chosen.

In the pantry, his mother mumbled something unintelligible but clearly was annoyed.

How did Billy live with this day in and day out? It was enough to drive even the strongest man to lunacy.

Anger gnawed at her throat. It wasn't her fault she was stuck with a crazy woman and a reluctant man. She had a clear-cut destination and a task to take care of. Only the storm had diverted her. *Lord, God, keep me safe, help me make it to town and enable me to accomplish my purpose.*

She ate slowly as she considered her situation and what she could do. Nothing for now. Except pray. She wished she hadn't told him the truth about being unmarried. It always made her feel dirty and stupid. She should have never listened to Wayne's promises. But if Billy felt the usual disgust at evidence of a woman with loose morals, to his credit he had hidden it.

Billy ate as if he'd never get another chance. He'd taken the platter she thought for serving food, and consumed the stack of potatoes, four venison steaks and well over a dozen eggs, used four thick slices of bread to clean his plate, then sat back with a huge sigh.

Aware she'd been staring these last five minutes, Vivian ducked her head but not before Billy noticed her interest.

"It takes a lot to fuel me."

She didn't say anything.

"Tea," his mother called.

"Coming, Ma." He tossed a handful of tea leaves into a big brown china teapot, poured in hot water and let it steep. "She's not always like this," Billy said. "Only when there's strangers about."

He was blaming Vivian, which wasn't fair. It wasn't her fault. As if aware of her upset thoughts, the tiny boy stiffened and whimpered. Her anger vanished and she murmured soft noises to the baby. "I'm sorry, son. I love you and will get you the sort of home you deserve."

Billy took a cup of tea to his mother. Vivian heard the woman mumbling her complaint, and Billy's deep voice responding, trying to reassure her. Somehow, despite his size and the timbre of his voice, he had the power to calm his mother. It seemed to work for the baby, too.

On his return, Billy offered Vivian tea.

"Thanks." Maybe it would soothe her nerves, growing tighter with each passing moment. In fact, if she listened carefully, she could hear them humming like frost-tight wires. She wanted only to get to Quinten. She hadn't been back since being whisked away to the orphanage seven years ago. She could hardly wait to start over as an adult, a mother and according to her plan, the wife of an upstanding citizen.

A cat rubbed against her leg, startling her. She gasped. Billy studied her. "You scared of cats?"

"No. I just never had one rub against me while I sat at a table."

"You never had a pet cat?"

"No." Mother had considered cats dirty. The orphanage didn't allow pets. And the Weimers had cats only in the mill—wild, mangy things you couldn't get close to. Or want to.

"Then I guess you might find it unusual to have so many."

"How many are there?" She'd tried to count.

"Eight in the house. More in the barn."

"I'm guessing you don't have trouble with mice."

He chuckled. "Would have to be the bravest mouse in the world to hang around here."

His easy humor caught her off guard but before she had time to analyze her response, the baby lifted his voice in a demanding wail. She had no idea what he wanted this time. Who knew a baby could be so challenging? She had to figure out what to do with him. Billy already expressed suspicion because of her lack of knowledge in caring for an infant. She wished she could assure him there would be no lawmen after her, but despite the paper in her pocket and Marie's assurances...

She balanced the baby in one arm, retrieved the abandoned bottle from near the fireplace and prepared it as she'd seen Billy do. She persuaded Joshua to take the bottle. He sucked eagerly. She burped him when it seemed appropriate, and changed his nappy realizing she would soon have to wash the soiled ones or risk running out of clean ones.

Billy stayed at the window looking into the emptiness or alternately watching Joshua. Then he caught her gaze.

She blinked before the compassion in his look, wondering at its source.

"I heard about your ma and pa. I'm sorry."

"What did you hear?"

"Them dying and leaving you alone. How you got sent to an orphanage. Must have been real tough."

Sympathy from this unlikely source unlocked a hidden store of pain that escaped in a rush of words. "You can't begin to imagine. I lost everything. My family, my home and security. I went from being a loved and cherished only child to being nobody." She struggled to contain her emotions. She'd felt lost and alone, not just on that dreadful day, but every day following. She knew if she ever let the full force of her feelings escape they would turn into a flood of furious proportions. She sucked in air, pushing down the words, the feelings, the anger and pain.

She'd learned to deny her feelings and accept her fate. Perhaps too well.

Until Joshua.

His birth seemed to have planted a strength in her. Granted, it took almost two months for it to grow enough for her to act, but she was here now—evidence it had reached its potential.

"You are valued and loved by God. Your circumstances don't change that."

She met his steady blue gaze, let her thoughts follow his words. "I know that." Her faith was part of who she was, part of what her parents left her, though people would have cause to wonder considering her present circumstance—a baby but no husband.

"You can trust God when you can't trust anyone else."

She couldn't break away from his look, guessed his words conveyed far more than she knew. "It's been tough for you, too." As soon as the whispered words were out, she wished she could pull them back. She didn't want to remind him of the cruelty of people; didn't know how he'd react.

Billy's expression went blank, almost stupid. "If you mean how people treat us, it don't matter to me. Ma and I don't need anyone else." He pushed to his feet. "I'm gonna clean up."

"I'll help." One thing she'd learned, you better make yourself useful or no one would bother with you. And despite her wishes to be somewhere else, she needed to stay here until the storm ended.

Joshua sucked his bottom lip as she laid him on his side in the stuffed chair. She touched his silky cheek. So beautiful. So sweet. So much responsibility but she would soon have help in raising him. As soon as she reached Quinten and contacted Wayne. One look at this beautiful child they had created together and marriage would be the first thing he'd want so they could give Joshua a loving home, and the benefit of Wayne's name.

She turned to help clean the table. Mrs. Black came to the doorway of the pantry, saw Vivian, covered her face and moaned.

Vivian halted. She didn't want to upset this woman any further. Slowly, she backed away. Mrs. Black did the same until she was out of sight.

"Just leave her be," Billy said, his tone mild, but she didn't make the mistake of thinking it carried no warning.

She wanted to protest. She'd done nothing to bother the woman except reluctantly find shelter under her roof, but that was obviously more than enough. She grabbed a drying towel from behind the stove. Billy had already washed several dishes and she dried them. They worked in silence.

One thought consumed her.

Would she have to stay here for the night? If so, she

faced long hours of forcing her eyes to remain open. M
Black's threatening looks made her afraid of what w
happen if she slept.

"Looks like you're stuck here."

Billy's words confirmed her worst fears, gave
body and strength.

From the pantry, his ma screeched.

The sound gave Vivian's fears flesh and blood.

She polished a plate. She needed to count her blessings
as Mother had taught her. She was in out of the storm
where she would have surely frozen to death. The baby
was safe and, best of all, they were together.

"I think it's dry."

Billy's slow words made Vivian realize how long she'd
been wiping the plate and she handed it to him to put
away.

"You'll be safe here. As safe as in your own home."

Vivian had learned the hard way you weren't safe even
in your own home. Yet his words—or perhaps his tone—
eased some of her tension.

They finished the dishes without further conversation.

"Ma," Billy called. "Come out now. You can sit by the
fire and card wool."

"Noooooo."

The sound sent shivers up Vivian's spine and she again
promised herself she would stay awake all night. Perhaps
with a poker at her side.

"You'll be getting cold."

"Bring me my coat."

"No, Ma. You can't stay there." He went to the pantry.
Ignoring a moaning protest, he slowly pulled his mother
from the room, his big hands enclosing her smaller ones.

Vivian hung back, half hidden beside the warm
kitchen stove.

Billy edged his ma toward the wooden rocker and ___ed until she bent her knees and dropped to its seat. ___ed his bulk toward the stuffed chair, saw the baby ___same time as Vivian cried out. Her heart rattled ___inst her chest at the close call.

Mrs. Black moaned and tried to regain her feet but Billy planted a hand on her shoulder and waited for her to settle back, then he scooped up the baby and handed him to Vivian.

Something cold and itchy washed down her back as she cuddled the sleeping bundle, and edged to a wooden kitchen chair and sat so she could see the pair. It looked to be a long, fright-filled night ahead.

Billy pulled a big Bible from the mantel and opened it. In slow, measured tones he read the Twenty-third Psalm.

Mrs. Black rocked, never once taking her eyes from his face, her expression desperate as if clinging to her last shred of sanity by focusing on Billy's voice, or perhaps the words of scripture.

It was not a comforting thought.

Billy finished and replaced the Bible on the shelf.

"I like that psalm," Mrs. Black said.

"It's a good one, for sure." Billy threw more wood on the fire and glanced toward the stove where Vivian sat.

She knew he wanted to stoke the fire, sensed he hesitated to move for fear of bringing an end to his mother's calm. Vivian didn't offer to help, nor move to do so for the same reason. She tried to stifle a yawn. The long day and the time spent afraid and freezing in the storm had sapped her energy. Her head drooped. She snapped to attention. There'd be no sleep tonight.

"Ma, why don't you go to bed?"

Mrs. Black scrubbed at her hair, tangling it even

worse. "I can't sleep with—" She tilted her head toward Vivian.

The way it made Vivian feel unwelcome was as familiar as it was despised. She pulled Joshua closer. She'd give him what she'd lost—a home. A place of belonging and acceptance.

She tried to picture the house where they would live but having never been inside as far as she could remember, she had to make up the details. However, she could picture the face of Joshua's father and she recalled every word he'd spoken to her. She should have taken them with a grain of caution but despite her many regrets at her foolishness, Joshua wasn't one of them. *My precious baby.*

As soon as the storm ended, she would head to town and her plan.

Billy's voice interrupted her thoughts. "Ma, you go to your bed and I'll make sure you're safe." Mother and son regarded each other for a long, tense moment, then Mrs. Black nodded.

"I'll not sleep."

"Nor I," Billy said.

Vivian silently echoed the words. Little Joshua was the only one inclined to sleep in this household tonight.

Mrs. Black disappeared into a doorway next to the pantry. She firmly closed the door even though they all knew it would also shut out the heat.

"You're welcome to take my bed," Billy said.

Vivian shook her head hard. "Thanks, but I'll just wait for the storm to end." She again tried to count her blessings—safety, a chance to start over and the determination to work hard to achieve her goal.

Her head drooped again. She jerked upright. What if she dropped Joshua?

"Best move closer to the fire," Billy said. "The kitchen stove is getting cold."

Her feet grew icy and her arm ached from holding the baby. She studied the warm glow of the fire and considered what it meant to move closer.

Billy sighed, lumbered out of the big chair and pushed it several feet from the rocker. "That make you feel safer?"

Heat raced up her neck and settled in her cheeks as if she stood too close to the flames. She'd been rude. She normally didn't shun anyone, but his size, his mother's mental state… Well, who could blame her for her anxiety?

She crossed the room and settled in the chair, shifting Joshua to her chest to ease the strain on her arm, then faced Billy squarely. "I didn't mean anything."

His eyes were flashes of blue ice. His gaze looked through her, past her as if she wasn't there. It wasn't an unfamiliar feeling, nor a welcome one. She was done with being invisible, though perhaps this was not a wise time to inform the world, especially when the world consisted solely of Big Billy Black and his mad mother.

Suddenly, his look connected with hers so intently surprise raced through her. Then he gave an unexpectedly gentle smile.

She floundered for a solid thought.

"Know you didn't mean anything."

Her eyes widened of their own accord. She seemed unable to break from his look that went past her fear and through her emptiness to a spot deep inside that warmed and quivered like flower petals opening to the sun. When was the last time someone looked at her so, as if she mattered solely because she was a person? Not, she knew, since her parents died. Oh, sure, there'd been exceptions—Marie and Joshua's father—but they were few and far between and in the latter case, short-lived. But why it should be Billy resurrecting that feeling of being valued made no sense. Any more than his soft assurances that he knew she meant no harm by her statement. "How could you know that?"

His smile deepened. His gaze warmed even more. "Because I remember you in school." He paused, and shifted his gaze to the fire and then back to her.

She saw something new in his eyes—was it longing? She couldn't say for certain, but the look brought a flood of sadness to her heart.

He nodded slightly. "I remember your kindness."

"My kindness?" She managed to stammer out the words. "I don't remember doing anything."

"I know." His words were soft, like a whispered benediction. "Your kindness comes natural. It's a part of you."

"It is?" Her mouth rounded with disbelief. No one ever said anything so approving before and it made her feel— She struggled to identify this sensation of…of being really seen. Valued. And from a source she least expected. "What did I do?"

"You offered me a cookie."

"I did?" She had no memory of the event. "Did you take it?"

He chuckled, a deep-throated rumble resounding in his chest and bringing a smile to her lips. "I have never been one to refuse food."

She laughed. "Maybe I knew it even back then."

"You were the only one who was nice to me. You didn't seem afraid of my size."

They studied each other. She didn't know what his

watchful gaze wanted. What she saw was a big, kind man
trying his best to hide his hurt at being treated poorly.
He wore a faded blue shirt that brought out the color in
his eyes. His fawn-colored trousers were sprinkled with
cat hair in variegated colors. He wore heavy socks knit
in raw wool and lounged in the chair as if life held nothing but joy for him.

She knew otherwise. And she knew more. This man
would never harm her. In fact, she would trust him to
protect her if the need arose. The thought comforted.
"I'm not afraid of you."

Hope raced across his expression and disappeared so
quickly she almost missed it.

Satisfaction smoothed away her tension. She'd brought
a bit of well-deserved well-being to this man.

He stared into the flames, the reflection of the fire's
glow softening his face.

She remembered how she'd sheltered against his shoulder as he carried her from the storm. It reinforced her
feeling he was the sort of man one could count on. If
not for his ma, this would be a safe and sheltering place.
She stopped her thoughts right there and stared into the
flames. She was letting the warmth of the fire and the
isolating roar of the wind divert her thoughts from her
goal. She must find Joshua's father. Together, they would
build a happy home even though she didn't know if she
felt anything toward the man except regret at what they'd
done, and gratitude for her son.

She stole a glance out of the corner of her eye, saw that
Billy watched the baby as he stroked a lap full of cats.
Other cats curled around his feet. The noise of so many
purrs made her laugh.

He smiled crookedly. "I spoil them."

"They're your friends." There was something oddly appealing about such a big man enjoying pets.

His eyes narrowed. "Better than friends. They don't judge or condemn."

She understood his reluctance to trust people. She shared the lesson. But through it all, she had Marie, a special friend whose support sustained her. "Not everyone is the same. I had a friend in the orphanage who always helped me." Even if Marie got herself into all sorts of awkward situations, she never failed to help Vivian when she needed it.

Joshua stiffened in her arms and wailed.

Billy bolted to his feet with surprising agility. "I'll get the bottle."

Joshua took the bottle readily and Vivian settled back, rocking gently. A person could get used to this so long as they knew what to do.

Billy snored softly.

Vivian smiled. So much for not going to sleep. She rested her head on the back of the rocker and closed her eyes. The storm still raged outside as questions raced around inside her head.

Who was she? Vivian Halliday. But who was that? She didn't know. She'd lost all sense of who she was when her life had been stolen from her. Or had she let people take it from her degree by degree?

It no longer mattered because from now on, her every thought and decision would be on Joshua's behalf and for his good.

She smiled, her eyes still closed.

True, taking the baby from the orphanage wasn't entirely an unselfish act. Yes, she wanted her baby to have more than a foundling home could offer, or even an adoption. But it had been to quench the hunger of her own heart that had spurred her to go against everything she'd been told to do.

Yes, Joshua's birth had given her a strength that had before been foreign to her.

Chapter Four

A sharp sound pierced Billy's sleep and he jerked awake. When he realized he slept in the big chair, he moaned. He'd promised Ma to stay awake and guard her. Not that he figured Vivian or the baby meant to harm them.

He scrubbed the sleep from his eyes. The rocking chair was empty. He bolted to his feet. Where had they gone?

The high-pitched sound echoed inside his brain. He shook his head to clear away the sleep fog. Vivian stood near the window now blackened by darkness and streaked with bits of snow. She jostled the baby—the source of such shattering noise. Her eyes were wide with distress.

"I'm sorry he woke you but I can't get him to stop crying."

"Maybe he's hungry."

"I tried feeding him."

"Wet pants?"

"No."

"Tummy ache?"

Her mouth dropped open. "Now how would I know?"

He chuckled. "I guess he's telling you the best way he can. He often have tummy aches?"

She turned her attention back to the baby but not before he caught what he guessed was a hint of surprise and confusion.

There was something odd about Vivian and this baby. Her affection and protective attitude were real enough, yet her inexperience seemed out of place.

She sighed.

He gave her a hard look now that the cobwebs had cleared from his mind. She looked as if she'd been wrung out and hung in a stiff wind to dry. "The little one been fussing long?"

"I've tried to keep him quiet so he wouldn't wake you or—" She tipped her head toward Ma's door. "But he simply won't settle down."

As if to prove her words correct, the baby arched his back and screamed louder.

Ma snorted.

Billy held his breath waiting to see if Ma would set up her own protesting racket. When he heard soft snores, he eased air out of his lungs. "Give him to me."

Vivian didn't argue. Didn't even protest. In fact, she seemed as eager as a Dakota spring was reluctant to rid herself of the squalling infant.

He cradled the baby to his chest and hummed as he walked the floor. The baby cried at first and then slowly quieted. Billy continued to walk because every time he stopped, the baby stiffened and whimpered.

Vivian curled up in the stuffed chair before the warm fire and in minutes fell asleep.

Billy walked until he was sure a pathway across the floor marked his journey. He hummed until he grew both hoarse and amazed a little critter could outlast the reserves of a huge adult. When the infant finally seemed relaxed, Billy dropped wearily to the rocker, sighing relief when the baby didn't fuss.

He closed his eyes, let his head fall back and listened. The wind had moderated. He figured the storm would end with first light and unless the drifts were impassable, he'd have Vivian and the baby in town by noon.

Then he and Ma could return to normal—the quiet calm of Ma working about the house, milking her cow, tending the chickens; his satisfaction in caring for all his animals and walking alone across the prairie. That was his life.

He closed his eyes, gritted his teeth and denied a desire for more. No point in wishing for stars when he lived in plain old farm dirt. His world was what it was.

He was unreasonably glad when Joshua started to fuss again and he could turn his thoughts to something else.

Vivian barely stirred so Billy fed the baby, smiling as the tiny fist curled around Billy's little finger. He rubbed Joshua's cheek, amazed at the smoothness of his skin, like a polished rock warm in the sun.

Vivian had washed out the nappies and hung them to dry. Billy wondered how to fold one to fit the baby. Had no idea. Best he wait and let Vivian do it.

He and the baby sat warm and content in front of the fire. He watched the flames twist and turn, and wondered about Vivian. Why had God seen fit to dump her on his doorstep? If she needed help, he would willingly provide it. He rested his face against Joshua's warm head. It pleased him to see Vivian and the baby together. God knew a child needed and deserved the love of his mother.

Billy snorted in surprise at the direction of his thoughts. This wasn't about what happened to him. It was about protecting Vivian and the baby until the storm ended. Then they'd be gone. Some unfamiliar portion of his brain wondered what it would be like if he could keep them.

The room lightened. The frost-covered window turned gray.

The baby stretched. Billy turned the little bundle into his palms and stared into wide eyes as blue as the deep pond of water where the best fish hid. Joshua puckered his lips in an expression as wise and knowing as an ancient sage. It was so serious and comical at the same time, Billy chuckled. "Never seen anyone like me before, have you?"

As the baby blinked solemnly, Vivian woke with a gasp. "I didn't mean to sleep."

"That's what most people do at night."

She snorted. "If they're safe in their own bed."

"You're just as safe." He understood people's fears of Ma's crazy behavior and his size. He'd grown used to it. Put it down to ignorance, phobia or just plain scared. But after sheltering Vivian and helping with little Joshua here, he figured it was about time she realized both he and Ma were harmless.

Of course, Ma had to pick that moment to scurry into the room, her hair as tangled as a crow's nest, her eyes wide. She paused to wave frantically at Vivian as if hoping her actions could chase her away. She mumbled something totally unintelligible before she darted past them and out to the lean-to to relieve herself.

He waited for her to return. He gave her a few minutes before he called, "Ma, get back in here."

Joshua, startled at Billy's loud voice, screamed as if he'd been stabbed. "Sorry, little fellow. Didn't mean to scare you." He rocked the baby.

Joshua stopped crying but his bottom lip stuck out, trembling, and his eyes remained wide.

Vivian jumped up. "I'll get a bottle ready."

Billy followed her to the table and waited while she prepared breakfast for the baby. As soon as Vivian took Joshua, Billy headed for the cold woodshed attached to the house. He yanked open the door and caught Ma's hands, pulling her gently inside. "You'll freeze out there."

Ma whimpered and clung to his grasp. "I don't like this," she whispered. "It scares me."

"Ma, she's just a young woman with a little baby."

Ma shuddered and pressed one hand to her chest.

"Look, the storm has ended." He should be glad but it was not relief he felt. It was regret, which he expertly ignored as he led Ma to a kitchen chair. "You sit here while I get the fire going and make breakfast."

Only by talking softly of the animals and the weather did Billy manage to get Ma to sit long enough to eat. He took a bowl of hot mush to Vivian in front of the fireplace without suggesting she move to the table. He didn't want to risk sending Ma running from the room.

As soon as Ma finished, she started to pull on heavy outerwear. "I have to milk Betsy."

Billy pulled on his winter coat, too. "I'll look after the other animals." He lifted the bar off the door.

"Leave the dishes. I'll do them." Vivian spoke quietly.

Billy gladly did so and followed Ma to the barn where he hurried through his chores. He would normally take time to brush the colt, stroke all the cats and play with Limpy, his three-legged dog. Billy had nursed the pup from birth. He was the only dog left from many batches. Limpy was getting old. Billy would soon enough have to find a new dog, though the idea branded a protest on the inside of his heart.

Poor Limpy used to love this weather but he was getting old and refused to leave the barn unless it was warm out. Today, the cold had a nasty bite.

Ma milked Betsy. "You'll get rid of her today?"

"As soon as I've done the chores." The sooner the better for all of them. He'd struggle for weeks after she left to control the longings buried beneath the rubble in his heart, longings that had wormed their way to the surface during Vivian's visit.

"Good."

Ma finished milking and handed him the bucket. "I'll stay here until you leave."

"Ma, it's cold."

"I'll sit beside Betsy."

He hitched up Blaze. "I'll be back in a few minutes for the wagon. Will you go inside then?"

"Maybe." She gave him a look full of regret. "I'm sorry. I wish I didn't act so crazy when—"

"Never mind. We both know you aren't crazy."

She snorted. "How can you be so sure?"

"'Cause I know. Though you put up with me. Many would think that makes you crazy."

She smiled and brushed her mittens over his chin, the wool rough and damp smelling. "If they knew the truth, they would know I am blessed to have a son like you."

"Ma, I love you."

"And I you." She patted his cheek. "Look after the milk."

Billy laughed because the look she sent the direction of the house had nothing to do with milk, and everything to do with getting Vivian out of her house.

The cold made his cheeks tingle as he crossed the yard. He wondered about Vivian and Joshua. Bitter weather for them to be outdoors. He'd keep them another day if not for Ma.

As he strained the milk and fed the cats, he told Vivian they would leave in a few minutes. She had already packed everything into the basket and wrapped the baby. Obviously, she couldn't wait to get to town. It would never enter her mind to ask Billy to let her stay. A long-denied ache pooled low in his belly. No one would want to stay here with the crazy Blacks. He sucked in air until the ache disappeared. He didn't need or want anything more than what he had grown used to. His heart set on accepting the facts of his life, he returned to the barn.

"Ma, I want to see you back in the house before I leave. I don't want to have to worry you might freeze to death."

"As soon as she's gone."

"I'll wait at the bottom of the lane to see."

He drove the wagon to the door, grabbed a heavy woolen blanket from the box and shook off cat hair. Vivian rushed out to meet him. She shivered in the penetrating cold and held the baby close to her chest under protection of the cape.

He grabbed the basket that held Joshua just yesterday. Still seemed impossible the soft-sided container kept the baby safe. He helped Vivian to the seat, and tucked the blanket tightly around her and the baby.

They started out. The drifts were hard but not impassable. They should make good time. He stopped at the bottom of the lane as he'd promised and turned back to the house, chuckling as Ma swept the step as if to remove all traces of this intrusion.

He kept his thoughts on the trail ahead as they turned onto the road. Within a few yards, they encountered a hard drift. Billy jumped down to stomp through it so Blaze could manage the wagon. The snow was deeper than he thought. He huffed from the effort. Should have a sleigh for this kind of journey. Would make more sense but he never had a need to go to town much in the winter and if he did, he rode Blaze.

He stopped twice more. The cold bit at his cheeks, nipped his fingertips. And he was working. Not sitting still like Vivian. She must be frozen clean through. And what about that little guy? He should never have brought them out. They could have stayed with the crazy Blacks until it warmed. He should have ignored her anxiousness to leave, he should have told Ma to settle down and wait for the cold to moderate. His thoughts twisted round and round each other like a tangle of ropes in a Dakota wind. If harm came to them... He couldn't think of it. Instead, he hurriedly broke the crust and led Blaze through the drift, lending his weight to the horse's efforts then climbed back to the seat. "How you doing?"

"Fine." The blanket she'd pulled over her head and across her face muffled her voice. Only her eyes peeked out and ice frosted her dark lashes.

"I ain't never took anyone out in this kind of cold." 'Course, he never took anyone anywhere. Not since the last time he took Ma to town and that was late fall with a warm sun, and...

He'd lost track of when it was, marking the seasons by the trees and the birth of foals and calves.

"The little one?"

"He's not moving much."

"He ain't?" He wanted to stop and fold back the covers, assure himself the baby hadn't been harmed by the cold, but until they found someplace warm it wouldn't be a good idea.

"The only warm place left in my body is where he is so I expect he's safe enough."

A whoosh of air escaped his mouth and he sucked in a big breath that stung his throat and practically froze his lungs. "We'll soon be there." Quinten lay down the road—a huddle of buildings covered with snow. Coils of gray smoke rose upward then bent to the south. "Hope the wind don't shift 'fore we get there."

Vivian grunted agreement.

They were but a few yards from town. He clenched his teeth until his jaw protested. He didn't usually go to town in the middle of the day. He didn't much care for the way women grabbed their children and ducked into the nearest doorway. "Where you want to go?" He'd see her to her destination and get out of town as fast as he could.

"To the Mercantile Bank."

He glanced about the approaching streets. Did he go boldly down the main street or turn aside to the alleys he usually used? Though he didn't have any call to visit the bank, it was close to Lucas's store. He made up his mind. "Don't mind if I don't go there directly?"

"Not at all." She lowered the blanket and looked about as eager as could be. "It's much the same as I remember." She craned to see down a street. "I lived down there," she whispered and shivered.

"Best wrap up. It's mighty cold." He had stopped feeling his feet several minutes ago. 'Course, he wasn't sure it was from cold or from the tension of this open visit to town.

But instead of pulling the blanket closer, she edged one arm out and touched her hair. "I must look a sight. I wish I had some place to clean up."

"'Spect the banker sees people come in looking half-froze all the time." He'd meant to be amusing. But she didn't laugh. She looked at him with big appealing eyes.

"I'm not going to the bank to conduct ordinary business." Her teeth chattered. "Joshua's father works there. I am going to speak to him."

Billy took a moment to digest the information. He knew little about the bank except the news Lucas relayed, but he knew who owned it—the Styleses. Mr. Big Shot Daddy and his equally big shot son, Wayne—one of his tormentors in school and one of the most likely to cause Billy grief even now. Far as he knew, the only other person working in the bank was the elderly Mrs. Bamber. "You going to see one of the Styleses?"

She pulled the blanket around her head and mumbled, "Wayne."

The news hit him like a load of bricks dumped on his head, sending protests down his spine and tingling along his fingers. Wayne Styles was the father of that little baby?

"I know he wasn't fair to you in school. But he's changed. He was very nice to me when…"

When he got what he wanted and left you. But it wasn't his business.

They were almost at the bank. Vivian sat up straighter and stared at the imposing brick building. "I…" She turned to face him. "I don't want to say what I have to say in the bank. Can you keep the baby while I speak to him and arrange to meet someplace more private?"

He didn't want to do anything to help Wayne Styles but he couldn't resist the desperation in Vivian's gaze.

"Please. This is what's best for Joshua."

He made up his mind. "We need to get Joshua in out of the cold." There was one place he could go and he flicked the reins, passed the bank and drew up behind the store. Lucas would be some surprised to see him in broad daylight. He threw a blanket over Blaze and hurried around to assist Vivian to the ground. She stumbled as she tried to take her weight and he caught her.

"I'm okay," she mumbled, but she wasn't. Ignoring her

protests, he scooped her up, pushed open the door and deposited her on a crate in the storeroom. He could hear Lucas talking to people in the front. The man would come to investigate the noise as soon as his customers left.

Billy fumbled at the blanket encasing Vivian, his fingers stiff with cold. Had to hurry. Had to make sure little Joshua... He folded back the blanket, parted the edges of the heavy woolen cape Vivian wore. More blankets covered the baby.

Shivering, her own movements clumsy with cold, Vivian lifted the covers to reveal the tiny face, eyes closed. He looked so peaceful. Too peaceful?

Vivian held her fingers a few inches from Joshua's nostrils. "I can't tell if he's breathing." Her whispered words edged with fear.

Billy touched the baby's cheek. "He's warm." He planted his big hand on the tiny body and shook it. "Joshua. Wake up." Nothing. Not so much as a whimper. He shook again. "Joshua."

A pair of blue eyes flew open. And the baby smiled.

Billy grinned. "Hardy little critter."

Joshua nuzzled at Vivian's neck as she and Billy smiled at each other with their shared relief.

Her smile eased. Her gaze grew darker, more intense. She looked beyond his relief over the baby, past his enjoyment of that little smile, deep into the secrets of his heart, secrets he didn't admit even to himself and yet suddenly they lay bare and exposed, raw and unformed yet very real and alive. Like a newborn foal struggling to get to its feet. He tried to bar his thoughts but he couldn't. Instead, they poured forth, reaching for her with a force that both astounded and frightened him, one he was unable to restrain.

"Billy," she murmured.

He surged forward, ready to lift her in his arms and take her back to his home.

"Thank you for being such a help."

He sank back. "You're welcome." Big Billy Black with impossible dreams. What a laugh people would get if they could read his thoughts of a few seconds ago.

"What brings you out on a day so cold the air is blue?" Lucas strode through the passageway and ground to a halt at the sight of a woman and child with Billy. He blinked as if hit by a blast of sunshine.

Billy grunted. He didn't have to act like the whole notion of Billy with a female friend was such a shock.

"Vivian, you remember Lucas Green?" Lucas was already working in the store when they were both in school. "Lucas, Vivian Halliday."

They exchanged greetings.

"How have you been, Miss Halliday?"

Vivian's smile was mocking. "Not bad, considering the circumstances."

Lucas fairly burst with curiosity, which neither Vivian nor Billy made any effort to satisfy.

"I have some business to conduct at the bank," Vivian said. She pulled a comb from the basket and looked around.

"Mirror over there." Lucas nodded toward the corner.

Vivian hesitated, her hands occupied with holding Joshua.

Billy reached for the baby who gave him a gummy smile. Realizing Lucas watched him openly, Billy settled the baby in the crook of his arm and pretended it was of no more importance than a bundle of papers. He got a perverse pleasure out of ignoring Lucas's questioning looks and furtive nods that invited information.

Vivian returned a few minutes later looking neat and tidy. "Do you mind watching him for a few minutes?"

"We'll be fine. You go about your business."

"He'll be wanting to eat soon, I expect. His bottle is in the bag."

"Fine."

She hesitated, her eyes filled with uncertainty.

He smiled, silently sending her encouragement. If this is what she wanted and what Joshua needed, he wished her all the best.

She patted Joshua's head and strode through the main part of the store.

Lucas barely waited for the door to close behind her. "So, what's going on?"

"I found them in the storm yesterday." Billy smiled, remembering his surprise, which had quickly shifted to pleasure. And now seemed to have turned into edginess at Lucas's curiosity and undisguised surprise. "She was returning to Quinten and got lost in the storm."

Lucas lapped up every word.

Billy let him drink eagerly and pant for more before he continued. "She's planning to start over here."

Lucas sat back. "She been with you overnight?"

Was that so hard to believe? "Yup."

"Your mother good with that?"

Billy chuckled. "Not quite."

Lucas shook his head. "Boy, you sure surprised me. Where's Vivian's husband?"

Billy didn't answer. It wasn't his place to spread tales about her. She'd face enough censure from the gossips without his help. But Lucas continued to stare, waiting for an answer.

"Can't say." It was the best he could do.

Joshua chose that moment to let them know he wanted

to be fed. "Can I use your kettle?" Lucas kept a pot of water on the stove to add moisture to the air.

"Surely."

Billy set the bottle to warm. Ice crystals had formed along the edge so it took a few minutes.

Lucas joined him near the stove. "You and a baby. Never thought I'd see the day."

The man's amusement failed to annoy Billy. "I've looked after lots of animal babies. Human babies aren't a lot different." Except the animals didn't smile or curl their little hand around his smallest finger.

The entrance door to the store slapped open. A cold breeze skittered across the floor and Lucas reluctantly returned to his business.

The bottle ready, Billy sat back to feed Joshua, who sucked greedily. In a few minutes, Vivian would return to collect the baby. They would begin their new life. One in which Vivian would be respected as the wife of Wayne Styles.

The idea burned through his veins like his blood was on fire. He tried not to think of the two of them together—Vivian so sweet and gentle, and Wayne, a self-righteous bigot. Instead, he forced his thoughts to the family the three of them would become, the ideal family, welcomed, treated warmly, accepted.

Joshua smiled around the nipple, allowing milk to dribble down his cheek.

Billy chuckled as he wiped away the milk. Twenty-four hours since he'd met this young fella and yet there was a spot in a warm and sheltered part of his heart that now belonged to Joshua. A spot that would ache like Betsy had stomped on it with her sharp hooves when Vivian returned and took him away. "I'm going to miss you, little guy."

For just a moment, he wished his world could be different. Long ago, he'd accepted it couldn't be. But he'd do everything in his power to make sure Vivian and Joshua got the sort of life he wanted. Yet he found it hard to pray the words asking for Vivian's success in arranging a meeting with Wayne.

Chapter Five

Vivian's footsteps echoed on the wooden sidewalk. She wanted to walk to the bank with her head held high, revealing none of the nervousness tickling her ribs, but the wind caught at her and she ducked, shrugging deeper into the protection of her cape. Cold fingers caught at the edges of the garment and blasted it open. She tugged it closed and headed toward the bank.

Lord, God, please give me the confidence I need to face Wayne and make my request. Make him open to my need. Joshua's need.

Wayne had sugarcoated his words, tempting her, making their action seem so right. She knew better all the time. She had sinned, but she could not bear that Joshua would suffer rejection and indignities because of what she'd done. She counted on Wayne to make things right and had every assurance he would. He'd been such a gentleman when she saw him.

A horse plodded past, steam billowing from its nostrils, the rider bundled up in heavy clothing, a woolen cap beneath his cowboy hat.

Reassured by the commonplace event, she glanced about. But the drifting snow reduced visibility to half a block of businesses—several frame, false-fronted buildings and more brick and stone structures than she recalled. The town had changed and flourished since she last saw it. She played a mental game with herself as she scurried toward the bank, trying to recall what businesses she remembered—Mr. Legal's Law Office. She smiled. Never before thought of the irony of his name in conjunction with his occupation. The hotel farther down the street. The—

She reached the stone steps of the bank and ground to a halt. *Lord, God, help me.* Knowing God's way was the right way had started her on this journey. She strengthened herself with the thought as she climbed the steps and paused in front of the thick, leaded-glass doors to glance back toward the general store where her son waited, safe with Billy.

Billy was a good man. Kind enough to take her out in this treacherous weather. A smile curved her lips. Someday, perhaps she could repay his kindness.

Now to face her reason for returning to Quinten. She pushed the door open and stepped into the hushed, warm interior. She'd been in this building as a child and the same awe she'd felt then sucked at her courage.

The oiled-wood floors gave off a unique lemon scent. The weary light shed soft muted tones to everything. Or perhaps the dark wood and yellow walls always made the interior feel that way.

An older woman with a coiled braid of white hair looked through the grate of the bank teller's cage and over the top of a pair of wire-rimmed glasses. She cleared her throat softly as if to suggest to Vivian that the woman awaited her business.

Vivian glanced about. In a side office, she saw an older man, a monk's bald spot the only part of his head visible.

She wondered if it was Wayne's father. In a smaller office, another man, his suit jacket removed, fiddled with papers. She could not see Wayne. Perhaps he was in a back office.

After the woman behind the counter cleared her throat again, Vivian crossed toward her, resisting the urge to tiptoe.

"Can I help you, miss?"

Vivian refused to let the imperious tone of the woman's voice deter her. "I'd like to speak to Wayne Styles, please."

"And what is your business with him?"

"Would you please tell him Miss Halliday wishes to speak to him?"

The woman cleared her throat again. A most annoying habit that grated across Vivian's tense nerves.

"I'm afraid I cannot do that." Another clearing of her throat. An upward tip of her chin as the woman studied Vivian through her reading glasses.

Although every nerve quivered with fear, Vivian would not give up. "Then I'd like to leave a message for him. Could I beg a piece of paper?"

The woman's gaze slipped past Vivian. Her eyelashes beat at a furious rate.

"Miss Halliday?" A male voice spoke behind her.

Vivian turned slowly, recognized the elder Mr. Styles with relief. "Thank goodness. Can you tell me how to contact Wayne? I need to speak to him."

"What is the nature of your concern? Perhaps I can help you?"

Vivian shook her head. "It's personal. I need to talk to Wayne myself."

The man looked as if the idea threatened all the money in his vault. "I'm afraid it isn't possible. Wayne is away."

"Away?" She'd never conceived of such a possibility. "Where? How long?"

"I don't see it's any of your concern but it's common knowledge he's gone east to visit relatives and friends."

"When is he due back?"

Mr. Styles sniffed. "I'm afraid I'm not at liberty to say. Now I believe any business we have with you has been concluded some time ago."

Vivian didn't realize he'd been shepherding her toward the exit until he reached it and waved her out. As the door closed behind her, she glanced back at the bank. Mr. Styles stood on the other side of the glass door, his expression far from friendly. She spun away, her heart frozen to the inside of her ribs.

Wayne was gone. What was she to do? She had no home. No family.

Ice edged her heart, immobilized her feet. She couldn't pull a single action from her scrambled brain.

"Vivian?"

She turned toward the sound. Billy? Her thoughts went no further.

"Come." He touched her elbow.

He wanted her to go with him. She understood that but her limbs didn't get the idea.

He caught her around the shoulders and steered her toward the store. And Joshua. Thinking of her son splintered her insides even more until she feared she'd disintegrate into a pile of kindling.

Billy pushed open the door, guided her through, past the shelves and counter and into the back room where Lucas sat holding her baby. He rose, and Billy steered her toward the vacant chair. Somehow she managed to fold her legs that felt like unwieldy stilts.

Billy took Joshua from Lucas and placed him in her arms.

She looked at the face of her son.

He smiled.

Her insides corrected themselves and with a strangled cry, she cradled Joshua to her chest.

"I'll leave you two alone." Lucas strode into the front of the store.

Billy squatted in front of her and with his thumbs swiped at her face, wiping away tears she wasn't even aware of shedding. "What happened?"

Vivian shook her head, unable to speak.

Billy nodded, seeming to understand. He stroked Joshua's head and patted Vivian's shoulder.

The tender gesture unlocked the tension inside her and she closed her eyes and sobbed silently.

Billy rubbed her shoulder, his silent acceptance of her tears releasing another rush of them. She cried until she was spent, her emotions drained. She found her hankie, dried her face and wiped her nose. A shudder shook her.

Billy squeezed her arm. "Better now?"

"Things couldn't be worse."

He held her gaze, his look soft and undemanding, silently offering nothing but kindness.

She searched his eyes, drawn by the intense blueness of them, drawn by something more, a deep understanding that likely stemmed from his own painful experiences. The realization that this man knew more about pain and disappointment than most released her fears. "Wayne isn't there. His father said he was away. Wouldn't tell me when he would be back." She cupped her hand to Joshua's head, pressing him to her chest. Her baby needed a father, a name, and acceptance.

Something Mr. Styles had said poked at the back of her brain. She tried to recall his exact words. When she did, they made no sense.

"Mr. Styles said something odd. He said our business had been concluded some time ago. I don't know what he could mean."

Billy gave a one-sided grin. "He's a banker. All they think about is business."

"But I've had no business dealings with him. How could I? I was twelve when I went to the home."

"Perhaps he meant Joshua."

"I don't see how he'd know."

"Wayne doesn't know?" His voice seemed tight as if the man was some sort of scoundrel for not knowing.

"He returned home before I knew and I never informed him. Didn't seem the sort of thing to put in a letter." And then there were all those months of being the obedient Vivian Halliday who hid from the harsh realities of life by doing what she was told. She closed her eyes as pain and regret twisted through her. She had made a profound mess of her life. There was only one way to make it right. Tell Wayne. He would be expected to marry her since she had his son. That would make things right for Joshua, but Vivian would never forgive herself for her sinful behavior. Guilt grabbed every other emotion and squeezed it lifeless.

Except her love for Joshua. She would fight for his right to his father's name.

Lucas peeked into the room. "Everything all right?"

"Yes, thanks," Vivian said. Mr. Styles said something about everyone knowing Wayne was away. Maybe they also knew more about his plans than his father revealed. "Do you know when Wayne Styles will return?"

Lucas darted a look toward Joshua as if putting together her reason for wanting to know. "Nothing more than he's gone east to visit. Do you want me to let you know if I hear something?"

"I'd appreciate it." What was she to do in the meantime? She darted a look at Billy.

He considered her with a furrowed brow.

"There someplace I can take you?"

She thought of the people she remembered. Perhaps some of them would allow her to stay. But she didn't want anyone to know about Joshua until… Well, the more that knew the more censure there would be to overcome. Best if she could stay out of sight until Wayne returned and they could correct this shameful mistake in the only honorable way. Mrs. Weimer had a favorite saying. Stuck between the wagon and the mill wheel. Described Vivian's predicament perfectly. But she would do what she must. "Will you take me back with you and allow me to stay until he comes home?" He had every reason in the world to refuse. What would she do if he did?

Billy straightened. Backed away. Shifted his gaze to Joshua then he shook his head. Hard. "Can't do that. You know I can't."

"I have no place else."

Again he glanced at Joshua.

She wasn't above using his obvious affection for her son to persuade him, and turned Joshua around so Billy could see his face and silently thanked her little son that he picked that moment to smile and wobble a little fist. "I think it's the best thing for Joshua, don't you?"

Billy dragged his gaze back to Vivian's face. "You planning to hide forever?"

"Only 'til Wayne returns." She was grateful Lucas had returned to the main part of the store to wait on a customer. "Think about it. If everyone knows about Joshua before Wayne can do the right thing…well, you know how harmful gossip is and how difficult to live down." It was an unfair argument considering Billy's experience, but surely he would realize how important it was that she shield Joshua.

A muscle in Billy's jaw bunched. He curled his fists into knotted mounds of power, then he nodded briskly. "You and Ma will have to figure out how to get along. Now, let's get going."

He spoke a moment to Lucas. She overheard Billy ask him to keep Vivian's presence quiet for now.

She smiled. Billy understood. She could trust him to protect her secret. And protect her, as well, she realized with a start.

They left town in a swirl of snow.

Billy had said she would have to get along with his ma. She wondered how she was expected to do that. She didn't know what she shouldn't do in order to prevent sending the mad Mrs. Black out of control. Nor could she guess what sort of action she'd precipitate by something even seemingly innocent.

She shuddered, and pulled the blanket tighter around her as if she could protect herself from more than the cold with the thick wool.

The temperature had dropped significantly since their earlier trip to town. She ducked her head. The cold sucking at her made everything else—including the specter of being stuck with the mad Blacks—fade into the distance.

It was, she admitted, only Mrs. Black that caused this itchy edginess to her insides. She didn't fear Billy. She recalled the strength of his arms holding her, giving her a sense of safety and protection. He was a man who would help her to his own cost. A man who would stroke a cat gently, rock a baby and sing to settle the fretful cries, a man who...

She closed her thoughts to visions of Billy's big hands

comforting away her fears. She buried her nose in the blanket and breathed in the smell of horseflesh.

The cold bit at her through the heavy blanket and she hunkered lower to protect Joshua. Nothing mattered more than keeping this infant safe.

By the time they arrived back at the Black homestead, the only warm spot was in the middle of her chest where the baby lay. She literally fell into Billy's arms and he rushed inside.

His mother jerked to her feet. "You brought her back?"

"Had to."

"I don't want her here." She waved her arms like a scarecrow caught in a whirlwind.

A bolt of fear went halfway through Vivian's heart before the frozen crust around her emotions stalled it. Not even Mrs. Black's madness mattered at the moment. All she cared about was getting warm.

Billy gently lowered her to the chair, paused to throw more wood on the fire then slowly unwrapped her. He pried Joshua from her stiff arms. "Ma, see to the baby."

"No." She sucked back a cry. "I'll not be touching anyone's baby."

Billy straightened. "Then go take care of Blaze. Put the kettle to boil before you leave. Vivian needs warming."

The heat from the fire touched Vivian but her skin seemed impervious. She couldn't remember being so cold. Not even when she'd thought she was going to die in the storm. A good deal of the chill came from inside, near her heart, as if an iceberg had found its way into her thoughts and feelings. She had not expected this delay. She couldn't have imagined how it caused her to feel so helpless. Knowing she was unwelcome here only intensified her sense of loss and confusion until she welcomed the way her thoughts had grown immobile with the cold.

Billy opened the blankets covering Joshua. He shook the baby gently and smiled when Joshua squalled. "You're a tough little man." He glanced toward the ceiling. "Thank You, God."

Vivian made a noise—somewhere between a grateful grunt and a cry of pain. She echoed his prayer of gratitude adding, *Please keep us safe*.

Billy carefully pulled her boots off and squeezed her toes. "Do you feel this?"

Her toes hurt—a good sign. She managed to mumble something she hoped sounded like yes. He pulled off her mittens. Her fingers hurt, too.

Billy grabbed a blanket from a pair roasting near the fireplace. He pushed back the snow-dusted one she'd huddled in and covered her with the new one. "You'll be okay as soon as you get warm."

He went to make tea, then returned to sit at her knees and lifted a spoonful toward her. "It'll warm you up quick."

At his gentleness, tears built up behind her eyes and stalled there. Even her tear ducts were so cold they refused to work.

"Here." He pressed the spoon against her lips and she opened her mouth. The warm liquid slid down her throat but did little to relieve the frigid state of her insides. The cold winding around her heart had nothing to do with the temperature in her body, and everything to do with the aloneness she'd lived with since her parents died.

"More." He continued, spoonful after spoonful of warm, sweet tea until the cup was empty. Each time his big hand brushed her mouth, she reminded herself he was only treating her as he would any of his pets if they needed special attention.

Slowly, in painful increments, feeling returned to her limbs. She wished the numbness could remain in her heart but feeling seeped back there, as well, making her keenly aware of her state. She tried not to think about the facts of her life, stuck where she wasn't welcome, with a baby out of wedlock and Wayne away.

Mrs. Black stomped back into the house. "I took care of your horse."

Billy put aside the cup. "Did you make dinner? I'm starved."

"I won't be cooking for strangers."

He snorted. "I'm not hardly one."

She glowered. "You'll find your food in the oven."

"Thanks, Ma."

Vivian closed her eyes. She didn't want to be here any more than Mrs. Black wanted her. But what choice did she have? "I'm sorry, Mrs. Black. I desperately need shelter." It wasn't even for herself she sought it but for tiny, defenseless Joshua.

The woman turned her back and spoke to Billy. "Ain't she got kin?"

"She's an orphan."

"Huh. Ain't she got friends?"

"She needs a place to stay."

"Not here."

"Yes, Ma. Here. Just for a time."

Vivian hoped and prayed it would be a very short time. She pushed to her feet, grimacing as pins and needles jabbed up her legs. "I won't bother you."

"Ain't cooking for uninvited guests," Mrs. Black informed Billy as she poured a cup of tea and sat at the table, keeping her back to Vivian.

When Joshua loudly announced he needed to be fed,

Vivian dug the bottle out of the basket, her fingers clumsy with cold.

Seeing her predicament, Billy took over.

She gratefully sank back to the rocker. It would be some time for proper feeling to return to her limbs.

A few minutes later, Billy lifted Joshua into her arms and handed her the bottle. She turned to thank him and realized he still bent over admiring Joshua, their faces almost touching. For the first time, she noticed the way his cheeks creased as if his mouth curved in permanent amusement. He was so close she could smell the metallic scent of cold from his skin. And ache for the comfort his arms offered.

She mentally scolded herself. Hadn't she learned her lesson about looking to a man for comfort? She'd promised never again. *Lord, God, forgive me for being so needy. Give me strength.*

Billy ambled to the stove to pull out a fry pan heaped with food. He dug into it with gusto and devout concentration. Not until he'd cleaned the pan did he look up. "You must be hungry."

Before Vivian could answer, Mrs. Black skidded her chair back, the sharp noise jerking along Vivian's nerves.

Vivian shook her head. "I'm fine." Though the cold had burned off breakfast and probably a few meals prior.

Billy sawed off two thick pieces of bread, spread them with molasses, put them on a plate and took them to Vivian. "It might tide you 'til supper."

Mrs. Black bounced her chair back to the table. "Ain't cooking."

Billy shrugged. "Then you all will have to put up with my form of cooking."

Vivian smiled in spite of her nervousness. "Supper last night was more than adequate."

His face broke into a sunny expression, smile lines fanning out from his eyes and mouth. "That was the extent of my ability."

Vivian glanced at Mrs. Black and lowered her voice. "I could cook."

Billy's eyebrows pushed furrows up his forehead. "Good. But—" He paused and his eyes crinkled in what she took as embarrassment. "I ain't a dainty eater."

She chuckled, keeping her voice low. She'd already noticed the fact but didn't think it would be kind to say so. "You show me the food and I'll concoct something to satisfy."

"I'll do that as soon as the little feller is done with his dinner."

Joshua finished eating and Vivian settled him in the chair then followed Billy to the pantry. He opened bins and showed her where things were, then led her to the cold woodshed attached to the house. A slab of some animal hung under a gunnysack shroud.

"I'll cut off a hunk of meat. What would you like?"

Vivian did some figuring. It was early afternoon yet. "A nice big roast."

She waited for him to saw it off and followed him back to the kitchen. When Mrs. Black saw she intended to work at the stove, she made a sharp sound of protest and jerked to her feet, crossing the room to settle in the rocker, favoring Vivian with dark glances.

Vivian's instinct was to keep her back to the woman and ignore her but when she did, her skin tightened. Better the enemy you could see than one you couldn't, so she turned. As she put the roast in the oven then prepared potatoes and turnips, Mrs. Black glowered relentlessly at her. Having no desire to sit in front of the fire and move the staring match into close quarters, Vivian went to the pantry and found dried apples and enough ingredients for a German apple pudding cake—something she'd learned to make at the Weimers'.

Billy had gone back to the woodshed and now returned with a crate lined with fur. "I made Joshua a little bed."

His mother whimpered.

Billy ignored her, and Vivian tried her best to do likewise as she went to examine the little nest he'd made.

"It's very nice. The baby will be warm and safe here." She thought of picking up Joshua and seeing how he fit, but Mrs. Black's dark look halted her at first thought.

Seeing her hesitation, Billy murmured, "She ain't gonna hurt you."

How could he be so certain? Vivian kept her face expressionless. Just because the woman had never hurt him didn't guarantee she would not hurt someone who seemed to step on her toes simply by being in the room.

Billy put Joshua in the box. The baby snuffled a bit and returned to sleeping.

Vivian smiled. "Thank goodness he isn't screaming like he did last night."

The pair of them hung over the box for a moment, watching Joshua sleep, but one could stare at a sleeping baby only so long. Vivian returned to the kitchen. Billy settled in the stuffed chair and opened the newspapers he'd brought from town. Mrs. Black glowered at the paper hiding her son's face then stomped to the quilt frame. She perched on a stool and bent over the quilt, studiously stitching the layers together.

"You want to read the news?" Billy offered Vivian a paper.

Grateful for the diversion, she glanced at the headlines, which held no interest for her. Her own problems were enough to contemplate without examining the troubles of others. She found the current serial and read the latest escapades of the pair in the story, chuckling aloud at the predicaments they got themselves into. When Mrs. Black made an angry sound, Vivian choked back her amusement.

As the light began to fade, Vivian put the vegetables to cook. A little later she announced, "Supper's ready."

Billy hurried to the table but Mrs. Black acted as if she hadn't heard.

"Ma, suppertime."

The woman shook her head and made a high-pitched sound of refusal or anger. Vivian had no way of knowing which.

Billy hesitated, his gaze devouring the food. "You got to eat. And it looks mighty good."

Still, Mrs. Black did not move.

Billy grabbed a chair and pulled it out. He hesitated again, seemed puzzled about what to do with his mother. Then he sat. "I guess it's up to you whether or not you eat but I intend to enjoy this." He tipped his head toward another chair, indicating Vivian should sit.

She didn't move. "I can wait. Let your mother eat."

The woman jumped to her feet. A pair of scissors clattered to the floor as she dashed to the pantry and again disappeared into the far corner.

Billy sighed. "Let's give thanks. Good Lord, bless these sinners as they eat their dinners. Amen."

A bubble of amusement tickled Vivian's throat. She tried to choke it back. After all, one didn't laugh about a prayer. But had he meant to be poking fun at the situation or was he being naively sincere? She stole a look from under her eyelashes, saw a twinkle in his eyes informing her he did it on purpose. She could no longer contain it and sputtered with laughter.

He grinned as he filled a plate and took it to his ma, then piled another almost as high as his chin. He ate several mouthfuls, came up for air long enough to say, "Good supper," then cleaned his plate. His eyes rounded with appreciation when she served a generous portion of the dessert topped with cream so thick she'd piled it on with a spoon. "Ma is gonna really like this." He took her a dishful. "Look, Vivian made dessert."

The woman mumbled something in an angry tone but Vivian noticed Billy did not bring the food back.

They did the dishes together then, as he'd done the night before, Billy drew his mother from the pantry to the fireplace. Joshua wakened and Vivian sat on a kitchen chair to feed him, listening as Billy read again from the Bible.

He read for some time, his voice calming his mother.

A little later, Mrs. Black rose and went to her room, not saying a word or making any unearthly noises, but closing the door firmly behind her.

"I have to tend to something." Billy went in and out of the woodshed and back and forth to the doorway next to his mother's room.

Vivian paid him little mind. After all, the man no doubt had things that needed doing.

"I've fixed my room for you."

"I couldn't. Where will you sleep? Besides, I'm fine here." But every bone in her body ached to stretch out and relax.

"I put up a cot in the other room for me. It's supposed to be a bedroom but we haven't needed it so it's gotten used for storage." He snorted. "A junk collection, really."

She wanted to refuse but truthfully she ached for a proper sleep. The baby woke, boisterously demanding to be fed, and she was saved from trying to find a way to refuse his offer.

He prepared the bottle and handed it to her. As Joshua settled down to sucking greedily, Billy sank into the other chair. "How did you get messed up with Wayne?"

His question hammered through her thoughts, drove spikes into her heart. How, indeed?

Chapter Six

She would have avoided the question but Billy's patient expression suddenly made her want to explain. "I don't know where to start."

He shrugged. "Does it matter where you start? Sooner or later you'll end up at the same place."

His attitude made her relax. "When I was fifteen, I was sent to work at the Weimers'. They owned a feed store, ran a gristmill and grain farm. There were always men to feed, customers to serve and the house and buildings to keep clean."

"Did you like it?"

"What? Working at the Weimers'?" His question startled her. "It didn't matter what I liked. I had no choice about where I went or what I did. An orphan has no say." How well she'd learned to live by that truth.

"Did they treat you right?"

His words slammed straight through the complacent attitude she had adopted after her few unsuccessful rebellions at the home. She'd quickly learned life was much easier if she asked no questions, made no demands. But behind her acceptance lay a sea of hurt. She had no choice about where she went and no one to care if she was treated kindly or otherwise. Thankfully, his words only skimmed the surface of that vast expanse.

"They were fair enough. If I did my work they didn't bother me much."

"Much? What does that mean?"

"They expected obedience, and quickly. A person learned not to dilly-dally around. They would tolerate no rudeness to them or the customers. But they didn't use the strap for no reason. Nor did they let the customers take advantage of me. They were decent people." Her obedient attitude had served her well. Yet all the time, the hunger for more—more being seen, being valued, being somebody—grew until her hunger for approval made her easy prey to her feelings when Wayne appeared on the scene.

"Wayne had business in the area. We recognized each other immediately. He spent several weeks conducting his business. I saw him every day. And soon—"

"What was his business?"

Her thoughts stalled. Somehow, his reason for being there had never come up. "I don't know. He never exactly said." They'd discussed other things. Done other things. Her cheeks grew hot with shame. Certain Billy could see the brilliant red of her thoughts, her regrets, she lowered her gaze. In her arms lay the evidence of her sin—Joshua. But for nine months—more if she considered the two he'd been in the foundling home—her love for him had grown until it almost swallowed up the shame of her sin. Almost.

She wanted to explain although she knew she was without excuse. "When Wayne showed up it was like a bit of home had been given back to me. I remember Wayne at school." She lifted her gaze to Billy. "I know he was unkind. Not only to you. But he grew up. Changed."

His eyes remained hard and unyielding as if he didn't believe her.

"He brought me little gifts—some candy, a new hankie with lace and—" Of course Billy didn't care about the fine hankie. Nor would he understand how important Wayne's gifts had seemed. "He took me to church. To a literary evening." How wonderful it had been to have an escort, to feel like someone cared that she'd fixed her hair special. No matter that she had only the plain gray dress the Weimers provided. She tried her best to fancy it up by folding the hanky into a fan and pinning it to her bodice. Wayne had noticed and said how nice it looked.

"We went for long walks. He told me how Quinten had changed, reminded me of the people I'd known. I thought…" She'd been so foolish to build dreams and plans on his words. "I thought he meant…" she swallowed hard "…to take me with him."

She pushed aside her shame, her regrets, her sense of having been a fool. "Otherwise…" She couldn't bring herself to give her awful sin a name. "I wouldn't have done it."

"But he never knew. When he sees Joshua he will do what any honorable man would do. He'll marry you."

She nodded. "And give Joshua a home and a name."

"Lucas will get a message to us when Wayne returns." His blue eyes revealed his weariness with the subject and lots more besides.

She thought she detected sadness, and likely an echo of the same shame creasing permanent pinpoints of pain into her brain.

He shifted to stare at the flames. As if he couldn't bear to look at her anymore.

She didn't blame him. Her own mirror threw back an unforgiving, condemning glance. Only one thing enabled her to face the present and contemplate the future—Joshua. Besides the baby, one other good thing had come of the situation. She'd learned to pray—urgent, soul-filled prayers—and her faith had grown strong. She could trust God to see her through this complication.

"He ever do any business that you know of?"

The sudden shift of focus stalled every thought. "I don't recall." Suddenly, she remembered the paper she'd signed. "I did give my signature to a form. He said it was a formality to close the debt my parents owed."

Billy's head cranked around. "Did the bank sell the house?"

"Yes, of course, but they didn't get enough from the sale. I think Wayne wanted to do me a favor and cancel the debt. He said there was no need for me to worry about clearing my parents' name."

"Huh. First time I heard of the Styleses forgiving a debt."

She gave a smile that felt like it struggled with the corners of her mouth. "Perhaps because he had some fondness for me."

"Could be." But his expression tightened even more.

She understood he and Wayne might have ongoing problems.

"What happened when you realized…?" He didn't need to finish his question for her to know what he meant.

Shame. Condemnation. "The Weimers allowed me to stay. Once I couldn't hide my condition, I had to stay out of sight of their customers." Not a day passed when the Weimers didn't remind her of her disgrace. Not that she needed it. Her own heart condemned her. Though after the first fluttering kicks of her baby, a love so profound she couldn't comprehend it had competed with the voice of shame.

"They let you stay after the baby was born?" He had reason to sound surprised.

Her insides wrenched as shame, regret, pain all twisted inside her until she wondered if her heart would burst. "You have to understand something about me. I was weak. I let people tell me what to do. I didn't think I had any choice."

He looked at her full on, quietly waiting for her to continue.

She couldn't break from his gaze even as self-condemnation made the skin around her eyes feel brittle. Something about the way his look seemed full of kindness such as she hadn't seen in a long time made her want to tell him everything, as if by speaking the truth she could rid herself of the guilt. She knew it wouldn't happen but yet a little bit of her hoped.

"I learned early to do what I was told in order to avoid punishment or a reminder of my precarious state as an orphan. When it was time for me to have Joshua, the Weimers sent me back to the home. As soon as the baby was born, they took him away. You see, unmarried orphan girls can't keep their babies and everyone says it's best if they don't see them. They wouldn't even tell me if it was a boy or a girl." She could barely squeeze the whispered words past the spasm in her throat. "I was allowed to rest for a week and then sent back to work." The first few days were a blur of physical and mental pain, of a sense of loss and failure like nothing she could imagine. Her body reminded her daily of the birth and the fact she had nothing to show for it but the cramps in her belly.

It was weeks before she could think at all without crying, though she learned quickly not to cry when anyone could see her.

She was totally unaware she cried now until a tear

dripped from her chin. She swabbed at her cheeks with a corner of Joshua's blanket.

"I only knew I had a son because my friend Marie cared for the babies in the home." She paused as another wave of pain engulfed her. "He was supposed to be adopted."

He nodded, his look so intent she felt as if she were wrapped in his thoughts. Kind thoughts. It was a surprising idea and one that eased some of the tension mounting as she told her story.

"I thought of Joshua every day. I prayed for him. And slowly, I grew strong enough to start thinking."

A slow smile filled his eyes. "And you ain't stopped since."

She chuckled. "I started to think how I could provide a home for Joshua myself. All it would take was finding Wayne. So I… You might not want to hear this part."

He chuckled. "You stole the baby from his new parents? I can see you doing it."

"No one had adopted him. Can you imagine?"

They both studied Joshua who sucked one fist and kicked his legs.

"Can't. No."

"Thank you." They exchanged a smile full of sweetness. It was good to share her love for Joshua with someone even if only temporarily. "I told the Weimers I was leaving. They weren't too pleased. I guess they appreciated my work though not once did they say so. I told a little lie. I said Wayne had sent for me. It was the only way I figured they'd let me go."

"Guess it ain't the worst thing a person could do."

"No. I'd already done worse." She held his gaze, wondering if he would reveal disgust.

Instead, he grinned. "I'm having a hard time thinking Joshua is wrong."

It was the kindest thing anyone could say and she hugged her son, though what she wanted to do was hug Billy.

She returned to her story. "I made my way back to the home. Marie helped me even though she was probably whipped for it. She let me know when Matron—that's what we called the head of the home—and her assistants were busy elsewhere and then she let me in to get Joshua. It was the first time I'd ever held him." She couldn't go on.

Billy leaned forward and squeezed her fingers. She turned her palm into his, let his big fist swallow her hand. His strength filled her.

She smiled. "Remember you asked if a lawman would be after you?"

"Wondering even more now."

"I have his birth certificate saying I'm his mother. Marie said that would be proof enough if Matron happened to send the law after me."

"Good to know." He squeezed her hand again and withdrew, leaving her feeling alone.

"So, here I am."

"Yes, here you are. Until Wayne returns."

She blinked. For a moment, she'd forgotten Wayne. She felt safe here. Except when Mrs. Black was up. "I hope it won't be long."

Billy's expression grew tight, his eyes guarded. "You and Ma both. Is the little guy ready for bed?"

Joshua chewed on his fist and showed no sign of being sleepy.

"I'll give him another bottle in a little while then put him down. Don't let us keep you up."

He lumbered to his feet. "I'll say good-night, then." He ducked into the narrow doorway and closed the door quietly.

Vivian let out a long, shaky sigh. For a few minutes, she'd thought Billy might care about how she fared and then suddenly he'd withdrawn. She couldn't blame him. She was a woman with a sinful past—a past that couldn't be hidden.

A little later, Joshua cried and she prepared his bottle, relaxing as he sucked back his milk. She burped him, changed him and tucked him into the fur-lined bed. He stiffened and screamed.

She picked him up again and tried to burp him. But Joshua arched his back and wailed. She wrapped him tighter and walked back and forth, jostling the baby. But he wouldn't settle. Was this his normal nighttime behavior? His crying seemed full of distress. Had he gotten too cold on the trip to town and back? Maybe he was sick or hurting. How did one know with such a little baby?

Billy strode into the room, his curls more unruly than usual. He wore hastily donned trousers with suspenders over his woolens. "Fussy again?"

"I don't know. Maybe he's sick or hurt."

"Is he hot?"

She pressed her cheek to the baby. "He's warm and damp."

"Probably from too much crying. Here, let me take him."

She gladly gave him the squalling bundle and returned to the rocker.

Billy cradled the baby on his barrel-sized chest and walked the floor.

He hummed as he walked and slowly the baby stopped

fussing. He continued to walk for fifteen minutes then eased down into the stuffed chair.

"How do you do that?" she asked.

"I don't know. But be happy it works."

"I am. I'm also annoyed he won't settle in my arms. What am I doing wrong?"

"He's just a baby. He doesn't make judgments. Probably has a tummy ache. Maybe my voice calms him."

"Then you better keep talking."

She invited him to talk? To sit and talk to her? Him. Big Billy Black. The monster of the county.

Warmth flared through him.

He looked at the fire to see if a log had burst open releasing an explosion of heat, but the flames simmered gently. The heat came from inside his own chest, bursting forth from a long-forgotten, always-denied spot, a spot he purposely neglected, where companionship and acceptance were normal.

Not that he needed anyone to talk to. He said plenty— to his pets, to the patient, good Lord up above and to the air. But within the space of a day, he'd discovered it wasn't the same as having someone with flashing brown eyes to acknowledge his words or challenge him with questions.

She'd be gone quick enough, though. He'd be back to having the cats, the good Lord and the clouds up above to talk to. Best not get used to eyes and mouth in a lively face. He would return to being alone, Big Billy Black.

But he'd had none of these rational arguments when Lucas called to say she stood in the middle of the sidewalk. Hadn't moved in several minutes. He hadn't even considered someone might see him as he rushed to her side.

When she'd told about becoming Joshua's mother, how

the baby had been sent to a foundling home, his insides had practically caved in. He sensed her pain and helplessness. He didn't know what it was like to be an orphan but he knew too much what it felt like to be treated like he had no feelings. His insides curled with anger that she should have endured such unkindness. Nor was it over. The future would carry its share of whisperings even after she married Wayne, though being a Styles would protect her as much as anything. He tried not to let it bother him to think of her marrying that man.

The baby snuffled. He patted the wee mite and made a low sound. The baby squirmed. "Guess he needs to hear my voice." He hankered to know more about Vivian and saw no need to waste a perfectly good opportunity. "What was it like when your ma and pa were alive?"

Her face softened in remembrance.

"We lived a simple life. Father was a carpenter. He made nice things for the house. He made me a beautiful dollhouse for my eighth birthday. I wonder what happened to it?" She stared into the distance. "Over the sofa were pictures in matching frames of Blue Boy and Pinkie. I liked to sit on a footstool looking at them as my mother read to me."

"You felt special as a child."

"I did. Didn't you?"

He closed his mind. "I prefer not to look back."

"Surely there must be good things to remember? I'm not meaning to pry but I'm... I guess I'd like to understand what happened to you."

How could she possibly begin to understand? His thoughts slid back to before—before everything turned upside down. Yet amid the bad things, he found surprising flashes of things special and comforting. He plucked the most vivid. "We lived in a tiny house, a settler's shack, on the edge of Indian territory. I remember picking berries with Ma. I 'spect I was eating more than went in my bucket. I recall how they were both sweet and tart. Ma said she'd make me a pie and maybe jam. She hugged me and laughed. Said she wouldn't kiss me 'cause I was sticky with berry juice. The sun was warm. I felt special that day.

"I'd plumb forgot about it. It was before—" He broke off. He didn't talk about before. Didn't think on it more'n he was forced to.

"Before? Do you mean before—"

"Ma's capture?"

"I'm sorry. It's none of my business."

"Hmm. Seems like everybody's made it their business."

"I'm sorry," she said again. "I don't mean to be curious, but how old were you when…?" She tipped her head toward Ma's door.

Billy shifted the baby a little, righted the tiny head, all the time holding Vivian's warm brown gaze. Something about the way she studied him, waiting, a little fearful perhaps, a little curious but maybe, just maybe, feeling a need to explore something they'd shared—the loss of a mother. Fear of what people would say. So many painful things came from the lips of people who seemed to have no compassion. She'd lost her father, too. For her, they would never return. Suddenly, he wanted to tell her how it was. How things could change. How life didn't stay the same. Though he guessed she knew that and expected to find a different future when Wayne returned.

"I was six years old when Ma was captured. She saw the Indians coming and hid me behind the wood in a cupboard much like that." He pointed to the cavity filled with firewood. "I was already a big boy. I don't know how she managed to put the wood back in good enough to hide me. She made me promise not to make a sound no matter what happened. I heard her scream and then it grew quiet. I didn't move until I heard Pa calling us." He stopped and took a deep breath. "She saved my life."

"How awful for you."

He shut away the pain—that was then—and focused on the contentment of now. "Not knowing if she was dead or alive was the worst. Pa said he thought she was dead. I heard him tell someone he prayed she was. When I heard that, I ran into our little root cellar and cried. I didn't want my ma to be dead. Then I got used to her being gone. She was gone six whole years."

Vivian's eyes glistened. "I can't imagine what she went through. It's no wonder—"

"She's crazy? Only she isn't. Just scared." He shifted the baby and when the little one didn't waken, put him into the bed he'd made. "He's settled, and I think we both need to get some sleep." As he headed for the door, Vivian touched his arm.

"Your mother is fortunate to have you."

Startled, he stopped and looked down at her. Remembering the berry-picking time before his mother's capture had enlivened a yearning long buried, long denied. Vivian's touch gave it power to burn upward to his heart where it gave a solid, insistent beat, then it headed straight to his eyes, making them sting with embarrassed heat. He blinked twice, grateful she hadn't noticed the awkward pause. "I'm fortunate to have her."

Chapter Seven

Billy pulled the covers to his chin. His suddenly exposed feet protested the cold. He shifted, adjusted his bulk, trying to find the usual comfortable spots in his mattress. But he'd given his bed to Vivian and this one wasn't big enough to accommodate his size. He groaned as he remembered the night before, how he'd let down a barrier in his mind and told Vivian about Ma. Something he'd kept to himself all these years.

He snorted in derision. Not that everyone didn't know, or fill in the details as they wished.

But only Pa knew he'd hidden while his ma was captured. He was only a boy and couldn't have stopped the Indians. He understood Ma would have suffered more if her son had been captured, too. Nevertheless, knowing didn't change the feeling he'd let her down.

No matter what was done or what people said, it wouldn't happen again. He would take care of Ma. He'd protect her from every kind of danger—physical or otherwise.

It was time to get up and he tossed aside the inadequate covers, yanked on his clothes and hurried from the icy room.

Vivian, dark shadows under her eyes, sat in front of the fire, rocking Joshua.

He hadn't heard the baby but she looked as if she hadn't slept. "He didn't fuss all night, did he?" He should have stayed up longer. Seems little Joshua would only settle for him. His chest expanded. He kind of liked knowing that.

"He slept some. He's just had another bottle and he's gone back to sleep." She put the baby in his little bed. "I'll get breakfast started."

Ma scurried from her room, jerked on her coat and boots, grabbed the milk pail and headed outside.

Vivian hung back until Ma left. "I don't mean to frighten her."

"It's not your fault. She doesn't like strangers." He pulled on his heavy coat and fur hat. "I'll feed the critters. Give you time to cook up a feed." He put a slight emphasis on the last word hoping she would make enough to fuel him for a few hours.

She laughed. "I've cooked for large crews. I think I can manage to make enough food to satisfy your appetite."

He grinned widely. "I don't eat quite as much as a threshing crew."

She lifted her eyebrows in a flash of disbelief. "Guess it depends on the size of the crew."

She was teasing. He could tell by the way her eyes seemed to capture the light seeping through the window and hoard it. He knew by the way the corners of her mouth tilted upward just enough to round her cheeks. And knowing it felt as if the spring butterflies had returned but instead of fluttering at the trees, they danced in his heart. A chuckle started slow and cautious in the pit of his stomach. It rolled, building up volume and speed until it burst from his throat, spilling out in deep, satisfying explosions.

His pleasure deepened when she laughed softly then said, "I'll do my best."

He still chuckled as he entered the barn.

Ma looked up. "What's so funny?"

"Vivian. She said she could make enough food for me 'cause she's cooked for crews. She was teasing me about my big appetite."

"Huh. Don't you be getting fond of that woman. She won't stay. She'll go and maybe…"

The knowledge sobered Billy and stole the pleasure of his amusement. "Is that what you're afraid of? That some woman will come along and persuade me to leave?"

Ma turned away but not before he caught the dark fear in her eyes.

"That will never happen."

"You ain't going to be happy with me the rest of your life."

"I'd never leave you. You know that."

They fell silent, but her words edged into his thoughts and poked unwelcome fingers into secret places. It might be nice to have someone like Vivian to laugh with. But like Ma said, no one would live out here. No one would ever be comfortable around Ma. Or maybe it was she who would never be comfortable around someone else, and would do her best to drive them away. He sighed. What did it matter? He had all he wanted right here— the mother he'd been deprived of as a child, his animals and the great outdoors. God's gifts were sufficient. He would not acknowledge his loneliness that had a Vivian shape to it.

He fed the cats, played with Limpy who needed little else but a pat on the head, put out some oats for Betsy's latest calf, already half grown, and gave Blaze a good brushing. He wanted to spend some time alone talking to the animals and collecting his thoughts, but Ma finished and waited for him. He sighed. She wouldn't return to the house without him. Not with Vivian there.

He put away the currycomb and left the barn.

The cold had a snap to it. He didn't need a thermometer to know the temperature had dipped to a new low. Despite the cold, it was beautiful outdoors. Even though his nose stung by the time they crossed the yard, if he didn't have to hang around the house for Ma's sake, he might have considered a walk to the creek just to see how it looked frozen over and snow dusted.

He stepped inside, and sucked in delicious smells of sausage, cinnamon, hot fat and coffee. Saliva flooded his mouth and a loud growl came from his stomach. It didn't take him a full minute to scramble from his outer clothes. He hurriedly washed his hands then sat at the table, greedily eyeing the stacks of food. A pile of griddle cakes, a bowl of hot applesauce, a heap of sausages, a steaming pot of thick porridge. "I see you found the rest of the supplies."

"You have enough to feed a small army."

He chuckled at the teasing in her voice. "Or one large man. Ma, you gonna sit down so we can eat?"

She shot him a look full of accusation and ducked into the pantry. Seems she'd decided to eat all her meals in solitude. "Suit yourself." He waggled a finger toward a chair, indicating Vivian should join him. His stomach growled demandingly.

She laughed. "We better hurry."

He bowed his head. "Lord, bless this food we are about to receive and bless the hands that prepared it."

He grinned at Vivian when he raised his head, pleased at the gentle blush in her cheeks.

Ma made a sharp noise of protest and he rolled his eyes. Vivian giggled, increasing his pleasure. Billy needed no invitation to dig in. He filled his mouth before he took a plate to Ma. He didn't bother waiting for her to say anything before he hurried back to his food.

Several minutes later, he paused. "Good food."

"Thanks."

"Where'd you learn to cook?"

"From Mrs. Weimer. She insisted I learn many of her German dishes."

"Awfully glad she did."

"Good. If you're stuck with me, I can at least do something useful."

He chuckled. "You keep cooking like this and I might be tempted to keep you."

Ma muttered.

He raised his voice. "I'm joshing, Ma."

Unappeased, Ma stomped from the pantry. He'd never seen her quite so angry and determined. She deposited her used dishes, then hurried to the stool by the quilt and picked up her needle. The way she jabbed it into the material made Billy feel like laughing. Ma wanted him to understand she wouldn't let him keep Vivian.

As if she'd stay.

He couldn't successfully ignore the silent cry that wished she would. Somehow, he forced his face to be expressionless as he turned back to Vivian. "Thank you for breakfast."

"It's me who should be thanking you for allowing me to remain here."

Ma grunted.

Billy shook his head, thinking he maybe preferred Ma

Dakota Child

all fearful to Ma all defensive, then as Vivian stacked the dishes and scrubbed the table, he filled the basin with hot water and washed the dishes as she dried. He and Ma did the same thing day after day after day. A change was nice.

Joshua woke as Vivian hung the towel to dry.

"I'll get him," Billy said. He liked feeding the baby, and settled in the stuffed chair with Joshua and took the bottle Vivian prepared. Ma studiously kept her head bent over the quilt as Vivian returned to hover by the stove. "Come and sit down," Billy called.

She hesitated. Ma stiffened in protest. "Look, we're all stuck inside. No point in either of you pretending you can't see each other." He ignored the anger boiling in Ma's gaze. "She ain't gonna hurt you." He didn't know if he meant the words for Ma or Vivian. Both needed to hear them.

Vivian edged over to sit in the rocker.

Billy smiled. "Isn't this cozy?" He didn't voice the rest of his thought. If not for the tension between the two women crackling like he suspected the ice on the creek would be doing, this would be kind of nice—a baby in his arms, a woman sitting across from him, Ma at her quilting. The contrast to real life made him laugh silently, mockingly. His hidden chuckle caused his stomach to bounce and Joshua stopped sucking to stare at him with wide-eyed surprise. "Someday you might understand," he murmured to the little one.

Joshua made a happy cooing sound.

Vivian leaned closer. "I think he likes you."

Billy's chest expanded several inches at the idea. And as quickly deflated when Ma snorted. There would be no little babies of his own to hover over. It was a fact of his life. He quickly quenched the wish that things could be different.

Hours later, Ma sighed and finally got up from the stool. Good thing. He was beginning to think she'd never be able to straighten if she didn't leave her position for something else. The only time she looked up was to give Vivian one annoyed look after another as Vivian puttered about the kitchen, mostly moving things from one spot to another and wiping under them. She stomped to the door and shrugged into her coat, stabbed her feet into her boots. "I'm going to give Betsy some extra feed."

A whoof escaped Vivian's lungs as the door closed behind Ma. He knew she'd been as aware of Ma's silent messages as he. She wandered the length of the room, touching pictures on the wall and lifting lamps and other things. She paused at the quilt and bent over to examine it. "This is beautiful. The stitching is an intricate pattern of—" She looked it over more carefully.

"Ma calls it The Garden of Eden."

"I'd like to learn how to do this."

Ma rushed into the room, saw Vivian studying the quilt and shrieked. Unmindful of her snow-covered boots, she rushed over. "Leave it alone."

Vivian backed up so fast she bumped into the stool. "Sorry. So sorry." She hurried to the rocker and sat down, breathing as if she'd run from the barn in a panic.

Billy fixed Ma with a hard look. Ma gave him an equally hard stare. "She was only looking at it. Admiring it. Said it was beautiful. Any reason that should upset you?"

Ma didn't answer.

Joshua cried to be fed and even though Billy enjoyed holding him, he sensed Vivian's increasing restlessness and let her feed him. And he made up his mind to do something for her. As soon as the baby curled in his bed in peaceful sleep, Billy went into the crowded room where he'd spent the night. Good thing Ma kept everything. In a few minutes, he found a warm coat and boots Pa wore when he was alive. They would be big for Vivian, but warm. He found a woolen cap with earflaps and added it to his pile, which he carried into the other room. "Put these on." He handed the items to Vivian. "I'm going to take you outside."

Ma jerked to her feet. "I'm not looking after the baby."

"We'll be back before he wakes up." He couldn't understand her dislike of Joshua. Ma liked all the other animals. Why not the baby?

Vivian rushed to her feet and pulled on the clothes, stood dressed and ready before Billy got his own coat on. She almost disappeared in the heavy clothing except for her eyes, which flashed with anticipation. It seemed she looked forward to this as much as he—for entirely different reasons, he reminded himself. He longed to enjoy her company. She wanted to escape Ma's.

She gasped as she stepped outside. "I didn't realize it was this cold."

"It ain't inside."

She laughed. "For which I am grateful."

"You grateful for anything else?" He knew she found Ma a trial.

Vivian turned full circle, her eyes squinting against the bright sun. "For all this beauty," she whispered.

"What do you see?"

"The snow sparkles as if the stars have been poured onto it. The tree branches are iced like a birthday cake."

He liked the way she put words to what he saw. "Do you want to see the animals?"

"I'd love to." Although her eyes crinkled half-shut

against the brightness of sun on snow, her face seemed alive with eagerness.

For a moment, he hesitated. Would she find it odd he had such a collection of animals, most of them useless as anything? Or would she see how special they all were?

They stepped into the barn and paused as their eyes adjusted to the muted light. But the cats didn't wait. They wrapped around his feet. Several of them stood with their front paws on his legs, meowing. Three of them studied Vivian for a moment as if to assess who this stranger was, then decided she would do to rub against.

Billy chuckled. "Meet the rest of the cats."

She looked around, counting. "Eleven?"

He nodded, feeling a tiny bit foolish. To cover it, he whistled and Limpy emerged from the straw pile, shaking himself.

"Oh. Poor dog. What happened to him?"

"Born that way. He's never seemed to mind. Never once heard him complain about missing a leg."

She laughed. "Don't suppose he would."

"When he was younger, he could catch gophers and chase rabbits like any four-legged dog so I guess it hasn't mattered much to him."

Vivian bent and took the dog's chin in her palm. She looked into Limpy's eyes and rubbed behind his ears.

Limpy managed to look as sad and unhappy as any animal could.

"He's faking," Billy said. "Trying to get your sympathy."

"Well, it's working." She patted Limpy's head. "You poor puppy."

Billy snorted. "He hasn't been a puppy for a decade."

"Don't listen to him. I know you're still a puppy at heart."

Billy groaned. The dog was lapping it up like fresh cream. The cats joined the party, pushing against Vivian for attention until she plunked down on the straw-covered floor. She laughed and let the cats crowd to her lap and Limpy push against her shoulder. "They can be very demanding, can't they?"

"They're spoiled rotten. I need to teach them some manners." But he sat on the floor beside her and shared the insistent attention of the animals. After a few minutes, half a dozen of the cats curled into furry balls around Vivian where they began licking their paws and purring.

Vivian laughed. "This is fun. They make me feel so welcome."

Unlike Ma. "Don't pay Ma any mind."

Vivian shrugged. "A little hard not to. Seems like she can't wait to get me out of her house."

"I told you. She's afraid of people." He paused then said the obvious. "And people are afraid of her."

"I remember the stories the kids told at school. About her acting like an Indian. I guess everyone was scared of her."

At least Vivian didn't pretend it wasn't true. "I'm aware of that."

She shifted so she could look him in the face. "Billy, why didn't you keep coming to school? You never gave people a chance to see you're just big, not scary."

Her words eased over his mind like a dose of soothing ointment. He could enjoy this for a long time—someone to talk to, to share his thoughts with, to enjoy simple pleasures with.

He jerked his thoughts back with cruel decisiveness. In reality, nothing had changed. He was the same, his situation, too. And Vivian would marry Wayne. "I knew they'd never accept me. And for sure, never let Ma forget she'd spent six years living with Indians. As if it was her fault. Pa hoped by moving here she'd get a new start, but everything just followed us. Only it was worse because we were strangers here."

"Maybe if you'd given them more of a chance."

"You mean listen to more nasty things about Ma? I lost Ma for six years. I did nothing to stop the Indians. I wasn't about to pretend I didn't hear what they said."

She tipped her head, her expression troubled. "You blame yourself for the Indians taking her?"

"I hid."

"You were six. You obeyed your mother. Don't you think that's what she wanted? Can you imagine how much worse it would have been for her if you'd been captured, too?"

"She said what kept her going was hoping she'd get back to me."

"There you go."

"I owe her for those years."

She stroked the cats and seemed to consider what to say. "I can understand how you want to protect her. I admire you for that."

As he looked into her eyes, something unfamiliar made itself known. It reminded him of when he found a wild animal and spent some time gentling it. It was like the first time he knew he'd earned their trust and the animal ate from his hand. Triumph, celebration and connection all rolled up and bound together with joy.

"But now you're both hiding."

His elation died like a bird shot from the sky. "What's wrong with that? If Ma could have hidden like I did, she would not have been captured."

"What are you hiding from now?"

"You've seen Ma. You know what people say about

both of us. You think I intend to let people say those things to her face?" He wanted to end this conversation but her gaze held him in a velvet-brown grasp he couldn't escape.

"Perhaps God has something new in store for you."

"Like what?"

"I don't know. Have you ever asked God?"

He searched his mind for a reply. He'd gotten Ma back. He'd always be grateful for that. And he'd found contentment in his life. Finally, he spoke. "I have learned to be content with what I have."

She shook her head. "That doesn't answer my question."

His words didn't satisfy him any more than they did her, but he had no other answer. He never allowed himself to look back, to ask questions for which there were no explanations. Nor did he allow a glance forward. Today was sufficient…until her questions pushed at him. But she didn't know that. Didn't know her questions took him to a place he didn't want to be, couldn't be. He got up. "We better get back." He held out his hand and pulled her to her feet.

Her small hand in his further unsettled his thoughts. He didn't know if he should drop it or continue holding it. He chose the latter without asking himself why.

"I haven't made you angry, have I?"

He tried to untangle his thoughts and decide what he felt. Not anger. Not contentment. Just confusion. "I ain't angry." Though he would almost welcome a good dose of anger. At least he would know what to do with it. A good brisk walk. Or chop a cord of wood. But he didn't like this feeling and had no idea how to handle it.

Vivian sat in front of the fire rocking as if her life depended on it. The trip to the barn with Billy had been a welcome break. But it seemed hours ago. She itched to grab a needle and help Mrs. Black quilt, but the woman made it clear she wouldn't be letting Vivian near her project.

Vivian went over every detail of her only diversion—the visit to the barn. The animals were sweet, obviously well cared for and loved. Seemed the only things that mattered to Billy were his mother and his pets. Too bad. No doubt if he ever let himself care for someone else he would be as loyal, loving and protective as he was with his mother.

A familiar, deep ache pushed at her insides. She wanted exactly what Billy offered his ma. It had been hers when she was a child in Quinten. She hoped to find protection with Wayne. If there was love and affection, so much the better. She hoped there would be. He'd said all the right words when she'd last seen him. But then he'd left and never contacted her.

Time to make supper. Billy enjoyed his meal as always and his ma ate in the pantry but cleaned her plate, so Vivian took that as approval of the food.

Dishes washed and put away, Billy sat before the fire and opened the Bible. "I'm going to read from First Timothy chapter six tonight." He spoke to Vivian then began to read.

She soon understood why he'd chosen this passage.

His deep voice in slow calm tones emphasized each word. "'But godliness with contentment is great gain. For we brought nothing into this world and it is certain we can carry nothing out. And having food and raiment let us be therewith content.'"

He read further but she thought of those words, aching to ask if it meant a person shouldn't want what people gave—friendship, acceptance, companionship? But she would not start such a discussion with his mother in the rocking chair.

Finally, the woman got to her feet and went to her room.

Vivian didn't realize how tense Mrs. Black made her until the door closed behind her and Vivian's shoulders lowered several inches.

Billy remained in the stuffed chair, staring into the fire.

When the baby cried to be fed, Vivian prepared the bottle and sat with the baby in the rocking chair Billy's mother had vacated. Perhaps now she would get a chance to voice her questions.

But it seemed Joshua thought the late evening was his time for attention. Again, he fussed and refused to settle until Billy took him and walked him for a while, singing as he paced. The baby finally quieted.

Billy barely had time to sit down and settle the baby on his chest before Vivian spoke.

"You read that Bible passage on purpose, didn't you?"

"It says what I believe."

"But doesn't it refer to things?" She paused, almost afraid to voice her feelings, knowing they revealed the ache of her heart. Would they trigger similar yearnings for Billy? She couldn't guess if he'd welcome such feelings. He seemed convinced he'd spend the rest of his life with nothing but his ma and his pets. More the pity. He had so much to offer—her cheeks burned as she realized she'd been thinking how he cradled her in his arms, comforted her with a touch… She couldn't remember feeling this way toward Wayne. Had he ever comforted her? Her thoughts seared her with shame. She intended to marry Wayne and had no call to compare him with another man. "Don't we all need friendship, companion-ship and acceptance?"

"Is it possible to have them without compromising who we are, perhaps even our moral standards?"

His words sliced through her like she'd swallowed broken glass. "I admit I compromised my standards because of my need for friendship and acceptance."

Chapter Eight

"No. No. I wasn't meaning you and your situation. I meant me. I learned I would have to make such choices if I was to have friends. I would have to pretend my mother didn't exist. I would never do that."

She perceived his invincible integrity and pushed aside her initial reaction of guilt to concentrate on where he intended the conversation to go. "That's very noble. But I'd be lonely."

He sighed deeply, shifting Joshua when he whimpered, and patting his tiny back. "Good thing you don't need to worry about it. You'll soon be back in town."

Yes, back to her goal. A twinge of regret tugged at her thoughts. Regret? No. Billy's gentle presence was comforting only because of Vivian's circumstances—difficult weather and the disappointment of not being able to see Wayne.

"I would have stopped them."

"Pardon?" She had no idea what he meant.

"I would have stopped them from taking you away."

Surprise jolted her limbs. She sat upright so fast the rocker kicked back, almost tossing her from the chair. Not since her parents died had anyone wanted to defend her. Trailing after her surprise came a flush of pleasure. She grinned widely, warmth creeping up her limbs and settling into her chest.

Suddenly, bits and pieces of that day lived in her mind—things she'd completely forgotten until now. "I remember two men and a woman like bats in their long black coats. Mrs. Griswald was one of them. She used to come when Mother had the ladies in for tea. She always wore black and had a ratty old hat with crinkled-up paper flowers on it." She paused, remembering her confusion as these people invaded her house.

"One man kept clearing his throat. It reminded me of a chicken scratching at a piece of wood. Mrs. Griswald stomped ahead of the others and announced in a voice like a summer storm, 'This child is to be removed to a foundling home.' I didn't know it meant orphanage. I didn't know what they wanted. I could barely understand that Mother and Father were gone and not coming back."

Another forgotten memory of that day flooded her mind. "Mr. Styles was there. He said something about the house being sold." Her throat had burned with anger at the words. "I screamed, 'You can't sell our house.' I screamed all sorts of protests. But no one listened. Mrs. Griswald marched me to my room and grabbed a few things. Most of the stuff she picked up and tossed aside. 'You won't be needing this where you're going.' It wasn't until I was on the train I found enough courage to ask when I'd be back. The lady laughed. She said, 'You won't ever be coming back.'" Vivian spouted out the whole story in one breath and stopped to gasp in air. "I didn't know an orphan was nobody. Had no rights. Couldn't even choose where they would live."

"I wish I'd been there."

She imagined him shooing the batlike adults from the house so fast their coats flared into wings.

She looked into his eyes, every heartbeat searing through her like a bolt of lightning. Every breath filled her lungs with a totally unfamiliar storm. The seconds ticked by, counted by the thunder of her pulse. The life-giving blood just below her skin's surface surged with such power it seemed the air vibrated.

And it had absolutely nothing to do with what she wanted in Quinten.

It came from the reassuring gaze of the man across from her.

The baby snuffled and began to fuss.

Vivian blinked and jerked her thoughts back in one sharp movement like snapping a whip. Embarrassed by how much she'd said and how her emotions had veered off path, she couldn't look at Billy. "I'll get a bottle ready."

She offered to take the baby when the milk had warmed but Billy said, "I like feeding the little guy."

Vivian sat across from him again, wishing she had something to occupy her hands—and her mind. She was much too aware of her emotional exposure. But also, she realized with a start, an assurance of being protected, validated, and found worthy. And from such an unlikely source—someone who didn't consider such things necessary.

She sighed. "It isn't as if I haven't done my best since that day."

"I'm sure you did."

She looked at him then. "How would you know that?"

He chuckled. "Because you have a very strong sense of right and wrong. That always includes doing a job well."

"I don't know how you can tell that from what little

you've seen of me." She clung to his gaze, something deep inside calling out to him for an answer.

"Vivian Halliday, you rescued your son. You faced a storm to protect him."

She snorted. "We would have both died if you hadn't stumbled on us."

"If God hadn't led me to you."

Again that sense of connection between them. And something else as right and fitting as it was unfamiliar. Vivian couldn't put a name to it. Or rather, she admitted, she circled around the word, afraid of what it meant. Fondness. Caring. Mutual regard. She closed her mind to further examination.

"I see a woman who will always want justice and demand mercy."

His words were a benediction to her soul.

"I thank God He led me to you in the storm." He looked uncomfortable, as if he'd said more than he should, and lowered his gaze to Joshua. "I'm glad I could rescue both of you."

He said no more. But long after Billy had gone to bed, and even after Joshua settled and Vivian lay on the bed in Billy's bedroom, his words surrounded her. She knew she would never forget them. Even after she married Wayne, she'd find comfort in Billy's blessing.

Guilt twisted through her. She shouldn't be thinking of Billy when she planned to marry another.

The next day was even colder. Frost built so thick on the window glass it dimmed the sunlight. Vivian stood before the kitchen window, scratching a peephole.

She needed to get to town. Not just for Joshua's sake. For her own. The thoughts she had about Billy had no place in her heart. She'd made one mistake. She wasn't about to make another. But she had nowhere to go until Wayne returned. How long would he be away? Days? Weeks? Heaven forbid, months?

"Have a look in this box." Billy's words pulled her from scratching at the window. "You might find a book you'd like to read."

She hurried to his side. "Thank you." Her eyes overbrimmed with gratitude at his thoughtfulness. It was so like him to think of how to help someone else.

With supreme effort, she jerked her thoughts from heading in that direction, and bent to look through the dozen books. She found one that sounded interesting. Mrs. Black sat at the quilt so Vivian chose the rocking chair and was soon engrossed in the story.

The next day the frost on the window thinned, indicating the temperature had moderated.

After breakfast, Billy said, "I'll slip into town and see if Lucas has heard anything, but no point in you and the baby going out."

Mrs. Black gave a strangled shriek then began to mumble.

The skin on Vivian's spine tightened. She avoided looking at Billy, not wanting him to read her fear, which she knew blared brighter than the winter sun. Was she safe alone with Mrs. Black? Would the woman grow more agitated? Even violent? Vivian glanced around. How could she protect herself? Would the broom or poker do any good if the woman went on a demented rage? Her gaze shifted to the baby bed and her heart kicked against her ribs so hard she gasped. Was the baby in danger? Mrs. Black continued to avoid all contact with Joshua even with Billy's urging.

She stole a look at Mrs. Black, trying to assess her strength. Could Vivian hope to overpower her if she had to?

The woman rocked back and forth mumbling.

Vivian's knees threatened to melt. Mrs. Black hadn't acted so weird since the first afternoon Vivian had invaded her home. Would she get worse when Billy left?

Billy, too, watched his mother, his forehead wrinkled with concern.

Something about Mrs. Black's mumbling caught Vivian's attention. She strained to catch the words.

"Denn Dein ist das Reich und die Kraft und die Herrlichkeit in Ewigkeit."

For thine is the kingdom, and the power, and the glory forever.

The Lord's Prayer in German.

Mrs. Black began again. "Unser Vater im Himmel."

Vivian took a step closer and joined her. "Dein Name werde geheiligt."

Mrs. Black stopped, her mouth working silently as she stared at Vivian. She muttered the next phrase.

Vivian spoke the words with her, never once blinking from the woman's intense look.

Together, they said the entire Lord's Prayer. Silence filled the room when they finished.

"What did you say?" Billy asked, scratching his head and looking curious.

She told him. "The Weimers said it before every meal." Vivian continued to look at Billy's mother, sensing her fragile state. She couldn't tell if the woman intended to retreat further into her past or step into the present, but she knew that she somehow had a say in it by how she handled this moment. She prayed for wisdom from above.

"I pray that all the time," Mrs. Black whispered. "I prayed it when I was with the Indians. It gave me courage. And the Indians feared me. Thought I was—" She circled her finger around her ear. "I pray it still because people think—" Again that circular movement of her finger. "I protect myself with the words."

"Mumbling in a foreign language only convinces them you are—" Vivian tilted her head to indicate the movement Mrs. Black made.

The older woman nodded. "They're afraid of me."

"Yes, they are."

She nodded again. "I'm afraid of them." She began praying in German again.

This time, Vivian accompanied her in English.

Mrs. Black stopped praying and looked confused, perhaps even frightened. Then her expression smoothed, she picked up her needle and returned to quilting.

Vivian's nerves relaxed.

"Well, I'll be," Billy said. He stood uncertainly at the door. "Will you be okay?"

"We'll be okay." The woman wasn't dangerous. Only afraid. And trapped in her fear.

After Billy left, Vivian moved about the room with a sense of freedom. Not that Mrs. Black was suddenly welcoming. She didn't invite Vivian to join her at the quilt, but then neither did she screech and moan. In fact, she seemed quite peaceful.

Until Joshua woke up, loudly demanding his bottle.

Mrs. Black bolted to her feet, sent Vivian an angry look, grabbed her coat and hurried outdoors before Vivian managed to scoop the baby from his bed.

She could only hope the woman would be safe outside. An hour later, Mrs. Black returned and Vivian almost laughed at her relief. Seems she couldn't quite decide what she wanted. She hadn't welcomed being alone with Billy's ma, yet worried when she left and sighed happily when she returned. She'd never known herself to be such a fickle creature.

* * *

Vivian waited at the window, watching for Billy's return. The sun hung directly overhead as he rode into the yard and took Blaze to the barn.

"It's so warm the snow is melting," he said, as he stomped into the house. "I 'spect at this rate—"

Vivian couldn't wait for him to finish his weather report. "Was there any news?"

He shook his head. "Lucas says Mrs. Styles was in the store. He asked outright when Wayne would be returning. The woman got all fluttery and said another week at least, then she mumbled something about unexpected news."

Billy tossed his coat and hat at the hook and rubbed his hands together. "A man gets mighty hungry riding to town and back."

Vivian stared at him. He seemed awfully happy for a man who just learned he was stuck with an uninvited guest for at least another week. She glanced at him. He avoided looking directly at her then slowly, he stilled his restless hands, swallowed hard and met her gaze, his eyes bright with meaning. She shied away, afraid of what she glimpsed, afraid of what he might see in her face, even more afraid of what she felt.

It was wrong to be relieved she had this respite, a few more days to enjoy the way Billy made her feel.

She hurried to the stove and dished up the food. "I made dinner. Expected you would be hungry when you got back."

"You can count on that." He parked himself and waited for Vivian to join him. He glanced at his ma, questioning her with a lift of his eyebrows.

Vivian held her breath as the woman hesitated, glanced at the empty chair, sent Vivian a considering look as if wondering if she was enemy or not, then slowly got to her feet and shuffled toward the table. Halfway across the room she paused, gave a desperate look in the direction of the pantry, then mumbled something Vivian thought was "deliver us from evil" in German and continued toward the table.

Vivian ducked her head as she smiled. Mrs. Black would soon learn Vivian meant evil toward no one.

Billy patted his ma's hand when she sat in the chair. "Let's pray." He bowed his head and for a moment, was silent. "Thank you, God, for happy hearts, for snow and sunny weather. Thank you, God, for this food and that we are together. Amen."

Vivian kept her head bowed for a second after Billy finished. She knew his gratitude was meant for his mother, yet it felt good to be included in *together* if only because she sat at the same table.

Billy hunched over his meal. Although he wasn't about to admit it to anyone, and didn't much care for having to admit it himself, he'd been glad when Lucas said Wayne would be gone longer. It meant Vivian and the baby stayed longer. He'd get to hold the little guy, settle him at night. Maybe he could show Vivian some of his favorite places—the path by the creek, the place where violets grew every spring. She might never see them, but he could tell her what it was like though it wasn't the same as sharing the event would be.

He slammed a fist into his thoughts.

He needed nobody. Managed just fine by himself, thank you one and all.

But holding that tiny little critter and having him smile up at him was about the greatest pleasure he'd known in some time. Except for one thing—Vivian's company.

Last night, sitting by the fire with her, listening to her story, he'd struggled to stop himself from cradling her to his chest like he did little Joshua. No one had the right to treat another the way those people had treated Vivian simply because she was small and helpless. If he'd been there, he would have fought for her. Even now, he'd do all he could to protect and help her.

He groaned silently.

The best way he could help her would be to see her and Wayne reunited and see that she and Joshua got the happy family he wished for.

Again he stifled a groan. What was he thinking? He had a family. He and Ma.

He concentrated on his food. He intended to keep his head squarely parked on his shoulders, but allowed himself one quick glance at Vivian.

She chased her food around the plate with no sign of giving it a lift to her mouth. She sighed. That sound was about more'n he could stand.

Again that ache in his arms as he fought the desire to wrap her to his chest and shelter her from distress.

He wanted to ease the worry filling her eyes with such darkness. "I'll go back to town in a few days and see if there is further news."

"Oh, but—" She shifted her gaze back to him and paused to suck in air. "I appreciate your help."

He couldn't stop his grin from widening, stretching his cheeks to their limit. "Don't mind at all."

Ma slammed her fork to the table. "Foolishness."

Billy only laughed. "Ma, I'd help an animal in trouble. Guess I can bend myself to help a human."

They finished the meal and he began to wash dishes, a job he'd despised until a few days ago. Now he eagerly dipped his hands into the soapy water. And he wasn't blind as to why he suddenly enjoyed the task. It gave him a chance to have Vivian at his side. He didn't have to move much to wash the stack of dishes, which saved him the possibility of crashing into anything. She fluttered from table to stove to the cupboards as quick and graceful as a deer he'd watched playing in a grassy clearing one day. It pleasured him considerably to have her twirl by him as she worked. Sort of gave him a solid feeling.

She brushed his arm as she reached for a dish.

Every bone in his body felt ready to melt like warm butter. If he moved, he'd surely stagger. Maybe into Vivian. His size often made him feel clumsy, but he'd never before had his body act like it had a mind of its own— wanting to reach for her to steady her as she spun past despite his intention of remaining indifferent. His heartbeat drummed in his ears. He needed air. He told his chest muscles to work. *Breathe, man.* With a noisy rush he filled his lungs, sucking in air until he could again feel his toes.

Vivian looked at him. "I know you're helping me out of the goodness of your heart."

The way she said it washed his insides with warm honey. As if she might look up to him. He grinned mockingly—everyone looked up to him. He ducked his head for fear she'd think he laughed at her. But to know her approval, well, if Ma measured his chest size right now she'd find it at least four inches bigger than usual.

Vivian paused at his side, wiping a pot. "I want you to know how much I appreciate it."

"Glad to help out." Glad to bring a smile to her lips and happiness to her life if only for a minute or two. Why, he'd walk through— And why was he thinking such foolish things? She'd go to town and her life with Wayne and he'd stay here with his ma and his life. Chances were they'd never see each other again once this little episode ended.

The plain, blunt, inescapable truth was he didn't want it to end.

He had to stop thinking along those lines.

Chapter Nine

He grabbed for something to talk about. Something that didn't remind him Vivian would leave as soon as Wayne returned. "Tell me about your friend at the orphanage." He scrubbed a pot with excess vigor.

"Marie?"

He nodded as if he had forgotten her friend's name but he remembered everything she'd told him. Down to the way her eyes looked and her mouth moved when she'd given him the information.

"She's twenty—a year older than me." Vivian laughed softly. "If not for Marie, I might have turned into a self-pitying, overly defensive person. She saw how hurt I was by what happened. And how frightened. I'd been pampered as a child. I didn't know how to do all the chores expected of me and I knew nothing about babies." She chuckled again. "I guess you must have seen how little I still know about babies."

He nodded, feeling his grin all the way to the corners of his heart. "Made me mighty suspicious."

"Marie taught me how to do my assigned chores, but more than that, she told me how to handle life. I didn't buy all her philosophies but she certainly turned me in the right direction when she said, 'You don't get a say in what happens to you, but no one can tell you how to feel or act or dream. Do your work, but keep your dreams.'" Vivian looked thoughtful. "Thanks to her, I did exactly that. Maybe too well. I agreed to everything I was told to do. Never allowed myself dreams, though."

"What about now? Any dreams?"

She paused, looked far away, thoughtful, her expression a little regretful. "My dream is to give Joshua the kind of home I had as a child. I want him to be loved and cherished."

Joshua started to squall.

She laughed. "He must know I'm talking about him." She put the last pot away, hung the towel and prepared the bottle before she went to get him. Angry at being made to wait, Joshua screamed.

"Hush, now. You're not going to starve," Vivian murmured.

Billy watched Vivian, her face glowing with love for her son. But he felt a tremor of sadness. Her only dream was for Joshua. Mighty noble. But didn't she have any dreams of her own?

That evening, Joshua set up his usual fuss and calmed only when Billy took him and walked him. After a while, Billy decided Joshua had settled enough to allow him to take advantage of a chair. Still bouncing the baby and humming, he sat across from Vivian. He looked forward to this evening time—a chance to hold little Joshua and visit with Vivian. He ignored how foolish it was in light of how soon it would be a thing of the past.

Vivian leaned back as if she enjoyed this quiet time together as much as he. "What did you and your father do while your mother was gone?"

"Pa's sister stayed with us a while, but then she found some lucky farmer to marry and left. We had a few other women come. I can hardly remember them so I guess they didn't stay long. Finally, Pa said we'd manage as best we could on our own. I soon learned to sweep the floor and do dishes and we cooked simple-enough meals. I weren't fussy so long as I got enough. Pa knew that better'n any of the women he'd hired. Seems they thought I should eat dainty meals. Did I ever start to grow when Pa let me eat as much as I needed." He chuckled, remembering the growth spurt he took. "I was twelve when Ma came back and she couldn't believe how big I was. Taller than her and I outweighed her considerably." He closed his eyes as he recalled the day the sheriff escorted her home. "She was thin as a straw." He shut his mind to remembering but couldn't stop the wayward direction of his thoughts. Ma so afraid. Acting so strange. Not at all like the Ma he remembered.

"Billy, I feel bad for both of you. Your poor ma must have suffered something awful and you must have missed her so much. And then she came back but she was—"

He opened his eyes and held her gaze in a hard look. "She ain't crazy."

"I know that." She gave him hard look for hard look. "But doesn't it seem she's stuck in her past?"

Her unspoken accusation he was somehow at fault annoyed him. "You don't know nothing about her. Besides, why does it matter to you?"

She ducked her head. "I'm sorry. I know it's none of my business."

He wanted to pull his words back, return the sense of connection they'd been sharing.

Slowly, she lifted her head, her brown eyes warm with compassion. "Don't you have any dreams?"

The words crashed through him, rolling like thunder into the far corners of his heart, reverberating across his thoughts like fingers over a scrub board. He had dreams. And sitting across from her, sharing time with her, seeing the dark stillness of her eyes, holding her tiny son, gave those dreams lightning-clear form. Inside him glowed a tender feeling that could easily grow into love if he wasn't careful. He tamped down his yearnings, bolted the door on his reaction. She would wed another. He would remain here with his mother. His dreams could not be acknowledged.

She waited, her eyes wide as if she'd seen a hint of his struggle.

"I got all I need right here. My ma. My pets. The great outdoors and God up in heaven."

She nodded slowly but her expression said she didn't accept it.

He hoped she would not pursue the topic. He had enough difficulty convincing himself without trying to convince her.

They settled into an uneasy pattern over the next days. Ma seemed to have accepted the presence of Vivian and the baby. She wasn't particularly welcoming but at least she was settled, spending quiet hours working at her quilt and joining them at the table for meals.

Billy had no complaints. Not about the food—Vivian continued to make meals that were not only filling but delicious. Most of all, he looked forward to the quiet evenings. He anticipated them far too much. Every day Vivian and the baby stayed increased his longing for more than he could have.

A few days later, the sun shone with such warmth he opened the barn door so all the animals could go outdoors. The frost melted from the windows of the house.

He finished the chores, spent time with the animals, giving them extra attention, trying to stay away from the house. Eventually, he ran out of busy work and leaned against the fence. He hadn't had a walk since Vivian and the baby came. Had the snow changed the shape of things? Done any damage to the trees along the creek? He wanted to see.

His breath escaped in an explosive sound. He wanted to show Vivian all his special places before she left. He gripped the board under his fingers as if holding on to the wood could enable him to hold on to his feelings. But his desire to share his pleasures, just this once, grew. He groaned. He was a strong man. Surely, he could control his emotions.

The sun warmed his face. It was a perfect day. They'd be able to see for miles. And he could just imagine the light on the ice.

One day. What would it hurt?

He headed for the house.

Vivian stood in the doorway, her gaze drifting into the distance as if she felt as restless as he.

Suddenly, his insides warmed and he didn't feel guilty. He was doing this for her. "Grab the baby. We're going for a walk."

She blinked as she realized what he said, then eagerness flooded her face. "I'd like that." She hurried to wrap Joshua in blankets.

Ma had shifted her chair so she worked in the sunlight. She shot him a hard look.

He wanted to assure her it was just a walk even though in the farthest corner of his heart, beyond reason and reality, lay a tender feeling, a sweet regard that he knew would look a lot like love if he examined it.

He had no intention of doing so.

Today, he would simply enjoy the sunshine and Vivian's company.

Within minutes, both Vivian and the baby were ready. "Where are we going?"

"To the creek." There was more to see. Lots more. But they'd turn back at the creek. He took the baby and shortened his step so Vivian could easily keep up. He liked having her at his side.

She lifted her face to the sun and laughed. "Such a nice day."

"Yup." Perfect in every way imaginable. If he could forever keep one day, this would be the one he'd pick. He paused as they passed the buildings and the open prairie lay before them. "Every spring, I see hundreds of antelope cross here. They're so curious, they will follow me at a safe distance. If something spooks them, they run off. I've heard they can outrun many a horse."

"Really?"

"Yup." When had that become his favorite word? He told her everything he knew about antelope though he couldn't imagine she cared. But her eyes sparkled as if the whole topic held incredible interest, so he rambled on.

They reached a little knoll and he turned her toward the open plain. Snowdrifts rippled across the prairie, creating black shadows in contrast to the brilliant light cast by the sun.

She sighed. "It's beautiful."

"In the summer, silver sagebrush dots the land. But for real beauty, you should see it on a moonlit night. It's all silvery white. So lonely and so peaceful. And in the spring, purple and yellow flowers patch it like one of Ma's crazy quilts. And in the fall, the leaves of those low bushes turn a deep red."

"I'd love to see it."

He stilled the ache squeezing up his throat, and shifted Joshua in his arms as if by so doing he could stop his thoughts from their wayward trek. How he'd love to show her this scene in every season.

"Maybe I can come back and visit when spring comes." She sounded wistful. They both knew once she married, there was little chance of her returning.

They stood a bit longer, drinking in the scene. Billy filled his mind with strength and determination born of the vastness before him. "Let's see the creek." But once he turned away, his weakness returned. He shifted Joshua so he could take Vivian's elbow as if she needed help navigating the trail when it was, in truth, not difficult. He welcomed the few drifts requiring his assistance.

They walked in companionable silence until they approached the streambed. Snow had drifted around the trees lining the bank. "Wait while I break a path." He handed her the baby and stomped a trail through the snow. And he tried not to think of the things he wanted and couldn't have, all wrapped up in a black woolen coat, watching as he flattened the snow. She was backlit by the bright sunlight, her face full of enjoyment, the baby in her arms peeking from his blanket.

He reached the other side of the drift. The creek lay before him, patches of blue ice swept to a polish, broken by fingers of snow scratching across the surface.

"It's so peaceful."

He'd heard her approach, but forced himself not to turn when every muscle of his body bunched up wanting to open his arms and welcome her into an embrace. "It is peaceful."

"Do you come here often?"

How often was often? "I come when I want to think

or pray. In the summer, I sit over there and watch the water ripple by."

"What do you watch in the winter?"

He smiled. He might be able to show her. "You want to sit down?" He whipped off his coat and put it on a spot where the grass had blown clear.

"You'll freeze."

"I'm tough."

She considered the coat, took in his heavy shirt, lifted her gaze to his eyes and studied him.

Feeling a little goofy because of how much he wanted to share some time with her, maybe doing nothing but staring at the frozen creek, he grinned. "Colder standing than sitting, I 'spect."

"Very well." She sat on one end of his coat.

He sat, too. Had to sit pretty close in order to share the fabric. Didn't mind a bit that it provided an excuse to touch shoulders with her. He noted with heart-swelling satisfaction that she made no move to shift away.

"This is nice."

He didn't care if she meant the scene, or the peacefulness. He pretended she meant sitting close to him. His mind flooded with things he wanted to say to her. But he had no right, and the words iced into great immovable blocks.

She looked to one side and gasped. "Look." She touched the back of his hand, sent a jolt to his heart.

He swallowed hard and followed the direction she indicated. A big buck deer tiptoed from the trees and picked his way to the creek. He appeared to examine it for a place not frozen, found a spot where snow had melted on top of the ice and daintily lapped at the water. He lifted his head, glanced about then drank some more.

Joshua gurgled happily.

The buck bounced away, gone as silently as it came.

Vivian's hand rested on Billy's arm. "That's one of the nicest things I've ever seen."

He studied her hand, amazed that such a small slim thing could cause such heaviness in his lungs, making it difficult to pull in a satisfying breath.

He forced his gaze away. A long sigh eased over his lips. "I guess we should head back before this little guy demands to be fed again." He scrambled to his feet and reached down to pull her up.

They stood facing each other. He feared all he tried not to feel pooled in his eyes, like the little bit of melted water pooling in the low spot on the river. He wished—

"Thank you," she murmured. She rested her hands on his crossed arms. "You're really a very good man. You should give people a chance to discover it." She stretched up on tiptoe and kissed his cold, whisker-roughed chin.

As she realized her boldness, heat flooded Vivian's cheeks and threatened to melt her borrowed coat off her shoulders. She hurried across the snowy path.

"You're welcome." He sounded as surprised as she was by her action.

She didn't hear his footsteps and turned.

He stared after her, his fingers pressed to the spot she had kissed. He looked as though she had shaken him to his toes.

A slow satisfaction warmed her. "Are you coming?"

He grabbed up his coat and tramped after her.

"I think he realizes what he's missing stuck out here," she whispered to Joshua before Billy caught up. Her satisfaction fell out the bottom of her heart. She would be missing something, too, when she left—a chance to see all the beauties he talked about, a chance to share more of these special times.

But she would be with Wayne. And she'd easily forget this pause in her life. After all, she must have felt just as pleased to spend time with Wayne or she wouldn't be in this situation.

But to her distress, she couldn't remember having this wonderful, scary sense of shared awe.

That evening, after Mrs. Black retired and Vivian and Billy sat around the fire with Joshua on Billy's chest, Vivian brought up something that had been bothering her.

"Billy, how long are you and your ma going to hide here?"

He did his best to reveal no surprise at her question but she'd seen the little jerk that made Joshua protest. "We ain't hiding. Everyone knows where we live."

"You know what I mean. You hole up here like there is no outside world."

"I been to town twice in the last week."

"On my behalf. I thank you for that. But when do you go for yourself?"

"Nothing in town I want." His voice grew more and more harsh.

"What about your ma? Wouldn't she enjoy visiting with friends once she got over her nervousness?"

"She's got no friends in town."

Vivian remembered something she'd heard so long ago she couldn't recall who'd said it. "Strangers are just friends we haven't met yet."

Billy snorted, quietly, careful not to disturb Joshua. "Or could be they're just people who'd be unkind if you gave them a chance."

"Not everyone is cut from the same cloth." She was concerned about his mother stuck out here without friends or a social life but she didn't mean for him to consider his options solely for his mother's sake. "You're a nice man. You should go out and meet others. Maybe some day you'll find a nice woman and get married." Something wrenched inside her at the thought. Something selfish and inappropriate considering she had a child by another man, and intended to make things right by marrying the other man. *Lord, send Wayne home soon before I lose my way again.* Not that she'd allow herself the same sin but she was dangerously close to falling in love with Billy.

And that just couldn't happen.

"That ain't possible, now is it? You see how Ma is afraid of strangers. And I could never force her to do something that would make her so unsettled."

A million arguments raced through Vivian's head as she considered his look that seemed as full of regret as her own heart.

She wanted to say it was time to push Ma into society. Surely, she would adjust. She wanted to tell him some things were worth upsetting the calm routine they had become slaves to. She wanted…

None of the things she wanted were possible and what Billy and his ma did was none of her business.

She had to keep her goal in mind. Had to accept responsibility for her sin and do what she could to make it right. But a wide beam of pain ploughed through her thoughts and bludgeoned her heart. If only she hadn't sinned. If only she'd paid heed to what she knew was right. Now she must bear the price.

But she would not make Joshua pay a similar price.

Lord, I'm so sorry. I'll do my best to do what is right from now on. Just send Wayne back so he can give Joshua the honor of his name.

There was so much she wanted to say to Billy. Like

how he had no reason to hide. Nor did his ma. They were decent people.

Like how she'd miss him and wished she'd glimpse him in town. Ahh. She mentally protested the pain that had not passed. How could she be such a wanton, wayward woman? A child by a man she hadn't married and aching for yet another man. Guilt and shame at her thoughts, her yearnings, her weaknesses, rolled through her like a giant wave.

"Something the matter?" Billy asked.

She could not let him guess at what bothered her. "Sometimes I am so full of self-loathing at the mistakes I've made." She might as well call a sin a sin. "I've sinned against God, and Joshua will bear the price unless I marry Wayne." She didn't mean it the way it came out. As if she didn't want to marry Wayne. As if the idea meant sacrifice.

To think so made her sin seem even worse. It was one thing to make a baby with a man she loved and hoped to marry. It was quite another to make one with a man who had done nothing more than offer her kindness.

But he'd done more. He still would. She just needed to see him and things would fall into order.

The look in Billy's eyes was gentle and she clung to it. Apart from Marie's support, she'd seen nothing but accusation and condemnation in the eyes of those around her since it became obvious she was with child.

"Vivian, there is a story in the Bible that I think you need to remember. It's the story of a woman caught in sin. A sin similar to what you refer to. Men dragged her before the Lord with the intention of stoning her to death. Do you remember the story?"

She shook her head.

He pulled down his Bible. "I think it's in John chapter

eight." He turned the fragile pages. "Yes, here it is." He began to read about a woman caught in adultery.

Vivian hadn't been caught in the act of immorality but there was no way to hide the fact she'd participated in it. Joshua was evidence. Poor baby. What she'd done to him was so awful.

Billy continued to read. "Now hear what Jesus said. 'He that is without sin among you, let him first cast a stone at her.' Then down a bit further, 'Neither do I condemn thee; go, and sin no more.'" He closed the Bible.

She'd never heard that story before. She'd heard the ten commandments. She'd heard all sorts of warnings about sin and be sure your sin will find you out. She had no reason to doubt that. Nor would Joshua. Her innocent little son would be marked by her sin. Tears flowed unchecked down her cheeks.

Billy shifted the baby and leaned forward to brush them from her face. "Vivian, none of us has the right to judge unless we are free of sin and none of us are. Jesus alone is sinless and what does he say? 'Neither do I condemn thee.'"

She shook her head back and forth, unable to speak, unable to believe the words.

"That's what the Bible says," he insisted.

"But it can't be true."

He smiled. "Why not?"

"Because that's not how it is. Having a baby out of wedlock is a great sin."

A dark expression crossed his face. "Maybe what you mean is that people judge some sins more harshly and this is one of them. Maybe because it can't be hidden."

"I don't want to hide Joshua. He deserves a normal life."

His expression grew almost harsh. "Then you must do what is necessary to give him that."

"Yes."

He sat back.

She felt his withdrawal in a more real sense than just the way he put physical distance between them. She saw it in his face and in the coolness in the air that made her shiver.

They both knew what she must do.

For Joshua's sake.

The coolness between them remained the next day. It confused her. Had she offended him by suggesting he should try and get his ma to visit town? Or had her talk about wanting a normal life for Joshua reminded him of the lack in his own life even though he insisted he was quite happy with nothing but the farm and his pets and no one but his ma?

After lunch, Billy jumped to his feet. "Someone is coming."

Mrs. Black shrieked and headed for the pantry. "Make them go away," she called.

"Ma, it's only the young Malone lad. You remember the Malones. They run the bakery next to Lucas's store."

Mrs. Black moaned but Vivian sprang to the window. Was the boy delivering the message she hoped for? And dreaded. Once Wayne returned, she would have to confront the harsh reality of her sin and throw herself at Wayne's mercy. He would have no choice but to marry her. She had no choice but to accept his marriage.

For Joshua's sake. For Joshua's sake.

And once she saw Wayne again, her feelings for him would return. He'd kiss her as he had in the past and all her uncertainty would vanish.

Billy strode out to meet the boy and nodded a couple of times then returned to the house as the boy reined his horse around and headed back to town.

Vivian couldn't breathe as she waited for him to relay the news.

"Lucas says Wayne is to return on the train tomorrow." Billy's voice was strangely expressionless.

"Tomorrow?" She took a step toward the baby sleeping in his little bed. Stopped. Turned back to look out the window. "I—" She tried to think what to do.

"The train arrives early in the day. I'll take you toward noon."

She nodded. *Calm down. This is what you came for.*

But her insides seemed to have been sucked clean, leaving nothing but an empty, scared feeling.

As if sensing her emotions, Billy patted her shoulder. "This time tomorrow things will be all sorted out."

That's right. Tomorrow. But she couldn't seem to pull her thoughts that far ahead. Tonight would be her last night shared with Billy.

Now why that should make her sad was inexcusable. By this time tomorrow, she would be making plans to marry Wayne. That's why she was here.

She strode over to pluck Joshua from the bed and pressed him to her chest. Her first and only consideration was doing what was best for him.

That night, Billy seemed as strained as she as they sat by the fire. This was the last time they'd do this. Vivian sucked in a deep breath. Maybe she and Wayne could do something similar. She tried to comfort herself with the thought.

Billy sighed—a long, lonesome sound that trembled over her own nervousness, setting her muscles to twitching.

"I'm gonna miss the little guy." He pulled the Bible

from the shelf. "I want to read you something." He turned pages until he found what he wanted. "Psalms twenty-nine, verse eleven, 'The Lord will give strength to his people; the Lord will bless his people with peace.'" He closed the Bible. "God's promise to you. My prayer for you."

Her throat tightened but she managed to speak calmly. "Thank you. I wish I had my own Bible. My parents had one but it disappeared along with everything else. The Weimers had a Bible but it was in German. I wouldn't have understood it even if I'd been allowed to read it."

But Billy's words would provide comfort in the days ahead.

Chapter Ten

For the first time in his life, Billy wished for a blinding snow storm. A three-day blow that would make travel impossible. He mumbled to himself as he hitched Blaze to the wagon. He was a man of simple wants. He accepted what life handed him and made the best of it. He did not build impossible dreams.

Limpy whimpered.

Billy patted the dog's head. "Not to worry, old friend. I ain't lost my mind." Though if anyone could read his thoughts they might have cause to wonder.

Absently, he scratched behind Limpy's ears and petted the cats. Yeah, he'd miss Vivian and Joshua. But he didn't regret what must be done. He'd spent far too many years as a social outcast. He'd do everything in his power to see that Vivian and Joshua didn't suffer the same fate. That meant seeing them safely into town and wishing them the very best in a life with Wayne.

"That's the way things have to be," he told his faithful pets. "At least you'll all be here when I get back."

He led Blaze and the wagon to the step and went to the door.

Vivian sat in the rocker holding Joshua. Her few belongings sat by the door awaiting their departure.

He expected she might be both nervous and excited. Instead, she looked like the sun had flown from her sky. Her eyes looked straight through him, wide as a deer's just before it dashed away after being startled by a sudden sound. Only Vivian showed no sign of moving. His heart went out to her. What she was about to do wasn't easy.

Ma sat at her quilt, her head down, but Billy saw she watched Vivian out of the corner of her eye and he wondered what she thought. Would she be glad to have the pair gone? Would she ever be willing to face the public?

He dismissed the thought. It was only Vivian's questioning that brought it to mind. He'd tried so often to get Ma to change. Every time had been disastrous until he finally accepted she either couldn't or wouldn't ever change. And he couldn't abandon her.

He shifted his attention back to Vivian. Wondered if she suddenly wished she could hide here, too. Just like Ma. But life had too much to offer her and Joshua. He moved to her side and touched her shoulder. "Vivian, it's time to leave."

She blinked three times and thrust out a sigh. "I'm ready." She took the hand he offered and let him pull her to her feet. "I'm ready." He knew this time she meant she was ready to deal with her future.

He loaded them in the wagon, thankful the weather made travel more pleasant than the last time he'd taken her to town.

He parked himself on the seat beside her.

Joshua peeked out from his covers.

Billy touched his nose. "You have no idea of what lays ahead, do you, young man?" He was going to meet his father for the first time and start a new life as the youngest Mr. Styles. How long would it take for Wayne and Vivian to marry?

The sun stung his eyes and he scrubbed them with the heel of his hand so he could see better.

He wouldn't think of how much he would miss Vivian's sweet presence, and the joy of feeding and rocking Joshua. He'd think only of how they'd be so well taken care of and accepted, how they would find their place in the social life of town.

They reached the bottom of the lane. "Would you mind stopping a moment?"

He did so, wondering what she wanted.

She turned to look back at the farm. She laid splayed fingers to her chest and seemed to stop breathing. Then she nodded, turned her gaze to him, her brown eyes revealing acceptance and determination. "Thank you."

There was little to say as they continued the journey. Several times she lifted her face to the sky, her eyes closed, the sun tracing feathery outlines of her lashes against her cheeks.

He thought she was praying and added his silent petition. *Lord, God, she is doing what is right and noble. Bless her. Give her courage to face this challenge and most of all, give her and the little one a happy life.*

Praying restored his peace of mind and purpose, and tension dropped from his shoulders.

They approached town. The familiar reluctance caught at his hands and he squeezed the reins. He had no desire to encounter the stares and whispers of the good, righteous townspeople so he again sought out the back route to the bank.

They reached their destination. But neither of them moved. Each, he supposed, for their own reasons. She, no doubt, a little afraid. He, reluctant for this final step.

He didn't know if she wanted him to keep Joshua again, like last time, while she made arrangements to meet Wayne in private.

As they hesitated, a man with a broad, shiny face tromped down the sidewalk leading from the front of the bank to the alley.

"I'll ask him if Wayne is in." He called to the man and asked the question.

The man answered with much arm waving and an accent so deep that Billy understood a fraction of what he said. He thanked the man and waited until he was out of hearing. "Did you get that?"

"I think he said Wayne was not at the bank."

At least they both understood that much. "Did he say Wayne was at his house?"

"I think so."

"Then I suppose it's best I take you there."

She pulled Joshua closer and nodded.

The Styleses lived at the south end of town. Meant he had to cross several streets. He avoided the main street as he made his way to the big fine house. He'd never been inside but the house had three stories, four dormer windows on the second story and on the main level, a big bay window facing the street. From the back where he stopped the wagon, there was a large, glassed-in porch, more dormer windows and a variety of outbuildings. The house was always painted. In the summer, the yard was always perfectly groomed. Not by either of the Mr. Styleses, though. They had a gardener. And a cook. Would they allow Vivian to enjoy preparing any of the food?

"We're here."

"Yes."

"I suspect you ought to go to the front door."

"I'll walk around." The house was on a corner lot.

He finally forced himself from the seat to help her down. He shifted his hands to her arms. "I hope things work out well for you and little Joshua."

"You've been a wonderful help. Perhaps I'll see you about town?"

"Could happen." She smiled up at him, her eyes round with so many emotions he couldn't begin to name them but knowing her nervousness made it impossible to let her go. "You'll do just fine."

"Thank you. For everything." She picked up the basket that held Joshua's things.

He dropped his hands to his side and stepped back. He wished he could see her safely inside but it wouldn't do her cause any good to be seen in his company. "Goodbye."

She nodded, tore her gaze from his and stared at the house. She shivered once, then lifted her head. "Goodbye and thank your ma for allowing me to stay."

He chuckled. "I'll be sure to do that."

She smiled, allowing her lungs to do their job. She'd be fine. After all, she'd faced far harder things than going to a man who must surely love her seeing as he'd given her a baby.

She headed down the sidewalk.

He waited until she turned the corner before he climbed back into the wagon and drove away. He did not look back as he returned the way he had come and pulled up behind the general store and went inside to get the papers Lucas would have for him and the thread Ma wanted.

Lucas joined him in the back room. "Where's Vivian and the baby? They still with you?"

"I left them at the Styles house."

"Then you haven't heard?"

Billy's scalp tightened at the sound in Lucas's voice. "Wayne came back with a wife."

Vivian didn't let her steps slow until she reached the front door. She put the basket down, adjusted Joshua in her arms so he faced outward, ready to smile at Wayne. She patted her hair and glanced down at her cape. She'd brushed it so it was clean enough. For the first time in days, she thought of the plainness of her dress and wished she had something nicer, but Wayne had paid court to her when she wore a dress no different than this one. He hadn't seemed to mind then. No reason why he should now.

She straightened her shoulders and prayed for God's hand of mercy on her. Not that she deserved it, but for Joshua's sake. She recalled the words Billy had read from the Bible. *Neither do I condemn thee.* Hardly seemed possible, but all that mattered for her right now was getting this meeting over with. She grabbed the brass knocker and clanged it.

She heard a voice call within and steps heading for the door and she held Joshua closer.

The door handle rattled.

Her heart clung to her throat.

The door opened. And Wayne stood as handsome as she remembered, his brown hair combed back in a perfect wave. He wore a fine, brown wool suit.

"Wayne," she whispered.

"Vivian." He stepped out and pulled the door closed behind him. "What are you doing here?"

He didn't sound welcoming. Though, of course, he was likely surprised to see her. But hadn't he said he would never forget her?

"Aren't you happy to see me?"

"No." His glance darted to Joshua.

She pulled herself taller. "Wayne, say hello to your son."

He made a noise full of harsh disbelief. "I take it he's your little illegitimate child. He's certainly not my son."

Her insides iced over at his harsh, condemning words. "Well, he is. If you recall your visit to the Weimers' almost a year ago, you might also recall how you took me out, how we…how you…"

"Dear?" Someone pulled the door open.

Vivian expected it would be Mrs. Styles wondering who had come to the door, but the woman who slipped out and took Wayne's arm in a most possessive way was young and pretty and wearing a gown that looked like it had been cut from a fashion magazine.

Wayne smiled at the woman. Much like the smile Vivian remembered he once favored her with. He faced Vivian, his smile still in place but his eyes cold.

She shivered at his look.

"It's just someone with a business question." He pulled the woman close. "May I present my wife, Isabelle Styles."

Everything inside Vivian died. She stammered something she hoped resembled a reasonable greeting.

"We have no more business to discuss." Wayne backed away and shut the door in Vivian's face.

She stood rooted to the spot. This was not how it was to be. Wayne was Joshua's father. As such, he was to marry Vivian and give his son a name. And a home.

What would she do now?

Billy stared at Lucas, unable to accept the news he'd heard. "What did you say?"

"He's married. Came back with a wife. A pretty young thing, everyone says."

"But I left Vivian there." He knew Lucas understood the reason.

"I don't imagine she'll be welcomed."

Alarm skidded through Billy's body, nailed him to the floor. Vivian would be shocked. She'd have no place to go. What would she do? "I've got to find her." He bolted for the door, leaped to the wagon and slapped the reins.

The fastest way was straight down the main street and he headed in that direction, the wagon box bouncing in the frozen ruts, Blaze leaning into the harness as he responded to Billy's wild yell. Billy saw startled faces as he flashed past. A rider jerked back on his reins to avoid a collision and the rider hollered for him to slow down. He yelled a warning to another wagon to get out of the way and skidded around the corner as he turned toward the Styleses' house. He paid no heed to his own safety and only a fleeting thought for those he passed. Vivian would be lost, alone, no place to go. He had to find her.

He cranked on the reins and rattled to a halt in front of the Styleses' house. The door was closed. The house silent. A flicker of a curtain in one window and then nothing. He glanced every direction. No sign of Vivian. Had they invited her inside? Decided to be civilized about this?

Only one way to find out.

He tied the reins, murmured to Blaze to wait and ran to the door, though anyone watching would likely call it a lumbering gait. He'd never been graceful running. Too big for that.

He took the three steps as one, rattled the knocker. Rattled it again then pounded.

Wayne jerked the door back, shielding himself with the solid slab of wood. "Would you stop that?"

Billy had never cared for this man. He was a bully. Whenever he chose to mock Billy as a child, he always made sure he was surrounded by friends or could easily escape to the protection of a teacher or other authority figure. Not that Billy would beat the man. He didn't care for violence.

Except for that one time. He'd come upon Wayne kicking a kid he accused of stealing a coin he'd dropped. Billy had stopped the abuse. Oh, he hadn't hit the man, though he was sorely tempted. He'd simply caught Wayne's fist and squeezed it until Wayne practically cried and forgot all about the defenseless child, which was all Billy cared about.

Wayne had been angry since that day. It was four years ago so he guessed Wayne wasn't the forgiving sort.

"Is she here?"

Wayne snorted. "That depends on who you are asking about."

"You know who I mean. Vivian. Is she here?"

"Why would she be here? Despite anything she might have told you, she's nothing to me. Nor is her little illegitimate child."

Billy's fist bunched. He took a step forward. "Why you..."

Wayne shoved the door toward him, his face white with fear.

Billy stuck his boot against the frame to stop the door from closing. "She deserves better than you, anyway." He turned and jumped off the step.

Brave little Wayne opened the door and followed him as far as the top step. "You are quite right. She deserves someone like you."

Billy growled low in his throat and turned to face the man but Wayne stepped back.

"Tell her I don't want to see her again. I got what I wanted a year ago."

Billy roared and leaped up the steps.

"And I don't mean the baby." Wayne slammed the door.

Billy steamed toward the wagon and climbed to the seat. He sat with the reins dangling from his hands. Illegitimate child. The words echoed through his brain. He'd never heard those particular words but he'd heard the tone often enough. Indian child. Monster. Freak. He couldn't bear the thought of innocent little Joshua enduring the same ridicule and cruel mocking. There was one way to prevent it. He would offer them a home back at the farm where they would be safe from such taunts.

First he had to find Vivian. He edged forward, looking from one side to the other. No sign of her. Where could she have disappeared to in such a short time? She wouldn't have gone far carrying the baby and dragging the basket.

He reached the end of the block. Still no sign of her. The church lay ahead. The hospital farther away. To his right, more houses. To his left and down the street, the livery stable. *God, show me where she is. Help me find her.*

A flicker of movement caught his eye. He turned toward the little cemetery at the back corner of the churchyard. There she was, crouched down in the snow.

"Vivian." She couldn't hear him. But the cry wasn't for her. It came from the depths of his being. He drove to the church fence, jumped from the wagon and strode through the snow to her side. He knelt beside her, wrapped his arms about both her and Joshua.

She turned her face into his shoulder and wept.

He closed his eyes against her pain. He would do everything he could to protect her. For always.

She cried until she was spent. Still, she clutched his jacket front.

He patted her back and held her, letting her work out her sorrow.

She finally spoke, her voice muffled against his shoulder. "I've made such a mess of things."

Billy wanted to say she shouldn't blame herself. If anyone were to blame it was Wayne. Something was off about the Styleses though he'd readily allow he had his own reasons for disliking them. But to deny your own flesh and blood. *I got what I wanted a year ago.* He'd never before been tempted to use his size to hurt someone but Wayne made him want to make an exception.

"You didn't do this alone."

She sniffled. "But it appears I will have to deal with it alone."

He eased her back so he could look into her face. Seeing her tearstained cheeks and reddened eyelids hurt more than he could imagine. He'd hammered his thumb with less pain. He kissed each cheek, capturing the remnants of her tears with his lips.

Her eyes flooded with uncertainty as he lifted his head and looked deep into her eyes.

"You won't be alone. You have me."

"What do you mean?"

"I'm taking you back home. I'll take care of you and this little fellow."

"But your ma?"

He pulled his lips back in a mocking grin. "Ma's getting used to you." She'd likely have a conniption when Billy brought her back yet again. But she'd just have to accept this was the way it was going to be. He wanted to make the arrangement permanent but it was too early to talk to Vivian of such things.

A thread of pleasure wound itself around his pain at how she'd been treated. Perhaps it was possible to have his dream. This seemed a gift from God. Especially considering where they were. "What are you doing here?"

She turned, pointed toward the crude wooden crosses. "This is where my parents are buried."

He could make out their names carved into the wood.

"If I can ever afford it, I want to put up proper stone markers."

The cold seeped through his bones. "You're going to freeze sitting here. So am I. Come on, let's go home." He pulled her to her feet, kept her tucked against his side as he led her to the wagon. He lifted her to the seat, wrapped the blankets more tightly around Joshua, who slept peacefully. "Wouldn't want this little guy getting cold."

A sob tore from Vivian's throat. "He called my baby illegitimate."

Billy jumped up beside her and pulled her into his arms. "We'll protect him from that kind of talk."

She sniffed and sat up. "You know what else he said?"

Billy prayed Wayne hadn't been as harsh to Vivian as he'd been to him but he sensed the man would get an unholy delight out of hurting Vivian.

"He said our business was completed a year ago. As if he'd set out to take advantage of my neediness. Not that I'm excusing my behavior. I'll live the rest of my life regretting it. But wasn't it cruel to make it sound like I was just a…a…" Her voice broke along with the outer shell of Billy's heart. "As if I was just some dirty, despicable task he had to do."

Billy kept one arm around Vivian, shielding her from

curious stares as they made their way out of town. He hoped anyone who saw him would be too interested in him to note the woman at his side. They took the back way from town and passed only two people, who seemed in a hurry to attend to their own business and barely glanced in Billy's direction.

He hadn't had time to think of it before but Wayne's statement did seem odd. As if he had set out to win Vivian's favor and once he had, considered he'd achieved his goal. He could think of no reason why Wayne should even care about Vivian. It just didn't make sense even for a worm like Wayne.

Chapter Eleven

Vivian leaned against Billy's chest, grateful for his support, both physical and emotional. When she'd learned Wayne was married, she'd fled in panic feeling like she had dropped off the world into nothingness.

And to hear from his mouth the very words she'd counted on him to protect Joshua from...

Panic swirled around her again and she pressed her face to Billy's jacket.

She had run, with no place to go. She didn't know how she ended up at her parents' graves. *Momma, Poppa. Why did you have to die and leave me homeless?*

Oh, if they knew the shame and sorrow she'd known since their deaths...

Being shunted off to the foundling home had been a shock she would never forget. She'd always been loved. Not so in the home. Children were simply stored there, made to earn their keep as much as possible, taught they were of no value to anyone and certainly not to society as a whole.

Working at the Weimers' had been a little different, except the work was harder.

And now—she groaned and Billy tightened his arm

around her shoulders—she was powerless to stop her precious son from facing an even worse situation.

Only Billy cared. And perhaps understood like no other. She'd go home with him and accept his kindness. She couldn't think past that. They reached the lane. She sat up and faced the house. Her insides had calmed somewhat with Billy's comfort but she now began to shiver so hard she felt dizzy.

Billy might welcome her back.

But even though they had settled into an uneasy co-existence, she doubted Mrs. Black would feel the same as Billy about Vivian's return.

They stopped at the house. She turned to look up at Billy. When she saw he stared at the door with a troubled look on his face, her fears exploded. "Your ma."

"She'll be fine."

His tight words did nothing to reassure Vivian but he jumped down and went around to take Joshua from her arms, then lifted her to the ground.

She clung to his arm, dreading Mrs. Black's reaction.

Billy pushed the door back and they stood in the opening.

Mrs. Black saw Vivian and bolted to her feet. "You were supposed to leave her in town."

The anger in the woman's voice trickled acid through Vivian's insides. All she wanted was a place where she and Joshua were accepted and welcomed. Seems her sin made that impossible. She gritted her teeth to keep from crying out. She would live the rest of her life regretting her action. But it wasn't fair Joshua would also be punished when he had done nothing except be born out of wedlock. Something he could hardly be blamed for.

"Ma, things didn't work out. She has no place to go."

"You can't keep her. Already told you that."

Billy put Vivian's basket down. He shifted out of his coat while still holding Joshua, who had started to fuss.

Vivian thought to relieve him of her son but she couldn't make her muscles respond.

Billy hung his coat, then edged Vivian's cape from her shoulders and hung it.

"I said—"

"Ma, I'm keeping her. Come, Vivian." He edged her toward the big chair and eased her down.

She melted into the chair as weak as a piece of old yarn.

Ma stomped into her room and shut the door with a harsh click.

"You hold this fella while I get his bottle ready." He placed Joshua in her lap and folded her arms across him.

She blinked and focused her attention on her son. With a groan ripped from someplace so deep in her gut she couldn't begin to think where it originated, she caught Joshua to her chest and rocked.

She'd ruined his life.

Her sin was ever before her.

She didn't cry. She was all cried out. She didn't speak. There was nothing to say. She couldn't think. Couldn't face the weight of her failure.

Billy returned, knelt in front of her, caught her chin and waited for her to look at him. "You are safe here. For always."

She nodded. At least she had that—safety. And she had Billy's kindness. She pressed her hand to his as he held her chin. "I will never forget this."

He smiled. "Well, that's a start."

She wondered what he meant but didn't have a chance to ask as Joshua let her know he had waited long enough.

Billy handed her the bottle. "Feed the little man while

I put away the horse and wagon." The door closed to signal he left.

Vivian sat alone with her little son—the evidence of
her sin and the one who would bear the brunt of public
censure. *Lord, I deserve it all. I know that. But Joshua?
He's done nothing. Show me how to protect him.*

No one would make comments about Joshua out here
on the Blacks' farm. He could grow up without hearing
those unkind words. Was this God's answer?

Billy returned. He paced about the kitchen, opened
the oven door and glanced inside. Grunted.

Ma called from her room but Vivian couldn't make
out her words.

Slowly, it dawned on her. Billy hoped someone would
cook supper. She reluctantly put Joshua in the little bed
that still stood by the chair and wearily went to the stove.
Food held no interest for her but the least she could do
was meet Billy's needs.

Ma stomped from her bedroom to join them at the
table. Her fierce frown made little impression on Vivian
except to deepen her sense of failure.

Billy bowed his head. "Bless, O Lord, this food for
Thy use, and make us ever mindful of the wants and
needs of others. Amen."

A smile tugged at Vivian's mouth at his words and his
ma's sound of disagreement. Some of her tension eased.
She and Joshua were safe. Her son would be free of public disgrace here.

Sourness suddenly rolled in her stomach and she
couldn't face the food she'd prepared. No matter where
she went, where she lived, who she saw, Vivian knew she
would never be free from the condemnation in her heart
that had sentenced her son to a life of being shunned and

ostracized. She pretended an appetite she didn't have to avoid attracting Billy's attention.

The next few days passed in a blur of emotions that tangled through her thoughts until she couldn't separate one from another—condemnation, determination, fear, hope and a sense of waiting.

Billy seemed to realize she needed time to heal, to recover and decide what was next.

Eventually, she began to think again. Not that she liked her thoughts. But she refused to look back. She had to plan a future for Joshua.

"Come to the barn with me," Billy said one morning, after he returned from doing chores.

She didn't need a second invitation. Joshua slept peacefully, allowing her to escape for a short time. The coat Billy had lent her still hung on the hook and she put it on.

He took her hand as they walked across the yard.

She liked how his hand engulfed hers. Suddenly, her heart stopped quivering with shock and returned to a normal beat. She liked this man. In fact, the only thing that had kept her from falling in love with him was she expected to marry Wayne. A plan that died a sudden death.

She no longer had to feel guilt at her fondness for Billy and she laughed with reborn hope.

He swung their connected arms. "I gotta tell you, that's the nicest sound I've heard in a long time."

"What?" She guessed he meant her laugh but wanted him to say so.

"I like to hear you happy." His voice deepened with what she took for tenderness. A peculiar sweetness washed through her heart, not quite erasing the shame and regret of her past, but cleansing it of some of its pain.

"I like to be happy."

They reached the barn but stood outside, the sun shining down on them with late-winter warmth. He pulled her around to face her. Her back pressed to the wood of the door. He rested his hands on either side of her without touching her and yet she felt as if he wrapped her in a protective embrace. He smiled down at her, his expression full of pleasure. "I'd like to make you happy every day of your life."

His words blessed her in a way that defied explanation. She couldn't speak. At least not with her mouth. She was certain her eyes spoke more than she knew or understood.

He leaned forward and brushed his lips to hers. A gentle, promising kiss. Warmth radiated from her mouth until it reached the far, secret places of her heart where her need for love and acceptance lay buried.

He lifted his head and searched her eyes. He must have read her surprise though she felt so much more.

"It's too soon to give an answer, but I'd like to marry you and give you and Joshua the protection of my name."

She nodded, still speechless.

He gave her another quick kiss, took her hand and led her into the barn. He talked about the cats. Told her the history of each one. Told her about dogs before and after Limpy. Twice he apologized for running over at the mouth, as he put it.

"I don't mind. It's interesting to hear your stories." Even more, she enjoyed being able to admire the gentle side of this big man. Like he said, it was too soon to make a commitment, but she liked the idea of his gentle strength being available for both her and Joshua.

The next few days, he seemed to delight in sharing every detail of his life with her. He took her for walks, carrying Joshua in his arms and explaining things to the baby as well as to Vivian.

Evenings—after he'd read the Bible out loud and his ma had gone to her room—continued to be the best part of the day as far as she was concerned.

One night, he pulled the Bible from the shelf again as she fed Joshua his bottle. "Vivian, I want to share something with you. Something I hope will ease the pain of your past." He turned the pages. "Psalm fifty-one." He started reading. She found the Psalms comforting and settled back to enjoy them.

He read, "'My sin is ever before me. Against thee, thee only, have I sinned, and done this evil—'"

She cried out as guilt swamped her. "Stop. Why are you reading this? I will never forget what I've done. I will never stop feeling guilty. I've not only sinned against God, I've brought shame and pain to my innocent child. I don't need a reminder. Why? Why would you do this?" Her insides churned with the pain of his unkindness. "I thought you understood. Accepted. What do you want from me?"

Billy bolted from the chair and knelt at her feet, squeezing her shoulders. "No. I am not accusing you. Never. I told you before, only one who is sinless has the right to judge and God, the righteous judge, does not condemn. That's why I wanted to read this to you. That's how King David felt after he'd sinned with Bathsheba. But he learned it wasn't the end of the story. Listen to the rest of the chapter." He pulled the Bible to her lap and ran his finger down the page until he found the place. "I'm going to skip some so you hear what David discovered. 'Create in me a clean heart; O God… Restore to me the joy of thy salvation; and uphold me with thy free spirit… Deliver me from blood-guiltiness, O God, thou God of my salvation.' See, it's a psalm of healing and forgiveness. God is saying He is willing to set you free from your guilt. He forgives you."

He ran his blunt fingertip across her cheek. "You can leave your past behind and start over."

Forgiveness, freedom. Could she even dream of such things? Not from what people said, she knew that, but from the accusation of her own heart? "Is it really possible?"

"It is. What's more, I think God is anxious to give it to you."

"It's a gift beyond comprehension."

"It is. But so is the gift of salvation. And if God did not spare His Son in order to provide us that gift, won't He even more readily forgive our sins as His children?"

"I never thought of it like that."

"Maybe you should."

She touched one of his wayward curls, let herself drink in every detail of this generous-hearted man. His broad, friendly face, the kindness in his eyes that blessed and loved her. She examined several more curls before she rested her hand on his shoulder. "Billy, you are the kindest man I've ever met."

He sobered. "It's not hard being kind to you 'cause I love you. I'm waiting for you to say you'll marry me."

She loved him, too. "I need to work through what you've just told me about God. I need to figure out who I am before I can be who you want me to be."

At that, he laughed. "I don't want you to be anything or anybody but who you are right now. But I'm willing to give you whatever time you need to work things out."

"Thank you. You're a good man."

He pulled her head down and kissed her slow and gentle. Billy would always be gentle. She knew that and she returned his kiss with a heart bursting with gratitude and hope—hope that she could be free from her guilt and free to start over.

Joshua screamed.

Vivian sighed. "Here we go again."

"Give him to me." Billy took him and began his nightly routine of walking and singing to the baby.

She watched him with her son. She loved him. She was certain of that. But could she make him happy? What had he said? That he liked her as she was. The idea gave her newfound delight. So much had happened in such a short time that she needed to sort it all out before she could give Billy the answer he wanted. And that she, too, wanted.

If Billy was at the house, he wanted to hold Vivian and tell her over and over how much he loved her. So, he would go to the barn where he'd tell Limpy. But after a few minutes in the barn, he would head back to the house to see Vivian and hold Joshua. And watch Ma shake her head in a pitying way.

Billy walked to the creek just so he could think. He'd be the first to admit he was acting like a man in love. And it felt good.

Every day he watched Vivian grow stronger, more confident. Every day he prayed for her to realize her sin did not stop God's love any more than it stopped Billy's. He'd gladly give her what she needed—home and belonging. And what her son needed—a name and a father.

Soon she'd be ready to forget the past and stride into the future, hand in hand with Billy.

He stood on the creek bank for a few minutes, paying scant attention to the pools of water on the ice. Spring would soon be here. A time of renewal and growth. He couldn't wait, though he didn't mean just nature with the soon-to-appear flowers and leaves, green grass and baby animals. He prayed it would be a time of renewal for Vivian, as well.

He knew she loved him and he anticipated the day she would agree to marry him.

Settled somewhat in his thoughts, he returned home in time for the noon meal. Vivian continued to prepare meals that satisfied in every way. And every meal he told her how much he appreciated her cooking.

Each time she would look pleased. "It's my pleasure. I like cooking."

"Good thing." He chuckled.

They had just finished when he heard a horse approaching and bolted to his feet. He'd never be comfortable with people visiting. "Someone coming," he called from the window.

Ma pushed her chair back and scurried to the middle of the room. "Why are so many people coming here?" She gave Vivian an accusing look.

Billy sighed before he turned back to the window. "Ma, you don't even know why he's come. Looks like the sheriff. Wonder what he wants."

"Go see," Ma said. "Tell him whatever he wants we don't have it. Tell him to leave us alone."

Billy was already on his way out the door. He strode a few feet from the house and met the sheriff, waited as the man dismounted. "What can I do for you?"

Sheriff pushed his hat back. "I got a complaint about a young woman I hear is living here."

Vivian? She'd done nothing wrong. "First I heard the law cared who I let live in my house."

"If it's just Miss Halliday, the law don't care. But if she's got a baby boy with her..."

"Sheriff." His voice came out soft but full of unmistakable warning. "What is it you're trying to say?"

"I hear tell she stole the baby."

"Now who would tell you such a thing?"

"Does it matter?"

"Seems to me someone is trying to make trouble where there ain't any." He suspected Wayne was at the root of this interference.

"You gonna let me speak to the woman?"

He heard the warning in the man's voice. "Do I have a choice?"

"No."

"The baby is hers."

"If she can prove that, then no problem. But I have to be certain. Kidnapping is a mighty serious crime."

If Billy were a vengeful man he'd make Wayne pay for this. But he'd learned long ago the futility of trying to give an eye for an eye. "Come along."

He led the sheriff up the steps and into the house. Sheriff yanked off his hat. "G'day, Mrs. Black."

Ma's eyes grew wide, she scurried to the bedroom and slammed the door.

"See she's still some jittery."

Billy almost laughed. Jittery was like saying there's a bit of breeze across the Dakotas.

"And this is Miss Halliday, I presume."

She stood in the middle of the room, clutching the baby to her chest as if she expected the sheriff would snatch him away.

"Vivian, the sheriff wants proof Joshua is your son."

"I got proof." She edged toward the basket holding baby things and dug into the contents to pull forth a piece of paper, which she handed to the sheriff.

He read it slowly. "I see your name as the mother. No name for the father?"

Vivian's face drained of color. "No."

The sheriff cleared his throat. "This is proof enough. I'll not bother you anymore. Your papers are in order." He hesitated at the doorway, his hat suspended from his fingers. "Miss Halliday, you need not hide out here. No one will threaten you in town."

He turned once more. "I'll inform Mr. Styles that there is no reason for concern."

"Wayne sent you out?" Vivian whispered.

"No, the senior Mr. Styles. Good day."

They stared after him until they could no longer hear the sound of horse hooves.

Vivian turned into Billy's arms and he held her tight. "Everything is fine. No one will bother us again."

She nodded against his shoulder. "I can't believe Wayne told his father. And why would he care if I was out here?"

"I don't know. Maybe he thinks you'll make trouble for Wayne."

"I don't care if I ever see the man again. I only hope no one figures out he's Joshua's father. He's not the kind of man I want Joshua to look up to."

Billy vowed he'd do all in his power—with God's help—to be the sort of man Joshua *could* look up to.

Ma stumbled from the room looking as if she'd endured a vicious ordeal. She made it to the rocking chair and collapsed.

"Ma?"

She moaned. "Will it never end?"

"The sheriff won't be back."

"Don't mean the sheriff." She rocked so fast it made Billy dizzy.

"Ma?"

She shook her head and stared into the distance.

He shuddered. She hadn't been like this since the first

day Vivian had entered their house. Why did such harmless things set her off?

Joshua fussed and Vivian laid him in the little bed as she prepared his bottle. Angry at being made to wait, Joshua screamed.

Ma sat in the rocker and as the baby's demands grew louder, she rocked harder. Pressing her hands to her ears, she made a mournful sound in the back of her throat.

Billy moved toward his mother as Vivian picked up the baby.

"Hush, now. You're not going to starve," Vivian murmured.

Joshua continued to raise his rather sturdy voice in protest as Vivian changed him.

Billy pulled his stool close to the rocker, watching Ma. Her distress never failed to make him feel powerless. Seems he could never do enough to help her. She lived with memories and hauntings that refused to leave her. As he watched, he prayed silently for her peace of heart.

Joshua stopped crying as Vivian stuck the bottle in his mouth, but Ma continued to rock and moan.

"Ma, what's wrong?"

She stopped rocking and listened. When she realized the baby had quit crying, she lowered her hands and stared straight ahead. As if looking into the past.

Billy shuddered.

"I had a baby." Her voice cracked on the words.

"I know, Ma. Fourteen pounds of baby." He grinned at Vivian. "I was the biggest baby they ever saw."

He laughed at the way Vivian's eyes grew round. Fourteen pounds was a lot of baby.

"Not you," Ma said, and began to rock. "I had another baby." She rocked harder. "When the Indians took me, I had a baby in my belly." She rocked so hard the chair creaked. "It was a little boy." She paused. "Much smaller than you as a baby." She resumed her frantic back-and-forth movement.

Billy struggled to accept this news. "A baby brother. What happened to him?"

Ma wailed and rocked harder and harder until Billy put his hand on the arm of the chair and stopped it.

"Ma, where's my brother?" If the Indians had him, Billy would get him back. Nothing would stop him.

Chapter Twelve

Ma sat perfectly still, her face a flour-colored pallor. He wondered if she even breathed.

"Ma, tell me."

Her shoulders fell. Her face seemed to crumple like a log dying into ashes. "He's dead. The Indians took him from me. They—they killed him right in front of my eyes." She buried her face in her hands and moaned like a tortured animal.

Shock ran through Billy in one powerful wave that rattled him from head to toe. Pictures flooded his mind of a baby—his brother—being killed. He closed his eyes. He didn't want to think about it. For sure he didn't want to see it inside his head. *Oh, God, stop this awful thing.* He meant the memories, the pain, the imaginations.

Ma's eyes were glassy. Billy shook her. "Ma, it's okay. It wasn't your fault."

She moaned, a sound so mournful Billy's heart squeezed like a giant fist. He rubbed her back.

"That's why I can't bear the baby's crying."

Before Billy could guess her intent, Vivian placed Joshua in Ma's lap, holding Ma's arms around the baby.

Ma shivered. She pulled back until she stared at Vivian who nodded, her eyes intent.

Ma lowered her gaze to the baby. At that moment, Joshua smacked his lips, smiled and cooed. With a moan that sounded half prayer, Ma cradled the baby to her chest. A look of surprise and wonder filled her face. She touched Joshua's cheek cautiously then smiled and relaxed, holding the baby as if doing so filled her heart.

Vivian handed her the bottle. "He isn't finished eating."

Ma fed Joshua, her eyes never leaving the baby's face. The baby studied her intently as he sucked. He smiled around the nipple, letting milk run down his chin.

Ma laughed. "He's a little scamp." Her voice broke and her eyes began to leak.

Billy scrubbed the back of his hand over his cheeks, surprised to feel them damp. He seemed to be leaking, too, and he ducked his head to hide his embarrassment. But when he stole a glance at Vivian, she wasn't looking at him. She smiled at his ma, and if he didn't miss his guess, her eyes were awash, too.

He settled back on the stool and watched Ma feeding Joshua. She alternately smiled at the baby and then sobered, her lips quivering.

Billy silently prayed for God to use this to heal Ma's hurts. Though he didn't expect she could ever forget seeing her own baby murdered.

Joshua finished his bottle and Ma raised him to her shoulder to burp him. As she patted the tiny back, she shifted to look into Billy's face.

"I never even tried to stop them."

He guessed she meant the Indians when they took the baby from her. Her mouth worked and he understood she had more to say.

"I was—" She swallowed loudly. "I was—" Her voice fell to an agonized whisper. "I was glad he died. I didn't want him raised there." Her eyes were bottomless pools of self-loathing misery.

Billy wrapped his arms around Ma and Joshua. "You couldn't have done anything. It wasn't in your hands. The baby is with God now."

She laid her head against his shoulder. "I know."

Billy patted Ma's back a few times then released her.

"Read from the Bible," she said.

He pulled it from the shelf. He could think of no appropriate scripture for this situation and paused to ask God to direct him to something of comfort. He opened the Bible to the Psalms and began to read chapter sixty-eight. "'Let God arise, let his enemies be scattered; let them also that hate him flee before him.'" He read on, letting the words of comfort and assurance cleanse his soul from the shock and anger of learning he had a baby brother who had been brutally killed. He prayed Ma would receive the same comfort and assurance.

He read for a long time, psalm after psalm. "'Save me, O God; for the waters are come into my soul.'" It seemed he couldn't get enough of God's word, and the way Ma and Vivian sat quiet and contemplative led him to think they hungered for it as much as he.

It wasn't until Joshua stirred that Billy closed the Bible and returned it to the shelf.

"I'll take him," Vivian said.

Ma released the baby. "I'm very tired. I think I'll go rest."

Billy pushed to his feet and hugged her. "Ma, I love you."

"I love you, too, son." She patted his cheek then went to her room.

Billy scrubbed his hand over his hair. He felt as drained as if he'd run four days without food. In fact, he was starved. "I'm going to have some bread and jam. You want any?"

"No, thanks."

"Tea?"

"That would be fine." She concentrated on adjusting Joshua's nightie and putting his booties on again.

Billy busied himself at the stove. He seemed alternately fatigued and then bursting with energy that he knew not how to handle. For a moment, he considered going outside and chopping wood. Or at least making a trip to the barn. But inside him there was a wad of words that needed saying, for his sake not anyone else's.

He carried tea to Vivian, who sat in the rocker holding Joshua, then he settled in the stuffed chair and attacked the stack of bread he'd slathered with jam. "Ma made this jam."

"It's good."

"Ma works hard."

"It shows. The sausages, the butter, the quilt."

He took a gulp of hot tea. "She's never said much about when she was with…them. I always figured she didn't want to remember."

"Can you ever forget the past?"

He didn't have a satisfactory answer and it left him floundering. "I don't know. I simply don't know." He wanted to forget the past. Wasn't sure he wanted to think too far into the future, either. "Seems we should do our best to enjoy each new day. God's word says, 'This is the day which the Lord hath made; we will rejoice and be glad in it.'"

She smiled. "That sounds like something Marie would say." She grew thoughtful, her gaze on Joshua. "The past is always with us. Look at your ma. It's been with her for so many years."

The way pain shafted through him felt like he'd stepped on a foot-long nail. He wanted to help Ma. He wanted to help Vivian. He didn't know how except to love them and pray for them.

Something about the sheriff's visit hovered at the back of his mind, a distant troubling voice. "What was it Wayne said to you when you saw him?"

Her eyes grew wide with shock. "That awful word about Joshua?"

"No. The other."

She considered the question. "About our business being completed a year ago? I assume he meant…" Her face deepened to the color of a summer rose.

He examined all the things that had been said. "Didn't Wayne's father say something similar when you saw him in the bank?"

"Yes." Her brow furrowed. "Isn't that strange?"

Billy wondered if it were more than that. "You said you signed some papers for Wayne?"

"Yes."

"Did you read them carefully?"

Again that flush of pink. "No. I trusted Wayne when he said they were only to erase the debt my parents left."

"I wonder…"

"What?"

"I wonder if there wasn't something more to those papers you signed."

"Like what?"

"I have no idea." The whole afternoon had been so full of shock after shock he could no longer think clearly. "I'll give it some thought."

Vivian couldn't imagine why Wayne or anyone would want her to sign papers that were other than what he said. And if they were other, why would he go to such lengths? Surely, Billy was being suspicious on account of his dislike for the Styleses—a dislike Vivian was learning to share.

She dismissed the whole affair as being nothing more than mistaken reaction. Right now, she had bigger things to consider.

Was it possible God would forgive her sin? Yes, she believed it but...

But did she? Her thoughts went round and round in ceaseless questions. She stared out the window. If she could be alone to think and pray.

Billy returned from doing his chores.

She barely waited for him to step into the house. "Would you mind watching Joshua while I go for a walk? I need to think."

He grinned and touched her chin. "Gladly. Nothing like a walk to ease a person's mind. Take your time. Little Josh and I can amuse each other."

She pulled on the warm coat and boots then headed out following the path to the creek. She reached her destination, found a grassy spot, pulled the back of her coat under her and sat. The air was so clear she could hear birds rattling about in the branches overhead. Puddles of mirrorlike water lay in spots on the blue ice. She breathed deeply, cleansing her lungs. *Lord, I need to talk to You. I need to understand what is happening to me. What You want. Where You want me. I need Your help to consider the future.*

She'd messed things up badly enough trying to do things her way. And now she had a baby son to think about. She couldn't afford to make another mistake that would affect him the rest of his life.

Peace and quietness surrounded her and she slowly exposed her worries to God.

My past. Can You truly forgive my past?

Forgive us our trespasses as we forgive those who trespass against us.

She had to forgive Wayne. She'd never blamed him for his part in her sin knowing she had the choice to say yes or no, but he had taken advantage of her hunger for love. Even that didn't make her angry. What she found impossible to forgive was that he would deny his son, call him that awful name.

They called God's son the same awful name.

"Oh, God, I guess I can't refuse to forgive when You do. I can't expect You to forgive me if I can't forgive others. Here before You, I forgive Wayne. I know I won't find it easy to forget what he's done. In fact, I never will. Not when every time I look at Joshua I have a reminder."

She also knew she would have to constantly remind herself of the decision she had made this day.

"Now am I forgiven?"

A verse that Billy had read some days ago whispered across her thoughts. *Neither do I condemn thee.*

She shook her head. God might forgive and let her into heaven but there was no forgiveness on earth for what she'd done.

She just had to move forward. Which necessitated her deciding what to do about her future. She loved Billy, knew she and Joshua would be safe with him, but something played at the back of her mind. Something she couldn't quite capture and name. And until she did…

She returned to the house two hours later, her mind made up, her spirit strengthened by the time she'd spent in prayer. Tonight, she would tell Billy her decision.

She waited until Joshua slept on Billy's chest and Billy

leaned back, patting the baby's tiny backside. Such a good, gentle man. He had so much to give—so much love and tenderness. Her throat tightened till she could hardly breathe. He deserved nothing but happiness. Was he really content hiding out here?

All afternoon she had thought of how to say the words to him. She had prayed, was certain of what she had to do, but suddenly none of her rehearsed speeches felt right. She loved him. It ought to be all that mattered.

He shifted his bulk.

It pained her that he thought others considered him a monster solely because of his size. If only they knew. If only he would give them a chance to discover it.

Time was running out for her to speak. And she didn't want to put it off to scratch at the back of her mind another day. "Billy, I did some serious thinking today."

His hand grew still. He watched her with a mixture of eagerness and caution.

Oh, how she dreaded hurting him. But perhaps he would listen to her plan. Agree to some changes. "Something the sheriff said has been bothering me. He said I didn't need to hide."

Billy opened his mouth.

"Let me finish. Part of me feels like I must. But I can't. I can't." She closed her heart to the way Billy's jaw muscles bunched up. "Hear me out." She drew in a slow breath and tried to sort out her feelings, rearrange her thoughts, find the right words instead of this sensation that everything inside had turned into hail stones bouncing about aimlessly, striking everyplace at once without warning, without reason. "I want to say this so you understand, so be patient while I try and sort out everything."

He didn't move. Didn't give any indication of what he felt.

She knew he had pulled shutters over his thoughts, allowing nothing to show in his eyes or expression. "I know what I did was shameful and marks Joshua. I expect all his life he will hear that horrible word. But I am not ashamed of him. He's a precious child. I pray he grows into a strong young man able to face challenges and ignore hurtful things so he can focus on what's important." She had to break through Billy's icy reserve and knelt in front of him, pressing her hands to his knees. "Billy, I love you but if I hide here, I will be saying to Joshua that I am ashamed of him. I will teach him to be ashamed of who he is."

Billy's expression grew more distant as he pulled farther and farther away from her.

She leaned forward, cupped her hands to the sides of his face. "Billy, I love you. You are the kindest, most gentle man I will ever meet."

He shook his head in disagreement but the movement also shook her hands away.

She settled back on her heels.

"I guess that means no to my offer of marriage." His words were little bullets of pain.

"I don't want it to."

"Then what do you want?"

She knew what she wanted. With all her heart. "Billy, don't you think it's time you moved on?"

"Leave the farm?" His voice was low, giving away nothing of what he felt.

"No. I don't mean that. I mean, leave the past."

He snorted. "Can't leave the past when it won't leave us."

"Things change. People change."

"Haven't seen it."

"You say you're here to protect your ma but hiding

from her past has only caused her pain. She's needed to confront it. Now she will start to heal."

"Ain't likely she'll forget about seeing her baby killed, now is it?"

"I don't mean she'll forget, but seems to me trying to hide it and pretend it didn't happen caused her unnecessary pain."

"You think if we parade through town we can pretend we don't hear what people say?"

"No. Yes. I don't know. I'm not saying what I mean."

"Then say it."

No mistaking the edge of anger to his words. She started over. "Billy, I love you but I can't hide Joshua out here. I want a normal life. I want to go to town proudly at your side. I want Joshua to be part of normal life. I want that for me. For you."

"I ain't going to make Ma go through torment just to try and be normal."

"Maybe it's time for a change. Maybe your ma is ready for it. You could give people a chance, you know."

"I gave them a chance. All they saw was an Indian woman and her monster son. Just 'cause I'm big don't make me a monster. 'Sides, Ma would never go to town."

"She might think differently if you ask her."

"I ain't asking her."

"Not even for me or our love?"

He shifted, pulled her close until she again rested her arms on his knees, looking up to him. "You could be happy here."

"Yes, I could. I could be happy anywhere with you."

He nodded. His eyes grew bright and he leaned forward to kiss her.

She closed her eyes as her love spread sweet honey throughout her heart.

"I love you," he whispered. "Can't it be enough?"

She wanted nothing more. For herself. But so much more for Joshua and so she let it go, praying Billy would think on what she'd said.

But two days later, nothing changed. Billy seemed set on proving his love. Not that he needed to and his tenderness left her feeling like a windblown tumbleweed, shifting to one thing when Billy was around—couldn't his love be enough?—to something else when he wasn't there—didn't Joshua need more? A chance to be accepted by those who would and the opportunity to learn there were those who wouldn't accept him but he could live with it. If they stayed here, she feared he would think there was only one opinion. She could not let him grow up believing everyone considered his birth a shame. Hiding out here would do exactly that.

She needed to talk to someone who could help her sort things out. "Who pastors the church now?"

"Pastor Morrow."

"Why, he was here when I was a child."

Billy laughed. "Still here."

"How is he?"

"Never heard anything indicating he was anything but fine."

She could remember the pastor in their house. He often came for dinner. How awed she'd felt when he said the table grace. Somehow, in her childish mind, she thought he spoke directly to God. She remembered other things, too. How he'd asked about her relationship with God and encouraged her to read the Bible and always speak to God. He had stood at the front of the church and held out his hand to her as she went forward to tell the congregation she had put her faith in Jesus as her savior. She was only eleven years old. Mother had said she didn't have to

go to the front for her faith to be real, but she'd wanted
to and Pastor Morrow had agreed she could. How she'd
shaken as she faced the people in the pews—so many
people with gray hair. It seemed they were all frowning.
And her school friends grinned in either curiosity or
teasing. The pastor had squeezed her hand. Her courage
had returned and she'd said her piece. Couldn't remember a word of it now. But she remembered how speaking
publicly had made her faith seem more real than ever.

She suddenly ached to see this old family friend.

"Would it be possible for me to borrow the wagon and
go to town?" Vivian asked the next day.

Her request reverberated through Billy like a clap of
thunder. It had been several days since she had said she
wanted a normal life, but she'd said nothing more and he
sort of hoped she'd changed her mind about it. He'd sure
gone out of his way to prove they could have a rich and
full life right here. What did they need with other people? Why would she want Josh to put up with the unkind
words he'd hear? And he'd hear them. Better to protect
the little guy. Give him lots of love. Lots of things to do.
Just like he'd been showing Vivian. She seemed to enjoy
walking with him, helping him with his pets. He'd even
started training the young colt simply for the joy of showing Vivian how to work with the animal.

"I could walk if you aren't keen to let me drive the
wagon." Vivian's words jolted him into considering an
answer.

"You ever drive a wagon before?" He 'spected she had
but he was stalling for time.

"A time or two when the Weimers needed someone to
take a wagon to the mill or bring something back. I can
handle it, I assure you."

He nodded. Knew she expected more than that. But for the life of him, he couldn't think of letting her go to town. Could she be setting out to find a different place to live?

"I want to see Pastor Morrow. I need to talk to him."

Pastor Morrow? His chest half caved in with relief. "I'll take you."

"No need."

"Got to pick up some things." They stood in the kitchen doing the dishes together and he glanced out the window. The warm weather of a few days ago had ended. It was sunny but cold. "I don't much care for the idea of taking Joshua all that way and back again. It's too hard on him."

He turned to study Ma as she poured milk into the cat dishes. Purring and the crackle of the fire were the only sounds. Comforting as they normally were—caught between worry about what Vivian said about not wanting to stay on the farm and concern for Joshua—this morning they jangled across his nerves.

Ma looked up from washing the milk things. "You leave that little feller here where he'll be warm and safe. I'll look after him."

Vivian jerked her gaze to Billy. They stared at each other and silently considered the offer. Ma seemed as sane as anyone since her confession about seeing her baby murdered. She'd fed Joshua several times and always held the baby tenderly. Billy figured she had conquered one of her demons. He sensed she'd protect the baby with her life if need be to make up for not being able to save her own infant.

But was it too soon to expect Ma to cope with this much change?

"Stop worrying about me," Ma said.

Although not completely at ease about leaving Joshua,

they'd been fortunate the baby hadn't suffered from exposure in his adventures. Vivian gave a slight nod.

"Okay, Ma. You can look after the baby while we go to town."

The two of them bundled up and hurried to the barn where Billy hitched up Blaze.

Vivian paced from the wagon to the door, clutching her hands before her. "I'm not being foolish, am I?"

Billy sighed. "It's impossible to believe you can have a normal life in town. No one will let you. I can testify to that."

She spun around, stared at him like he rattled away in a foreign language, then burst out laughing.

"What's so funny?" He was being completely serious. Speaking from the hunger of his heart. It kind of stung that she found it amusing.

"I was thinking about whether it was safe to leave Joshua with your mother. After all, it's only been a few days since she wouldn't so much as look at him."

He ducked away to hide his embarrassment at being caught thinking of how to persuade her to stay while she was thinking of something else entirely. "Ma would protect him with her life to make up for losing her own baby." The knowledge he'd had a younger brother he never even got to meet knuckled through his insides.

Vivian nodded and stared at the side of the wagon. "I guess so. Unless something upsets her. Then what?"

"She ain't crazy."

"Oh, Billy. I know that. But you got to admit she's pretty spooked around strangers. After all, she seldom sees one."

"Seen her share the last little while."

"And she's managed fine. Maybe…"

He heard the hesitation in her voice and prepared himself for more arguments.

"Maybe it's time for a change. Time to persuade her to widen her world. Perhaps just a step at a time."

He led Blaze out and helped Vivian to the wagon seat. "You think she can be normal? That anyone will ever think I'm normal? And don't be fooling yourself. No one will ever let you forget you have a son without the benefit of a husband."

His words hurt her. He could tell by the way she sat up straight, looking neither to the right nor the left and tried to shrink into herself so her shoulder didn't rub his. The last thing he wanted was to give her pain. "Let's not argue and ruin the day."

She kind of collapsed forward and let her breath out in an airy sigh. "You're right." She turned suddenly and faced him, her face gleaming with determination. "I believe our love will find a way."

He took her hand. He wanted to believe as stubbornly as she but he couldn't forget she'd said she wanted a normal life. So long as she insisted on that, how could their love be? His teeth felt bathed in vinegar. He'd been alone so long. Ached for more for years. And here it was within reach. Except for who he and Ma were—the Indian woman and her monster son.

He hated the taunts. Hated how it made him feel powerless despite his size, which didn't defend him against unkind words. Even so, he might have put up with what they said about him. But not how they tormented Ma. She hadn't shown her face in town in five years or more. He quit even asking because it upset her so much.

Chapter Thirteen

Vivian knocked on the door of the manse as Billy waited in the wagon to be sure someone was home.

Mrs. Morrow opened the door. "Yes?"

Vivian recognized the woman immediately. "Do you remember me? Vivian Halliday?"

"Vivian!" The woman pulled her to her ample bosom and hugged her tight. "I wondered if we'd ever see you again. You know, I think of you often and have prayed God would uphold you. Child, how have you been?"

Vivian clung to the woman, the scent of peppermint triggering a burst of memories. Mrs. Morrow had taught Sunday school and handed out peppermint candies to good little boys and girls. Vivian had always earned one. This poor saint of a woman would be shocked to discover that Vivian was no longer a good girl.

She remembered Billy waited and turned to wave him away. He planned to visit his friend Lucas while Vivian visited at the manse.

"Come in, child. Come in." Mrs. Morrow led her into the well-used parlor.

Again, Vivian was assaulted by memories. "The horsehair sofa." She remembered the feel of the hide against her legs, rough, poking through her clothing if she didn't sit just right on it. And slippery if she sat so the hair all ran smoothly toward the floor. When Mother wasn't looking, she liked to slide downward.

Mrs. Morrow chuckled. "You were like every other child who liked to slip and slide on it."

Vivian giggled. "I didn't think you noticed."

The woman gave a sideways hug. "I didn't mind in the least. Now sit down. I'll make tea and you can tell me what you've been doing."

Vivian chose the little chair with wooden arms and pink-and-rose brocade upholstery on the seat and back. She looked about at the room, seeing a few new things like the picture of the Morrows' grandchildren and a painting of a prairie sunset.

The woman returned with a large silver tea tray.

"Is the pastor around?"

"He's upstairs studying but I've called him. He'll join us in a minute. He's as anxious to hear what you have to say as I am."

Vivian pretended a great interest in adjusting her skirts so they lay neat. They might be less pleased to see her once they heard her story. She lifted her head, her breath stalling in her throat as she heard footsteps descending the stairs. And then the pastor entered the room. His gaze fell on Vivian and a welcoming smile creased his face.

"Vivian, my dear child."

She rose and went into his arms, struggling to control her emotions. This dear elderly couple was so much a part of her childhood that she felt like she had almost returned home. A lump landed heavily in the bottom of her stomach at the shame she must confess.

Mrs. Morrow poured tea and handed Vivian a dessert plate with a generous slice of lemon cake.

Vivian laughed. "This was always my favorite. I remember worrying when we had church socials that I wouldn't get a piece before it was all gone."

"The good Lord knew you were coming today."

Vivian hadn't realized she'd sighed so loudly until the pastor patted her hand.

"I'm glad you're back. Whatever is burdening you, we're here to help, but first, enjoy your cake."

Vivian welcomed the chance to sort her thoughts. This time, she could voice them to two gentle friends. She finished her cake and put aside the plate. "I guess you know I went to a foundling home."

Mrs. Morrow grabbed her hand. "We both had the flu at the time or we wouldn't have let it happen. For a while, I wasn't sure Mr. Morrow was going to survive." Her voice thickened.

"I'm glad he did." Otherwise, she would have no one to turn to now.

Slowly, one strangled word after another, she told her sordid story. "I'm so ashamed of what I did but I don't want Joshua to think I'm ashamed of him. I fear if I stay on the farm with Billy and his ma that is exactly what I am teaching him." For a moment, she couldn't go on, as her throat closed off with sorrow and regret. Her poor little son should not be made to pay for something his mother had done. "I don't mind facing what people say. I deserve it. But how can I face what they say about my son? He's a beautiful little boy."

"Does his father know about him? That would seem the first avenue to pursue."

"He's not interested."

"I could speak to him. Remind him of his duty. Do we know the man?"

Vivian considered her answer carefully. "I don't ever want anyone to know who his father is."

"I understand. Your secret will be safe with us if you choose to reveal his identity."

She knew that. And she wanted to tell them. They might as well know the whole truth. "It's Wayne Styles."

To their credit, neither of them revealed shock or surprise, though they likely felt both.

"He's now married," she added unnecessarily. "So, he can't do his duty to me and Joshua. And he doesn't want to. He made it very plain."

"So, you must face this on your own. Only you won't be on your own. You'll have our support and even more importantly, God's help."

"I don't expect God's help. I know I deserve whatever punishment He chooses to send my way. I only want to do what I can to protect Joshua, apart from hiding him."

Pastor Morrow slipped his chair closer. "Vivian, I can't say what people will say or think or how they will act but I can tell you what God says." He opened his Bible. "None of us is without sin."

Vivian nodded. Billy had said the same. But knowing she was like everyone else did not ease her sense of shame.

"Here in First John chapter one, verse nine, God's word says, 'If we confess our sins, he is faithful and just to forgive us our sins, and to cleanse us from all unrighteousness.' He will cleanse away the guilt of your sins. All of them."

"I hear the words. I know they are true. But… I don't know if they apply to me. I mean, this isn't like telling a lie or sassing your mother. This is a big sin."

"And one you can't hide or relegate to the past because of your son. Is that what you mean?"

"It is also one other people won't let me forget."

"The first thing to deal with is to believe that God forgives you. Do you believe that?"

She knew the correct answer was yes but did she believe it?

"God is in the forgiveness business."

Billy had said something similar when he'd pointed out that forgiving sins after they were God's children was no harder for God than forgiving for salvation.

"You must choose to believe God or not."

Was it really that simple? Just choosing. *Lord, God, is it really possible that You can forgive me for such an awful sin?* Would He have said it if He didn't mean it? All that stood in her way of forgiveness and cleansing was her lack of belief? "I don't know how to make myself believe it."

Mrs. Morrow leaned forward. "May I say something?"

Vivian nodded.

"I remember the day you chose to believe God for your salvation. You were always such a single-minded child. I had just finished a lesson explaining God's plan of redemption. You waited until the others left then said, 'I'm going to do it. I'm going to do what you said.' I thought I might have to walk you through a prayer or something but when I offered, you politely refused. 'It's done. I already decided.'"

"I remember."

"My mother used to say something. 'God said it. I believe it. That settles it.'"

Vivian replayed the words in her head and slowly she nodded. "I believe it." A swell of peace raced up her insides, caught in her throat, pushed at her tears. She blinked and laughed as a burst of joy exploded inside her.

Both of the dear folk reached for a hand. Pastor Morrow prayed aloud. "Heavenly Father, Merciful God, wonderful Savior, how we rejoice that Vivian has found the forgiveness You generously extend to each of us every day. Keep her joy strong and help her face the challenges of her life. Amen."

Vivian sobered. "I can face whatever life hands me but I don't know what the right thing is for Joshua."

"God will guide you."

Confront your accusers. The words were so clear Vivian knew immediately what she wanted to do and she told the Morrows.

"It's not necessary," the pastor said.

"I want to do it this way."

The Morrows looked at each other and smiled.

Mrs. Morrow spoke. "I'm not surprised. You've always been very clear about how you wanted to handle things, even as a child."

"You can certainly do it if you want."

She nodded. Now if God would just send a solution so Billy would consider living a normal life. She closed her heart to the pain her decision would bring if he continued to hide out at his farm.

The conversation shifted back to ordinary things— news of people she vaguely remembered, plans for an upcoming social, and as always on the prairie, talk about the weather.

Pastor Morrow refilled his tea cup. "I was surprised to hear you'd sold your house to the bank."

"Is that what I did?" She gave an embarrassed laugh. "Wayne brought out some papers for me to sign to get rid of my parents' debt at the bank."

The pastor's brow furrowed deeply. "How odd. If they had an outstanding debt against the property, the courts would have allowed them to sell the house years ago. They had an auction sale and sold the contents shortly after your parents died. Why would they wait to sell the house?"

Vivian knew nothing about legal proceedings but she wished she'd at least read those papers before she signed them. "All our things were sold?" She wondered what had happened to the family Bible and the pictures of Pinky and Blue Boy.

"Much of it went to friends and neighbors."

"I have nothing left of my family but I learned to live with that as an orphan." She was more fortunate than many of the children. At least she had experienced a loving mother and father. Some of them never had and never would. It had been that knowledge that spurred her to action on her son's behalf. She wouldn't let him grow up in the home thinking no one loved him.

Nor would she let him grow up thinking he was too shameful a secret to be out in public. Not even if she had to sacrifice her love for Billy. The thought dragged sharp stones through her heart and tossed them, blood-stained, to the bottom of her stomach where they exerted cruel pressure.

Billy headed the wagon out of town. His insides felt wound too tight all morning but seeing the smile on Vivian's lips and the determination in her eyes released some of the tension. Whatever she had discussed with the pastor had eased the strain that had been in her eyes for days.

"I take it you had a good visit."

"Very satisfactory." She explained how she'd decided to let God forgive her. "It's that simple. And that hard."

She opened the tea towel containing the sandwiches she'd brought along and handed him a thick one filled with hefty slices of meat.

"How was your visit with Lucas?"

"Got a bunch more papers to read."

"That's nice." They continued in peaceful contentment.

"There's something about this business with Wayne and his father that isn't sitting right with me, so I asked Lucas about your parents' house. He said he found it mighty peculiar that the bank waited this long to sell it."

Vivian stopped eating. "Pastor Morrow said much the same." She told him what the good man had said.

Billy pulled back on the reins. He reached for another sandwich. "This is getting more and more suspicious sounding. I think you should talk to a lawyer."

"A lawyer? What for?"

"Whatever you signed for, Wayne allowed them to sell the house. I think it's time to ask some questions."

She turned away. Stared into the distance. "I don't want to."

"Why not?"

She swallowed hard enough to make her throat bob. "Because it will prove how foolish I am to sign something without reading it." Slowly, she faced him, her eyes wide, her lips trembling. "Just because he was kind to me."

Her distress cracked him open from stem to stern. He folded her against his chest and rocked her. "Vivian, you were alone and lonely. It sounds to me like Wayne took advantage of that. But you don't have to be alone anymore. I'm here."

She nodded against his lapel, her fingers clutching the fabric of his coat.

He would protect her against all threats.

"Will you go with me to the lawyer?" She sat up, her gaze demanding so much from him.

Could he give her all she wanted? He didn't know but he would do his best.

He bent and kissed her, feeling the dampness on her cheeks from recent tears, tasting the salt on his lips. He wanted to head the wagon for home where he could protect her from the cruelness of life but she had asked this one thing of him. "I'll take you."

There was no back entrance to Mr. Legal's office so Billy gritted his teeth and headed down the street. He hadn't been this way for years. Suddenly, he realized he had been out in public view at least two times in the past few weeks—the first time to rescue Vivian from her stunned state in front of the bank, and the second when he'd heard Wayne was married and drove as fast as he could to the Styles house, not caring that people saw him. Was that close enough to normal for her?

He pulled the wagon to a halt and helped her down.

She tucked her hand into the crook of his elbow.

He smiled. Knew if anyone saw him they would see a big goofy man with a tiny little gal at his side and shake their head in wonder, but he liked feeling big and protective with Vivian.

Inside the office, a man with glasses parked on his nose glanced up. "May I be of service?" He looked at Billy as he spoke.

Billy's smile fled. Vivian could speak for herself. "Miss Vivian Halliday would like your advice." Suddenly, he realized that neither of them had come prepared to pay the man cash. "If she can't pay you, I will."

"Fine. Now that we've taken care of the important things, why don't you both take a seat and tell me your problem."

Billy knew from the gleam in the man's eyes that he was teasing about the money. It made Billy relax and he held a chair for Vivian then perched in the not-quite-adequate one at her side.

"It's about my parents' house," Vivian said, and told the lawyer the whole business.

Mr. Legal nodded, asked a few questions and made some notes.

Vivian finished and sat twisting her mittens into a knot. "I know I should have read the papers but I didn't. However, I did sign them so that would make them legal."

The man tapped the top of a square glass paperweight. "I'll do some investigation and let you know. Where might I find you when I have news?"

"She's at our house." Billy made sure the lawyer heard *our*. "With Ma and me." He wanted to give no cause for gossip.

"I know where it is. When I have something I'll ride out and let you know."

"Thank you," Vivian whispered, and pushed to her feet. She waited until she sat on the hard seat of the wagon and they again rode away from town to speak again. "I don't know why I went there. I'm sure there is nothing to be done."

"Wouldn't it be nice to know the nature of those papers you signed?"

"It would ease my mind a bit."

"Well then, that's something." He draped his arm across her shoulders and pulled her close, satisfied when she leaned against his chest.

"I had a good talk with the pastor."

"Good. It's nice to hear you more at ease."

"Letting God forgive me is a load off my mind."

He tightened his arm about her and kissed her head,

wishing he could feel her silky hair instead of the woolen cape. His love for her filled him until he wondered how he would contain it.

"It was good to talk to someone who remembered my parents and recalled me as a little girl." She laughed gently. "They saw me as strong minded."

He chuckled. "Guess they knew you pretty well."

She gave his chest a playful slap. She sat up so suddenly he feared she would tumble from the wagon and grabbed her. "Billy, I want to go to church again. I'm..." She drew in a breath and seemed to hold it.

He sensed her fear and tried to pull her close.

She pressed her palms to his chest. "I've decided I am going to face the congregation and confess my sin."

"What? Why would you do that?"

"Because of something you said."

"Me?" He'd never stand in front of the mocking crowd. Knew the futility of it. People thought what they wanted, said what they wanted.

"Remember when you said Jesus said, 'neither do I condemn thee'?"

He'd told her that all right. Even read it from the Bible. "It's got nothing to do with standing in front of the whole church."

Her smile was full of sweetness. "I figure if God doesn't condemn me then I have nothing to dread from people. Now, do I?"

"You'd think that's the way it should be. But it ain't."

She trailed a cool finger down his cheek. He should tell her to put her mittens on but not until she finished touching him—a touch that went far deeper than the pores of his skin. It landed somewhere south of his most distant thoughts and burrowed beneath all his secrets and longings, giving them life.

"Billy, I know you've endured so much but you are a good man. A man I'd be proud to walk into any business in town with. I want to let people see me with you. See what a good man you are. I want you to stop hiding at the farm."

"You want a normal life."

"Normal can be many things. But yes, I want to live proud of who I am, who my son is and proud of the man I love. Billy, you have no reason to hide."

He'd longed for such acceptance all his life. She offered it to him. But it came at a price. She wanted him to live in the open. "Your love makes me proud. But what you want is not possible. Don't you think I tried? I'm afraid this is as good as it gets." He had found what he wanted. Love. A chance to marry and have a family. But what she wanted wasn't possible.

They would soon be home. Somehow, in the next few minutes, he had to make her understand the truth.

"I can never abandon Ma. Never."

Vivian sat up. "Maybe she's ready to move on. I'll pray she's willing to change."

Easy for her to say. She'd never seen how Ma reacted to any suggestion of doing anything normal like going to town. "I hid in a cupboard when I was six and couldn't help her. I ain't gonna ever again do something to hurt her. I will stand by her as long as she lives."

He let the wagon slow to a snail's pace and turned to Vivian. "My normal is what you see. If you love me, you have to accept that." He waited, hoping against fear she would nod agreement. Instead, her eyes grew watery. Her lips trembled but her jaw muscles tightened. He knew before she spoke she would not give the answer he ached for. "I love you. I accept you but I can't hide. I have to give Joshua more than that."

Chapter Fourteen

Vivian knew there was no easy answer to their dilemma. She prayed Mrs. Black would change and Billy would believe it, even as he must believe her love despite her decision.

She watched Mrs. Black, hopefully assessing her behavior. They had arrived from their trip to town to find her contentedly rocking the sleeping baby. The older woman smiled as they stepped inside. "We had a good day."

The first, Vivian hoped, of many such days that took Billy's ma further from the comfortable cocoon she had buried herself in, and closer to starting a normal life.

She sensed Billy's restlessness in the way he shuffled the newspapers without reading them, and in the way he often hurried to the barn to see his pets. It hurt her clean through to think she caused him mental anguish.

"I want to see to the animals," he said yet again late one morning.

Vivian finished preparing the pot of soup then checked on Joshua. He slept. Shouldn't need feeding for a little while. "Do you mind watching the baby while I go outside?"

Mrs. Black looked up from working on her quilt. She'd made great progress. The frame had been rolled several times. She was almost at the center. "Go ahead. Me and the little one will be fine." Mrs. Black often asked to feed Joshua and spent hours rocking him or talking to him when he was awake.

It would soon enough be spring but a cold wind today denied the possibility. Vivian pulled on the borrowed coat and boots. She'd worn them so often she almost thought of them as hers. She slipped outside, closing the door as quickly as possible to keep out the cold and hurried, head down, to the barn. Billy had to have heard the squeal of the door and noticed the splash of light as she stepped inside, but he didn't look up from where he sat on a length of log surrounded by his cats and Limpy.

"Mind if I join you?"

"'Course not." He positioned another butt end of a log for her to sit on.

She sat and let half a dozen of the cats crowd around her, pulled the littlest to her lap, finding comfort and courage in cuddling it. "Billy, I don't like to think I have upset you."

"I been thinking."

"Come to any conclusions?" She ached for him to hold her and assure her everything would be fine, but she knew no matter what either of them decided, they would face problems. Life could not be easy like it was when she was a child.

"I thought you were happy here."

Her heart flipped over and lay like a frightened animal. She'd hoped for more than insistence that living here was all one needed. She prayed quickly before she answered him. *Lord, I need wisdom to make him under-*

stand that he needs to change as much as I do. "I am happy here. But it isn't enough for the future."

"It's a fine place to live. I have the animals, a solid house—"

"Billy, this isn't about where you live. It's about how you live. I love the farm. I've found peace and contentment that I'd forgotten was possible. But I don't want to be a recluse. If I just had myself to think about it would be different but there's Joshua. And if we married, I hope there would be more children."

His face turned a glorious red then faded to white. "Children? You and me?"

She couldn't help but smile. "It usually happens to married folks. I wouldn't want them growing up afraid to see people. Would you?" Her words were very soft.

"No. But I wouldn't want them teased and tormented, either."

The argument was an endless circle. "I guess we couldn't be guaranteed it wouldn't happen but there'd be those who welcomed them. Like the Morrows. Like your friend Lucas. Like Mr. Legal. There's probably a lot of people who would be friends if we give them a chance." He'd lived here so long, hidden from the public for his own sake as well as his mother's. How could she hope to persuade him it didn't have to continue? "Your ma is ready to move on."

"How can you know that?"

"She's taken many steps forward of late, hasn't she? Doesn't that indicate her readiness to change?"

"I gave up expecting any changes a long time ago."

She rested her hands over his fists. "I know you did. But it's time to try again."

"I don't know if I can."

"I think you can. If you want to."

He cupped his hand to the back of her head and pulled her forward to kiss her eyelids and her cheeks and finally, her mouth. She leaned into his kiss. She wanted this man as her husband to live together, to share their joys and sorrows. She said so to him.

"But not here?"

She grinned as she patted his chin. "Here is fine. I already said that. But not hiding. No more hiding."

"If you don't stay, where will you go?"

She jerked back, her heart crying silent tears that threatened to drown her. "You're saying no?"

"I don't know what I'm saying. But it seems to me you have no place else to go."

His words stung worse than she could imagine possible. "You think I have to stay by default. So you don't have to even try and change things?"

"I want it that way."

She jerked to her feet, scattering cats every direction. "Billy, it can't be that way. I won't let Joshua grow up afraid to face people. Thinking I don't want anyone to know about him because I'm ashamed of him."

Billy scrambled to his feet, too. "And I can't ask Ma to face the cruel things people say and do. She's content here. I can't take that from her."

The anger fled, leaving Vivian so weak she grabbed a post to steady herself. "Stop blaming your choice on your ma. It's because of your own fear of what people say that you won't go out in public unless you're forced to. It's time you stopped being afraid." She turned and stormed out.

She made it a few feet before she collapsed to the cold hard ground. *What was I thinking? That my love would be enough to change him. Give him the courage to face people.* How foolish she'd been. Again. Only this time, it hadn't been a sinful, shameful foolishness. It was an honorable, cherished thing that she would carry in a special place in her heart for the rest of her life.

Her heart heavy as field stone, she looked about at the low house, trees surrounding it, struggling for survival in a harsh land.

Here she'd found everything she'd longed for since she lost her parents. But now, it seemed she would be forced to choose between what her heart wanted and what she knew was best for her son. It was a far harsher choice than she could deal with. *God, help me do what is best.* She must move on. She must give Joshua the life he deserved. *If You see fit, help Billy to see that he can move on, too.* Yes, he protected his ma, she understood that and honored it, but he hid from his own fears, as well, whether he realized it or not.

She huddled over her knees and prayed for strength and wisdom, found comfort in recalling the scripture verses she'd heard from Billy's lips and from the mouth of Pastor Morrow. If only she had a Bible of her own to strengthen her soul in the days ahead—days she feared would be dark and difficult unless she kept her thoughts focused on God's Word.

Her limbs grew cold and she stiffly gained her feet and returned to the house, keeping her face turned away from Mrs. Black lest she see the depth of her pain and guess its source. She could not deal with questions and curiosity right now.

Billy plunked back down on the log end and let the cats crawl to his lap, his attention to them somewhat distracted.

Vivian loved him.

He nailed his heart and his hopes to that fact.

She felt she could conquer the world with her determination.

He knew she couldn't. Facing the people in church was only giving them more reason to whisper and gossip. And why would she want to do that? Create more for Joshua to endure?

Yet, his only defense was she had no place to go.

'Course she could find work somewhere, perhaps as a housekeeper or chambermaid in the hotel.

The very thought made him grind his teeth. He didn't want her in someone else's home. He wanted her in his.

He prayed fervently that no such opportunity would come her way.

She'd accused him of hiding because of his own fears of the public eye. It wasn't fear. It was unkind reality, which she would soon discover if she followed her plan. Nothing a person said or did could change the way people looked at him.

He would spare her the pain of discovering it for herself.

Dear God, look down on Vivian. Make a way to keep her here until she realizes how useless her plans are.

He returned to the house some time later but it wasn't the welcoming place he had grown content with. The air felt brittle as the argument they'd had crackled between them. He wanted to cradle her to his chest and assure her things would be fine. She just had to give herself time to sort them out. She soon announced lunch and he let the worries of the day slip away as he enjoyed the thick soup she'd made with bits of browned meat and a variety of vegetables.

A few days later, the midday sun slanted bright rays across the table. Full of warmth and the promise of spring, the bright light made Billy glad to be alive, especially with Vivian across the table from him and Joshua in her arms. She seemed so happy. So content. A Sunday had passed without her mentioning going to town. Perhaps she already reconsidered her plan.

Ma jerked to her feet, her eyes wide and filled with nervous fright. "Someone coming."

Billy blinked. He'd been so busy thinking how he enjoyed watching Vivian talk to the baby he hadn't even heard. "Sit down, Ma. I'll go see who it is." He strode outside to meet the rider. Mr. Legal.

His heart bounced against the soles of his boots. Did the man have news that would benefit or hurt Vivian?

Mr. Legal swung from his horse and rearranged his coattail before he thrust out a hand in greeting.

Billy shook it. "You've found out something?"

"I have. Is Miss Halliday still here?"

"Yup."

"Could I speak to her?"

Billy wanted to refuse. *Tell me. And I'll decide if I want you to tell her.* But it was Vivian's business. He had no right to interfere though his only concern was protecting her...and his own desire to keep her here, he reluctantly admitted. "Come along." He waved the man to the house.

Ma jerked from her chair as she saw the man with Billy and skittered headlong into her bedroom. Billy shot Vivian a pointed look. Did she really think Ma would ever be comfortable around strangers?

Mr. Legal didn't wait for an invite to sit but pulled out a chair and spread some papers. "I'm pleased to say you are the proud owner of your parents' home."

Vivian stared. "How can that be?"

"It seems your parents didn't owe more than a pittance

at the bank. The proceeds of the auction were more than enough to pay off their debt."

"But Wayne said…" She stopped, her face flooding with guilty color.

"From what I can piece together, I think Wayne showed up at the Weimers' because he had business not with them, but with you. It would seem he went with the express purpose of getting you to sign papers giving the bank your house."

Vivian scrubbed her lips together and widened her eyes but not before Billy saw the glisten of tears. He knew she must be calling herself every kind of fool. He slipped to her side and squeezed her shoulder. She clung to his hand.

"I don't understand," she whispered.

"You were the sole heir and beneficiary of your parents' estate. The bank was to act as your agent until you were eighteen. They've been renting out the house and recently sold it. You're entitled to the rent monies."

She shuddered. "You said I owned the house. Didn't I foolishly sign it over to the bank?"

"The documents weren't witnessed legally. The Styleses realize their claim would not stand up in a court of law and have wisely backed away. The people who bought the house under false pretenses are not legal owners."

"I'm sure they acted in good faith."

"Certainly, but they don't want to have anything to do with such dirty dealings so asked to have their money refunded. I think it would be only decent to do so. Now, let's get down to business. I need your signature here, here and here." He paused. "This time let's go over the documents and make sure you understand them." He explained the papers, paragraph by paragraph, and only when he was satisfied Vivian understood them did he allow her to sign.

A few minutes later he gathered up the documents and returned them to his brown leather carrying case. He shook Vivian's hand. "It's been a pleasure doing business with you. I should have the funds sorted out by Friday. Your house will be ready for you to move in around the same time."

Move in! The words blasted through Billy like a burning summer wind, drying up hope and blowing away his plans and dreams. Now she didn't have to stay. She could move into town and become part of normal life if anyone would let her. He spun around and stared out the window as his heart bounced around madly in his chest seeking a place to hitch its reins.

Vivian stared at the papers the lawyer had left her. She owned a house. Her childhood home. Her stomach reached for her backbone in a spasm of joy. She could hardly wait to see it.

Another thought grabbed the heels of her joy, dragging it bottomward.

She could move into town, begin a new life, face her past, build a future. The weight of the idea sucked at the skin on her face. She wanted things to be different. So much different. She wanted to share her future with Billy.

Billy had stayed at her side throughout the lawyer's visit, lending his support, but now he had moved away. Not just physically but mentally and emotionally.

She would make another appeal. Her strongest, most intense one. *Lord, please give me words that will convince him.* "Billy, I love you. You know I do. I love your home. You have made me so welcome. You have protected me and helped me. But my first concern must be what I think is best for Joshua. And now all of a sudden, I have a way of doing it."

"What if you're wrong?"

"What if you are? Billy, give people a chance. Give yourself a chance."

His ma came out of the room at that point, and Vivian could say no more to try and convince Billy, but from the look on his face she knew she had failed to change his mind.

She could do no more than pray and leave it in God's hands, but the joy of getting her parents' home tasted dry and dusty as she faced following through on her choice.

Billy waited up for her as usual that evening. Their time alone contained a bittersweet element as she realized there would be so few of them. If only he would take a chance. They talked about everything but what really mattered as if he found it as painful as she.

She prayed fervently for things to change but Friday arrived and nothing had.

"You'll be wanting to head to town." Billy spoke with a sad note.

"The lawyer is expecting me." Her insides echoed his tone in increasing volume until she wanted to wrap her arms around herself and moan. How could they love each other and yet each be determined to go in separate directions? It just didn't seem right and yet she knew not how to change it. All the way to town she prayed for God to give them a way that would work for both of them.

But they drove up before the lawyer's office with no solution.

Billy remained in the wagon holding Joshua as Vivian went inside. She emerged a few minutes later feeling like she'd taken a step off the end of a walk and encountered nothing but thin air. Billy reached down to pull her to the seat. He sat considering her.

"You look as if a hard wind blew you off course."

"I've got money."

He chuckled. "Well, ain't that supposed to make a person happy?"

"I've never had more than a nickel in my pocket, ever." She now had a house and enough money to survive until she found a job or a position. This had to be God's way of assuring her she was doing the right thing. If only she didn't have to do it alone. But last night, Billy had reminded her of how his mother reacted to the lawyer's visit.

"Ma ain't ever going to be comfortable around strangers." His voice thickened.

She knew he ached over the impasse they had reached as much as she, which only intensified her pain until she wondered if she could contain it behind a smile and pleasant words. She pulled her thoughts back to her latest shock. "I have enough money to buy some nice things for Joshua. Maybe a toy." She could even make a new dress to replace the gray shapeless wonder provided by the Weimers. She should be excited. Instead, all she felt was a dull ache in the back of her head. She'd put off moving on as long as she could.

"Mr. Legal said I could go look at my house. It's empty."

"I'll take you."

She offered directions to the place. "There." She stared at the front door. There had once been a swing from that tree branch. And a special place beside the narrow veranda where she played with her dolls.

"Are you going in?"

She nodded and he jumped to the ground, Joshua still in one arm. She waited for Billy to assist her down and clung to his hand. "Come with me." Her insides quivered as she stared at her past with her future tucked against Billy's chest. It was an odd, disorienting feeling, like swinging too high and getting that little feeling of sailing onward free of the ropes just before the descending swing carried her backward.

"Come on. Let's have a look." The thickness of his voice was almost enough to make her change her mind and forget the whole business. But he headed up the path, pulling her along.

He thrust open the front door and stepped aside, giving her a chance to go in alone.

She took one tiny step and then another. The place was cold and empty except for a wing-backed chair with stuffing escaping the cushions, and an upturned bookshelf. The air still carried the smell of coal smoke and cinnamon. She stared straight ahead, mentally reviewing the rooms. Mother and Father's bedroom the first one on the left. Hers the second one. The kitchen through that door to the right with three more doors. One to a small storeroom, one to the guest bedroom and the third to the backyard where a big garden provided plenty of vegetables. Vivian had carried wash water out to the plants. Mother had also grown flowers along the front edge of the garden. "Beauty and practicality together," she always said. "Makes a good combination."

Most of all Vivian remembered how her parents had loved her. How her home had been a place of safety and warmth. She would provide the same for Joshua. She sucked in air until the quivering of her insides subsided.

"You going to look at anything else?"

Billy's voice jarred her into action. They explored the rooms. The former occupants had left behind a small table and two chairs in the kitchen. She found a chipped bowl in the cupboard. A bed frame had been left in the guest room and a dresser with a broken drawer in her bedroom.

"Not much to start over with," Billy said.

"I'll have to buy some supplies." She didn't need much in the way of furniture. "I'll fix the chair."

"You're determined to go through with this, are you?"

She faced him, her heart pressing hard against her ribs as she tried to be brave. "I have to do this." She touched Joshua's cheek. "For my son."

Billy caught Vivian's chin and tipped her face toward his. Their eyes met. At that moment, the sun dipped below the top of the window and poured golden light over them. Her insides felt kissed and blessed by the look of love in his eyes flashing back the glow of the sunshine. "Vivian, I love you." He bent his head and caught her mouth.

She leaned into him, drinking in his love. She wanted nothing more, nothing else, at least not for herself.

As if to remind her she must think of more than her own desires, Joshua kicked as if protesting being sandwiched between his mother and Billy.

She eased back, breaking the kiss with reluctance and only after two unsuccessful attempts. *Oh, Lord, how I love this man. There must be a way for us to be together.* "Billy, I love you so much I can't imagine not seeing your welcoming smile every morning across the table. But I have Joshua." She shuddered as the bright light of love faded from his eyes, replaced with a stormy sky of resignation.

"And I have Ma."

She wanted to beg him to forget his mother but if he would do so, he wasn't the man she loved. She wanted to tell him he could come and visit without his mother.

But she knew his own fears were as strong as his ma's. "I can only pray that God will provide a way."

"In the meantime, you plan to move into this house?"

"Yes. As soon as possible. Tomorrow." She'd stay tonight but she wasn't prepared and she wanted just one more night at the farm, sharing the evening hours with Billy and seeing his smile over the breakfast table. She would etch those moments on her heart and carry them forever or until God saw fit to provide an answer for them.

They made the trip back home in relative quiet as if neither of them could think beyond what the morrow held.

And that night, as they shared their customary evening hours, Billy shifted the conversation to his past.

"Pa used to take me to church."

"Did he have a strong faith?" Suddenly, it seemed she must know everything about Billy from the time he was a baby. She might not get a chance to ask him later.

"Pa said, 'A man takes what God gives him and tries to make the best of it.' I guess I've tried to do the same."

Vivian knew he meant taking care of his mother. "My mother said it's darkest just before the dawn."

At the meaning of the words, their gazes locked. Could dawn be approaching for them? She didn't see how. She'd gone so far as to suggest to Mrs. Black that things might be different now if she were to go to town. Perhaps she'd find she could be part of normal life. The woman had scrubbed her hair into wild disarray and dashed outside, pausing only long enough to grab her coat. Perhaps Mrs. Black had lived this way too long, couldn't change now.

She blinked, pulling back the pain that crawled up and down her insides, dragging cruel nails in its fist. "Tell me about your pa."

He shifted as Joshua fussed, and hummed until the baby settled again. "Pa seemed to shrink after Ma came back." He chuckled softly, mindful of the content baby on his chest. "I just realized it wasn't Pa who shrank but me who grew way bigger than him. He was a good man, patient, unruffled by…" He stopped as if surprised by his thoughts.

"Yes?"

"He never let what people say bother him. Said they only spoke out of their own fears or ignorance and we wouldn't act any differently if the shoe was on the other foot."

Thank You, Lord. You are at work. Wisely, she didn't choose to comment on Billy's observation, certain he would realize the importance of what he'd said without her help.

He continued to talk about his father until they retired to bed.

Chapter Fifteen

If Vivian thought her prayers had been answered, her hopes were flattened the next morning. Billy carried items from the room where he'd been sleeping—a small rocker he fixed a broken rung on, a battered pot and some dishes. "If you're going to live in town you'll need more than a bed. Good thing Ma keeps everything."

Vivian kept her disappointment stuffed in the pit of her stomach as she prepared breakfast and Billy continued to haul things out to the wagon. He soon had a fair-sized load. "I can't take all that stuff."

"Nothing we've any use for, ain't that right, Ma?"

Mrs. Black watched Billy make the trips back and forth, her expression growing more and more troubled. "You're leaving?"

"I told you, Ma. She got her parents' house back. She's going to live in town."

"You'll be taking Joshua?" The woman's voice quivered.

"You can come visit anytime." Vivian watched carefully, hoping to see a hint of agreement.

Instead, Mrs. Black windmilled her arms. "I don't go to town. Never go to town. Never."

Vivian pressed her lips together to still the cry of disappointment. She met Billy's gaze and saw his resignation and remembered his words of last night. *Try and make the best of things.*

She didn't want him to accept this way of life. She turned away so he couldn't see the depth of her pain. There was nothing he could do to change things. She had to accept that. But the bottom of her heart threatened to push clear up her throat and choke her.

They ate in silence. Vivian didn't know what either of the Blacks felt but she felt like she ate the condemned man's last meal.

She and Billy did dishes together, sadness making her limbs heavy. Mrs. Black huddled over her quilt now almost finished. She'd removed it from the frame a few days ago to begin stitching the edging on.

Vivian loved the design and wished she could see the quilt completed. But watching Mrs. Black working feverishly as if each jab of the needle could poke holes in the tense atmosphere filled her with such a long, dark ache she wanted to cry. Why couldn't the woman change? Just a little. Just enough to set Billy free.

Vivian was almost grateful when they finished the dishes and scurried to gather up the last of her things. She wrapped Joshua against the cool air and paused. "Goodbye, Mrs. Black. Thank you for allowing me to stay. And if you ever get the notion to visit me, I'd be pleased to see you."

She waited. Mrs. Black didn't even look up. "Goodbye."

Just as she stepped out the door, Mrs. Black called, "Wait." She bundled up the quilt and rushed to Vivian's side. "It's yours. Take it." She pushed the quilt into Vivian's arms.

The woman had been in a hurry to finish so she could gift Vivian with the quilt. Vivian was so surprised she couldn't speak. She swallowed hard, forced words to her wooden tongue. "Thank you. I will cherish it always."

"Well, I'll be," Billy murmured, as he helped Vivian into the wagon.

Vivian didn't speak all the way to town. She couldn't. She was too busy trying to control emotions that raced through an endless circle of surprise, sadness, determination and hope. Hope that this gift was a sign Mrs. Black was changing. As quickly as she thought it might be possible, her doubts and sadness returned. Giving a gift was a far cry from changing how she lived.

They arrived at her house and Billy quickly unloaded the things he'd brought. He carried in a feather tick and slapped it into shape on the bed frame he'd moved into her former room.

Too soon, the wagon stood empty.

Vivian tried unsuccessfully to still the panic pressing against her heart. Soon she'd be alone, facing her future. Joshua lay in the little bed Billy had made. She stared at her son. For him. She was doing all this for him, but at her side Billy stood, his hands stuffed in his pockets.

"I guess I better be on my way. Leave you to get settled."

She turned slowly, her limbs rubbery. She managed a strangled whisper. "Stay. I'll make supper."

Regret wreathed his face, making his blue eyes cloudy. "Vivian, I can't. You don't want people to start talk, now, do you?"

She shook her head, although at this very moment she didn't care what cruel things the neighbors might think or say. But look where not caring had gotten her.

"'Sides, Ma will be 'specting me." He made no move toward the door.

Vivian's face felt as if the skin might sag off the bones. Her chest, on the other hand, had turned stiff except for a spot in her chest where all the pain of this parting burrowed deep, with agonizing insistence.

"I don't want you to go."

Billy groaned. "Then come back with me. Marry me and live on the farm."

From somewhere inside, an indisputable argument forced its way into her thoughts. She loved the farm. Would gladly live there but she wouldn't hide. Especially not hide Joshua. "When life at the farm can be normal."

"Vivian, it won't happen. Not while Ma's alive."

She nodded. They both knew it. They both had to live with the fact. But oh, how it hurt to say goodbye. She searched his face, memorizing every dear, familiar detail. She pressed trembling fingers to his cheeks. "You will visit me, won't you?"

He shook his head. "It wouldn't be appropriate." His words caught. He closed his eyes and turned his face to kiss the palm of her hand. Then he caught her to him and held her securely against his big chest.

She wanted to beg him to change for her sake. Somehow, they could work this out. He could protect his mother and still live a normal life if he would only…

What? What did she expect he would do? He felt this was the only way he could make up for hiding when his ma was captured—sharing a life that put no expectations on her. She understood. But she wished it could be different.

"You must do what you must do for Joshua and I must take care of Ma."

"You're right. Tomorrow, I will go to church and confront the congregation. I will start over with God's forgiveness and whatever forgiveness people choose to extend to me."

"And I will take care of Ma."

She clutched his shirtfront and breathed in his warm familiar scent. "If only things could be different." She had only one hope. "I pray something will change."

He cupped a big, protective hand to her neck. A shudder shook him. "Since I became a man, all I've wanted was a wife and family. Then I accepted I could never have it. Not with Ma the way she is about seeing people. And then you and Josh came into my life." He tipped her head back so he could examine her eyes, her hair, her chin.

The hunger in his eyes filled her with an ache as deep as a canyon, as wide as the Dakota sky and as dry as the winds that blew across the prairie.

Billy continued. "I will cherish each moment I have spent with you. I will see your face in every sunset. I will hear your laugh in the wind through the treetops. I will see your smile each time Limpy greets me. I will pray for you every day and fall asleep with your name on my lips. And I will miss you with every beat of my heart."

Vivian quivered with emotion. Never had she heard Billy so eloquent. His words were sweet as dew on the petals of a rose and as painful as the thorns on the same bush. She didn't realize she cried until he thumbed the tears from her cheeks.

He bent and tenderly claimed her mouth, his kiss lingering.

Greedily, she returned his kiss, wanting to weld him there forever.

He broke away and with long strides headed for the door. He paused, turned. "Vivian, I love you."

"I love you, too." More than he could know. More than

she thought possible. She'd never felt anything as powerful as this before.

But he left in such a hurry she didn't know if he even heard.

Billy couldn't remember the trip home. He couldn't remember putting Blaze in his stall. He ate the food Ma set before him without tasting it and he must have washed the dishes because the kitchen was tidy. He sat in his big chair before the fire and stared at the flames without seeing them.

He'd been content enough before Vivian blew into his life on the tail of a storm. But he would never know that contentment again. Every corner of the house echoed with memories of her and the baby. Every breath he drew vibrated with his loneliness. How he'd endure he did not know. He only knew he must somehow convince Ma it didn't matter.

"Is Vivian's house nice?"

Ma's question startled him. He'd almost forgotten she sat in the chair across from him, carding wool for her next quilt.

"Pretty little house." He didn't have to close his eyes to see Vivian hurrying about, putting things away, adjusting the position of each piece of furniture until she was satisfied. He crossed his arms over his chest to still the hunger for her.

"She'll be happy there?"

Why did it matter to Ma? No doubt she was glad to have the woman and child out of her home. Billy sucked in air until he coughed. No need for him to blame Ma for things beyond her control.

Missing Vivian was a pain so real, so demanding, he

had to chance upsetting Ma. "Ma, do you think you might like to go to town in the future?"

He waited, hoping, praying.

She stopped rocking. "I ain't been to town since…" She shook her head. "I can't."

He knew her answer before she gave it. Yet unless she changed—

She rocked furiously, her eyes wide with fright.

His hopes wilted. She could not change and he would never walk away from her. He'd been powerless at six to defend her, protect her. He wasn't now.

He flipped open a newspaper but the words made no sense. He couldn't stop thinking about Vivian. If only it was possible for them to enjoy their love.

He rattled the pages and forced himself to continue reading. Ma was not an obstacle. She was his glad responsibility. She must never guess at how much it cost him to give up Vivian. He did not want to make her feel bad for something she couldn't help—her fear of people and of change.

Why had God sent Vivian into his life? Was it meant for good? *It's time to start new.* That's what Vivian said.

But Ma would not change. He didn't want to upset her. He'd long ago learned to do so meant sending her into one of her spells.

Loving Vivian had changed things for him but unless Ma changed, he must endure this pain until it somehow developed a scab. Even then it would fester. Forever.

Could he trust God to change Ma so their love was possible?

He bowed his head and prayed for a long time, confessing that he hadn't trusted God nor asked His help. *Lord, let Ma be willing to change.* If she wasn't, he must be ready to let this whole business rest in God's hands.

No longer did he feel so powerless. Surely, God would work things out.

"Ma, we've hidden long enough. I want to start living again. A new life." He sucked in air. If she knew how important it was and why— "Ma, I love Vivian. But I can't expect her to hide here like we do."

Ma stopped rocking. Only her hands continued the restless motion. Her gaze darted to the fire, remained there a moment then slowly came to him.

He saw the dark fear in her eyes. His conscience smote him. How could he torment his ma like this? "Ma, I won't go. I'll always be here for you."

She nodded. "I'm sorry. I'm sorry. I'm sorry."

He caught her hands. "Ma, stop. It's fine."

She held his gaze in an endless search.

He wished he could read her thoughts and guess what went through her mind as she studied him.

She picked up her project and resumed the soothing routine of combing the wool.

That should have been the end of it for him. He would not upset Ma anymore. But he lay again in his own bed where Vivian had slept these past weeks, every breath full of her scent, every inch of skin missing her, he could not stop wishing and dreaming, missing and aching.

He didn't sleep much. He prayed. He thought of Vivian and Joshua in town. He thought of Vivian standing before the congregation in the morning.

And he made up his mind.

He told Ma at breakfast. "I'm going to church."

She dropped her knife. "Church?"

"Yes, Ma. Vivian is planning to publicly confess her sin before the whole congregation. I can't let her do that by herself. I will be there to stand at her side."

Ma kept her head down as if his announcement signaled his departure forever.

"Ma, I'll be back but I can't let her face this alone."

"I did some serious thinking last night." She faced him, her eyes wide, her lips trembling. Something flickered through her eyes. "I've kept you here long enough. I've hidden long enough." Her voice hardened with determination. "I'll go to church with you." She shivered.

"Ma, that's great."

"Maybe only this once. Depends."

It was a start. God willing, it would be more than that.

They hurried through chores and donned their best clothes. He eyed Ma. "You might enjoy going to town and picking out fabric for a new dress."

"Billy, I'm not promising anything but this one time. Besides—" she smoothed her hands over her skirt "—I quite like the fabric you pick out."

A few minutes later they sat side by side on the wagon seat and headed for town. Billy had been so many times in the last few weeks that it was almost commonplace, but this time he would confront a crowd of people, many who had been cruel in the past.

Ma's anxiety pulsated along her arm and up his until his nerves vibrated.

Only one thing kept him going—the thought of Vivian standing at the front, alone and vulnerable.

The service had started by the time they arrived.

He hesitated, sucked in air. "Let's go, Ma."

She clutched his hand. "I can't. You go ahead."

Aah. Pain caught him just below his ribs and knuckled deep and hard. He'd hoped this was the beginning. He'd hoped this meant he could dream of a future with Vivian. It took all his strength to push back his disappointment. "Ma, I must go in."

"I'll wait here."

He didn't have time to argue. He didn't want to miss being with Vivian.

He jogged to the door and paused, remembering. Now was not the time to think of the way he'd been laughed at in the past. He closed his mind to such things and slipped in as quietly as he could to stand in the entryway where he had a good view of the front of the church.

Vivian stood before the congregation, holding Joshua proudly in her arms. It was so quiet. Was he too late? He stood, his hat in his hands, trying to decide what to do.

Vivian smiled. "Thank you for the chance to speak to all of you. This is my son, Joshua. Now I could pretend I am a widow and that would it make too easy for all of us. But I'm not. What you see before you is a woman who has sinned. I confess to my shame and sorrow. Except I am not ashamed or sorry to have this precious child. He is a treasure and it is for him that I am willing to face you and make this confession. Yes, I have sinned. For a time, I thought I must live condemned and guilty, but Pastor Morrow showed me many verses that prove God's love and forgiveness for even one like me. One verse I will cling to is First John, chapter one, verse nine. 'If we confess our sin, he is faithful and just to forgive us our sins, and to cleanse us from all unrighteousness.' I don't deserve His mercy and forgiveness but I won't refuse it, either.

"I'm very glad to be back in the town where I spent my happy childhood. I look around and recognize some of you. I remember how good and kind you were to me in the past.

"God has forgiven me and I pray you can find it in your heart to forgive me, too. And if you don't, well, I don't blame you."

Billy thought he would burst with pride at her strength and confidence.

She drew in a shaky breath and adjusted Joshua. "For Joshua's sake, I ask you not to blame him for what I've done. But whatever each of you decides, I am going to live here even if I have to walk alone."

Billy pushed into the sanctuary. She would not be walking alone. Ignoring the startled whispers, he strode to the front of the church and went to her side.

Her smile was trembling, her eyes grateful.

"I'm here." He didn't know what else to say. He wanted to promise her he would walk boldly at her side always but a great gulf of fears held him back. Ma's fears only, he realized. He no longer cared what people said or did. But he still must provide Ma with the security she needed. He owed her that much.

A surprised ripple had people turning to the back of the church.

Both he and Vivian gasped. Ma stood, arm in arm with Mrs. Morrow. Ma caught his eyes and nodded. He knew exactly what she meant.

She and Mrs. Morrow sat in a pew close to the back.

The congregation settled and faced forward again, all eyes on Billy and Vivian.

He knew they expected something more and, with a wide grin, he prepared to give it to them. "Vivian, you will not have to walk through town on your own. I'll be at your side each step of the way. If you will have me, I will be your husband and Joshua's father."

"I will have you," she whispered.

Billy drank in her eager smile, then faced the congregation. "It is time for a new start."

He noted some of the elderly ladies dabbing hankies to their eyes.

Pastor Morrow stood at the pulpit. "Billy is right. But I doubt that Vivian and Billy or Mrs. Black are the only ones who need to put things right or find a way to start over. Whether it's with friends or family or with God, why not do it today?"

Billy and Vivian sat in the front pew as the pastor spoke.

"Let us pray." The pastor prayed for forgiveness, honesty and humility and for those who needed cleansing to have the boldness to seek it. When he finished, more than a dozen people made their way to the front and knelt at the steps.

A holy hush filled the place until the organist played, then people quietly departed, leaving behind those who wanted to pray.

People gathered in the yard. Many went to Ma and shook her hand. She looked more stunned than afraid. Billy hoped because she found the welcome overwhelming.

He stood, his arm around Vivian. A continual parade of people came to congratulate them. Some shied away, averting their eyes. Billy knew not everyone would welcome them. He didn't expect it. In fact, this was more than he'd thought possible.

"Come to my house for lunch."

"Ma?"

"Her, too. It makes it respectable, after all." Her eyes twinkled and he laughed.

They slipped away. After they ate, Ma offered to feed little Josh.

"Come for a walk?" Billy said.

She nodded and grabbed her cape.

Spring was in the air and they walked away from town, enjoying the sound of returning songbirds and the warm breeze. She tucked her arm around his and snuggled close. "I love you, Big Billy Black."

The nickname that had once made him feel like a monster sounded like a trophy on her lips and he laughed loud and hard, not caring if people would hear him and wonder.

He waited until they reached the edge of town and found the shelter of a budding tree to pull her into his arms. "I love you, Vivian Halliday. My love, my dream, my everything. When can we get married?"

Vivian's laugh was silenced by his kiss.

Epilogue

Vivian held the squirming Joshua in her arms as they waited for Billy. At the sound of the approaching wagon, Josh kicked and babbled with excitement and leaned toward the door, his arms extended for the greeting he knew he would get. "Hang on, Daddy will be here in a minute."

Thank you, Lord, for the love of this good man and for the love he has for my son.

They married that spring and had enjoyed six months of wedded joy in a summer as warm and wonderful as their love.

Billy burst through the door. "You ready?" He kissed Vivian on the nose and Josh on the top of his head.

Vivian laughed. "You're almost as excited as I am."

He took Josh and shepherded her out the door. He offered his hand to help her up, then kissed Josh before he put the baby on her lap. "I'm excited just to be alive." The wagon creaked as he climbed up to sit beside her. "I can't believe how wonderful life is." He slipped his arms around her and kissed her thoroughly before he took up the reins. "Blessed, I am."

She tucked her hand around his arm and nuzzled her

cheek on his thick solid arm. "Me, too, my sweet man. Me, too."

It seemed only moments before they arrived in town. Several people looked up as they passed and waved. Vivian squeezed Billy's arm. People had been so good to them. Not everyone, of course, but it grew easier and easier to ignore those who turned away.

She still regretted that Wayne had turned his back on his son but it was a relief when the Styleses had moved. She didn't know how many people knew of their shady dealings with her and she'd never tell. In fact, she would do all she could to protect Joshua from being identified with his biological father. Someday, when he was older, if he wanted to know she might tell him all the sordid details, but for now...

"Want to leave Joshua with his gramma while we tend to business?"

"She'd have our hide if we didn't."

They looked into each other's eyes, openly, silently loving each other and sharing their amazement and joy at how far his ma had come from the frightened, strange lady of the past.

"Vivian, I can now readily admit what I once denied, that I was hiding for my sake as much as for Ma's."

She understood more than he knew. "And now?"

"I'm proud to walk openly because people see how much you love me. I never want to hide that from people."

Her throat tightened at the way he looked at her all proud and grateful. He turned the wagon down the side street toward Vivian's house where his mother now lived. She had a circle of friends who were as avid about quilting as she. Her interests had grown to knitting. She and her friends had a passion to supply quilts and knit goods to those less fortunate. Vivian's heart drank in sweet delight at their latest project. A woman in their group had opened her house to a family of three children left orphaned. She vowed to keep them together and give them love and nurturing. Ma Black and her friends promised to help in every way they could. Some of the money the bank had given back to Vivian had helped purchase goods for the newly formed family.

They left Josh in the loving arms of his grandmother and turned down the street toward the church where Billy stopped the wagon and helped Vivian to the ground.

She clung to his hand as she crossed the yellowed grass. With a start, she realized fall was upon them already. Then she forgot everything but what she had come to see.

A simple stone marker she'd purchased with some of her windfall money.

Two names were carved into it.

Joshua Halliday. His birth date, the date of his death. Isabelle Morton Halliday. The dates of her birth and death. And a verse Vivian had chosen. "Nothing shall be able to separate us from the love of God, which is in Christ Jesus our Lord."

She knelt on the ground before the graves and bowed her head.

Billy cupped his hand across the back of her neck.

Momma, Poppa. I made so many mistakes. Some so big. But not even that can keep me from God's love. I will see you some glad day in glory. Until then, goodbye. I love you.

She scrubbed tears from her cheeks. She would miss them always. But she had a new family—a husband, a son and a mother-in-law who had observed much and thought deeply during her years of isolation and now seemed an endless fount of wisdom and keen wit. Perhaps, God willing, there would be more children. How her parents would have loved to see her grown and with a child.

And she had a husband who grew more dear with each passing moment. She pushed to her feet and turned into his arms. "I love you, Billy Black."

He kissed her soundly and tucked her against his chest as they returned to the wagon. "I have one more stop to make before we go home."

They drove straight down the main street toward the store. "Wait here." He strode in the front door as bold and at ease as if he'd done it all his life.

He returned almost at once, carrying a large package. Lucas, at his side, carried a smaller one.

Curious, she demanded, "What do you have?"

"Something for my sweet wife. But you have to wait until we get home."

"Not fair." They had to stop and visit his ma and then there was the ride home. "I can't wait that long."

"You don't have much choice."

"I could climb in the back and unwrap it right here."

His eyes twinkled. "Think you can outwrestle me?"

She giggled at the absurdity, then crossed her arms and faced straight ahead, determined she wouldn't let him know she was dying of curiosity.

But by the time they reached home she had practically crawled out of her skin.

And Billy knew it. He took his time about carrying Josh inside and sitting him on the floor to play with a soft ball his grandma had knit for him.

"Now?" she asked.

"You sit, and I'll bring it in."

She sat and folded her hands.

Satisfied, he returned to the wagon. First, he brought

in the bigger parcel and set it on the stool. She scrambled to tear off the brown paper.

She gasped when she saw what it was. Her throat closed off with a rush of emotions. "Blue Boy. Where did you get this?"

"Lift it up."

She did so. "Pinky." Tears flowed like a river. She shook her head and choked out, "How?"

"You spoke of them so often I had to see if I could track them down. I found the auctioneer who had sold your parents' things and he kindly gave me the name of the people who bought the pictures. The people gladly sold them back when I explained why I wanted them."

"Thank you." She tipped her face upward, inviting a kiss and was rewarded with a gentle one.

"Where will we hang them?" She glanced around, choosing a place.

"Don't you want to see the other parcel?"

She'd forgotten it. "I can't imagine anything better than this."

"I could take it back, I suppose."

"No, you don't. Bring it in."

He placed the parcel in her lap. Some solid object. She folded back the papers to reveal a Bible. She opened the flyleaf and read the family registry of her parents and their wedding and her own birth. "It's my parents' Bible." She stroked the cover, ran her finger over the names and felt a cord of belonging in her connection to these names. "I can't believe you found this."

"It is rightfully yours. Now you can add our marriage and Joshua's birth to the family history."

She hugged the Bible to her chest. "It feels like I have come full circle from the love of my parents to the love of a good man."

"Full circle. I like that." He knelt before her and wrapped her in his warm love. "And we build another circle on top of that."

Their love would go on and on—a circle of endless love.

* * * * *

DAKOTA FATHER

I will praise thee;
for I am fearfully and wonderfully made.
—*Psalms* 139:14

To my grandparents and great-grandparents, who faced challenges in moving to a new land. I am in awe of the hardships they endured and conquered. We owe them and the pioneers like them a debt of gratitude.

Chapter One

Buffalo Hollow, Dakota Territory, 1884

Nineteen-year-old Jenny Archibald spared a moment to dab at her forehead. If only she could escape the heat sucking at her pores and driving two-year-old Meggie to fretfulness. Jenny sensed the annoyance of those who shared the passenger rail car, cooped up in the same hot box as she and Meggie and having to endure the fitful cries of a child.

She pulled a clean cloth from the valise at her feet and spread it over the leather seat across from her. "Meggie, lie down and I'll fan you." They'd both be considerably cooler if Meggie didn't clutch at her neck and struggle in her arms.

Meggie whined a protest but allowed Jenny to put her down and, as she promised, Jenny waved over the child the book she had hoped to read on the trip. She'd naively thought Meggie would sleep the entire way from Center City, Ohio, or be happy to stare out the window at the passing scenery.

After a few minutes of fussing, Meg stuck two fingers in her mouth and her eyelids lowered. Jenny let out a sigh of relief. And hid a smile as the other occupants let out echoing sighs.

She glanced about the car. Apart from a withered old lady mumbling in the far seat, Jenny was the only woman aboard. Across the aisle sat two men who seemed to be business associates. They had persevered in wearing their suit coats for the first hour of the trip but now had shed them and waved paper before their faces trying to cool themselves.

Further along, a cowboy hunched over, his legs stretched out beside the seat in front of him. He spared her a sharp look then pulled his hat low and let his chin fall to his chest.

Jenny told herself she would not look at the man who sat across from the old lady. She'd been aware of him since he joined them several stops back—dressed in black, with black hair, and black eyes that seemed to see everything.

Pa was right when he said to her, "Pepper, you must learn to restrain your impulses. Think before you leap."

Only it wasn't that she exactly jumped at the sight of the man. Or the thought of him sitting there so calm and self-contained. More like her heart did a funny little jerk and her eyes jolted to him and away as if controlled by a power beyond her mind.

Like now. Despite her best intentions, she glanced at him. He watched her, his eyes bottomless. Her breath caught in a pool of heat somewhere behind her heart and she couldn't look away.

It took Meggie's wail to free her from his intense stare.

"Mama. I want Mama."

Jenny's heart ached for this child. How could she begin to comprehend the loss of both parents? As Lena and Mark lay dying of the raging fever that had taken so many lives Jenny promised them she would see their child delivered to Lena's brother and his wife and stay long enough to see her settled.

She did her best to soothe Meggie and fan her without resorting to picking her up.

The men across the aisle sighed. One muttered loudly enough for the whole car to hear. "You'd think people would know enough to teach their children how to behave in public."

Jenny stung under the unfair criticism. Meggie wasn't her child but even if she had been, the child could be excused her crankiness. No doubt she felt the heat even more than the rest of them.

If only she could find some cool refreshing water for her. She'd tasted the water from the jug at the back. It was hot and smelled funny. All she needed was for Meg to take sick. But even that inadequate supply had disappeared a short time ago.

The conductor assured her they would soon reach Buffalo Hollow where she could find fresh water before the next stage of her journey.

The muttering of the old woman increased in volume. She was clearly annoyed with Meggie's fussing. The slouching cowboy sat up straight, pushed his hat back and fixed Jenny with a belligerent look.

"Needs a good whupping."

Tears stung the back of Jenny's eyes. She blinked them back, tossed her head and pursed her lips. She would not let their comments affect her.

"Leave her be. The kid's as hot and cranky as the rest of us." The low words from the black-clad man made Jenny's tongue stick to the roof of her mouth. If only she could find a drink.

She glanced at the speaker, again felt that funny sensation deep in her heart. Knowing her feelings were spilling from her eyes, she ducked her head.

Guilt stung her ears. She'd promised Pa to return as quickly as she could, promised she would then hear Ted's offer of marriage. It was only a formality. Ma and Pa both highly approved of Ted Rusk who worked with Pa in the store. When Jenny protested she didn't feel like settling down despite her age, Ma cautioned, "Jenny, you must learn to think with your head not your heart."

"Ted is steady," Pa said. "He'll settle you down."

They knew what was best for her. And didn't the scripture instruct her to honor her father and mother? She intended to obey God's word. Didn't intend to follow her foolish heart into any more disasters.

Both parents had given cautious consent to her plan to take Meggie to Lena's family. No doubt they figured this adventure would get her restlessness out of her system.

She hoped it would, that she'd be ready to take her role as Ted's wife and partner as she intended to. Having given her word, she would fulfill it. Her word was her bond. She would learn to still the restless voice whispering from the dark corners of her imagination. She knew too well the risks of listening to that voice and would never again do so.

Meggie wouldn't settle and begged to be held. They were both sticky with heat but Jenny gathered the baby in her arms and rocked her, crooning soothing sounds which did little to ease Meggie's fussing and nothing to ease Jenny's feeling of being watched.

Stealing a glance from under her eyelashes, she saw the dark-eyed man studying her, a tightness about his mouth. He realized she looked at him and nodded, giving a smile that barely widened his mouth and pushed the tightness upward to his eyes. Yet he didn't look so much disapproving as simply hot and tired like the rest of them.

She nodded, her own smile small and polite even though inside she felt such an unusual touch of excitement. Again she ducked her head and studied the back of the bench before her.

Lord, I have promises to keep. I have tasks to do. And You know me. I have a side of me that rebels, overreacts, enjoys a breathless gallop. She thought of the verse Ma had drilled into her head and heart, 'Godliness with contentment is great gain.' There was no point in longing for things she couldn't have. She tried to find contentment even as she wondered that God had made her a woman—one who must abide by the tight restraints of society when she longed to be free to explore and adventure. She smiled as she thought of how she had—in the not so distant past—tried to talk Pa into heading for the Black Hills to look for gold.

Pa laughed. "Pepper, don't let the glitter of gold make you blind to the beauty of stability."

She loved Pa. He understood her better than anyone, perhaps even better than she understood herself. That's why she'd promised she and Ted would be engaged as soon as she returned. Pa approved of Ted and thought he would be the perfect mate for her. She trusted Pa's love and wisdom.

The conductor came through the car calling, "Buffalo Hollow next stop." He paused at Jenny's side. "I'll help you with the little one when we get there."

Her insides did a tumble as she thought of what faced her. She must find transportation to Lena's brother's ranch and turn Meggie over to the man and his wife. She would see Meggie settled as she promised then return home. But—she allowed a trickle of excitement—the settling-in period would surely give her a chance to explore the countryside. Just the thought made her shift so she could watch out the window. The golden prairie drifted past. The sky seemed endless, making her feel small yet light, as if she could float forever under the blue canopy.

The train jerked to a halt, puffing and groaning. The old woman muttered about having to endure the ride longer. All the men rose and headed for the door. Only the black-haired man paused to indicate she should precede him.

Flustered at his kindness, she fumbled to pull the two traveling bags from the overhead rack—an impossible task with Meggie clutched in her arms. She tried to put Meggie on her feet so she could manage but Meggie clung to her and refused to stand.

Jenny grew even warmer as the man patiently waited. "I'll take your bags. You carry the child."

She managed to untangle her thoughts enough to murmur "thank you," then hurried down the aisle and let the conductor assist her to the platform.

The stranger set her bags on the wooden platform. He considered her with a dark intense look. "Ma'am, if I might give you some advice?"

She nodded.

"Go home. This is no place for a woman and child." He tipped his head in good-bye and strode away.

"Go home?" she sputtered, but he continued on without a backward glance. No place for a woman and child? Who was he to make such a statement? Lena said her brother had sent for his intended six months ago. That woman had come out—no doubt happily married by now. Besides—she sniffed—did he think women were too fragile for frontier life? Too fussy? Too soft? She sniffed again. She could prove him wrong if he cared to hang about and see.

But of course he didn't and would never know how she would welcome the challenge of this life if it were offered to her. However, that wasn't going to happen. She would deliver Meggie and return home to her stable life. But not—she glared at the place where the man had disappeared from sight—because she couldn't stand the challenge of living out West.

As Burke Edwards rode from town he restrained the urge to lean forward and gallop all the way home. He wouldn't find any sense of peace and release until he could shed his Sunday-go-to-town clothes for jeans and chaps, and ride out on the prairie. He'd wished for a different outcome to his trip though in the back of his mind he knew the futility of hope. Had known, he supposed, from the first, but he had fought it. Perhaps if he'd accepted it from the beginning, made the necessary changes, all this would have turned out differently.

He sighed and settled back into the saddle, letting the rhythm of riding and the familiar scents and sights of the open prairie soothe his troubled mind.

Unbidden, unwelcome, his thoughts turned back to his recent train ride.

He'd noticed the girl the minute he got on the train— her hair trailing in damp disarray from the roll coiled about her head, her bonnet askew as the baby batted at it, her brown eyes both weary and patient. When he sat facing her he saw how her smiling brown eyes darted about, taking in everything. He admired her for coping with the fussy little girl, for smiling and nodding politely when the other passengers complained of the noise.

But the way she peered out the window in awe brought

such a surge of heat to his brain, he'd seen stars. He wanted to tell her, yup, that's what most of Dakota Territory was like—flat, endless prairie. Great for cows and horses. Deadly for women.

He'd studied her. Held her gaze steadily when she glanced his way. In that moment he'd felt something promising, even hopeful as if she dared him to venture into the unknown with him.

Just remembering that fleeting sensation made him snort. "I guess I've learned my lesson," he muttered to the silent prairie and uninterested horse. This was no place for a woman. He'd told her so then marched away without giving her a chance to reply.

A smile lifted the corners of his mouth. Her eyes had fired up a protest. She'd sputtered. Would have argued if he'd given her opportunity. If he hadn't learned his lesson a little too well he might have paused long enough to see her let off steam. Instead he marched away. Heard her words of protest follow. Had to steel himself not to turn and satisfy his desire to see how she looked all het up.

For a moment he wondered at her destination. He knew most people from the area who did business at Buffalo Hollow. Hadn't heard of anyone expecting a visitor. From what he'd overheard the woman explain to the conductor, this was more than a visit. She'd said something about joining an uncle. He'd heard her mention the child's father dying from a fever and guessed she was a widow.

He shrugged. He'd not see her again, of that he was certain. He only hoped she'd heed his words of warning and leave this country before it destroyed her.

The thoughts he'd been trying to avoid all afternoon flooded his mind, tearing up his plans, his dreams, his future. He'd known it was coming but had refused to accept it. But today had been final. The words left no room for doubt or hope. At twenty-five years of age, he, Burke Edwards, knew his future would take a different shape than the one he'd had in mind when he headed West three years ago with big ideas and bigger dreams.

The ranch came in sight. The house was intended to provide a home for a growing family. It would not happen now. Or ever. The house was only partially finished. He'd intended to extend it further to create a large front room where he and his growing family would gather in the dusk of the evening and enjoy each other's company. He figured there would be a woman in a rocking chair knitting or mending, he in another chair reading the paper or making plans for the future and someday, children at his feet or on his lap. Knowing it would never happen didn't make it easy to push those imaginations into the distance, never to be revisited.

Guess he'd known what the final outcome would be because he had abandoned all pretense of work on the house several months ago. It no longer bothered him that it looked forlorn and neglected. He would probably never complete it. No need to. It was adequate for his purposes.

He reined back to study the place and analyze his feelings. Shouldn't he feel something besides disappointment that there was no reason to finish the house? Shouldn't he be mourning the fact he and Flora would never marry?

"Guess I've known it for a long time. I've just been going through the motions of asking, waiting, hoping because I knew that's what I should do. But you know what, horse? I expect I'm happy enough to let it go. In some ways it's better that it is over and final." Still he couldn't quite shake a sense of failure. He should have walked away from the ranch when he'd seen how Flora felt about it. He didn't need her parents pointing out that her present condition and her current incarceration in the insane asylum was due, in no small part, to his failure to do so.

He flicked the reins and rode into the yard, turning toward the barn. He dropped to the ground. "Lucky," he called to the squat little man hanging around the corrals, wielding a pitchfork. The man was past his prime, one leg all gimped up from an accident. But he was handy around the place and had proven to be a loyal friend. "Look after my horse."

"Okay, Boss." He dropped the fork and sprinted over to take the reins. "Good trip, Boss?"

"Glad to be home."

Lucky chuckled. "Absence makes the heart grow fonder, they say."

"What's new around here?" He'd only been away two days but it felt like a month.

"Nothing, Boss. Though Mac said he thought the spring over to the west was drying out."

"I'll ride over tomorrow and check."

"And the mosquitoes been awful bad. I'm about to start a smudge over past the barn for the horses."

"I'll do it." Burke welcomed the chance to be out in the open doing something mindless and undemanding. He didn't want to think of Flora or his failures. He smiled as he recalled the look on the young woman's face as he warned her this territory was too tough for a woman, then he shook his head.

He didn't want to think about her, either.

His restlessness returned with a vengeance matching the vicious prairie winds. "Lucky, throw my saddle on another mount. I'll ride out and have a look at things." He strode to the house with an urgency that had no cause and quickly changed into his comfortable work clothes. He paused long enough to build the smudge, smeared some lard on the back of his neck to protect himself and rode into the wide open spaces where a man could enjoy forgetfulness.

Forgetfulness was all he sought—all he needed.

Jenny jolted to one side as the buggy bounced along the trail. She feared little, hadn't blinked when caring for Meggie's parents in their final days. Nor had she felt anything but a trickle of excitement at the task they had given her before their death—deliver their child to her new guardian. But trepidation gnawed into her bones as the miles passed. She'd soon have to meet Lena's brother and his wife and inform them of Lena and Mark's deaths, then turn Meggie over to their care.

Jenny smiled at the child in her arms. It was appreciably cooler riding in the open buggy and Meggie had fallen asleep. She loved this little girl. It would be a wrench to leave her.

"How much farther?" she asked the man she'd hired to take her to the ranch in the far corner of the Dakotas.

"Lookee there and you can see the buildings in the distance."

She followed the direction he indicated and indeed, saw a cluster of buildings. "Looks almost as big as Buffalo Hollow." The little prairie town had proved dusty and squat but friendly. The store owner had allowed her to wash Meggie and tidy them both up as best she could. Customers had offered greetings and given her details about the ranch she was about to reach.

"Big place."

"Boss works his men hard and himself harder."

"Too bad about what happened."

When she pressed for details on that latter bit of information she found the people of Buffalo Hollow suddenly reticent.

Too bad? A fire perhaps or a broken bone.

Now, as she studied the far-off buildings, she wished she'd insisted someone tell her what they meant. She could almost hear Pa's voice and she smiled up into the sky. 'Pepper, you must learn to guard your inquisitiveness. Sufficient to the day is the trouble thereof.' He meant everyone had enough troubles and trials of their own without borrowing from others. And that included wanting to know more than she needed about other people.

She turned her attention back to Meggie. Despite her attempts to clean them up in the tiny town, they were both dusty and soiled, and smelled of coal smoke and sour milk. Not the way she would have wanted to arrive on a stranger's doorstep. She could only hope Meggie's new guardians cared nothing for such things and only for the well-being of their orphaned niece. Suddenly she wanted this meeting over with and had to remind herself to be patient. Like Pa would say, "Settle down, Pepper. You can't make the world turn faster."

They rounded a corner, ducked between two sharp embankments crowned with a jagged row of rocks and headed toward the buildings.

She strained forward, assessing everything. A barn surrounded by rail fences with a horse in one of the pens. Several low buildings on either side of the alleyway running from the barn to the rambling frame house that sat like the crowning jewel a little apart. Smoke twisted from the rock chimney.

She squinted at the house as they drew closer, anxious for a good look, wondering what sort of life Meggie would be thrust into.

A roofed but wall-less lean-to covered the sides of the house —a sort of veranda though it seemed to come to an abrupt halt midway down one wall.

Even several hundred yards away she could see an untidy assortment of things under the roof of the lean-to. As if the barn wasn't big enough to accommodate the tools of ranching.

"We's here." The driver's announcement was redundant as he pulled to a halt before the house.

"Could you please put my things on the porch?"

He yanked the two bags from the buggy and deposited them. One contained her traveling things and Meggie's few clothes. The other held most of Lena's and a few of Mark's belongings. The bulk of Mark's possessions had been claimed by his brother, Andy, who also wanted to take Meggie but Lena had been insistent that Meggie go to a married man.

"I don't want her raised by a bachelor. How would she learn to be a refined lady? No, promise me you'll take her to my brother. He sent for his bride six months ago. They'll be happily settled by now. My brother and I were always close. They'll take good care of my baby."

Jenny had gladly given her promise and would very shortly fulfill it.

She allowed the driver to help her from the buggy, carefully shifting Meggie from one arm to the other as she descended. The baby wakened and whimpered.

The man stood by his buggy. "I'll wait and see if anyone has letters to post."

Meggie hesitated. Why had no one come to the door or strode from one of the outbuildings? She'd glimpsed the shadow of a man in the barn. Seems someone should show a degree of curiosity if not neighborliness but apart from the creak of a gate blowing in the wind and the far-off cry of a hawk, there was no sound of welcome. "This is the right place?"

"The Lazy B. 'Spect all the men are out working but Paquette should be in the back. Want we should go that way?"

"Paquette?" What was that? But if it meant admission to this house, she'd follow the man most anywhere.

"She's the housekeeper. A Métis."

She'd heard of the part Indian, part French-Canadian people, many of them descended from the fur traders.

They left the baggage where the man put it and picked their way past overturned buckets and around a huddle of chairs.

They found the back door open. The driver stepped inside with complete confidence and Jenny followed hesitantly. In her world, one didn't walk into a house unbidden. This, however, was a strange, exciting new world. A thrill trickled through her lungs.

The enormous size of the room surprised her. A scarred wooden table with plank benches along each side and a chair at each end took up the area nearest the door. At the far end, cupboards and a stove—presided over by a little woman so bent and crippled Meggie wondered if she could walk. Her graying hair hung in twin braids down her back, tied with a length of leather. The frayed ends of each braid were black.

"Hullo, Paquette. The boss man about?" the man at her side called.

"I hear him soon ago. Out by de corrals, him. He ride away 'gain. I hear horsesteps. I help you? Me?"

Jenny edged past the driver. "My name is Jenny Archibald. I need to speak to the Edwards. Could you tell Mrs. Edwards I'm here?"

Bent as she was, the woman appeared to regard Jenny

from beneath her gray-streaked, black hair with eyes so dark the pupils were indiscernible. "Be no Missus Edwards." She gave a jerky sort of laugh that seemed oddly full of both mirth and mockery.

"But—" Jenny fell back a step. "There must be."

"No, Ma'am, there is not." The deep voice behind her jerked Jenny about so fast it hurt her eyes. She blinked. It was the man from the train. Except—

She narrowed her eyes and looked at him more closely. He looked like a wild cowboy now but with the same dark intense eyes. Yes, it was the same man.

She gathered her thoughts and chose the most obvious one. "Mr. Edwards, I presume?"

"That would be so, though I prefer to be called Burke. But tell me, why must I have a wife?" His words were slow, his voice deadly calm.

She shivered at the way he spoke as if she had insulted him and he was about to demand some sort of retribution. Suddenly the strength drained out the soles of her well-worn black leather boots. As her knees turned soggy, she groped toward the table and plunked down on a bench.

"Perhaps you better explain what it is you want." He signaled to the woman. "Paquette, bring us coffee, please. Unless…" He silently questioned Jenny.

"Might I have tea?" she whispered.

"Tea, for the lady, Paquette."

"Yes, boss. Fer de lady. I get de tea."

Jenny pulled in a long, strengthening draft of air, hot from the stove and rolling with scents of many meals past and present. An explanation, he wanted, did he? Well, seems he had some explaining to do himself. Maybe she'd misunderstood. "No wife?"

"No wife now or ever."

"But—"

Mr. Edward's expression stopped any comment she'd been about to make. Lena said he had sent for his intended six months ago. They should have been married by now.

She reminded herself of all the times Ma had warned her to control her emotions, speak like a lady. *Mama, how would a lady speak and act in this situation?* Thoughts of Ma settled her and common sense replaced her shock. She'd deal with the facts one at a time.

"Mr. Edwards, I have come with some bad news."

His eyes narrowed and he sat down a few feet away, forcing her to shift sideways to look into his face.

Ignoring the thunderous warning in his face, not even pausing to wonder what it meant, she rushed on. "I'm sorry to have to inform you your sister, Lena, and her husband, Mark, succumbed to the fever a few days ago. And I have brought your niece to you."

The man jolted like she'd stomped on his foot and she knew a certain satisfaction at surprising him as much as he'd done her. Her inappropriate feeling fled as quickly at it had come, replaced by sympathy. He'd lost his sister and brother-in-law. "I'm so sorry. Please accept my condolences."

And somehow he'd managed to lose the woman who was to be his wife. What had happened to her? Why didn't Lena know this? It sounded very suspicious and she glanced about as if the corners held secrets.

"They're gone? Both of them?" He swallowed hard and shifted his gaze to the little girl. "This is Meggie?"

Meggie whimpered at the sound of her name.

"She's hot and tired and missing her parents." The details regarding his lack of a wife could be sorted out later, after Meggie had been tended to. But what the baby needed most was a new mother figure.

There was no Mrs. Edwards. She tried to get her thoughts around the unwelcome information. Jenny glanced at the man in continuing disbelief.

His gaze held hers in the same steady probing look that had trapped her on the train. She tried to free herself. Tried to think what she must do now.

Paquette set steaming cups at the table.

The driver sucked back black tea.

Jenny bent her head, ran her finger along the tiny handle.

This was not how things were to be.

Chapter Two

Burke stared at the young woman. Lena was dead? His baby sister and her husband? The only family he had? A sour taste like gall stung his throat. He'd cared for Lena after their parents died when he was sixteen and she fourteen. He'd found work, provided them a home, been her chaperone at outings. Only when she had Mark to care for her had he felt free to head west, full of plans for the future. He'd never considered Lena wouldn't always be there. He should have stayed and protected her. But shouldn't Mark have been doing that?

They were both gone. Taken by something no one could control but God. And God seemed not to care about the troubling affairs of individuals. No doubt He had his hands full running the world and taking care of the stars in space.

Burke had gotten his ranch. He'd planned to be married by how, perhaps even have a new little Edwards boy or girl to look forward to.

That wasn't going to happen now. Suddenly he felt very alone.

He considered the fussing child. This baby was Meggie? He'd never seen her except for a likeness Lena had sent in a letter. He hadn't seen Lena and Mark since their marriage just before he headed west.

He choked back the thick bitterness clogging the back of his throat. Meggie was the only family he had left. A fierce protectiveness clawed at his gut. This child was now his. But what was he going to do with a little girl? If she'd been a boy…

The young woman coughed discreetly. "This changes everything. Lena was very clear that Meggie was to be raised by a mother and father. I'll take her back home and raise her myself. After I marry."

His fists clenched of their own accord. He uncurled them and planted his hands on his knees, deceptively calm while inside raged a storm a thousand times more fierce than the one he had endured only yesterday at Flora's side. The thought of losing Meggie about tore his heart out. And who was this stranger that she thought she had a say in it?

"I think we better start at the beginning. I'm Burke Edwards, Lena's brother and now Meggie's guardian. This is my home." He waved a hand to encompass the room where they sat, suddenly aware of the inadequacies of his home. The leather straps he'd been soaping tossed in the corner, the clutter of pots hung on the wall because the cupboard he'd started to build sat in the back of the barn, unfinished. The rest of the house offered even less. The front room only a thought in his head, the bedrooms, intended for a family, used mostly for storage except for the one Paquette occupied.

To her credit the woman before him revealed little shock as she glanced about. "Pleased to meet you. I'm Jenny Archibald." She held out a very tiny hand clad in soft kid leather.

He spared her a closer look. She wore what he expected was a fashionably appropriate but totally impractical bonnet. Her traveling outfit was of fine gray broadcloth although it now showed signs of her trip. She was every inch a city girl though her eyes blared with challenge.

"How did you know Lena?"

"We became friends when they moved to Center City, Ohio."

"Ahh."

"Lena and Mark were very specific in their instructions regarding their daughter."

Did he detect a hint of defiance in her voice? And the sheen of tears in her eyes. No doubt she found this whole ordeal most taxing. Well, he could relieve her of her problems immediately. "No need for you to concern yourself further about my niece. I will assume responsibility for her here and now. You can return with Mr. Zach." He indicated the man she'd hired from the livery barn who watched the proceedings with avid curiosity. By the time he was back in town in fifteen minutes, everyone would know Burke's current situation. He drew in a breath that had to struggle past an angry tightness. Adding this to the speculation about Flora and Burke would provide enough fodder for many a delicious evening of head shaking and *tsking*.

Jenny drew herself tall and gave him a look fit to brand his forehead. "And how, may I ask, do you intend to care for a two-year-old child?"

"I'll manage."

Paquette mumbled something in French or perhaps Cree in the background.

"It isn't like I'm here alone."

Jenny's eyes flickered in disbelief and if he wasn't mistaken, amusement was the reason her eyes crinkled at the corners. "I suppose you intend to put her on a horse and teach her to hold the reins as you chase cows."

It was so close to what he figured he'd do that he lowered his eyes lest she see his acknowledgement. Meggie had the same golden brown hair and light brown eyes Lena had. "She's very much like her mother." The way his voice had grown soft revealed far too much of what he felt—loss and pain that twisted through him with the cruelty of an internal auger.

"She is." Jenny's voice softened too and trembled slightly. She cleared her throat. "I realize she's your niece. I'm sure you feel a sense of responsibility toward her, but be honest. You can't possibly hope to provide her with a proper home." She pushed to her feet, ignoring Meggie's wails. Perching the child on one hip she turned to Paquette. "Thank you for tea."

"Baby need food. Need loving. Need sleep, her." The two women considered each other silently, some unspoken message passing between them.

Burke watched, wondering about the way Paquette's eyes flashed from Meggie to him.

Jenny turned to Mr. Zach. "May I ride back to Buffalo Hollow with you?"

Zach scrambled from the table. "Certainly, ma'am."

Jenny took two steps toward the door, Meggie clutched to her side, before Burke realized what she had in mind.

He bolted to his feet. "Now hold on just one minute. I am this child's uncle and as her last living relative, I am most certainly her guardian. You can ride back to Buffalo Hollow with Zach and catch the next train back home but you are not taking Meggie with you." He reached for the little girl.

Meggie's eyes grew wide. Her mouth opened in a perfect O. She clung to Jenny's neck. For a moment, Burke struggled to extract the child from Jenny's arms. Jenny would not release her and Meggie fought him.

"Let her go," Burke ordered.

A fierce, angry look crossed Jenny's face and then it fled. She nodded and released her grasp.

Meggie screeched fit to stampede every cow within a hundred miles. She threw her head back, arched her little body and turned into a writhing bundle of resistance.

Burke almost dropped her in surprise. His ears hurt from the noise. But he had to prove he could handle this. "Meggie, I'm your Uncle Burke." He had to shout and even then he doubted Meggie heard a thing. She was every bit as hard to hold as an eight hundred pound steer as she reached for Jenny. Burke backed up so she couldn't touch the woman. But Meggie refused to come with him and hung suspended between the two.

Jenny watched, silently challenging him to admit defeat.

He would not. He turned his back on her and held the child so they were face to face. "Meggie, look at me."

But Meggie tossed her head side to side, still screaming, tears washing her face. He sat her on the table hoping that would calm her. It didn't and he struggled to keep her from throwing herself flat-out.

Paquette shuffled over. "Boss man not know babies. Boss man need help, no?"

Obviously he did. He nodded toward Paquette indicating she could help him.

She shook her head. "Paquette not strong no more. Paquette not look after baby." She waved toward Jenny. "Give baby to lady."

"No!" He shouted the word. Startled, Meggie gulped back a sob and stared at him, her eyes wide and filled with fear. It burned clear through that she should be afraid of him. But it was only because they were strangers. "I've lost everything, everyone. Meggie is all I have left." Seems God was prepared to allow him this much and he wasn't about to let it go.

At the sound of her name, Meggie again shrieked.

Paquette shook her head. "Boss man biting off big chunk of tough meat." She retreated to the stove.

Surely Meggie would soon run out of steam. But she showed no sign of relenting.

He flung a look over his shoulder.

Jenny and Zach stood at the doorway. Zach looked ready to fly away in a heartbeat. Jenny simply stood patiently, her arms crossed as if she knew he wouldn't be able to handle the child and waited for him to admit it.

At that moment he knew nothing in the world would induce him to let this child go. "She isn't going to settle so long as you're there. Please leave. Go back to town with Zach."

Meggie's wails did not let him forget how powerless he was to deal with her.

"Mr. Zach, you can go," Jenny said. "I'm not going to leave Meggie like this."

The man nodded and strode away.

Jenny knew her eyes flashed defiance. It was an attitude she'd tried hard to quell but Burke's behavior undid all her carefully fought gains. How dare he tell her to leave? As if she were to blame for the fact Meggie was crying. As well she should. She'd never seen this man before and he had rudely wrenched her from Jenny's grasp.

Being her uncle gave him no right.

As she boldly, defiantly met his startled look, she realized what she'd done. This was not what she'd planned. A few days. A week. Two if she pushed it, to allow Meggie time to get used to her new guardians, with a Mrs. Edwards taking over Meggie's care. Then Jenny would return home to her promises. Now what?

It wasn't like she had a lot of choice. She glanced around. A crippled old woman who mumbled and fiddled with things on the cupboard and made it clear as the air outside the door that she wasn't up to looking after a child. As if she needed to speak the words. Her first look had given Jenny the necessary information. Paquette was so crippled Jenny wondered if she could lift a pot of water which she did so right before Jenny's eyes. Barely. The woman must be in constant pain.

She shifted her attention back to Burke. He looked like he wanted to throw a brand on the baby.

She could hardly leave Meggie here under these circumstances.

"Where is your...fiancée?"

Paquette grumbled loudly but Jenny couldn't make out what she said.

Burke scowled. "She's gone. That's all you need to know."

Well, fine. He was entitled to his secrets, as was she.

Then the enormity of her situation hit her and she plunked to the hard bench. Here she was with a man who looked like he cared nothing what people thought and an old woman who—what would Ma and Pa think? What would they say? Pa had warned her to act wisely, speak carefully and live a life that gave people no cause to whisper about her. She knew her reputation was a precious thing and didn't intend to compromise it. She shivered. Not after her narrow escape.

Meggie thrust herself into Jenny's arms and Jenny held her close, finding comfort in the way the baby clung to her. She had a responsibility to this little one. But would everyone understand her choice?

She fired another look at Burke. "I intend to stay until suitable arrangements have been made for this child and she is settled." Her decision raised all sorts of quandaries. "Where do you...will I—?" Heat crawled up her neck and stung the tips of her ears. She couldn't even voice her concern. Where did he sleep? Where would she sleep?

Burke leaned back on the heels of his dusty cowboy boots and grinned. "Got yourself into a predicament, did you? Didn't check out the situation before you made your bold decision?"

Bold. The word clawed through her mind. How often had Pa said she was too bold? How often had Ma said it would get her into trouble?

Boots thudded on the wooden floor outside and Mr. Zach appeared, carrying her luggage. "Thought I'd carry your bags inside."

"Not too late to change your mind and go back with Zach."

Burke's voice was low, insistent, as if he not only thought she should do so, but felt an urgency she should.

Meggie in her arms, she pushed to her feet and faced him knowing her determination blared across her face. "If I can take Meggie."

"'Fraid I can't let you do that."

Slowly she nodded. "Then I'm afraid I must stay with her until you get married."

Ignoring Burke's sputter of protest, she thanked Mr. Zach, who hesitated then slowly retreated. As she listened to the buggy rattle from the yard she knew she was irrevocably committed to this decision.

She stared hard at Burke, each of them taking stock of the other's reserve of stubbornness. She narrowed her eyes, hoped he would see she would not back down. Not now. Not ever. Not until arrangements were up to what Lena would expect.

The look he gave her might have made her shiver if she had been the quiet, refined lady her parents hoped for instead of one who acted first, thought later, afraid of nothing and no one. She remembered Ma's admonition to moderate her boldness and lowered her gaze. "I hope we can arrange a suitable living arrangement."

Burke snorted. "And what do you intend to do if we can't? Shouldn't you have thought of that before you sent Zach away?" He sighed. "It's too late to ride with him but I'll take you back."

"Why are you so determined to get rid of me?"

"Because you don't belong. Better you accept it right now before you get in over your head."

Little did he know that she was already in that situation, but it would not cause her to abandon Meggie whose warm arms clung around Jenny's neck, her face buried against Jenny's shoulder.

"It's not too late to change your mind."

"I'll let you know when I'm ready to leave. But I can assure you it won't be until I'm satisfied Meggie will be properly taken care of."

His gaze darkened. "I don't think that's your call to make."

"I disagree. Lena and Mark trusted me with seeing Meggie properly settled. I intend to do just that. Now—" she glanced about "—if you would be kind enough to show me where we might clean up."

He didn't move a muscle or give any indication he would help in any way.

Jenny shot a glance toward Paquette who met her gaze

with what Jenny could only take as a mixture of pity and compassion.

"Boss, she and baby use room next mine. It be big 'nough."

Burke groaned. "This is a mistake we'll all live to regret."

Jenny didn't know if he addressed her or Paquette but she understood her decision to stay was the mistake he referred to, and it undid all her efforts at being reserved. "I fail to see why you should view this as a disaster in the making. I simply have a job to do—see Meggie is settled." She refrained from adding she would insist on several other changes, too—but a glance around revealed a hundred things that would be dangerous to a toddler. And it didn't require more than a fleeting acquaintance with the setup to realize there was no one in the present company who could care for Meggie. Until she solved that problem she would be staying. "I think if we all co-operate things should go swimmingly."

He looked at the roof as if hoping for divine help.

Exactly what she needed. *My Father in heaven, guide me and protect me as I help Meggie settle in. Help me be wise and cautious.*

"Paquette, show her the room." He headed for the door then paused. "Miss Archibald, I will say it again. This is no place for a woman. You might do well to heed my warning."

Before he could escape, Jenny spoke. "I'll leave when I deem it's appropriate but I won't be run off. I won't be scared off. So don't even try."

He turned slowly, his expression full of pity. "Don't flatter yourself that I'd bother. You'll find plenty of challenges without my interference."

What on earth did he mean? A trembling worm of

warning skittered across her neck. Was there some sort of danger she should be aware of? But he was gone before she could ask. That left Paquette as her only source of information. "What was he talking about? Is there something I should know?"

Paquette grinned, her black eyes snapping. "Boss be…" She fluttered her hands as if to indicate the man was unstable.

The trembling in Jenny's neck developed talons. Was the man dangerous? She'd heard tales of men losing their minds out in the vast empty prairie. Why, Pa had saved a newspaper story just to show her, warn her. "You need to be on your guard, Pepper. Strange things happen out there and you'll be on your own." For proof he'd allowed her to read the story of a bachelor who had gone out of his head from the loneliness and ran out into the cold clad only in his union suit, firing his rifle into the air. The report said it was a miracle no one had been shot.

"He's not given to doing strange things, is he?" She needed answers, needed to know what to expect so she could be ready.

Paquette looked surprised then chortled. "He not the crazy one."

Somehow Jenny found that less than assuring. "Who is?"

The older woman shook her head. "Lots people crazy. Lots people. Now come. I show you de room."

Jenny wanted more information. Who was crazy? Were they a threat to her? Or more importantly, Meggie? Then she followed Paquette into a room and her questions were forgotten.

"Need cleaning, it."

Jenny almost laughed at Paquette's understated words. From what she could see the room served as a catchall for both farm and home. Bits of wood were scattered on one side along with hammer, saw and nails. As if a building project had come to a halt at that very spot. As obviously it had. The walls were unfinished uprights. The window only roughly framed. It looked like the abandoned building materials had served as a magnet to other forgotten items—an overcoat, foot warmers, a bundle of canvas....

She shuddered. She and Meggie were expected to sleep here?

"Boss man sleep bunkhouse. Wit de men, him. For long time now. Since—" She didn't finish.

Another secret. "Since when, Paquette?"

Paquette shook her head and backed from the room. "You be fixing room, no?"

Jenny understood she would be getting no answers from Paquette. All she could do was keep her eyes open and be alert to anything out of the ordinary. In the meantime...

She stared at the room. Only one way to get it ready for habitation...start hauling out stuff. She cleared a spot for Meggie in the center of the bed, retrieved her bags and found a little blanket for the baby to sit on. She pulled out the little rag doll Lena had so lovingly stitched and settled Meggie to play.

As she worked, words raced through her head—crazy, warning, mistake. There were far too many unanswered questions for her to feel safe. She heard the sound of horse hooves and picked her way across the room to the window in time to see Burke ride away, his well-worn cowboy hat pushed low on his head, leaning forward as if anxious to be away from this place. She shivered. Should she be afraid of him?

He turned, saw her at the window. His gaze drilled into her, dark, powerful, full of—

She jerked back and pressed her palm to her throat.

Promise? Hope? Or was it despair? Warning?

Was she seeing things she wanted to or things that were real?

In a flash she thought of the way he watched her on the train. Had he been kind or something sinister? No. He'd been kind and polite. Her imagination was simply getting out of control. He'd defended her before the others in the train. He'd helped her with her bags.

And he'd warned her not once but twice that she didn't belong here.

Why? What lay behind his warning? Kindness or something else? What secret lay behind his not being married?

Sufficient to the day is the trouble thereof.

Pa's oft-spoke words released her tensions and she laughed. None of those things mattered. She had a task to do and she would do it. She would keep her promise to Lena and Mark.

Meggie had fallen asleep, the rag doll clutched in one hand.

While she slept, Jenny quickly changed into a dark skirt and a wrinkled shirtwaist. It could do with ironing but at least it was clean and considerably cooler than her traveling outfit. Then she surveyed the room. There was nothing she enjoyed more than a task of significance and this was a big one. She tackled the job with vigor, singing softly as she worked.

Burke rode for half an hour, a leisurely, enjoy-the-quiet type ride. Out here he found peace and solitude—something he feared he would not find at home in the future.

He reached the spring Mac had expressed concern about, took his shovel and attacked it, tossing out heaps of dirt. The work did its job—releasing the tension that started at the first sight of Jenny in his house, and built steadily throughout her announcement that Lena and Mark had died until it peaked when she informed him she would stay. He should have insisted she leave. Before this country sent her screaming into the distance.

He paused to suck in air. Lena was dead. Her husband, too. He let sorrow drench his pores, let it ease out in the sweaty drops beading his skin. He would miss her.

The Lord giveth and the Lord taketh away.

He would not finish the sentence...*blessed be the name of the Lord.* The taking held no blessing in his opinion. Only regret and sorrow. Deep sorrow.

He returned to digging out the hole until water broke loose and flowed freely into the shallow pit he'd fashioned last year. At the scent and sound of water, a nearby cow bellowed and headed toward him. The call echoed across the short grass and was picked up and passed along by other cows until he could see them running like a living, shrinking circle.

The first cow saw him and balked. A human on foot made her nervous.

He obligingly swung into the saddle.

The cow tossed her head and raced onward, her calf skipping at her side.

The herd neared. As they crowded in for water, he smiled. A man could forget his troubles out here.

And just like cows heading for water his thoughts headed for home. What was he going to do about Jenny? She didn't belong out in this country. But he couldn't seem to persuade her otherwise. And until he did, he was stuck with her.

How could he best prove to her he didn't need her?

He thought of little Meggie crying and struggling in

his arms and amended his question—he didn't need her for long.

He considered his options. First, he didn't want any pretty young woman languishing out here in order to care for Meggie. He would manage her care. All he had to do was give her a few days to get used to him and then he would simply take her with him as he worked. She'd grow up as his sidekick.

Someone to share his life with. The idea gave him a jolt of pleasure.

Carefully, he laid out his plan. A few days for her to get to know him, and then they'd ride and work together.

And Jenny could return to her safe home back east. Before it was too late.

That settled, he reined around and headed back to the ranch. Paquette would wonder at him returning before suppertime but he figured the sooner he got working on his plan, the sooner it would be fulfilled.

A few minutes later, he strode toward the house, try-ing to think how he should start getting to know Meggie. Only two years old. No doubt shy. Certainly frightened. Like a barn kitten seeing a human up close for the first time. He'd tame Meggie the same way…slow, patient and with…he laughed. Doubted she would like milk straight from the cow in a warm stream. What did a child like? Perhaps Paquette would know.

He slipped inside. The kitchen was empty but sounds came from the far side of the house. He followed the voices around the house and stopped short at what he saw.

Jenny stood before a stack of boards and blankets, boots and saws all in a heap fifty feet from the house. She'd taken off the ridiculously impractical thing she wore on her arrival and wore an ordinary shirt and skirt. Not that he thought it changed who she really was.

She spoke to Paquette. "I'm sure it can be arranged for someone to haul this stuff away where it will pose no threat to a small child."

Paquette stood on the veranda shaking her head and making disapproving noises. "Boss not like stuff throw out like dis."

"Meggie and I can't sleep in the midst of debris and dirt. She's a baby. She needs a safe, clean environment."

Burke sighed and filled in the other things Jenny no doubt figured Meggie needed—things like neighbors, church, town activities, pretty clothes. He'd heard it all. Tried to convince Flora those things weren't necessary but it was the land itself that defeated him. Flora thought the prairies desolate; the wind haunting. She swore they would drive her mad.

She was right in the end.

But he would teach Meggie to be different.

He could only do it without some city gal filling her mind with frivolities.

He cleared his throat to announce his presence.

"I finish de supper," Paquette said and shuffled indoors.

Jenny dusted her hands. "I'm cleaning out the room you've allotted me."

"So I see. Is all this necessary?"

She smiled. "I guess only you could say. But necessary or not, it won't be sharing my quarters."

He knew from the way her eyes flashed that she had purposely misunderstood him. He meant was it necessary to move everything out to the middle of the yard. But he let it pass. "Where's Meggie?"

"Sleeping. I better check on her." She would have slipped past him except he moved to block her path.

"I think you better accept that we have different agendas here."

Her eyebrows headed for the sky. "Really? I thought we both had Meggie's best interests in mind. Her health and safety and happiness. Am I mistaken in thinking so?"

Her quiet challenge edged through his arguments and completely disarmed him. "On Meggie's behalf, we are agreed. But you won't be staying any longer than it takes for me and Meggie to make friends."

Her eyes clear as the sky above, she stared at him. "I'll leave when I decide everything is as it ought to be for Meggie." She swung away then turned back. "Unless you figure to have me bodily removed."

The idea tickled his insides. Somehow he suspected it would require three strong men and a long length of sturdy rope. His amusement trickled into his eyes. He felt them crinkle. Then it caught his mouth and filled his throat and he laughed. "Let's hope it doesn't come to that."

She blinked at his laughter then her stubbornness seemed to melt away. "I do tend to get all bristly, don't I? I'm here to see Meggie is settled. We should be able to tolerate each other long enough to accomplish that." And she marched away.

He scrubbed his chin with one finger. Tolerate her? Now why should she think that? But perhaps she'd been thinking she would tolerate him. Ah well. He had nothing to offer a fine lady. He knew it. His life consisted of the vast lonely prairie and the company of cows and cowboys. He'd teach Meggie to appreciate it all but he had no such misconceptions regarding any young woman. He'd put up with her tolerance only as long as he needed.

Mac and Dug rode to the bunkhouse and Burke sauntered over to see how things were.

"Good to have you back, boss."

"Good to be back." He better warn them before they stomped into the house for supper. "There's company up at the house."

"Yeah?"

He could almost feel their ears perk up with interest. The last time he'd had company…no point in thinking about that. It was history. A lesson well learned for them all.

Lucky joined them. Burke felt their cautious curiosity but it was Mac who broke the barrier of silence. "Flora?" His voice was courteous, revealing nothing though Burke knew they likely all hoped to never put up with her dramatics again.

"Flora won't be back. Ever."

A silent sigh filled the air.

"She's still in the—"

Burke nodded. "Her parents are with her. They told me not to come again. Blamed me for how she is." No more than he blamed himself. He shouldn't have pushed her, shouldn't have asked so much from her.

The four men turned and stared at the house. Burke realized he still hadn't provided them with the necessary information. "My niece is here. Meggie. She's only two."

He chuckled at the way all heads turned and surprised eyes stared at him.

Dug swallowed hard, his long thin neck working all the way down. "A little gal?"

Mac, ever practical and blunt said, "Why?"

"My sister and her husband died. I'm now Meggie's guardian."

"Sorry, boss," the three mumbled in unison.

He joined them in staring toward the house. "A young woman brought her out."

The men shuffled but no one spoke, as if waiting for Burke to say more.

"Name's Jenny and she's staying to get Meggie settled in."

Dug took a straw from his pocket and picked at his teeth. Mac crossed his arms and stared at the house, his expression dour. Burke didn't bother glancing at Lucky. He felt again their reluctance to voice their concerns about another young woman visiting the ranch.

"She won't be here long."

A couple of grunts.

"She hauled all the junk out of the second bedroom and piled it in the middle of the yard on the other side of the house."

Cautious nods.

"Guess we best haul it away." He strode across the yard, the men in his wake. They rounded the corner and viewed the pile of junk.

"Boss, all this was in a bedroom?"

"Yup."

"What was ya thinking?"

He shrugged. "Had no need of another bedroom. Paquette only needs one." He didn't say the bedroom had been meant for him and Flora. Suddenly the men figured it out and shut up. Except Mac.

"You say this young woman hauled all this out by herself?"

"I came from cleaning out the spring and found it here."

The men grabbed armloads. "Where you want it?" Dug asked.

"I don't know. In the barn. Beside the barn. Wherever you think it should be."

Lucky paused at Burke's side, his arms loaded with

lengths of lumber. "Must be a right spunky gal to drag this all out by herself."

Spunky? Huh. He didn't know about that. "All I seen was her stubbornness."

Mac chuckled softly. "A bird of a different feather maybe."

The men seemed cheered by that thought as they moved the pile of stuff.

Burke didn't care what sort of feathers she wore so long as she nested them far away from here. As soon as possible.

Chapter Three

Jenny held Meggie's hand and led her to the kitchen. Her job at the present was to get Meggie settled and that included introducing her to the house and its occupants.

"Meggie, say hello to Mrs. Paquette."

"It be only Paquette." The woman bent forward even more until she was almost eyeball to eyeball with Meggie. The beaded necklace she wore hung within easy grasp. "Pretty baby." She patted Meggie's head.

Meggie chuckled and reached for the necklace.

"Don't touch, Meggie," Jenny warned.

"Baby not hurt it." Paquette slipped the necklace over her head and hung it around Meggie's neck. "You play with."

"Paquette, are you sure? She might break it or lose it."

"Not break. Leather string. Not lose. Too big."

"Thank you. Meggie, tell the lady thank you."

Meggie looked up from patting the beads. "Pretty. Thank you for pretty."

Paquette seemed satisfied and turned back to her chores.

"What can I do to help?"

The woman grew very still, her back to Jenny. "I not need help. I be strong as bear."

Jenny immediately realized the woman felt challenged, as if Jenny had suggested she couldn't manage. "I'm sure you do very well but I can't sit around and watch you work. I intend to make myself useful while I'm here."

Paquette turned slowly and studied Jenny with bottomless eyes. Finally she nodded. "Set de table."

"Great. How many?"

"Burke and three men. Me."

She hadn't included Jenny and Meggie. Was it intentional? Was she not going to be allowed to eat with the others? That wasn't going to work. Not if Meggie were to feel at home with whomever lived here. Her mind made up, she nodded. "With myself and Meggie that would be seven places."

She held Paquette's startled gaze, refusing to back down. Finally the older woman nodded. "Seven." And turned back to the big pots on the stove.

Jenny found the plates and silverware. She found battered tin cups and put them on. "Shall I fill a jug with water?"

"Water at pump."

Jenny already had noticed the pump at one end of the cupboard. Much more convenient than having to run outside for water. She found a large enamel jug. As she pumped the water, she looked out the window.

Burke stood at a low building with three men at his side. They all stared toward the house as if waiting for something. Burke reached up and pushed his hat back. The sun hit his face, making each feature sharp. Suddenly he grinned, his gaze still aimed at the house. Her heart skittered in alarm. Did he see her? She backed away.

But if he did, he wouldn't likely smile. He had been less than welcoming. And she had been even less compliant. She had forgotten her upbringing. *Father God, forgive me for being so quick to speak my mind. Help me cause no offense.*

She vowed she would not react to any further comments from Burke about how soon she would leave and how glad he would be for that time.

The jug was full. As she lifted it Burke and the men trooped across the yard and past the house. A few minutes later they returned, all with their arms full of the things she'd hauled from the bedroom. She chuckled.

Paquette looked out the window to see what amused her. "Boss not like moving stuff."

Jenny shrugged. What could he do about it? "What else does the boss not like?"

Paquette turned as fast as her crippled body allowed and her mouth worked as she stared at Jenny.

What on earth? It was a simple enough question meant only to help Jenny know how to avoid any upsets. Why did the woman look so sad? Or was it anger?

Paquette ducked away. "Boss not like be hurt."

"Ahh." So it was probably both sadness and anger. "And has he been hurt somehow?"

"He not say. I not say."

That was extremely unhelpful but Jenny knew Paquette would say no more. She couldn't help admiring the woman for not dipping into gossip or sharing secrets. A most honorable trait.

Paquette checked the pots again. "You ring for men."

"Sure. How?"

"Out de door."

Jenny took that to mean the bell hung outside the door. "Come on Meggie, want to help me ring the bell?"

"Me help."

Hand in hand they went outside. Jenny looked around for a bell. Saw none. She looked again. Saw a metal rod hanging from the rafters. Another piece of rod hung from a nail nearby. This must be the bell. She banged the rods together creating a great clatter.

"Me help."

She gave the metal bar to Meggie and held her up to bang the bell. Meggie laughed. "Me do more." She banged and banged, giggling with each crash. Then she handed the rod to Jenny. "You do again."

Jenny batted at the rod, the racket vastly satisfying. A great way to deal with frustration and she hit the swinging bar as hard as she could. It went flying. She followed its journey and gulped as it landed at the tip of a pair of boots.

Jenny was almost certain she had seen that particular set of footwear already today. Knew they belonged to a man who wasn't terribly glad to have her here. This would not make him any more glad. Slowly she raised her gaze until it connected with a pair of dark eyes. "Whoops. Guess I got a little too vigorous."

"Either there's a fire or the meal is about to dry up and blow away."

She swallowed hard.

The men she'd seen earlier flanked Burke. She couldn't look at any of them as embarrassment journeyed up her neck and seared its way across her cheeks. She shifted Meggie closer, feeling the child's wariness of all these strangers.

"Supper's ready." She fled indoors.

Paquette chuckled. "Big racket. Bring de man fast. No?"

"Yes." Next time she would be more circumspect,

more controlled. But a grin tugged at her mouth. It had been fun and maybe next time she'd ring it every bit as hard.

The men had paused at the washstand outside the door and now trooped in and began to take places at the table. Suddenly they saw the number was off and paused, glancing around for someone to direct them.

Jenny hung back, Meggie still in her arms. It wasn't her place to say where they should sit but all eyes darted at her. If she wasn't mistaken they all held a bit of nervous wariness. "Please, just go ahead as you always would."

Paquette placed the heaping bowls on the table. "You be sit at end?" She indicated one of the chairs. The other chair stood at the far end and Burke stood at it like it was his customary place.

Why the sudden cautiousness? Was there a secret order or something? A place she could choose that would usurp some subtle hierarchy? One way to find out. "Where do you usually sit?" She directed her question at Paquette.

Paquette didn't answer but her gaze sought out the chair.

"You take the chair. I'll sit wherever is con-venient."

"Sit," Burke ordered.

A general shuffle followed. Jenny hung back until the men sorted themselves out. The only empty places were next to Burke. She would have chosen to be closer to Paquette but the die was cast and she sat. Meggie refused to leave her lap so Jenny held her.

"Jenny," Burke said, "Let me introduce my men." He turned to his right. "Dug—

A man who appeared to be in his early twenties, as lean as a twist of rope, but with a friendly enough expression, grinned at her.

"Lucky—"

The man she'd glimpsed in the barn. Short, stocky and with a wide grin that made Jenny feel more welcome than she had since she landed on the ground in front of the house.

"Welcome, Miss Jenny," Lucky said.

Burke's gaze shifted across the table to the man at Jenny's left. "And Mac."

The man had red hair and a red beard and even though he smiled at her, he looked like he'd better fit a frown.

"Pleased to meet all of you and I look forward to getting to know you better during my visit."

If she wasn't mistaken they all shot wary looks at Burke. She wondered if he had told them she wouldn't be staying long.

"Eat," Paquette said. "Before de fat form."

Hands reached for the bowls.

Jenny cleared her throat. "Shouldn't someone say grace?"

The hands jerked back and disappeared under the table. A startled silence filled the room.

Jenny met Burke's eyes. "Lena would want Meggie raised in a Christian home."

Burke's eyes were hard and unyielding. "I ain't much for praying."

Wasn't he a Christian man? Lena certainly thought so. Or was it just discomfort at praying aloud? She waited. The men waited. The room pulsed with waiting.

Burke looked about the table. "Anyone else willing?"

The men mumbled. Only words Jenny made out indicated they thought the boss should do it.

Finally Dug cleared his throat. "Want me to do it?"

"Please." Burke sounded like he'd been saved some dreadful disaster.

They all bowed their heads. Paquette crossed herself.

Dug sucked in air. "We thank you, Father, for this food. And pray you'll bless it to our good. Help us live your name to praise, in all we do through all our days. Amen." He gasped as he finished the words in a rush.

Mac cleared his throat.

"Eat," Paquette again ordered and the men dug in with haste as if they had to make up for lost time.

Meggie watched them for a moment, silently measuring and assessing.

"Meg, how about some food?" It had been ages since they'd had a good hot meal and the aromas coming from the pot roast and rich gravy made Jenny want to imitate the men in attacking her food. But she had Meggie to think about.

Meggie opened her mouth and waited for Jenny to feed her. She'd abandoned feeding herself after her parents died. Jenny understood it was only her way of coping—going backward a little to a safer, kinder time in her life.

No one spoke as they focused their attention on the food.

Finally Mac swiped his plate clean with a slice of bread and leaned back. Paquette placed a pot of coffee in the middle of the table and he poured himself a mug full.

"Hauled out all that stuff by yourself, did ya?"

Jenny realized he meant the junk from the bedroom. "I did."

"Not a nice job."

"Wasn't bad."

"Must have been pretty dirty."

"I sneezed a time or two." The others filled coffee cups and leaned back. For some reason they seemed mighty interested in this conversation. "Stomped a few spiders but nothing much."

Lucky chuckled. "See any big spiders." He held his hands out to indicate one about six inches across.

As a greenhorn Jenny knew she was open season for teasing but she wasn't falling for that one. She decided to turn the tables. "Phew. One that big is nothing." She held out her hands to the size Lucky indicated. Slowly she widened the distance between her hands until they were twelve inches apart. "There was one behind the stack of lumber that came at me with a piece of wood. But I fixed him."

All eyes were on her now. She glanced at Burke, saw his guarded expression. His eyes seemed to grab her and invite her to follow him into exciting adventures. She jerked her gaze away. She was being fanciful. Only place he wanted her was out of here.

"How'd you fix him?" Dug asked.

She glanced around the table, delaying the moment. When she felt everyone waiting for her answer she quirked an eyebrow in a dismissive, doesn't matter way. "I trapped him in a boot. Tied it shut. Put it on the veranda with its mate. Guess you all better be checking your footwear before you put it on."

The men stared. Burke laughed first. "She gotcha."

Startled laughter came from the others and Paquette cackled.

Jenny allowed herself a glance toward Burke. The skin at the corners of his eyes crinkled. His eyes weren't black as she'd first thought but dark brown and full of warm mirth. She couldn't pull away. Couldn't break the moment as they grinned at each other, something silent and sweet passing between them.

"I think she got *you*, boss," Mac murmured.

The laughter had ended. How long had they been staring into each other's eyes? Jenny jerked her gaze away and fussed with Meggie, who worked on a crust of bread.

Burke pushed from the table. "I got things to do."

The men all bolted to their feet and followed him from the room.

"I'll help clean up," Jenny offered as she rose from the table.

"It not for lady," Paquette protested.

"I'm not here to be pampered." She carried dishes to the cupboard and tackled washing them. Work was a good way to control her wayward thoughts. As she worked she had but to lift her head to see Burke outside doing something at the corrals, Lucky at his side. Burke moved with a sureness revealing his strength and confidence.

A man who belonged in this new challenging land.

A man who drew some deep longing from a secret place behind her heart.

She jerked her thoughts to a standstill.

She'd listened to those siren voices before—adventure, excitement. It had led to disaster.

She pulled her gaze away.

Father God, help me be wise. Help me heed the counsel of my parents.

She washed the last dish, wiped the table clean. "I think I'll take Meggie out for a walk before bedtime. She needs fresh air and exercise."

She took Meggie's hand and together they went outdoors. She let Meg run the length of the veranda, smiling at the fun the child got from her shoes echoing on the wooden floor. When Meggie climbed down the three steps to the ground, Jenny followed. They wandered down the path toward the open field. The land rose almost imperceptibly but enough that suddenly the countryside lay before her like a great huge blanket. The sun dipped low in the west casting shadows across the land, filling it with dips and hollows. The light caught higher objects almost lifting them from the ground. The land went on and on. Amazing. Awesome.

Jenny lifted her arms to the sky.

She could almost touch the clouds. Float on them across the endless sky.

"Oh, Pa," she whispered. "If you could see this. Feel what I feel, you'd understand the restlessness of my soul." She didn't want to be confined within four walls, constrained by the bounds of town life.

But she would honor her parents. She lowered her arms and crossed them over her chest.

She would keep her word and return.

Surely, once she was back she would forget this moment.

She knew she never would. In fact, she stared at the vast prairie for a long time. She didn't want to forget. She wanted to brand it forever on her brain, a secret place she could visit in the future and find again, this wonderful sense of freedom.

Burke watched Jenny and Meggie head past the corrals. His arms tingled with apprehension. How would she react when she saw how empty the prairie was around her?

At his side, Lucky watched, too. "She's different."

Burke knew what Lucky meant—Jenny was different than Flora.

Lucky went on as if Burke had asked him to explain. "She's got a sense of humor, for one thing. And she sat with us like she didn't think she was better."

Flora had made it clear she would not share the table

with servants. She'd wanted Burke to join her at eating separately, expecting Paquette to wait on them.

Burke had refused. It was only a small thing. He should have found a way to compromise. Perhaps it would have made a difference. He watched Jenny as she reached the end of the path and drew to a halt.

In the end it was the emptiness of the land that did in Flora. As it did so many. Why, just a few months ago the marshal had taken away Stan Jones to the north of here and Mr. Abernathy had packed up and gone back east because his wife couldn't take it anymore. Burke had heard Mrs. Abernathy now had a personal nurse to care for her.

Jenny raised her arms over her head. What was she doing? Trying to hold the emptiness at bay?

Lucky watched, too. "Is she laughing?"

Burke threw down the hammer he held and headed after her. If he didn't need her to help Meggie settle he would send her back to town first thing in the morning. Before her laughter took on a shrill note.

He had gone but twenty feet when she turned and headed back toward the house. A smile wreathed her face. She looked positively happy—excited even.

Burke shifted direction and returned to the fence he'd been repairing with Lucky's help.

Lucky continued to stare at Jenny. "She's different, I tell ya."

Burke wouldn't watch her but he couldn't stop himself from glancing up from pounding a nail. She walked with a carefree swing. Her face glowed as she glanced skyward. Her laughter rang out as Meggie said something. From his first glance he'd been attracted. But nothing had changed—not the land and not him. "She's only been here a few hours and she isn't staying more than a few days. No need for her to concern herself with anything but Meggie." No need for her to think about what life was like out here, how living here day after day would feel.

"Boss, not all women are like Flora." Lucky made his soft comment then grabbed the other end of the plank and drove in a spike, making conversation impossible.

Burke stuffed back his response. It didn't matter whether Jenny was different or not. He wasn't about to repeat his hard-learned lesson.

Jenny and Meggie went inside and a crackling tension he'd been unaware of—or maybe just unwilling to admit—eased off.

He should ride out into the prairie until his thoughts settled into acceptance of the reality of his life, but he lingered in the yard listening to the sounds coming from the open windows of the house.

Jenny must have put Meggie to bed. He heard the baby fussing then Jenny singing a lullaby. The notes caught his memories and teased them forward. He remembered his mother holding Lena and rocking her to the same tune. He hadn't thought of his mother in a long time. Not since he'd moved out west.

Now Lena and Mark were dead of a fever and he was guardian to their child. It was a repeat of when he became Lena's guardian.

They had done well together.

Only Meggie was so much younger.

Jenny's singing grew softer.

He strained toward the sound. It had stopped. Meggie must have fallen asleep. He drew in a relieved breath. Must be hard on such a little one to lose her parents and all.

But once she settled in, he would teach her how to have fun, how to enjoy the wild land. Satisfied, he headed for the barn.

A wrenching sob stopped him in his tracks. Meggie again. Poor child sounded heartbroken. No doubt she was.

Burke longed to be able to comfort his niece. Knew she wouldn't accept any offer from him. Jenny's soft, soothing tones underlay Meggie's cries and the child quieted again.

His heart flooded with gratitude to Jenny for comforting Meggie when he was powerless to do so.

He thought again of the way she'd flung her arms skyward, the brightness of her smile as she returned from her walk. He smiled remembering the spider joke she'd told the men. And how she'd sat at the table with everyone. Pictures of her calmness on the train brought again the flicker of admiration and interest he'd felt at the time.

He snorted. He would not be mistaking gratitude for attraction.

There were things he could do to keep himself busy in the barn and he headed that direction. As he checked harnesses and cleaned out a pen, he strained to catch any sounds from the house. No more crying. A relief. No more singing. Too bad—no, he was not disappointed.

The interior of the barn grew dark and he headed out into the dusk.

Against the darkening sky, at the end of the path, Jenny stood outlined, standing in the same spot where she'd been when he watched her with her arms raised.

From deep inside him a strident voice called, demanding acknowledgement. Something about this woman pulled at his heart, made him want things that were at cross-purposes with his intentions.

Drawn by a silent, invisible cord, he sauntered over to stand at her side. "Mighty lonely place."

"Listen."

He did so. "It's silent."

"No. It's full of whispers. I hear the breeze tickling the grass. It almost sings. And way off a bird is calling good night."

He listened, hearing tiny sounds he'd grown used to until he no longer heard them. The sky faded to gray. Pink hovered at the horizon.

"It's so pretty."

A mournful wail came from one side.

She turned toward the sound. "What's that?"

An answering howl came from another spot and a sharp yapping sound from another.

"Coyotes." He waited for her to shiver and head back to safety.

"They're singing." She sounded pleased rather than scared.

Flora had fled to the protection of the house, shivering and frightened. "Wild animals. This place is so uncivilized."

Seems Lucky was right. Jenny was different.

Not that it changed a thing. This country was hard enough for a man, not at all suitable for a woman.

They stood watching the last light fade, listening to the coyotes sing and the prairie whisper.

Unwilling to break the spell of contentment, he didn't speak though a thousand words flitted across his mind, questions about who she was, what her dreams were.

Finally she sighed. "I guess I better get back and make sure Meggie is okay."

She headed for the house and he fell in at her side.

Meggie. A topic he could safely mention. "It took her a long time to settle."

"Poor little girl. She's lost everything."

"She still has me." And you, until you leave.

"I'm sorry. I meant everything familiar."

He'd been too quick to take offense but wasn't sure how to correct it without drawing undue attention to the fact. "She'll soon settle in and feel at home here." Why did the idea not feel as good as it should?

"I expect so."

They'd reached the veranda and paused. "Good night," she said.

A lamp sat on the kitchen table and sent a golden glow through the window putting Jenny's face into a shadow.

He told himself he wasn't disappointed he couldn't see her expression as they parted ways.

He strode to the bunkhouse and headed for the bed he'd claimed as his own six months ago when he'd convinced Flora to visit the ranch. He'd been so sure she would learn to love the place as he had even though she had insisted on staying in town for weeks.

He'd been wrong.

Jenny enjoyed the coyotes singing.

"Seen you out walking with Miss Jenny," Dug called. "Pretty gal."

"She ain't staying," Burke growled. He didn't want her to. Wouldn't ask her to consider it.

He turned on his side, giving the men a good view of his back, indicating this topic of conversation was over. He felt their watchful stillness then rustling as they settled themselves at something else.

If only his thoughts would obey as quickly but they kept painting pictures on the inside of his eyelids—Jenny walking and laughing with Meggie, Jenny at the table telling a joke. Jenny reaching for the sky.

He opened his eyes so he couldn't see the pictures, but then sounds filled his thoughts.

Jenny singing to Meggie. Jenny laughing. Jenny whispering at the magic of the prairie evening song.

He groaned silently.

How long would it take for Meggie to settle in?

It couldn't be too soon for his peace of mind. The sooner Jenny left, the better.

Chapter Four

Jenny lay on her bed fighting her thoughts. It was wrong to think of Burke as she did. After all, she was all but promised to another man. She'd given her word to her parents. Yet here she lay with every word Burke had said, every gesture he'd made playing over and over in her mind. But even those memories weren't as condemning as her wayward reactions.

She'd almost grabbed his hand in excitement when she heard the coyotes howl—a mournful sound that made her want to sing along. If Burke hadn't been at her side she might have tried imitating them.

Besides being wrong, her thoughts were so futile. He made it clear she wasn't welcome here. And there was still the mystery of the missing fiancée. What happened to her? He said he'd never marry but perhaps he was only angry with the woman. A lover's quarrel.

She focused on that thought until her wayward imaginations came into order.

Father God, be Thou my hiding place. Keep me safe from my impetuous nature.

Finally she fell asleep.

Twice during the night, Meggie wakened and Jenny sang to settle her.

Next morning, she rose with her resolve returned. She had a task to complete. Today she would start doing things necessary to get Meggie ready for her to leave.

She knelt at the bedside, careful not to disturb Meggie who still slept. *Father God, I need Your guidance today. Put a watch before my mouth so I speak only kind words. Show me the things I need to change for Meggie's sake. Most of all enable me to guard my heart so I don't think and feel foolish, inappropriate things.* She didn't say exactly what those things were but God saw her every action, heard her every word, knew her every thought. He knew how she loved the sense of adventure in challenging a new, forbidding land, just as He knew something about Burke drew her eyes to him more often than was appropriate.

Meggie yawned and stretched. She turned to see Jenny kneeling at her side and smiled as sweet as an angel. She patted Jenny's cheeks with her warm soft hands.

"Good morning, little miss. How are you this fine day?"

Meggie babbled excitedly.

"I'm sorry, sweetie. I don't understand."

Meggie caught Jenny's face between her palms and looked intently into her eyes and repeated the indiscernible words. Jenny couldn't look away from the intensity in the child's eyes. It filled her with sorrow that she was unable to understand what Meggie wanted.

Sounds came from the kitchen. Pots rattled. Boots scraped across the floor.

"I think we might have overslept. How about we get you dressed and then you can go see your uncle Burke."

Meggie had jumped from the bed at the idea of getting up but at the mention of her uncle, her face crumpled.

Jenny scooped her up before she started to cry. "Your uncle Burke would like to play with you. Wouldn't that be fun? Perhaps you could show him your dolly." As she talked, she slipped the nightgown over Meggie's head and pulled on her clean dress. Quickly she put on socks and tied the little boots. As soon as she released Meggie, the child grabbed her doll and hugged it close.

"Do you think you'd like to show her to Uncle Burke?"

Meggie shook her head.

"That's fine." It would take time but that was first on her agenda. Right alongside urging Burke to hurry and resolve his differences with his fiancée. She ignored the way her heart quivered at the idea. She pushed resolve into her thoughts. Getting Meggie properly settled was her only concern.

Hand in hand, they stepped into the kitchen. Paquette stood at the stove, stirring a bubbling pot of porridge. Two huge frypans sizzled.

Burke put a bucket of foaming milk on the cupboard. Good. There would be milk for Meggie. That was essential.

"Good morning, Paquette, Burke." His name clung to her tongue. She forced herself not to duck away as he met her gaze, even though she knew her cheeks likely hinted at her awareness of him. She swallowed hard and dismissed those awkward, wayward feelings.

Intending to begin the way things should continue, she turned to Meggie, still clinging to her hand. "Meg, say hello to Paquette and your uncle Burke."

Meggie's chin quivered. Her eyes glistened but she read Jenny's silent insistence. They'd done battle before.

Meggie knew she'd have to give in eventually so made the wise choice to do so from the beginning.

"'Lo, Pa—" She stumbled on the name, shot Jenny a look.

Jenny nodded encouragement.

Meggie tried again. "Pa—et."

Paquette chuckled.

Jenny waggled Meg's hand and indicated she should greet Burke.

Meg gripped Jenny's hand hard and hung her head. "'Lo Unca Burke."

Burke knelt to Meggie's level. "Hello to you, too, little Meggie. Did you sleep well?"

Meggie nodded without looking at her uncle. Burke shifted his gaze to Jenny. From this position she could see how his black hair glistened, how slight waves formed across the top of his head. Then she realized he'd spoken to her asking how she'd slept.

She cleared her throat and hoped he'd think her hesitation was from being thirsty or anything except the truth—she'd again been distracted by her wayward thoughts. "Well. Thank you."

He rose slowly, holding her gaze as he did. Her heart rose with him, pushing against her ribs as if wanting to rush out into open space. "Heard some crying," he murmured.

She nodded, forcing her gaze to leave his face and return to Meggie's upturned, watchful face. Meggie held her doll in one hand, watching them with an expectant look. "I think she wants you to say hello to her doll."

Burke blinked.

Jenny grinned. "It's a great honor." It somehow pleased her to see this tough cowboy faced with the challenge of a little girl and her doll.

To his credit, Burke knelt again and touched the doll gently. "Is this your baby?"

Meggie nodded and allowed him to stroke the yarn hair on her precious dolly.

"She's very nice, isn't she?"

"My dolly." She cradled the toy against her neck and stuck her fingers in her mouth.

Jenny suspected Lena would have scolded her daughter for sucking her fingers but Jenny had decided to overlook it, allowing the child whatever comfort it provided.

Burke studied his niece a moment more. She considered him with equally serious intent. Neither of them made any motion toward the other.

His quiet caution around Meggie, giving her space to get used to her new surroundings, gave Jenny another moment's struggle with the reactions of her heart.

Burke straightened. Her eyes followed him, never leaving his face. Meggie pulled away and climbed up at the table to play with her doll.

"She's very attached to it, is she?"

Jenny struggled to make her tongue work, to bring her thoughts back to where they belonged. Seeing Burke with such interest was definitely not where they should be. What would Pa think if he could see her, read her thoughts?

Sudden guilt dried her mouth. She'd promised to marry Ted and yet here she stood with her heart pounding, her pulse racing at the sight of another man.

Hot regrets at her foolishness made it easy to turn her attention to Burke's question. "She's very fond of it. Lena made it for her just before she got ill. In fact, she put the finishing touches on it when she was almost too weak to work."

"That makes it extra special." His voice held a rough

note as if his throat threatened to close off, which only made Jenny forget her resolve to keep her thoughts on practical things. A man who made room for emotions, who honored the effort that went into creating a pretty doll, touched a chord deep inside Jenny, making her want to laugh and cry at the same time.

Burke cleared his throat. "I better get back to the chores."

Jenny nodded and turned to Paquette. "What can I do to help?" She didn't look back until she heard the door close and Burke's boots thud on the veranda floor.

"You not work. You company." Paquette watched Jenny without looking directly at her. She'd refused help before. Suggested Jenny expected to be waited on. Jenny realized Paquette was somehow testing her.

"I'm not company. I'm only here on an errand. What kind of person would I be if I sat around instead of helping?" She rubbed her hands together. "Do you want me to fry the bacon?"

Paquette moved to one side, allowing Jenny to stand at the stove. The fat spattered. "Oh, I should have brought an apron."

Paquette reached under the cupboard and brought out a big apron made from white flour sacking but decorated with a red and gold geometric pattern. "Wear dis, you."

"Thank you." Jenny examined the design. "This is beautiful. Did you do it?"

"I learn from ma mere. She use beads and quills. I use..." She sought for a word. "From plants."

"Dyes?"

"Oui."

Jenny hesitated. "It's too nice to use for frying bacon."

Paquette laughed, a merry sound unlike the usual chortle. "It can wash."

So Jenny reluctantly donned the apron feeling she had stepped into another world, one full of adventure and excitement, bold cowboys and women with strange accents. She was dangerously close to stepping over a line she had firmly drawn for herself, one forbidding her to follow wayward paths, yet she couldn't keep back a smile as she turned the meat.

A few minutes later the men trooped in for breakfast. Jenny had the table set, the bacon fried, the bread sliced and piled high. She'd made coffee under Paquette's guidance while the other woman fried potatoes and eggs.

Jenny had thought of claiming a place at Paquette's side. After all, didn't she need to be available to help the woman? But she couldn't make herself do so. No matter where she sat, she would be aware of Burke with every beat of her heart and every breath she sucked into her tight lungs. Sitting next to him would enable her to encourage a friendship between him and Meggie and so she settled in the place she'd sat the night before.

Again the men reached for food as soon as everyone sat. Paquette cleared her throat. Everyone stopped, suddenly remembering Jenny's request for grace.

"Who's going to pray this morning?" Burke asked.

Dug shook his head. "I did it last night. It's someone else's turn."

The others mumbled.

Amused at how this was like a bunch of young boys arguing about whose turn it was, Jenny ducked her head to hide her smile.

Mac sighed loudly. "I'll say the words rather than starve to death."

Jenny snorted as she tried to contain her laughter.

Mac, beside her, grunted. "I know how to pray. Me old mam taught me." He bowed his head and murmured,

"May God be with you and bless you. May you see your children's children. May you be poor in misfortune, rich in blessings. May you know nothing but happiness from this day forward. Amen." He sucked in air like he had forgotten to breathe throughout the recitation. "Pass the bacon, please."

Jenny stared. It was the most unusual grace she'd ever heard. "That was beautiful." God's blessing. Children's children. Happiness. No doubt what they all wanted.

She couldn't meet Burke's eyes even though she felt him watching her. She didn't want him to see the ache she knew would be evident. Didn't want to acknowledge it. God's blessing required obeying her parents. *Honor thy father and mother that thy days on the earth might be long.* Sometimes it was hard to quench her rebellious spirit. Remembering how often she'd failed to do so and the near disastrous consequences of one such time, she prayed for a submissive spirit.

The meal was almost over. She had to begin implementing her plans. Her heart had settled and she could face Burke without revealing anything but a calm, disciplined spirit. "Perhaps you would give us a tour of the ranch after breakfast." She rushed on before he could say anything. "I need to familiarize Meggie with her new home and teach her safe boundaries. As well, it would give you two a chance to get to know each other."

"Not a problem." He seemed unconcerned, as if this day was like any other. Hadn't he felt any of the emotions she had at Mac's prayer?

Of course, he hadn't. Why should she expect he would? He'd made no secret of what he wanted—her to be gone as soon as possible. Only she was foolish enough to want something more—something completely out of her reach.

She resolutely pushed aside a dying dream of adventure, excitement—why should she long so for things she couldn't have? It was this country. The open spaces grabbed her heart and wrenched out her childish dreams, pouring them into the sunshine like a stream of golden honey. When she returned home, she would realize how foolish all this was. "I'll help Paquette clean the kitchen first."

"Fine. Come outside when you're ready and I'll meet you."

It was all Burke could do to walk calmly from the house, the men at his heels. Everything in him wanted to race away from the warmth of the kitchen and the snarl of his thoughts. Mac's prayer had almost been his undoing—God's blessing, children's children? Where was God's blessing in Burke's life? He certainly hadn't seen any evidence of it. First, the fiasco with Flora and now Lena dead.

His gaze had rested on Jenny. Something about her made him remember his big dreams of a short time ago—home, blessings, family.

He shifted his gaze to Meggie. This was his family. He supposed that was a blessing from God. Yes, of course it was. Only somehow it didn't satisfy.

"Where's the fire, boss?" Lucky asked.

Burke realized how fast his steps had become and slowed. "No fire."

"Maybe anxious to get back to that little gal?" Mac's teasing always sounded so serious that many took offense.

Purposely misunderstanding, Burke said, "I'll need to spend some time with Meggie getting to know her so she'll be happy here." He pretended he didn't notice the sly glances the men exchanged. Every one of them knew Mac hadn't meant Meggie. It didn't matter. They'd soon enough realize Jenny and he would part ways. He ignored the ache twisting through his gut at the knowledge. "Dug, you ride out and bring in the rest of the horses. We need to get them broke before fall round up. Mac, check the pasture to the north. Lucky, see if there's any hay to cut south of here."

He strode to the barn, leaving the men to follow his orders. In the dark interior he could think of nothing he came for. The cow was out grazing, the cats had finished their milk and sat washing themselves in patches of sunlight.

"Jenny's waiting for you," Lucky called, his voice carefully neutral but Burke heard the men chuckling before they dispersed. Let them get as much fun out of this as they could. Not that he could stop them if he tried.

He scrubbed his hands on the thighs of his jeans and adjusted his hat then strode toward the house. This was only about Meggie. He needed to keep reminding himself.

He paused at the bottom of the steps and carefully kept his gaze on his niece. "What would you like to see first? The cats or the horses?" The mounts in the nearby corrals were used to people and posed no danger.

"Kitties?" Meggie sounded cautiously eager.

"Scads of 'em. Come along." He straightened and finally allowed himself to face Jenny. Her eager expression almost undid all his harsh self-talk. Oh to see that eagerness every morning, to share it about the ranch. Whoa. Stop right there. This was about Meggie, not him.

He stepped aside and waited for Jenny to descend. Meggie skipped along at their side as they headed for the barn.

"Tell me about your ranch," Jenny said.

Her words caught him off guard, left him struggling to find an answer. "We raise cows and horses," he said tentatively, not knowing if she wanted any more information.

"Your animals range free?"

"To some extent. Most of the ranchers let the animals roam, but with more and more settlers things are changing." He had his own ideas of how things should be done. "Most ranchers let their animals graze during the winter, too, but I think it's too risky."

"Why?"

Her eyes brimmed with interest and he willingly told her how he considered the risks of having them unable to find enough to eat if they should get a lot of snow. "Cows can't dig through the snow like horses or buffalo. I prefer to contain them closer to home and have hay ready to take out if there's a need."

"That's very forward thinking of you. How do the other ranchers react?"

How did she guess there were mixed feelings about the way he did things? "Some think I'm overly cautious. Survival of the fittest, they say, produces the strongest cows."

"I suppose there's something to be said for that, but still, cows are not created to survive certain elements."

He realized they had stopped walking and stood talking intently. For his part, he was lost in the interest and knowledge she showed.

Meggie had paused to examine a bug crossing their path.

"Let's see if the kitties are still around."

They reached the barn. Most of the cats had disappeared but the old mama cat still lay in the sun, enjoying her rest from her newly weaned kittens. This old cat was the tamest of the bunch, having been around since

Burke first arrived, and having learned humans meant warm milk and a gentle rub behind her ears.

"Go slow, little Meg," he warned.

Meggie, who'd been about to pounce on the unsuspecting cat, stopped.

Jenny caught Meggie's hand and knelt at her side. "Let her get used to us first. After all, we're brand new here."

Good advice for befriending both human and animal.

Jenny held her hand out to the cat and called softly.

Old mama meowed but didn't move.

"She's lazy. Or maybe wore out. Just raised a bunch of kittens."

"Kitties?" Meggie looked around expectantly.

Burke laughed. "Three of them went to neighbors. The other two are wild. You wouldn't want to hold them." He wished now that there were tiny kittens available but he knew of none.

Meggie turned back to the mama kitty. Squatting down she jiggled forward in a funny little frog walk.

Burke grinned.

Meggie reached the cat and touched it with one finger. The cat meowed and purred, obviously glad for the attention.

Meggie plunked to her bottom and the cat wrapped paws about her leg. The little one giggled. Soon the two were busy being friends.

Jenny stood back at Burke's side. "This is good for her. There's something about pets that eases sorrow."

"Maybe I should get myself a new dog." He wanted to groan at the way he sounded, as if he had so much sorrow to deal with.

"I thought it strange there was no dog. Don't all ranches have one?"

"Mine died a few months ago."

"I'm sorry. How'd it happen?"

"Don't know. Just found him dead one morning." Suddenly he remembered things he'd ignored. Old Boy had gone missing after one of Flora's visits. They found him dead out past the barn a day later. He looked a little beat up. They'd suspected coyotes. But knowing what he did about Flora now, he wondered—

Nah. She would never hurt the dog. Had no reason to.

"We lost a dog when I was about twelve. He and I were best friends. I told him all my secrets. Never loved another quite so much." She gave a little laugh. "Guess I outgrew pet friends."

He wanted to ask what kind of friends she had now. Was there a special someone in her life? But her life was none of his business. They would soon say their good-byes and never see each other again. He would not acknowledge any discomfort at the idea.

Something caught the cat's attention and she raced off, leaving Meggie teary eyed.

He reached for her hand. "Let's go see the horses."

Meggie studied the outreached hand for several seconds then slipped hers into his. So small. So soft. Made him feel ten feet tall that she trusted him enough to do this.

Jenny, at his other side, touched his arm, sending jolts of warmth to his heart. He could get used to this—a child at one side, a woman at the other. He ground his teeth at such foolishness.

"This is a big step for her," Jenny whispered.

"I know." Surely the hoarseness of his voice was due to the fact Meggie had taken his hand, not because Jenny had touched him. But deep in the recesses of his mind he couldn't deny one meant as much as the other.

He led them from the barn to the pasture fence and

whistled. The half dozen horses still at home lifted their heads and trotted toward him.

"Me touch," Meggie begged as the horses crowded around.

"I'll lift you." She made no protest as he did, and love for this little gal filled him. He wanted to hug her but didn't for fear of frightening her. He felt Jenny watching him and met her gaze. Her eyes filled with warmth and love—for Meggie, of course. But something real and alive passed between them, a mixture of pleasure and pain. He didn't try and sort out the source of each but the reasons came anyway. Pleasure at sharing love of this tiny child, pain at knowing he would only share it with Jenny for a short time.

Jenny jerked away first, a pink color blushing her cheeks. She reached out a hand and touched each of the horses, stroking their heads, scratching behind their ears, giving them equal attention as she murmured sweet nothings to them.

At least she wasn't afraid of them nor did she complain about how they smelled. He used to tell Flora they smelled like horses. What did she expect?

One of the horses tried to nibble Meggie's hair. Meg squealed and buried her face against Burke's chest. Love roared through him. He would do everything in his power to protect this child.

Meggie realized what she'd done and squirmed to be put down.

Burke released her. Afraid his emotions would be blaring from his eyes, he wouldn't look at Jenny to see if she'd noticed. Instead, he turned toward the alley. "Do you want to see the rest of the buildings?"

"I want to see everything." She sounded so eager that he stole a glance at her. Her eyes shone, a smile wreathed her face. Suddenly she sobered. "Meggie needs to become familiar with her surroundings." She stared toward the outbuildings

He nodded. It was all about Meggie. He needed no reminder. Yet her words left him feeling strangely hollow.

Chapter Five

Jenny wanted to stuff a rag into her mouth. She'd revealed far too much eagerness. Allowed herself too much interest in the ranch. In the man who owned the ranch.

With firm determination she forced her thoughts back to her purpose—settling Meggie. She needed to find out about the fiancée and encourage Burke to go ahead with his plans so Meggie would have a suitable home.

But they arrived at a long low building—the bunkhouse.

"I should show Meggie the inside."

Jenny wondered at the hesitation in Burke's voice. She was curious to see Burke's quarters—where the men lived, she corrected herself. "I'd like to see, too."

Burke hesitated. "I warn you, it's the home of a bunch of cowboys."

"What do you mean?" She pictured beds covered with brightly colored blankets, saddles at the end of each bed, bridles hung from hooks on the wall between them. Likely a stove in the middle of the room with a table nearby and chairs circling it.

A slow release grin started and made its way across his mouth and deep into her heart. The man had a smile to melt every one of her good intentions. "I guess I'll let you discover for yourself." He opened the door and waved her in.

"Come and see where Uncle Burke sleeps, Meggie." Holding the little girl's hand made Jenny feel less like she'd entered forbidden territory.

The first thing she noticed was the mess. No colorful blankets—only tangled bedcovers. No saddles. No neatly hung bridles. Instead a jumble of tools and ropes as if things had been tossed aside and forgotten.

The second thing to hit her senses was the smell. It was all she could do to keep from gasping. She tried to control her breathing but couldn't contain a cough.

Burke chuckled. "Some of the men are so familiar with the smell of animals they claim they can't sleep without it."

"I'm surprised they can sleep in here. Period." Jenny could have bitten her tongue. When would she learn to keep her thoughts to herself?

Burke shrugged. "I guess you get used to it."

She spun on him, her vow of self-control forgotten. Again. "Do you enjoy these conditions?"

His eyes grew wary. "I tolerate them."

"Why do you sleep here when you have a perfectly good house?"

"You and Meg are in one bedroom."

"Oh come on. No one has slept in there for ages." There was another room across the hall. She hadn't opened the door, expecting the same disarray.

"It's only been a few months."

"Really. I'd have said at least two years." Her curiosity raged. "Why did you move out?"

They had moved away from the bunkhouse to the clear, fresh air of the nearby pasture and stopped to lean on a rail fence. Burke's gaze sought the distance but

Jenny directed her attention to him. She was not just curious; she wanted to know why things were not as she expected. Something was wrong here, hidden under a current of secrecy and more. For Meggie's sake she needed to find out what it was.

Burke sighed and slowly brought his gaze back from afar. He stared at the grass at his feet. "I suppose Lena told you about Flora?" He glanced at her.

"Your fiancée?"

"She was."

Was? But before she could shape or voice the questions roaring through her like wildfire, he sucked in air.

"Flora stayed with a lady in town most of the time. Circumspect, she said. But she came for visits, staying a few days at a time. I gave her the third bedroom and moved out here." His voice was soft, as if he had gone back to his memories.

Jenny sensed that to say anything, ask any of her burning questions, would make Burke stop talking so she forced herself to remain quiet. But after a few minutes she decided he wasn't going to say more. "But you said no one has stayed there for months. What happened? What did you argue about?"

"Nothing." He drew his mouth down in a fierce frown. "Or maybe everything, though I didn't realize it at the time. She didn't want to marry until she got used to the place. Maybe I hurried her too much."

"I'm sure it's not too late to mend your fences, so to speak."

At the look in his face, she drew back. Anger. Frustration. Defeat. And then amusement. "Believe me. It's too late."

"You need to reconsider. For Meggie's sake. She needs a mother—"

He made a harsh sound. "Once Meggie gets used to me we'll do just fine. Be assured, Flora won't be coming back." His whole face tightened. "I have no need of a wife."

Jenny couldn't find a response. She would not admit that a tiny part of her—a corner of her heart not brought into submission—was glad he seemed so certain Flora no longer had any part in his life. She scolded herself. It made no difference to her. In a few days she would be back home and shortly thereafter announcing her engagement to Ted.

Shouldn't she have felt something besides resignation at the idea? It was only because this place was so far removed from her real life that the two couldn't coexist in her mind. Once she returned, she would realize this was only a dream. But what didn't change were Meggie's needs and her promise to Lena to see her daughter properly cared for. "Someone needs to take care of Meggie."

Slowly he faced her, such coldness in his eyes she almost stepped back. Only her stubborn nature enabled her to meet his gaze without flinching.

"I am perfectly capable of caring for her."

"But—"

"I'll hear no more argument on the matter." He turned and called Meggie. "I'll take you back to the house."

Anger roared through her. How did he think he could care for a two-year-old and run a ranch? She reached for Meggie's hand. "I can find my own way, thank you very much." She hurried away as fast as Meggie's little legs allowed.

Partway back she realized the humor of her situation. She'd asked God to keep her thoughts pure. To help her remember her promises. She'd thought it would be a fight to deny her attraction to Burke but his rude behavior had cured her. She laughed. God had uniquely answered her prayer. But by the time she reached the steps she didn't feel so much like laughing as crying. She only wanted to help. Keep her promise to Lena. Burke had no need to act like she'd done something wrong.

She went inside and begged Paquette for a job.

"Clean veranda, you?"

"I'd love to." She hurried out to tackle the job, leaving Meggie playing in the kitchen. She sorted out bits of harness and hung them from nails. She tossed the boots to the ground, carted shovelfuls of debris to the ash pile back of the house and set fire to it.

She had swept the floor and was on her hands and knees with a bucket of sudsy water and a brush when she heard the thunder of approaching animals and the whistles of men driving them. Leaving her task, she hurried around to watch. Burke threw open the corral gate and Dug drove a herd of horses into the pen. The horses milled around, tossing their heads, manes and tails catching the wind. Black horses, every color of red, a couple of buckskins and two or three pintos.

Jenny laughed softly as excitement coursed through her veins. It was glorious. So much power. So much activity.

Burke dragged the gate shut behind the last horse. Jenny couldn't make out his words as he called to Dug who edged toward the gate. Burke opened it enough to let him ride through then climbed up to sit on the top rail. Lucky joined them and the three men pointed and nodded.

Jenny wished she could hear what they said about the horses, wished she could join them and be close enough to feel the surge as the horses milled about.

After a few minutes, Dug moved away, taking his horse to the barn. Burke watched the wild bunch a bit longer. Jenny told herself it was the animals she couldn't take her eyes from but it was Burke she watched. Why was he so set against marriage? No. That wasn't what she meant. Why was he so set against making up with Flora? Her thoughts bounced around inside her head as if seeking an open door and escape. Regret warred with hope. Caution fought with adventure. Her thoughts were wayward children needing discipline. How often had both Ma and Pa warned her she must learn to control them? She sucked back air until her lungs released then returned to scrubbing the veranda floor. Several times she paused to listen to the horses whinny and neigh but she would not allow herself to return to the side of the house to watch the activity.

Only later, after the men had eaten dinner, full of talk about the horses, and after Meggie had fallen asleep for her afternoon nap, did Jenny slip around the veranda until she could see the pen.

The men seemed to be sorting out the animals. She wished she knew why they were put in different pens. Finally there was only one in the main pen.

Burke threw his lasso around the remaining horse and snubbed the end of the rope to a post before the rearing animal could jerk it from his hands. He edged toward the wild-eyed thing, speaking calmly.

Dug stood by with a blanket and saddle.

Burke intended to ride the horse!

Jenny's heart leapt to the back of her throat and stayed. She slipped from the veranda and, hoping no one would notice, crossed the yard until she pressed herself against a large post, hiding from view as best she could. She didn't want to draw attention to herself but she would not miss a moment of this drama.

Burke deftly drew the rope tighter until the horse couldn't rear. He snagged the blanket from Dug and eased it to the horse's back.

From where she stood, Jenny saw how the animal's eyes widened and its nostrils flared. It quivered all over.

Burke waited a moment, all the time talking softly. She couldn't make out his words but his tone of voice was soothing. A man in control. A man who knew how to still fears. A man—

Stop those wrongful thoughts.

Burke eased the saddle from Dug and gently lowered it to the horse's back. When he reached under the belly for the cinch, Jenny's lungs stopped working completely and refused to start again until the saddle was secured and Burke stood back safe and sound. Even then her breath jerked past tense muscles.

He managed to get on a bridle.

He caught the saddle horn.

Every muscle in Jenny's body quivered as he swung into the saddle.

"Let him go."

Dug released the rope and the horse exploded, head down, hind legs in the air.

She flinched with every pounding jump but Burke held the saddle like he was glued there. Her tension shifted from fear to excitement and admiration. She no longer watched the horse. Her eyes were on Burke. The alertness in his face as if anticipating every move, the set of his jaw, the way his arms exerted such control. .

Her eyes burned with longing. Her throat tightened. Oh, if only she could be part of this every day.

The horse stopped bucking.

Dug yelled. "Way to show who's boss."

Jenny clapped and cheered. Then she clamped her palm against her mouth. She hadn't meant to reveal her presence. Did a lady hang about the corrals watching cowboys break horses? She didn't expect they did and could almost hear Ma's soft admonition. But it was too late to slip away. Burke had seen her and smiled.

She needed to explain herself. "It's the first time I've seen someone break a horse."

"These horses are already broke for the most part. Just haven't been rode in a while so they pretend they've forgotten." He patted his mount's neck. "Just trying to see if I'm still boss."

She knew her eyes shone with excitement, admiration and things she wouldn't confess even to herself. "Will you ride them all like this?"

"Me or one of the boys. It's not hard work."

She'd seen the pounding his body took. Looked like hard work to her. Hard and thrilling. "I wish—" She stopped before she could say how much she'd like to try riding a wild horse.

"If you ever want to ride, let one of us know and we'll saddle up a quiet horse."

"I might like that."

Dug cleared his throat. "Hey, boss, did you forget there's more horses? You want me to ride 'em?"

Burke blinked as if caught at something he shouldn't have been doing.

Jenny had the same guilty feeling. "I better check on Meggie." She picked up her skirt and hurried to the house.

Burke watched her go. She'd observed the whole time. He'd seen her slip across and hide behind the post as if she didn't want anyone to notice her. He noticed all right. With every thought and every nerve ending. She was like a magnet drawing from him feelings he didn't know he owned. Didn't want to deal with. It had taken every ounce of his self-control to keep his attention on riding the horse.

And then she'd clapped and cheered. He knew by the way she covered her mouth she hadn't intended to and it thrilled him more than riding the horse to know he'd managed to edge past her cool exterior. What else lay beneath? What was she really like?

Stupid thoughts. He needed to rope them and ride them into submission.

Instead he watched until she disappeared inside the house.

"She's different, boss," Dug said.

"Different than what? Old cheese? Fresh bread?" He hoped his tone would tell Dug to cease.

Dug only laughed. "Different than that other one."

Seems the men couldn't bring themselves to say Flora's name. Not that he could blame them. Flora had been rude and nasty to them. And that was at her best.

"Flora was different, too, to start with."

Dug was silent—not an easy silence.

Burke turned to see the stubborn look on his face. "What?"

"You only tried to tell yourself it was so."

"I tried to tell myself lots of things." That she would change. That he could persuade her she'd get used to things. He no longer believed it and wouldn't try and convince himself or someone else ever again. "Let's get another horse."

He needed to work away his foolishness and he rode horse after horse until his whole body ached. Still every time he paused, his thoughts headed for the house to wonder what Jenny was doing.

He should pack his saddlebags and head out into the distance. He could check the herd. Explore the countryside—

But he couldn't. He now had a little girl to look after.

Things would be a great deal more complicated when Jenny left and Meggie became his sole responsibility. Of course, Paquette would help as much as she could.

He needed to stop worrying. Meggie would adjust quickly and as she grew older, she would learn how to look after herself. Why, by the time she was three, she'd be riding all over with him. Maybe he'd see if he could find a small pony for her....

Jenny wished she could avoid Burke. It seemed the only way she might hope to control her thoughts. But even when she couldn't see or hear him, her thoughts wouldn't be so easily controlled.

And then there was Meggie. The sooner she got Meggie used to things, the sooner she could leave. She had hoped to see a more suitable arrangement concerning Meggie's care, but Burke was her guardian and it was up to him to see to that. She ignored the pricks of her conscience that said Lena expected more.

She could only do so much. She shivered as she admitted her weakness—how this adventure pulled at her thoughts, how Burke was a magnet to them.

She needed to return home before she did anything foolish she'd regret the rest of her life.

Over the next few days, they settled into an uneasy routine. After the evening meal Burke and Jenny would take Meggie for a walk. First, they visited the cats. If it was cool enough they strolled down the trail away from the house; otherwise they wandered about the yard, pausing to speak to the horses or the men.

Jenny often waited until Meggie was asleep for another walk, which took her down the path to the open prairie. She loved the open plains, especially in the evening. Sometimes Burke joined her. Like tonight.

To keep her thoughts from running in forbidden directions she spoke of her family. "Mary is a year older. She got married last fall." She'd married John Stokes, a man Ma and Pa fully approved of. So many evenings she had overheard their conversation—*John is steady. He'll be good for Mary. A man with a solid future.* She heard the unspoken words—they feared their daughters would choose unwisely and suffer a dreadful future. She understood their concern. But sometimes a safe and solid life threatened to imprison her. Surely it was only her current situation—so foreign and exciting—that made it so difficult to control her thoughts. She pulled them firmly back to obedience and continued telling of her sisters.

"Sarah is fifteen." She chuckled. "Going on eighteen. I think she's been trying all her life to catch up to Mary and me." They were a strange trio of sisters. Mary wanting only to be like Ma and Pa. Jenny longing for adventure and excitement and little Sarah trying to grow up too fast.

"Tell me how you met Lena."

"The first Sunday they came to church I introduced myself. We just seemed to suit each other. She was so full of life. Not afraid of anything." Only Mark's opinion carried any weight with Lena. And then Meggie's needs became foremost. "She was a devoted mother right to her death." Jenny's voice thickened. She owed it to her best friend to follow her wishes to a tee. Who would care for Meggie when Jenny left? Paquette? She was fond of the child but so crippled she couldn't even lift her.

"Have you known Paquette a long time?" Perhaps he would replace her with someone who could manage the child.

"Since I arrived here."

"She come with the place?" Jenny wanted to know more about the woman and what options might be available.

Burke laughed.

It was the first time she'd heard him so amused and the sound roared through Jenny's defenses, leaving her struggling to keep from staring at him. Finally, in order to stifle the thrill bubbling to the surface, she bent, plucked a blade of grass and examined it with devout concentration. "Didn't realize I said anything amusing."

"This place didn't exist when I came out here. I've built it up from scratch." His voice rang with pride. "Nothing will make me leave here."

She wondered at the harshness in his voice. "Can't see why anyone would want you to." Her gaze swept the circle of the horizon.

"What do you see?"

A smile started in her eyes, spread to her mouth and smoothed her heart. "I see space. Opportunity." She allowed herself to meet his gaze. Knew immediately she'd made a mistake as his dark eyes sought and found entry into her heart. They regarded each other silently, exploring—

It was only because she envied him living out here in the open, inviting prairie. Nothing more. Nothing that knocked at forbidden doors in her mind.

She sought to escape her treacherous thoughts. When she felt in control, she straightened. "Paquette?" Did her voice sound as hoarse as it felt? "Where did you find her?" She tried to force herself to look some place other than into his eyes but she couldn't pull away. She realized what she'd said. Find. As if he'd gone looking for Paquette. Hopefully he would understand what she meant to say. "I mean where did she come from?"

His eyes creased with amusement. "You're right. I did find her. Literally. In a little shelter made of animal hides. She was so sick she couldn't walk and was on the verge of starving to death."

"How awful." The horror of the idea allowed her to shift her gaze away from his intense look. "Why was she alone?"

"She'd been abandoned by her Métis husband when she got sick."

"That's terrible. How could he walk away from her, leave her to die?"

Burke sighed. "I expect he figured she was going to die anyway so the best thing he could do was take care of himself."

Slowly, knowing she risked being caught in a struggle with her wayward thoughts, she brought her gaze back to him. "Is that how people out here feel?" She thought she knew the answer but wanted to hear it from his lips.

"A person ought to be prepared to deal with challenges, inconveniences, whatever they must, in order to fulfill their promises."

She nodded. "What sort of promises?"

"Like the promise of marriage, whether an engagement or a signed, sealed marriage."

His voice rang, conveying just how important this was. He would be shocked to know she'd once or twice over the past few days considered reneging on her promise to Ted—or more accurately to Ma and Pa.

Burke continued. "I think there are unspoken promises about family, too. Like Meggie. I will provide her a home no matter what it takes. And even this ranch. I've committed myself to it. What sort of man would I be if I simply walked away when things got tough?"

She couldn't speak as her mind whirled with words—

commitment, marriage, family—he was a man who faced challenges. Oh to stand at the side of such a man. Face those challenges together. Conquer them.

Firmly, with every ounce of discipline she'd been taught and tried so hard to learn, she pushed the ideas from her head. "So you rescued Paquette and gave her a home?"

"As soon as she got her strength back she took over running the house. She rules the roost."

"Is that what happened to Flora? Paquette wasn't willing to relinquish her position?" Somehow she couldn't see Burke allowing such a thing especially after what he'd just said about promise and commitment. But something had happened and the very fact he wouldn't speak of it made her unduly curious.

Burke snorted—a sound ripe with something she couldn't identify—perhaps bitterness or maybe mockery. "Flora had no objection to Paquette doing the work."

She stared at him, knowing her surprise showed in her eyes. "Was she overwhelmed by the work, then?"

"That's a good way to describe it. Yes, I guess you could say Flora was overwhelmed."

She waited, suspecting he meant something more than Flora was overwhelmed by work, but he seemed disinclined to explain. She ached to know. To understand the tension drawing his shoulders upward. Oh, if only she had the right to reach out and brush her hand across his arm and offer comfort.

But she did not. It would be well to remember that fact.

Chapter Six

Burke shifted so Jenny couldn't see his face as a blast of emotions swept through him. Disappointment that his plans had been thwarted. Sorrow at his loss, though he had to confess the loss of Lena far outweighed Flora's loss. Then determination settled over it all. As he said, he was committed to this ranch.

He'd let himself swim in the silent messages blaring from her brown eyes. Allowed himself to think what it would be like to share his love of the land, his determination to conquer it with a woman of like mind.

Hadn't he thought that's what he and Flora would be doing? They'd corresponded three years. She'd written words glowing with hope for a new life, a fresh start—as if life back East was not to her liking. Then she came for a visit. They'd planned for the visit to end in their marriage.

Overwhelmed? Guess that explained why she refused to help Paquette, refused to eat with the men. Why she shuddered when she looked at the prairie and why eventually she had run screeching across the land. Her screeching hadn't stopped even when he brought her back. The marshal said he'd seen it before. "Prairie madness," he'd called it and told stories of both men and women suffering the effects of days of loneliness and emptiness. Burke didn't see how loneliness applied to Flora. She had him, Paquette and the men. In the end it had been the land she couldn't take. He'd had no choice but to let the marshal take her to the insane asylum. She'd lasted two months out here.

Burke had never told Lena. Couldn't find the words to explain what happened.

Jenny touched his elbow. "I don't know what happened but I'm sorry it didn't work out."

Slowly he turned to face her, allowing himself to drink from the kindness in her eyes. Something shifted in his heart. He felt an uncertain hope for the first time in months.

Hope? He pretended it wasn't so. He didn't hope for anything but success in running the ranch. And now being Meggie's guardian. Nothing more. Not God's help nor any woman's help. "I demanded too much from her. I won't make that mistake again."

Something closed behind her eyes as if she didn't want him to guess at her thoughts. "Not everyone would be overwhelmed by this country."

Again hope swept through him. If only—he shook his head, driving such thoughts into nothingness.

"What about Paquette?" she persisted, as if she must prove a point. "She's survived this country even when she was ill and abandoned."

"She's born and bred in the wilds and even then, it almost destroyed her."

"Then what will happen to Meggie?"

"She'll be raised to survive."

Jenny turned away to stare out at the darkening landscape. "Seems to me you're expecting failure from all women just because Flora somehow failed."

"Not all women. Just eastern-raised ones. This is not a life for them."

She spun to face him, her eyes blazing. "I don't think you are equipped to make that kind of decision for others. After all——" She clamped her mouth shut. Then she headed toward the house, her breath rushing in and out so hard he feared she would pass out.

He strode after her. "No reason for you to take this personal, is there?" Did she love the prairie and wish she could help tame it? Hope again reared its persistent head.

She slowed considerably. "Of course not but it's still presumptuous on your part."

"Maybe." But she hadn't said anything to indicate how she felt or to give him any basis for his flagging hope. Even though he could easily catch up to her and walk at her side, he stayed several feet behind, as he reasoned his way back to the truth—words were easy. Even Flora had no trouble writing the right thing. But living the life was far different. Overwhelming, as Jenny said. "I'll say good night here. I have things to tend to." He didn't wait for her to answer but headed for the corrals as if he could outrun his thoughts.

"Good night," she called.

Next morning, he watched her more closely than usual. She helped Paquette. Did she do it out of a sense of obligation or did she enjoy the work as much as she seemed to?

She normally took Meggie for a walk after breakfast and he hung about outside until she showed up then joined her. He didn't miss the way Dug chortled as if this simple event meant impending wedding bells.

He told himself it was only so he could spend time with Meggie. But he knew it was far more. Something about Jenny had drawn him from the beginning and

now her comments about some women not being overwhelmed had him curious. Did she mean herself?

And if she did?

Only curiosity made him want to know. It wouldn't
make any difference to his decision. Would it? He
couldn't answer the question. Instead he fell in at her
side. "She's settling in well, isn't she?" He nodded toward Meggie.

"Yes, I think she is."

Meggie caught his hand and pulled him toward the
barn. She pointed to the opening for the loft. "Kitties."

He understood immediately what she wanted. All the
cats had disappeared. She'd noticed they often went that
direction. He made a low whistling.

Meggie laughed. "More."

He did it again.

Meggie held out her arms. He lifted her. When she
allowed him to hug her, his love for her burned through
him, stinging his eyes.

"'Gain," she said, touching his lips.

He chuckled, which of course made it impossible to
whistle. At her insistence, he sobered and again made
the sound.

Mama cat meowed as she came to the familiar call.

"Kitty." Meggie almost launched herself from his
arms.

"Hold on there, little miss." He released her so she
could go to the cat.

"She's certainly warming up to you."

"That's good." He avoided looking at Jenny, feeling
slightly foolish at how tight his lungs were and how his
eyes stung at Meggie's acceptance.

Meggie had a routine she insisted they follow so they
moved on a few minutes later to greet the horses, then

she raced down the trail until she found something on the ground to study.

"She's settling so well, I'll soon be able to leave."

Leave? The idea seared his mind. "No need to rush away." They walked side by side in Meggie's wake. He didn't dare look at her for fear he would reveal how much he wanted her to stay.

"My family might not agree."

"Only your family?" The question hung between them.

"Pa has picked out someone for me. I promised to give my answer when I return."

He stumbled a bit. Not enough for Jenny to notice and wonder what had tripped him when the ground was worn and smooth beneath his feet. Picked out? Promised? "Does that mean you haven't made up your mind?"

She didn't speak for so long he turned to study her and watched determination replace confusion. "Pa knows what's best for me." For one fleeting second she met his eyes. He would have said she seemed regretful. And then she jerked her chin upward. "I'll accept his choice. I'll say yes."

"You're letting your father pick out your husband?" Doing so wasn't unusual. But it didn't seem to fit what he'd learned about Jenny. "I thought you were more self-sufficient. More…" He sought for a word to describe the way she swung her arms over her head, the way she clapped when he broke a horse, the way she asked questions about the ranch, the way she touched dark corners of his heart, made him hope for things he thought were over. "I guess I took you for a woman with lots of grit." He knew his sentence ended on a bitter note. He had only himself to blame that he'd let thoughts of the future include her. She'd certainly never given him any reason for hope.

"It is sometimes a mistake to follow your own wayward heart. Doesn't God warn us that 'our hearts are deceitful above all things, and desperately wicked'?" Satisfied with her explanation, she nodded. "I prefer to trust God for the details of my life. I believe He is concerned about them and sends guidance through my parents and…other means, too, of course."

He wanted to argue but he couldn't. God seemed little interested in guiding the details of his life and yet following his heart had proven to be a mistake. Still—

"I guess if you love him." Speaking the words felt like arrows striking his soul.

"Ted's a good man."

Ted. The man had a name. He wished he didn't know it because he disliked him for absolutely no reason. Other than he was a good man. Good enough for Jenny to choose to marry. "I better get to work." He strode away so fast his boots kicked up clouds of dirt.

The truth could not be avoided. Jenny was anxious to get back home. She only needed to be reasonably certain Meggie would be fine without her. He lifted his face to the sky. Did God delight in manipulating the affairs of man to see their reaction? To see them bleed with sorrow? Wilt with unfilled hopes? He would never understand why God allowed bad things to happen.

Such questions were too profound for him. He had to accept that God ruled the universe but seemed to have little concern for the everyday little things of puny man. Not that he blamed God. He must get tired of the way people messed up.

Well, Burke didn't plan to mess up again. An eastern-born woman did not belong out here where there was nothing to see except the horizon on all sides and where life required day after day of unrelenting labor.

The sooner Jenny left, the better for them all.

He needed a plan for getting Meggie settled into ranch life so Jenny could go home to her Ted.

Meggie lay stretched out, snoring gently. Her afternoon nap usually lasted an hour or two.

Restless, Jenny wandered outside. No men lingered about. That was just fine. She didn't want to see Burke. Things had shifted between them since she'd told him about Ted. Though in reality she'd said very little about him. But Burke insinuated she was somehow weak in following Pa's advice. But why should she care if Burke seemed disappointed with her? She knew her own weaknesses, knew God, in His almighty, infallible wisdom, had given her a father to guide her.

She wandered toward the corrals. Many of the pens were empty. The men had taken some of the horses they'd broken and moved them to another pasture. But behind the barn she found one horse alone. A big horse black as polished coal. "You're a pretty one, aren't you?"

The horse reared and snorted, backing into the far corner.

"Got to put on a good show, do you? I know how you feel. Lots of times I feel like I have to put on a good show, too."

The horse tossed his head.

"I guess I don't know what kind of show I'm putting on right now. Am I pretending to be an obedient daughter, an obedient Christian when I long for adventure?" She thought of sharing life with a man like Burke. Her heart kicked into a gallop. Despite her resolve, she was drawn toward him, aching for the chance to work side by side in conquering this land, establishing a successful ranch. "You know what?" She waited for the animal to paw the ground as if asking for an answer. "I think I'm just confused because I'm so far away from home and everything here is new and exciting."

The horse waggled his head as if agreeing.

"You, too?"

Jenny chuckled to herself.

"I should write a letter home telling them I've arrived safely and explaining I'll have to delay my return until I'm satisfied Meggie will be provided for as Lena and Mark would want."

Soft noises from the horse made her laugh.

"You're a regular font of wisdom. Come here and let me pat you." But the big black animal shook his head as if saying no. "Fine. Maybe next time. Now I'm off to write a few words." She hesitated. "Nice talking to you." Laughing, she returned to the house and penned a letter. She didn't know when she'd get a chance to mail it but she felt better after she'd written to Ma and Pa.

When Burke came in to fill his canteen she asked when she could hope to post the letter. "Dug will go to town Saturday night. He'll be glad to take it. He picks up any mail for the ranch at the same time." His words were clipped as if he had too much work to deal with her questions.

Fine. She wasn't here to be amused.

She spent the rest of the afternoon pulling weeds from around the house.

She would have skipped the evening walk but Meggie insisted. Her disappointment that Burke didn't join them far outreached reasonable. "He needs to spend more time with Meggie," she murmured to the silent prairie.

* * *

Next morning as soon as breakfast was finished, Burke turned to his niece. "Meg, do you want to go with me today?"

Jenny wondered if he had read her thoughts of the previous evening and decided to act on them.

"Me go." Meg jumped down and headed for the door.

"Hang on. I'm not quite ready." He turned to Jenny, his expression hooded so she couldn't guess at his thoughts. "It's time Meggie and I got used to spending our day together."

She nodded, hoping she hid her feelings as well as he. "Where are you taking her?"

"I thought I'd show her more of the ranch. After all, it's to be her home."

Jenny stomped back an unreasonable burst of jealousy. No one had offered to show her more of the ranch. Of course they hadn't. She was here to get Meggie settled. Nothing more. "How far will you walk?" Maybe he'd ask her to accompany them.

"We'll ride."

Ride? "But she's only two."

"How old do you think children are when their parents pack them across the country to start a homestead?"

What that had to do with taking Meggie for the day, Jenny couldn't begin to comprehend. She studied her empty dish. Remembered a lady did not vent all her feelings. Recalled Ma's word to temper her reactions.

Apparently Burke took her silence for acquiescence. "Would you like that, little Meg? To ride with your uncle?"

"I ride." She pulled at his hand, urging him to come.

"It's settled then." He paused at Jenny's side. "We'll be back for dinner."

"Dinner?" she murmured. That was five hours away.

"Sooner or later we have to learn to get along without you. Best get at it." He strode away, his words like bees stinging at her thoughts. Plainly, he couldn't wait for her to leave.

"Man not know babies," Paquette mumbled.

Her words did nothing to soothe Jenny's concerns. But she was powerless to stop Burke from taking Meggie anywhere he chose. As she helped Paquette clean the kitchen, she watched Burke ride from the yard, Meggie perched in front of him babbling away excitedly.

Burke noticed her at the window and nodded curtly.

She ducked her head and gave undue attention to the pot she scrubbed. Of course she had to leave. The sooner the better. But for him to be so eager for it....

Well, what did she expect? From the first day, even before he'd known who she was, he'd said this was no place for a woman. Seems he still believed it.

Not that it mattered. She had other plans.

But the ache filling her almost drove her to her knees. She rushed to her room and flung herself on the bed to gasp for air. Finally calm, she prayed for God's strength to guide and uphold her. *And keep Meggie safe. Help her adjust to her new life.*

On the other hand, if this went as poorly as Jenny feared it would, perhaps it was God's way of showing Burke he couldn't manage without a wife. Maybe if things didn't go well, he would consider being reconciled to Flora.

She fell back on the bed and again struggled for composure.

Meggie squirmed in Burke's arms, wanting to pet his mount. He held her so she could do so and she laughed.

"This is going to work out just fine, isn't it, Meg peg?" The two of them riding the range together, enjoying the land. She'd grow up to be a real little cowgirl.

They flushed out a pair of partridges.

Meggie squealed. "Birdies."

"Partridges. Good to eat." He pointed out other birds. An antelope watched them then raced away.

Meggie laughed and jabbed her finger in the general direction, almost falling from his arms in her excitement.

"Careful, little one." He chuckled. This was going to be a great morning. "Let's go find some cows."

"Cows?" She looked around. "No cows."

"Soon." Well-being slowly eased away the knot in his thoughts he'd been dragging around like something caught on his spur. But there remained twin ropes of regret and hopelessness that tightened every time he thought how Jenny would soon be able to go home to her Ted.

He would not let disappointment turn the day sour and urged his horse to a faster gait.

Meggie giggled as she bounced.

"You're a natural little cowgirl."

They rode up an incline and he stopped to look around, trying to pinpoint clusters of cows.

"Down please."

"Not yet. See those cows way over there? We'll stop when we get to them."

Meggie stiffened. "Down."

"Not yet, Meggie." She wasn't used to riding. He'd let her take a break when they reached the little grove of trees where some cows grazed.

Meggie settled back for the ride. A good kid. She'd adapt quickly. Before they reached their destination, she started to whine. "Want down. Want down."

"Soon."

His promise did not make her patient. By the time they reached the trees, her fussing had sent the cows racing away. Burke struggled to hold her. He swung from the saddle, scarcely able to keep her from squirming out of his grasp until he reached the ground.

She staggered a few feet as if her legs had forgotten how to work and then ran in wide circles waving and yelling. Something about her excitement reminded him of Jenny. She'd lifted her arms to the skies the first day she arrived at the ranch. Was it excitement she felt? She'd said it was presumptuous on his part to think all women would fail on the prairies. He'd thought long and hard on that. What did she mean? But there was no point in trying to decide if she thought she could be different. She'd be leaving as soon as possible and return to her Ted, hand-picked for her by her pa. She wasn't any different than Flora. Flora retreated to a madhouse. Jenny would retreat to her father's plan and protection.

"Come on, Meg. It's time to move." He wanted to check the watering holes and run his eyes over the cattle and make sure they were all well.

Meggie dropped to the ground and wailed. "I want Mama."

Burke stared at the sobbing child. How did one deal with her cries for a mama she would never again see? Where did one get wisdom for such a situation? He could almost hear Jenny's voice telling him God was concerned with the details. He didn't buy it because if it were true, where was Lena? And why was Flora where she was?

He scooped the child into his arms and ignored her protests as he swung into the saddle.

After a moment she settled, glancing about with interest. He let out air that had grown stale in his lungs. This was all strange to her but she'd adjust.

A few miles later though, she started to squirm. "Go home. Wanna go home."

"Not yet. Soon."

She wailed. She threw her head back. Her cries intensified. He remembered her behavior on the train and his admiration for Jenny grew. How had she coped hour after hour? He didn't know if he could manage until noon. A glance toward the sun informed him he had at least two hours to go.

Never had a morning promised to be so long.

His leg suddenly felt warm. He lifted Meggie and saw a dark spot growing on his jeans. She'd wet herself. And him, too. "Meggie, why didn't you say something?"

She hung her head and sobbed.

"Never mind. We'll both just have to endure it until we get home."

An hour later, he admitted defeat and turned the horse toward the ranch. He thought he'd never get back. A hundred yards from the house Meggie's cries brought Jenny to the veranda, Paquette peering over her shoulder mumbling about the poor baby. At least Jenny held her tongue though her eyes spoke accusation. Lucky came to the barn door and shook his head as if to say Burke was a cruel guardian.

"She needs clean clothes." He handed the squalling child to Jenny. The smell had grown pungent. He reined around and headed for the bunkhouse. He needed a bath and clean clothes, too.

Lucky backed out of sight as Burke rode toward the corrals. "Look after my horse," Burke called, knowing the man could hear him even if he pointedly avoided him.

An hour later, he tramped back to the house feeling

restored by a soak in the metal tub behind the bunkhouse and a set of clean clothes. He took his place at the table. Mac was away tending to work but Dug and Lucky sat at the table, their gazes carefully averted. Jenny wasn't so cautious. The look she sent him practically left a brand. He sighed. "Who is going to say grace?" They'd all taken turns except him.

No one volunteered.

"Guess it's about your turn, boss," Lucky said, when it became apparent no one else was offering.

"Me?" The men gave him an unyielding stare. Jenny's gaze challenged him. Even Paquette silently warned him to expect no sympathy from her. He knew what was going on. They were all angry with him for making Meggie miserable. "Very well." He bowed his head. He didn't feel a lot of gratitude. Truth was, he didn't know exactly what he felt. God had been relegated to the ruler of the universe. Not concerned with the details of life. Yet didn't saying grace imply acknowledgement of His hand in the most basic of needs—food?

Lucky cleared his throat, reminding Burke they all waited.

Burke searched for something appropriate to say, remembered a verse his mother had taught him. "Heavenly Father, kind and good, thanks we offer for this food—" There was more—*for thy love and tender care, for all the blessings that we share*—but he couldn't give voice to the words. He had once believed them. No more. Was it because of Flora? Suddenly he realized he'd stopped thinking life was so simple after his parents died. That's when he began to doubt God's tender care. The events since had only served to entrench his belief more firmly. "Amen."

"Food be cold," Paquette complained but everyone else dug in without comment.

Burke, for his part, was content to eat without enduring any conversation. It had been a difficult morning. As if to emphasize the failure of his experiment, Meggie wouldn't meet his eyes or respond to anything he said.

It didn't require anyone to point out Meggie wasn't ready for accompanying her uncle on long rides. But he knew from the unblinking looks Jenny gave him she wouldn't be letting the episode go without saying something.

Somehow he suspected he wouldn't care for her observations. He sighed. Seemed the afternoon would be as unpleasant as his morning.

Chapter Seven

Meggie should have fallen asleep instantly but she fussed like she had the first day, as if reminded of all she'd lost. Jenny rubbed her back and sang to her. When she finally gave in to sleep, Jenny was exhausted but she had a task to tend to. She'd prayed God would use this to show Burke how much he needed a wife. Now she had to make sure Burke understood that's what it meant.

A glance out the kitchen window revealed no one about. No doubt Burke guessed she would tackle him on his outing with Meggie and had ridden off for the day. Well, he might delay it but he wouldn't avoid it. Sooner or later they must talk.

In the meantime she needed some company. She grabbed a carrot from the bin and headed to the corrals and her new friend. She'd named the big black horse Ebony. As she approached the pen, Ebony whinnied.

"Hello, big boy. Glad to see me, are you?" He seemed eager for her visits but still shied away from touching. Today she hoped to overcome his fear. She held out the carrot. "Look what I have for you. Come on." The horse quivered as he took a step closer. "That's a boy." Slowly, as she murmured, he crossed the pen, stopped almost within reach then raced away. "Come on. You know you want it." She shook the carrot. Again he started toward her. She talked softly. "Sometimes a person just has to confront their fears to discover they're all a mirage." That's what she hoped Burke would discover. Surely if he gave Flora another chance they could work things out. Ebony's lips brushed her fingers. Laughter bubbled up but she closed her mouth and held it in for fear of frightening the horse away. He took the carrot. She touched his muzzle. He quivered but didn't run. "Oh, you are a pretty thing, aren't you?" She ran her hand up his warm neck and scratched along his jaw.

"What do you think you're doing?" Burke roared.

She hadn't heard him approach and his angry voice made her yelp and jump. Ebony reared away snorting and tossing his head.

"Can't you see he's a renegade? He'd as soon stomp you as let you pass. Why, if this isn't just like a woman. Can't leave 'em a minute without them getting themselves into trouble."

Her alarm gave way to anger at being scolded as if she had done something so foolish it defied explanation. "We were doing just fine until you came along yelling your fool head off."

He grabbed her elbow and dragged her away from the pen. "Are you out of your head? He's a killer."

"Phew. He's a pet. Watch." She yanked from his grasp and headed for the pen. "Come on, Ebony. I won't let him hurt you. Come on, pretty boy."

She made two steps before Burke practically jerked her off her feet.

"Don't you ever listen to advice?" He scowled so hard his eyebrows almost touched.

She wondered if her own brows did the same. "I listen when the person giving it knows what he's talking about." She planted her fists on her hips and leaned forward. "You obviously do not."

He refused to give an inch. "Right. I've been ranching for four years and you? How long now?"

"Fine. If we're going to talk about experience let me ask you, how long have you been caring for two-year-olds? How many do you know who ride all day?"

He snorted but did not yield.

Her conscience pushed at her anger. This was no way to convince him of what he needed to do. But right now she wanted only to—

To be part of his life.

Her anger fled—all fight defeated. She was never going to be that. "You're right. I sometimes forget to listen to advice." She'd paid for it in the past. Vowed she wouldn't pay for it in the future. "Pa is often telling me to listen to those older and wiser."

"I guess that explains why you're letting him choose your husband. Afraid to follow your heart. However—" He leaned closer so she felt each word on her cheeks. "That's not the same thing at all."

She fought her rebellious spirit and won. "But sometimes it is."

"Care to explain what's behind that statement?"

"I do not."

He snorted, sounding an awful lot like Ebony. Both afraid of too many things, both hiding it behind a tough exterior. "Should have guessed you'd be too self-controlled. A real lady. All eastern ways."

Fire burned through her veins at his mocking. It stung her eyes. "You know nothing about me."

"So tell me. What makes you so set on doing exactly

what your father decides is best for you?" His voice softened. "Jenny, what do *you* want?"

His quiet question almost loosened her tongue. But what did he care what she wanted? Besides, what did she want except to see Meggie settled happily? Her anger died as suddenly as it flared. "Do you have time for a little walk?"

"Sure." He answered too quickly. Did he think she would answer his questions?

They turned down the path and headed away from the buildings. Jenny didn't speak, not certain how to broach the subject. *Father God, give me the right words. Help me say only what helps.*

They paused as they reached the end of the corrals. Jenny looked around, letting the wide-open spaces lift her heart and carry it along, soaring above the fragrant grass, almost touching the clouds. "I could never get tired of this view." She hadn't meant to speak the words aloud and rushed on before Burke noticed. "You said I should listen to advice. Are you willing to do the same?" She turned so she could watch his reaction. Caught a flash of something warm and promising before he understood her question and his expression turned cautious.

"I listen if it's wise."

"I don't claim to be wise but may I offer some advice anyway?" She didn't wait for his nod but appreciated it when it came. Willingness on his part made what she had to say easier. "I think you can see Meggie isn't ready to be a cowboy." Again a reluctant nod. "She needs a mother. Can I be so bold as to suggest you contact Flora and ask her to reconsider?"

No mistaking the dark thunder in his expression. "I'm afraid that's totally impossible."

"Nothing can be that bad. Whatever your disagreement, if you talk I'm sure you can resolve things."

He sucked in air until she feared he'd sweep up the dust from the trail. Then he let it out in a gust that would surely move leaves if there had been any on the path. "In this case I am sorry to say you are wrong. It is that bad."

She shook her head preparing to argue.

He grabbed her elbow and shook her gently. "Flora is in an asylum." His eyes were cold though she detected pain behind the anger.

"Asylum?" Sick or—

"She's insane."

Jenny gasped. "No."

"I was returning from my last visit to her that day on the train."

She thought how she'd been attracted to him even then, knowing it was wrong of her. And though it was still wrong, her heart reached for him in a way that both frightened and thrilled her.

"Her parents were there. They told me not to come again. My visits visibly upset Flora. They said a lot more."

At the pain in his voice, she squeezed his elbow, felt his tension. Oh if only she could somehow ease his sorrow.

"They blamed me but no more than I blame myself. From the beginning she was afraid of the prairie. Said it was too lonely. Too empty. Said it sucked at her insides. I wouldn't listen. I figured she'd get used to it. Instead—" He shook his head. "It was awful. The way she screamed and wailed. It took two men to get her into a buggy. The last sound I heard was a shriek. I will never forget it."

"That explains why you think this country is no place for a woman."

"It isn't."

"Oh, Burke. Not everyone sees lonely and empty when they look out there." Without breaking eye contact she tilted her head toward the prairie. "Some find it exciting." She stopped. Explaining her reaction to the land would serve no purpose. "Don't blame yourself. Don't condemn others."

His gaze drove deep into her soul as if seeking healing.

"Burke, don't give up on the future. Not now when you have Meggie to consider. The future is full of wonderful possibilities." She pushed aside regret that her future was set by the desires of her loving parents. She would no doubt find it satisfying once she adjusted. "You're a good man, Burke Edwards. Don't forget it."

The hunger in Burke's gaze slowly grew. "You almost make me believe."

"Believe. It's true."

He studied her mouth and lowered his head.

She knew he intended to kiss her. Knew she should back away, refuse it. But he needed the comfort and reassurance a little kiss would give and she lifted her mouth to meet his.

His lips were warm, gentle, questioning.

She leaned into him, his arms at her elbows anchoring her. He tasted of sage and sunshine, strength and adventure. To her shame she clung to him, seeking more.

This was wrong. It took every ounce of self-control, memory of every well-taught lesson to pull away.

His hands on her elbows kept her from fleeing.

She kept her head down, staring at the ground between them as guilt washed through her in waves.

"Jenny?"

She backed away. "I didn't come out here to be kissed." Or to kiss.

"Oh." He grinned. "What did you come for?"

She intended to convince him to reconcile with Flora. That was out. But Meggie's need was still the same. "You need to find someone to care for Meggie."

He caught her arm, his fingers burning through the fabric of her dress, shredding her resolve. "I have the perfect person in mind."

She knew he meant her and surprise and sorrow intermingled. It would be a good solution for Meggie's needs. It hurt Jenny clear through to contemplate leaving the little girl. She would think no further. She controlled her thoughts so her eyes would reveal nothing. "Good. Who?" She tried to inject a teasing note to her voice and wondered how successful she'd been.

"You." He gently rubbed her arm making it impossible to think clearly.

"Me?" She croaked the word.

"You're perfect for the job. Meggie knows you. You and Paquette get along. Dare I think you even like the prairies? A rare thing indeed."

She couldn't look at him, knowing her hopes showed on her face, naked and raw, aching to be acknowledged. She could not allow them freedom and closed her eyes. *Father God, help me. Give me strength.*

Slowly her world returned to normal and she faced him squarely. "I can't. Ted—"

"Ted." He spat the word out. "Your father's choice." The pain in his eyes almost melted her resolve. "You won't tell me what you want. Or do you even know? Maybe you're too weak to have an opinion. Like I said. This is no country for weak women."

Originally it had been women in general. Then women from the East. Now it was weak women and that's how he saw her. If only he knew how hard it had been for her to learn to be submissive. But that was a story she would never share.

He spun around on his heel. "Forget it. We will manage fine on our own. There are five adults here to help with Meggie. We don't need outsiders."

Burke swung into the saddle and kicked the horse into a gallop. He didn't slow until his mount was lathered and breathing hard and then only to rest the animal. Why had he let himself think Jenny was different? Just because she seemed to enjoy the prairies didn't mean— what? What did he want it to mean? Besides, it wasn't the prairies he wanted her to care about. It wasn't only Meggie he wanted her help with. He wanted her to care about him enough to consider staying, consider making up her own mind about who she would marry.

He touched his lips, remembering how she'd yielded to his kiss. Slowly he smiled. No mistaking her reaction. There was something between them whether or not she admitted it.

He slapped his thigh. Great. Wonderful news. Because it made no difference. She intended to return home to the man of her father's choosing. He couldn't believe it. He'd accused her of being weak but he knew better. Or at least, he thought he did. He'd seen her deal with a cranky Meggie on the train and remain unruffled. He'd watched her help Paquette. Of course, maybe it was only good breeding.

He'd been so angry when he'd seen her with that black rebel of a horse. She could have been killed if the animal struck out with his hooves as he invariably did when any of the men approached him, and yet he'd watched her stroking the animal's head. Maybe it was simply blind good fortune, not courage or perseverance.

He had no solid reason to think she was anything other than a well-trained Easterner. In fact, the more he thought about it, the more convinced he grew that's exactly what she was.

Believing so made it easier to plan to take her back to town and put her on the train to her pa and her Ted.

He'd inform her of his decision tonight.

Regret threatened to suck his insides out.

Maybe he'd wait until tomorrow to give himself time to get used to the idea.

By morning the idea was no more welcome than it had been the day before. He milked the cow, fed the cats and tended to his chores, taking lots of time, delaying his return to the house when he must make the announcement.

Finally he could find no more excuses. He sighed. Knowing what he must do did not make it any easier. He stood outside the barn and stared at the rank horse she'd been petting yesterday. Fragments of her actions dashed across his thoughts. Her head close to the horse's black head, almost touching. The way she lifted her face to the sky and laughed. The sight of her standing several yards from the buildings, gazing into the distance. The touch of her lips on his. He sighed. Those sights and sounds and feelings would be difficult to erase. But he must put them behind him. Never think of her back East with Ted. The name burned a bloody path through his mind.

He shoved a load of determination into his body and ordered his boots to march toward the house. He grabbed the neglected bucket of milk and crossed the yard. Halfway across he heard Meggie wailing and Jenny's soothing tones as she tried to calm her. Meggie hadn't cried like this since the first day or two.

Meggie's cries paused.

Burke relaxed. Only a momentary upset. Nothing to worry about.

He hadn't even completed the thought when Meggie started again, long shuddering sobs filled with shrill anguish.

What was wrong?

He rushed the last few yards, dashed in the door. Jenny sat on Paquette's chair struggling with Meggie, who tossed her head back and forth.

Burke swung the pail to the cupboard without taking his eyes off the pair. He crossed to squat before them. "Meggie, what's wrong?"

She screamed.

He sought Jenny's gaze. Read her frustration and something else—worry?

"I'm trying to get her clothes on."

Seemed ordinary enough. Shouldn't upset Meggie. He turned his attention to the child. "Come on, sweetie, let Jenny dress you."

Meggie gave him a defiant look without letting up on the racket.

"Give her to me." He plucked Meggie up and struggling to hold her, took the little socks and boots Jenny handled. Impossibly small. He struggled to handle the tiny things and at the same time, corral Meggie. But he would manage. He had to prove to himself and Jenny that they didn't need her.

He caught Meggie's foot.

She wailed and twisted away leaving him with a stocking and no foot.

He snagged her thrashing limb and held on. He could do this…if he had another set of hands.

Jenny yanked the stocking from his tight grip and slipped it on as he held Meggie's foot. Working as a team they managed the other stocking and the little boots. By the time they finished, both were disheveled and sweating. Meggie was a sopping mess of tears.

Jenny wiped her face with a towel. "Honey, what's the matter?"

Meggie screamed.

"This is unacceptable." Burke shifted the baby so she was facing him. It was like trying to corral water. She slipped through his hands every time he thought he had her. Finally, he gave up trying to make her face him and simply held her. "Meggie, behave yourself."

His firm tone made no impression.

"Meggie, stop or I'll put you in your room."

No change.

He marched to the bedroom and sat her on the bed. "You can come out when you're done."

She curled into a ball with her back to him and sobbed.

He could hardly stand it. She sounded so miserable. Made him feel so helpless. How did one deal with a squalling child? No doubt some would suggest a spanking but he couldn't bring himself to do so. She barely knew him, had lost both her parents and been transported halfway across the country. Seems it was enough to drive an adult to tears let alone a child. But how to console her?

He would hold her, rock her. "Meggie, come here." He touched her shoulder.

She curled tighter and wailed louder. "Mama."

The cry made him want to join her. His parents were dead. His sister dead. The woman he intended to marry in an asylum. And he was prepared to send a woman he could see himself growing to love back East to marry another. Meggie's cries reached into the ache of his heart, gave it breath and life. *Oh, Meggie, I know how it hurts.*

Ignoring her resistance, he scooped the baby to his lap

and cuddled her close, rocking back and forth. "Hush, little baby, don't you cry. I will sing you a lullaby." He crooned words from some deep forgotten corner of his memories. He didn't even know he knew these words. He must have heard his own mother sing them. Perhaps to him. Or to Lena. His throat tightened so he couldn't go on. The pain of all his losses brought hot tears to the back of his throat.

After a few minutes, Meggie's sobs settled into shuddering gasps. Burke got his own emotions safely relegated to the back rooms of his mind. Along with every speck of feeling toward Jenny. For his sake, his sanity, for all of them, she needed to leave. Before he couldn't let her go.

He and Meggie would do just fine with Paquette to help.

Jenny heaved a sigh of relief as Burke took Meggie into the bedroom. She'd been at her wit's end to quiet the child. What was wrong with her? Was the reality of her loss making itself felt? If so, they would all be hard-pressed to provide her some measure of comfort.

Burke's voice came to her. First, pleading words and then a song. A lullaby. He was singing to the baby, his voice deep and calming. Plucking at something unfamiliar deep inside.

Drawn by curiosity and an invisible thread that bound her to this pair, she tiptoed to the bedroom and drew to a halt at the doorway.

Burke cradled the baby and crooned, his head bent as if he intended to shelter Meggie from every danger, every hurt.

She reached toward the pair, wanting to add her comfort, share the way they clung to each other. She wanted to hold them both close. Be held close by them. Or perhaps be held by Burke as they closed their arms around Meggie.

This was wrong. How could she yearn after him when she'd given her promise to another?

Why did she continue to find submission so difficult? Had she not learned her lesson? She shuddered. Her eyes stung with shame. Yes, she'd learned the risks of ignoring her parents' wise guidance. They only wanted to protect her even as Burke wanted to protect Meggie. She lifted her fingers as if she could touch the pair and be part of them. Then she spun away, unnoticed by either and returned to the kitchen.

Shc would leave immediately. In fact, she'd announce her intention at breakfast.

Burke and Meggie would manage well enough without her.

Chapter Eight

Her resolve was firmly in place when Burke entered the room with Meggie in his arms. It faltered only slightly when Burke met her eyes. She imagined regret and longing in his gaze, but knew it was only concern about Meggie. He had no idea of her foolish imaginations. She ducked her head lest her eyes give her away.

Now was the time to act.

She was about to make her announcement when the men trooped in, ready for breakfast.

Burke stepped to her side. Was he going to say something to try and change her mind? She stomped back the little thrill on the heels of the idea. Her mind was made up. He only wanted someone to look after Meggie, but they would manage on their own. Though she wondered how well they'd do.

"Time for breakfast, little Meg peg."

She silently mocked her thoughts. He only wanted to put Meggie in her customary place at Jenny's side.

Meggie stiffened and refused to let go of Burke.

Jenny closed her eyes against the feeling sweeping over her. She could understand Meggie's reluctance to leave those comforting arms.

"I guess you can sit on my knee. Just this once. Remember, Meg peg. This is just once."

He settled in his place and awkwardly tried to fill his plate while struggling to hold a squirming baby. Meggie simply wasn't going to be content. Jenny took pity on him and dug out a generous portion of scrambled eggs to place on his plate.

Thinking Meggie might be hungry, she offered her a taste of Burke's eggs.

Meggie started to cry again.

"I can't imagine what's wrong with her." Jenny studied the fretful little girl.

Paquette made clucking noises. "Child not happy."

That was an understatement if Jenny had ever heard one. But why? Was she sick? Sad? Naughty? Spoiled? She didn't believe the latter. Besides, she was certainly getting her share of attention at the moment.

Burke eyed his plate of food. She could almost feel his mouth watering. Then he sighed. "You eat first, Jenny. Then maybe she'll settle for you so I can eat." He pushed from the table and strode outside.

No one spoke as they listened to his boots thudding back and forth on the veranda floor as he sang to Meggie, who settled into a fitful fuss.

"Do you think she's sick?" She meant the question for anyone at the table but directed it at Paquette.

"Not sick. Hurt."

"Hurt? How?" Had she fallen? Been dropped? Had Paquette seen something?

"She be on horse day before." Paquette rubbed her legs and then her neck. "Hard work for baby."

"Ahh." Of course. "Anything we can do for her?"

Paquette mumbled some foreign sounding words. "I

make the rub." She finished her meal then left the table and hurried to her room.

Jenny stared after her then slowly turned back to her food.

Mac touched her elbow. "Paquette knows Indian cures."

Jenny nodded though her thoughts weren't easy. Was this something Burke allowed? She cleaned her plate and went to take Meggie from his arms. "Paquette says Meggie is sore from the ride yesterday."

Burke blinked. "I did this to her?"

At the shock and regret in his eyes, she wished she hadn't said anything. "Paquette is making a rub."

"I only meant to make her part of the ranch."

"I'm sure she'll be fine."

"How could I expect her to ride like a man? She's a baby. It was wrong of me." He grunted. "Seems I'm always misjudging the females in my life." His eyes grew hard. He flexed his jaw muscles then spun away and returned to the kitchen.

From the look he'd given her, Jenny knew he included her in his misjudgments though he had no right to do so. She'd been honest from the beginning. She'd told him she would return home and fulfill her promise to Pa to marry Ted. He had no right to ask her to stay.

Did he really think she would?

Her heart begged to be released so she could.

She quieted it.

Adventure was not in her future. Nor was the thrill of sharing life with a man like Burke. Only a long slow obedience. It was for the best. But acknowledging it did nothing to ease the pain threatening to bring her to her knees.

Meggie's pitiful cries anchored her in her responsibilities, her duty. She couldn't leave today. Not with Meggie fussy. It wouldn't be fair to her. Or Paquette. Or Burke.

Nor did she object to the delay.

Her conscience accused her of unkindness that she could be even faintly happy that the situation gave her an excuse to stay another day. After all, Meggie's suffering was responsible for buying her a reprieve.

I'll do everything to help Meggie. It was faint comfort to her guilt.

Burke poked his head out the door. "Paquette is ready." He waited at the door and touched her upper arm as she stepped through. She felt his urgency, knew he sought comfort from his guilt.

"Burke, don't blame yourself. No one guessed this would happen."

"I wouldn't have listened if anyone suggested it. My mind was made up. Well, it's made up again. From now on Meggie stays with Paquette until she's old enough to saddle her own horse. Unless…" He sought her eyes, silently asking her to reconsider her refusal to stay.

"I can't."

"Then let's get on with it."

She didn't know if he meant taking care of Meggie, or her leaving, or both. But she would not allow herself to think beyond her boundaries. She would focus on Meggie.

When she tried to put Meggie down so she could take the bowl of thick paste Paquette handed her, Meggie plunked on her bottom, leaning her head over her lap and crying hard enough to make Jenny want to sob along with her. "I didn't realize her legs hurt too much to stand."

"I'll put her on the bed." Burke scooped her up.

Jenny took the concoction from Paquette.

"Wipe on legs and back. Not get in eyes."

Burke already had Meggie stripped down to her petticoat. They perched on the edge of the bed, gently smoothing the pungent rub as Paquette had instructed. As they worked, they murmured to Meggie, assuring her she'd be feeling better real soon.

After a few minutes, Meggie relaxed and fell asleep. They remained at her side.

"Poor baby," Burke murmured. "To think I did this to her."

"She'll be fine."

"Will she? She needs a mother."

Jenny couldn't argue. She'd been saying the same thing since her arrival.

He continued. "She had a mother. God saw fit to take her. Makes me even more convinced God is busy with the universe and has no time for petty details of our lives."

"Oh no. God is concerned with details."

"And you base this surety on what?"

She sought for the basis of her conviction. "Have you ever turned a leaf over and studied the intricate pattern? Have you compared leaves from different species of trees and seen how they vary?"

"What's leaves got to do with humans?"

"Think about the birds. How each is so different. The variety of flowers. Why, even the sky. Such a display of color every morning and evening and never the same."

"Yes?" He sounded impatient.

"Do you think a God who specializes in such variety is unconcerned with the details of our lives?"

He shrugged. "Seems to me nature simply repeats itself. Hardly proves a thing." He fixed her with a demanding stare. "Tell me of a time when you knew beyond a shadow of a doubt that God cared about the details of your life."

She didn't doubt God cared even about little things in her life, but she knew she also had choices to make. She wasn't sure how to reconcile the two. Too often her choices seemed to bring dire consequences. But she could hardly blame God for them.

"What brings that little frown to your forehead?"

She quickly forced her muscles to relax.

"Do you have doubts you aren't willing to admit?"

"My doubts are regarding my own ability to do the right thing. I have no doubts about God's sure hand."

"Ahh. Now I see."

"What?"

"Why you allow your father to choose your husband. You are afraid to take responsibility for the choice." He leaned closer, his eyes dark and demanding. "You're afraid to be who you were meant to be."

She snorted but couldn't find a response, afraid of where her natural instincts led her. "I have reason to be cautious."

"Is it caution or are you hiding? They're different. I think—"

She didn't want to hear what he thought and half rose.

He caught her hand and stopped her, pulling her close until she practically bumped into his legs. Heat flared up her neck, and she dropped back to the edge of the bed rather than deal with such intimate closeness.

"I think the things you desire frighten you because they go against the constraints of your Eastern society."

She wanted to deny it, but how could she when she struggled with the very thing every day? But she wouldn't let him guess how correct he was. "Yeah. Like what?"

He leaned back, pleased with himself, as if he knew he

had struck close to home. "Like adven-ture. Challenge. Risk. I think I have to amend my opinion."

She couldn't tear herself away from his amused, prob-ing stare.

"Perhaps there are women who belong in this country."

"You mean apart from the ones bred and born out here?" She couldn't keep the sarcasm from her voice. Didn't want to. Wanted to use it to stop him before he went further, probing into territory forbidden to every-one, including herself.

His expression shifted and grew distant.

Instantly she regretted her sarcasm. Wanted to pull the words back and return to that challenging, tempting place of a few minutes ago.

"However, we both know you won't admit what you really want. Jenny, what happened to make you so scared of who you are?"

She opened her mouth to deny anything had happened. The words wouldn't come. Because they'd be false. Some-thing had happened. Something she couldn't undo. But never again would she listen to that inner voice calling for adventure. *Lord God, my heavenly Father, help me remember how dangerous that inner voice is. Help me hear Your voice guiding and protecting me.* The voice she heard came from scriptures she had memorized. One had become her motto. 'Honor thy father and thy mother that thy days may be long upon the land which the Lord thy God giveth thee.'

"Jenny, are you pretending you can't see me? Can't hear me?"

She realized she sat with her eyes closed and opened them. Forced herself to meet his gaze. Her heart cracked at the concern she saw. Quickly, she patched the crack and smiled, knowing it probably looked as false as it felt. "I see you just fine."

"You aren't going to tell me what happened, are you?"

"Not ever."

He chuckled. "At least now I know for sure something did."

She heaved out hot frustrated air. She'd revealed more than she wanted. But it didn't change anything. Her secret would never be revealed. "It doesn't take two of us to sit with Meggie. Do you want me to stay with her?"

"I'll stay. After all, this is my fault."

"Fine. I'll go help Paquette."

"Jenny?" He reached for her.

But she slipped away. There was nothing either of them could say to change the reality of their situation. She would stay another day or two—only as long as it took for Meggie to recover. And then she would return home.

Burke watched her leave, wishing things could be different. He said she might be the sort of woman to live here. It was only wishful thinking on his part. She belonged no more than Flora, though he knew she wouldn't likely end up in an asylum. What had quenched her vivid spirit he'd glimpsed at unguarded moments? He tried to convince himself it didn't matter. But he longed to know, longed to see her enjoy life to the fullest.

Did God care about such details?

His mother seemed to think so. As did Jenny. But so far, he'd managed quite well without God's help.

Or had he?

Would God have changed things for Flora if he asked? He hadn't, but almost certainly her parents had, so the answer was probably not.

But could he manage to raise Meggie without making mistakes? Big mistakes that would create calamity? Maybe he needed God's help in that area, though he wasn't sure how he could expect to see it. How would he know if God did intervene in some way? Could he ask for something specific—sort of a test?

He didn't like the idea one bit. It felt like challenging God, which he wasn't about to do. Guess he'd just continue as he had been doing. Managing on his own as best he could, accepting the consequence of his mistakes, hoping to learn from them and do better in the future.

Meggie wakened and cried. Jenny hurried in. "Paquette says to smear her again."

He welcomed Jenny's help caring for Meggie. Wished he could have it into the foreseeable future. But no point in wanting things he couldn't have.

But if it didn't feel so wrong he would almost be glad Meggie's pain had given him reason enough to put off telling Jenny it was time to leave.

But he couldn't put it off forever.

Knowing the time would come far too soon, pain drove cruel fingers through his gut.

By evening Meggie seemed better, though she still refused to walk so he hung about, carrying her from place to place.

She did allow him to seat her at Jenny's side for supper and she ate a small amount.

While Paquette and Jenny cleaned the kitchen Burke took Meggie outside. He hoped Jenny would go for their customary evening walk even though she'd been cool and businesslike since their morning conversation.

Paquette came out first, a buckskin bag hung over her shoulder, and headed off across the prairies without a backward look.

He watched her.

"She says she's going to find more healing plants."

He hadn't noticed Jenny coming out and jerked around at her voice. She stood framed in the doorway, the sun pooling in her features and bathing her in a golden glow. She looked as if she'd been kissed by sunlight. His heart drank in the sight, letting it drench every corner, revealing secrets hidden in the dark.

He wanted to share his life with her.

He swallowed hard. It wasn't possible. She had promised to marry another even though he suspected she didn't love this Ted fellow. To please her pa. Or was it because she didn't want to admit to being the person she truly was?

The woman created by God.

One thought triggered another in rapid succes-sion.

If she was running from who she was, wasn't she running from God? And would God see fit to intervene if that was the case?

He didn't know. But somehow it felt as if God was on his side. He held the thought carefully, wishing he had time to examine it more closely.

Perhaps, in this case, it was fine to ask God to listen to his prayer. *God, you know my doubts, my uncertainties. But this one thing I'm certain of. Jenny is hiding from something. Show her how to deal with it. Help her.*

He wanted to ask for more. For Jenny to be willing to stay on the ranch. To help with Meggie. To stay for him.

But he couldn't ask for all that. It was too selfish.

"Ready for our walk?" he asked.

She quirked an eyebrow as if to ask when it had be-come "our walk." Then she nodded. "I could use some fresh air."

Meggie rested happily in his arms as they headed for the barn. She sat on the floor as mama cat greeted her but insisted on being carried again as they went to see the horses. He held her as she touched each muzzle and giggled.

Then they headed for the open prairie.

Sure she needed fresh air. However, she didn't need to accompany Burke to get it. But for the life of her she couldn't refuse the opportunity even though she'd been angry with him for poking at her deepest feelings. How often had she wondered why God made her a woman bound by the constraints of her society? She looked about the rolling grassland. Out here, the boundaries were different—pushed back like the horizon was. Perhaps if she'd met Burke earlier....

There she went again, chasing after dreams, ignoring her parents' wise counsel. She reined in her feelings. She would not be making that mistake again.

Some persistent voice whispered, "How is Burke a mistake?" The mistake was in thinking this visit could be anything more than that—a visit with a task to do.

Meggie babbled away contentedly in Burke's arms.

Jenny wondered if Meggie's legs still hurt or if she was enjoying the attention so much she intended to pretend they did. Not that she could blame the little girl. And if it meant Meggie and Burke grew closer, well, all the better.

She sought for something to talk about that would take her mind from these wayward travels. "Is there church in Buffalo Hollow?"

"Not that I know of. Why?"

"Nothing's been said. I've seen no sign of anyone attending. So I wondered. Lena would surely want Meggie raised to go to church."

Burke sighed. "I expect that's so."

"But?"

"I hadn't thought about the necessity. Didn't seem important until now."

She chuckled, knowing he'd likely given the whole idea little if any thought. "Would you have gone even if there was a church?"

He gave her a mocking grin. "You have come to know me too well, I fear."

The thought burned through her careful self-control. Did she know him? Not as well as she wanted. She tried to think of Ted. Did she know him any better? She had no idea how he felt about God. Did he go to church out of habit or conviction? Had he faced troubles? If he had— or when he did—what would his reaction be? Would he be like Burke and say it proved God wasn't interested in details of human existence? She'd never asked him any of these questions. In fact, they had never discussed anything but daily occurrences—how many people had come into the store, the pleasure of the new shipment— mundane stuff about his business interests. She knew practically nothing about Ted and had absolutely no curiosity about him. How odd when her heart yearned to peel back every layer of Burke's thinking until she saw the pulsing core of his thoughts.

She realized he watched her with a bemused expression, as if aware she'd done a mental side trip. It required a great effort to bring herself back. "So would you have gone?" She guessed he might have with Flora's urging but not otherwise.

"I would have considered it when Flora was here."

She laughed, pleased she had guessed correctly. "And never before or since. Funny, I thought that might be your answer."

He shifted Meggie to one arm and caught her hand.

"I might see the value of attending if I had someone to go with me."

He was asking again for her to stay. Using his need to go to church as an incentive. Her thoughts ran away like wild horses turned free. She imagined sitting beside him in a church, singing together, worshipping together. It held appeal like she'd never before felt at church attendance. The skin across her cheeks shrank as guilt flared up her throat. She'd let her willful spirit turn worship into a—she swallowed hard—a romantic event. God forgive her. "I guess you'll see what can be done to start services so you can attend, seeing as you have someone to go with."

Hope flared in his eyes. "I do?"

She couldn't pull from the warmth in his eyes even though she knew it was wrong. His dark gaze seemed to seek and find secrets in her heart. Secrets she longed to share with someone who wouldn't consider them scandalous. But they were. Furthermore, even her present thinking was wrong and shameful. She had promised to marry another. Yes, of her parents' choosing, but she trusted her parents, knew they understood her, cared only about what was best for her. They'd seen where her rebellious spirit led and had protected her from the damage she might have incurred.

Her fingers cramped. She realized she curled her hands into tight fists and used the pain to fuel her resolve. "You have Meggie to go to church with you."

Disappointment flared through his eyes. His smile flattened and his cheeks appeared wooden. "I see you're still running."

His assessment stung. "I am making what I consider to be a wise decision."

He snorted—a sound ripe with mockery. "Wise or

safe? Or is it fear that makes you cling to what your father decides for you?"

She breathed so hard she wondered if her nostrils flared. "I am not afraid of anything. Never have been. Never will be."

"Then why are you prepared to return home to marry a man you don't love?"

He touched her arm so gently she couldn't pull away, couldn't deny herself the comfort his touch brought, melting away, as it did, her anger and fear. Yes, she feared where her own desires would lead her but at this moment, with his fingers warming her elbow and his eyes kind and pleading, none of that mattered.

"Jenny, tell me you don't feel a little excitement at the idea of being part of building something solid in this new land. Then I will believe you don't secretly long to stay here." His voice lowered and he brushed his hand up to her shoulder. She thought he meant to kiss her by the way he looked at her. She couldn't think past her longing for him to do so.

But he waited.

She realized he expected her to say something but couldn't, for the life of her, remember what they'd been talking about. All she could think was how nothing else mattered but being here with Burke, Meggie safely sheltered in his arm. It would take only one step for her to be as safely sheltered in his other arm.

"No," she wailed. She would not allow it to happen. Not again would she allow her emotions or her longings to control her actions. "This is all wrong." She fled back to the house, remembering only after she stood panting inside the kitchen that she had to put Meggie to bed.

She struggled with her thoughts. She knew what was right for her. Being here threatened that. As soon as Meggie felt better she would be leaving. A trickle of guilt pulled at her conscience. Paquette was not able to deal with an active two-year-old. However, that was not her concern. It was Burke's.

But what about her promise to Lena?

Surely, Lena would understand she'd done the best she could. Her resolve firmly under control, she put on her most calm face and turned to face Burke as he stepped through the door. She moved to take Meggie. "It's time for this little one to go to bed."

Meggie protested weakly at the idea then came to Jenny arms.

"Good night." She waited for him to leave.

He hesitated, correctly reading the dismissal in her face. She wasn't prepared to discuss this any further. "Very well. If that's how you want it. Just think about what you're giving up."

She quirked an eyebrow questioningly before she could stop herself and pretend she didn't wonder exactly what he meant. Before he could respond she headed for the bedroom. She tried but failed to stop her thoughts from making a list of what she was giving up—the open prairie, the sense of adventure, a chance to conquer the land as he'd said. All of those things paled in comparison to the knowledge she would give up a chance to share her life with Burke. Not that he had exactly said that. He wanted someone to help with Meggie. That's all. She needed to keep the truth clearly before her.

She didn't love him. She couldn't. As she prepared Meggie for bed, she prayed. *Father God, keep me pure and true. Strengthen my resolve.*

Meggie fell asleep almost immediately and Jenny returned to the kitchen. Paquette had not come back and she used the chance to write another letter home. She had to fill the pages without revealing the truth of her heart—that she cared for Burke far more than she should. So she described the prairie.

I want to laugh with joy when I see the wind ripple the grass. And the sunsets and sunrises are so beautiful they make my heart glad. It's a bold, new land that requires strong people. The men are adventuresome. I've met few women but the ones I have seem full of grit and good humor. It makes me want to get to know them better.

She went on to describe how Meggie was doing.

Burke took her for a long horseback ride yesterday and we are all paying for it today. She is very sore. Paquette mixed up some native ointment that seemed to relieve her suffering. Meggie is sleeping now.

I wonder how she will do when I leave. A two-year-old needs so much attention.

Should she explain Paquette would be helping Burke? She could see no reason not to do so.

Burke expects Paquette to care for Meggie while he is out. I try not to worry how it will work. As soon as I am reasonably happy with the situation in regards to Meggie's care I will return home as promised.

She closed a few lines later and sealed the letter, ready to be taken to town the next time someone went.

A glance out the window revealed it was almost dark. Paquette was not yet back. Of course she would be fine. As Burke said, she was born here. Could probably find her way home blindfolded. But for her peace of mind, Jenny decided to wait up until the older woman was safely back home.

Chapter Nine

Jenny stared out into the night. A lamp glowed from the bunkhouse window, an echo of the lamp on the table behind her. Otherwise, the prairie was dark and silent.

Several times she'd gone to the veranda and listened. Apart from the evening rustle of the horses settling down and the gentle lowing of the milk cow, the only sound was the far–off yipping of coyotes. She strained to hear something indicating that Paquette had made her way back.

Nothing.

Jenny's neck tingled. She couldn't shake her tension. Didn't know if she should be worried or not.

She turned from the window and walked to the bedroom. Meggie slept. On the off chance Paquette had slipped in unnoticed—and Jenny knew it was impossible—she peeked into Paquette's room. The narrow, fur-covered cot was empty. She glanced around the room, noting the herbs hanging from the rafters, the little baskets lining a shelf. She smiled. It looked and smelled like Paquette—a comforting presence.

Where was the woman? How long did she wait before she notified Burke?

She returned to staring out the window, feeling alone

and abandoned. Burke and the men were only a few yards away, yet were totally unaware of the situation.

Her heart squeezed out a flood of worry. Surely Paquette should be back by now. Something must have happened. She refused to think of what that "something" might be.

She checked again to make sure Meggie slept soundly then obeyed her instincts and marched over to the bunkhouse. The sound of laughter and deep voices came from inside; she heard the creak of wood, like someone tipping a chair or—she swallowed hard, knowing she approached forbidden territory. Forbidden or not, she must talk to Burke. She rapped on the door. Instant silence greeted her knock.

She called, "It's me, Jenny. I need to talk to Burke."

Lots of shuffling and whispering ensued and then the light shifted. It reappeared when the door opened, held in Burke's hand.

"You need me?"

Was she crazy or did she hear a welcome longing in his voice? Now was not the time to let her emotions take over. "It's Paquette."

Burke's expression shifted through a range of emotions—surprise, disappointment and then concern. "What's wrong?"

"She's not back. I don't know if I should be worried or not. But I thought you should be the one to decide." The words came like a bolt of lightning. She didn't realize until she spoke just how concerned she was. "Should she be out this late? Is she safe out there after dark? What if something has happened to her?"

"Whoa. Slow down." He gripped her shoulder.

His touch calmed her. He would know what to do.

He turned to the men. "Boys, we need to find Paquette."

"Aww, boss. I'm tired," Dug moaned but grunted as if getting to his feet. From the thumping inside the bunkhouse, she guessed they all pulled on boots.

"Meet me at the veranda. Bring me a horse." Burke took Jenny's hand and led her to the house. "You need to stay here with Meggie. If Paquette returns before we do, I need you to signal us."

"How will I do that?"

He pulled a rifle from the cupboard. "Fire this off, three shots about fifteen seconds apart. Do you know how to shoot this?"

"I've never even touched a gun."

He showed her how to load it and pull the trigger. "Most important thing—press it hard to your shoulder and brace yourself for the kick. Oh, and aim at the sky. I wouldn't want you killing one of the horses or blowing a hole through the bunkhouse."

Her giggle revealed her nervousness.

He looked at her with narrowed eyes. "You'll be able to do this?"

She tipped her chin upward. "Of course." In fact, it was exciting to contemplate. Who'd believe she might get a chance to fire a real gun? Pa would be— well, she didn't know if he'd be shocked or surprised or what. "I'll be fine. Go find Paquette and, Burke, God be with you and help you find her safe and sound."

"You really believe God will help?"

"I certainly do. I pray He will give you eyes to see and ears to hear."

He squeezed her hand. "You pray and we'll look."

The men rode up to the door, leading a horse for Burke. They all carried lanterns and handed one to Burke as he mounted. He ordered the men in different directions. Just before he rode away, he turned and nodded to Jenny as if they shared something special. Perhaps they did. A shared concern over Paquette. An agreement to pray.

And something more. Something tenuous and forbidden but real. For tonight she was glad to acknowledge at least a fraction of her feelings for him—her confidence in his ability to find Paquette and a certainty that he trusted her to pray.

Burke hoped Jenny hadn't guessed how concerned he was over Paquette's absence. It wasn't unusual for her to wander the prairie but she always returned by dark. She knew better than most the dangers of being out after that. How easily one could get turned around if the stars and moon were hidden as they were tonight. The danger of tripping in a gopher hole, falling and breaking something.

Finding her in the dark required a miracle. Why, they might ride three feet from her and if she couldn't call out…well they would miss her as much as if she were ten miles away.

Jenny said God would help. He wasn't sure he believed it, but she seemed to believe enough for both of them.

He rode slowly, pausing often to call and listen. He heard the men doing the same thing. "Paquette!" The sound echoed across the land, the only answer the whir of birds' wings as they startled from their sleep.

His search took him farther and farther away from the ranch and with every step, his worry grew. Where was she? How could he hope to find her in this pitch-black night?

The darkness and the light are both alike to thee.

The words came softly from some distant room of his

memories. He remembered his mother saying the words.
They were from the Bible.

He didn't doubt God saw as well in the dark as in the
light. But would He allow Burke the same ability? Or at
least guide him to Paquette? Jenny seemed to think He
would. He certainly needed help beyond human ability.
Now might be a good time to forget his doubts and believe in God's divine help.

*Lord God, you made the universe. You made night
and day. They are the same to You. You know I have
trouble believing You bother with the numerous details
of mankind but if You do, please be so kind as to show
me where Paquette is.*

It was a weak sort of prayer yet the first real one he'd
offered in too many years to count and it felt good. As if
he'd turned from showing his back to God, to showing
his face. Whether or not it would make a difference…
well, time would tell.

He continued on. Riding a few feet, stopping, calling
and listening. Nothing. His doubts returned. Seems God
couldn't be bothered with man's many problems.

He got off his horse. Couldn't explain why he did.
Wasn't like he was tired of riding. Shoot, he could ride all
night if he wanted. He waved the lantern around more out
of desperation than hope. Saw nothing and lowered the
light. Something on the ground caught his eye. A flash
of something bright. He plucked it up. A bead necklace.
Like the ones Paquette wore. He straightened and turned
again, the light above his head. Did he detect a movement
on the edge of the patch of light? He stepped closer. This
time he was sure a shadow shifted. Two more steps and
he made out a shape. "Paquette, what are you doing?"

She didn't move, her only response a soft mutter.

His nerves tensed. "Paquette?"

She shifted as if startled. Lifted her head then wilted and resumed her mumbling.

He strode over, shining the light in her face. "Paquette, are you hurt?"

She acted as if she hadn't heard.

He touched her shoulder, felt the chill of her body. "Come on, let's go home." He urged her to her feet. She hadn't walked upright since he'd met her, but she seemed to have curled closer to the ground, her steps agonizingly slow. He didn't ask her any more questions. All that mattered at the moment was getting her home.

Ignoring her mumbled protests, he lifted her to the saddle and swung up to ride behind her. Several times she swayed. Only his arms around her kept her from pitching headlong to the ground.

She'd be fine as soon as she got back to the shelter of the house, as soon as she got warm. He had to believe it. But his nerves twitched with worry. Paquette was quiet and withdrawn. Flora had been loud and aggressive. Still the similarities stunned him. Seems this land was too much, even for those bred and born in it. He would do well to remember. Expecting any woman to settle here and survive the challenges was not reasonable. He quietly and firmly pushed aside the picture of Jenny in his kitchen every day for the rest of his life. It simply wasn't possible. It would eventually destroy her, and he couldn't bear for that to happen.

He concentrated on getting Paquette back to the house. "Jenny, I found her."

Jenny was already racing across the veranda, alerted by the hoofbeats of his horse.

He swung down, catching Paquette in his arms as he touched the ground.

"Is she hurt?"

"I don't know. She's cold though."

Jenny rushed back inside, calling over her shoulder. "Bring her in and I'll tend her."

He was hot on her heels. As she ran for a blanket, he dragged a chair out with his boot and deposited Paquette. She slumped forward.

Jenny returned and wrapped her warmly. She rubbed Paquette's hands. "Are you hurt? Did you fall?"

Paquette stopped mumbling, slowly lifted her head and stared into Jenny's eyes as if searching for answers.

Burke's heart beat loudly against his chest. This was so unlike Paquette. The woman had fought for survival after being abandoned on the prairie. To see her so small and weak…

Paquette shook her head. "Not remember."

"I'll make some tea." Burke filled the kettle and while he waited for it to boil, took out the teapot and tossed in a handful of tea leaves.

Paquette rocked and mumbled. Several times Jenny caught the blanket as it fell from Paquette's shoulders and rewrapped her.

As soon as the water had any color, he poured a cup of tea and laced it with sugar. He knelt at Jenny's side and held the cup to Paquette's lips.

She stared at him, a look of such confusion in her eyes that he sat back, the tea momentarily forgotten. "Paquette, do you know where you are?"

She glanced around. "Dis not 'ome. My 'ome gone. Gone."

He slanted a look at Jenny. Saw his worry reflected in her eyes. Paquette had lived here three years. This was her home. Yet she seemed to have retreated to an earlier time. "I wonder if she fell."

"Do you hurt anywhere?"

Paquette blinked as if she didn't understand.

Jenny gently ran her hands over Paquette, checking her limbs, feeling her scalp. "She seems uninjured." She again knelt and faced Paquette, studying her face. "Do you know who we are?"

Paquette studied first one then the other. Burke felt as if her gaze reached far into his heart and found nothing she could connect with.

"Maybe I see you afore."

He remembered the cooling tea and held the cup to her lips, urging her to drink.

"I'll help her into bed," Jenny said. "Chances are she'll feel better in the morning."

"Right."

He stepped outside and signaled the men then plunked to a chair and waited, listening to Jenny's soothing tones. He stayed until Jenny returned. "How is she?"

"She seemed glad to see her bed. I'll check her through the night just to make sure. What do you think happened?"

"She must have banged her head somehow." It was an easier answer to swallow than to contemplate that she'd lost more than her way out on the prairie.

He rose and found two mugs. The tea was now strong enough to use as dye, and he poured in more water before he filled the cups and carried them to the table.

"Thanks." To her credit she didn't grimace when she tasted the strong brew. But perhaps she didn't notice as she stared down the hall.

He was worried about Paquette, too. "She's tough. Likely she'll be fine by morning."

Horses approached the yard. One by one the men stuck their head in the door to ask after Paquette. "She's home safe and is sleeping," Burke told each in turn.

When the last had made an appearance, he and Jenny continued to sit side by side.

"Tell me how you found her."

"Almost didn't. I was only a few feet from her, calling her name but she didn't answer. Should have known then something was wrong with her."

"God certainly guided you tonight."

He'd forgotten his prayer. "Maybe He did. I thought we'd look all night without finding her so I—" He turned so he could see her better, observe her reaction. "I prayed. Sort of a doubters' prayer but I asked for help and not more than a few minutes later, I found her." He recalled the events, telling her every detail—how he'd gotten off the horse, seen the beads, noticed a flicker of movement. "Did God do that?"

She reached for his hand and squeezed. "You know He did, don't you?"

With her warm touch and gentle smile he could believe anything. "Guess so."

She chuckled. "I know it's hard for you to admit you might need to change your mind, but I think you know as well as I that God guided you to her. I think if you allow yourself to believe, you'll see Him at work in many areas of your life."

"I guess God helps in emergencies." He still couldn't believe God cared about everyday, ordinary things.

"'If then God so clothe the grass, which is to day in the field, and tomorrow is cast into the oven; how much more will he clothe you, O ye of little faith?' How much more basic can we get than clothes and food?"

He recognized the Bible verse. Another his mother had quoted often. "Says nothing about food."

She chuckled. "But if I remember correctly, it does in

the verse before that. Another verse says He has the hairs of our head numbered. He cares about us. He loves us."

His heart yearned to believe wholly and simply as he had as a child. But life wasn't simple. Nor did it seem to be whole. "What about Lena dying? Did He care about that? Or Flora. Did He do anything about that?" His questions sounded soulful, as if he wanted everything to be fixed, put back to his ideal. It couldn't be. A man simply had to make the best of things, roll with what life dealt.

She continued to hold his hand and without thinking what he did, he turned his palm to hers and interlocked their fingers.

"I can't explain why bad things happen," she said. "Maybe I don't want to. If I understood all the intricacies of life, the end from the beginning, the purpose of pain and suffering, why I think I'd be overwhelmed. I prefer to leave that in God's hands. He is all-wise, all-knowing and all-love. I choose to simply trust Him."

"You make it sound simple."

"In some ways it is."

He wanted to believe, yet at the same time wanted to challenge her because he was certain there were areas where she didn't find trust any easier than he did. "Is it trust or fear that makes you let your father choose the direction of your life—pick your future husband?" He wanted her to confess it was fear and then choose to trust God enough to decide she needed and deserved a man who would honor her strengths. He wanted to be the one she chose, but even if she did that desire must be denied. As soon as Paquette felt better he would send her away— back to safety and sanity.

She twisted her hand away and wrapped her fingers together in her lap to sit with her head bowed. "It is obedience. God says we are to honor our parents. I have learned to my disgrace the result of not listening to their counsel."

Another hint of having done something she regretted, something making her fearful of following her strong nature. "I don't know what horrible thing you think you did. Maybe someday you'll tell me." It couldn't be as bad as she thought. He captured a bit of hair that had escaped its bounds and played with it. "You are a strong–natured young woman who can boldly face risks and challenges. Yet you intend to pretend you are a docile woman content to follow the lead of your father and then, I suppose, this man you intend to marry. Jenny, I fear you will live a life of regret, always wishing you'd taken the riskier path, the one that led to adventure and—" He couldn't finish. Couldn't say what was in his heart.

He released the bit of hair, curled his fingers over his thumbs and squeezed until his knuckles protested. She would not be at his side. He would not allow it. Far better to know she was safe with another man than to see her spirit slowly die right before his eyes.

Jenny kept her gaze on her hands twisting in her lap. She'd never tell him what happened. Never confess it to anyone. It would remain tucked into a corner of her thoughts. But the idea of being part of this great adventure warred with her determination. Her control was further threatened by the way his fingers brushed her neck as he played with a strand of her hair. Only once before had a man touched her. And that had been so unexpected she hadn't known what to do. It had ended frighteningly. She shuddered at the memory and jerked to her feet. "I'd like to check on Paquette then go to bed, if you don't mind."

He nodded. "Sorry to be a bother." He strode out without a backward look.

She hadn't meant to sound rude or dismissive, but she knew the risks of forgetting her upbringing.

She had difficulty falling asleep as memories twisted through her head, intermingling with worry about Paquette and wishes for things she could never have. Three times she rose and checked on Paquette, who jerked her head up and grumbled at being disturbed.

The morning sun woke her, assisted by Meggie jabbing fingers in Jenny's eyes.

Groaning, she sat up. She'd overslept. No sounds came from the kitchen. Was Paquette not up? She scrambled into her clothes, dressed Meggie hurriedly and let the child run ahead, her sore legs thankfully a thing of the past.

The kitchen echoed with quiet. "Wait here, Meg, while I check on Paquette." She tiptoed to the bedroom. Paquette curled in a ball snoring softly. Poor woman was tired. She'd let her sleep.

That left her to make breakfast for them all. She rubbed her hands in glee. An adventure.

Meggie seemed to remember her sore legs and whined.

Jenny settled her on the floor and handed her some pots and pans to play with while she cooked. A few minutes later she banged the iron bar, smiling at how it had been secured with a piece of stout wire nailed into place with a six-inch spike. Burke wanted to make sure she didn't send it flying in his direction again.

Her thoughts stuttered. She would miss all this when she left. She would miss the prairie, the big kitchen, ringing the bell…and Burke.

The men trooped in for breakfast.

"Where's Paquette?" Burke asked. "She's not—?"

"She's sleeping peacefully. No need to disturb her."

He took in the food she prepared. "You did this by yourself?"

"I did." Satisfaction made her words strong and round.

"And enjoyed it, I venture to say." His eyes spoke approval and something more—a silent challenge.

She nodded. "It was fun."

"As life should be, don't you think?"

His statement was reasonable enough, but she knew he referred to his argument of last night. He seemed to think she was running from things she would enjoy. Well, she was, knowing where such wild abandon, such reckless seeking after adventure led. Why had God made her thus? Or was it only temptation seeking to lead her into dangerous territory? Likely a bit of both, she thought.

His eyes narrowed and she realized she'd allowed him to see too much. He scooped Meggie off the floor and tickled her then put her beside him.

Jenny placed the heaping serving dishes on the table then sat in her customary place. She waited for someone to choose to say the grace, felt a flash of surprise when, without any prodding from the men, Burke announced he would.

He thanked the good Lord for Paquette's safe return and for good food for their hunger. "And thank you Jenny is here, capable of making us a great meal. Amen."

She couldn't look up for fear he would see how his gratitude pleased her. She only did a job that needed doing. Yet it had been a challenge to get everything cooked and ready at the same time and in quantities large enough for the huge appetites of these men. She'd embraced the challenge. It had been fun.

She wouldn't get to do such things when she returned home. No doubt Ted would hire a housekeeper when they got married. Jenny would be expected to entertain, perhaps be allowed to grow flowers, might occasionally help in the store, though she expected Ted shared Pa's opinion that women belonged in the home. How she would manage to keep boredom at bay she couldn't imagine, but Ma seemed to do so. She would likewise learn how.

But until then, she could enjoy this chance to expand her world.

The men left. Jenny did the dishes before Paquette staggered out, her clothes askew, half her hair hanging in her usual braid and the other half out as if she'd gotten sidetracked before she finished.

"Good morning. How are you feeling?"

Paquette ground to a halt beside Meggie, who had returned to playing on the floor. "Where baby come from?"

Alarm skittered up Jenny's arms. "This is Burke's niece, Meggie. We've been here for days, Paquette. Don't you remember?"

"Not see before. Not know you. Where I am?"

She allowed Jenny to lead her to her chair. "I'll get you coffee and breakfast."

The older woman hunched over as if life had become too heavy to bear.

Jenny served her then played with Meggie so she could unobtrusively observe Paquette.

At first the woman stared at the food then picked at the bacon, but she eventually cleaned her plate and had two cups of black coffee—her usual morning routine.

Jenny eased out a sigh. Whatever had happened would right itself in time. She had to believe that. So why then did she feel a tiny trickle of excitement that for now, she had no choice but to stay and run the kitchen?

She made dinner while Paquette remained at the table, muttering from time to time or letting out long sighs.

Other than that, she seemed unaware Jenny did the work she usually did, often refusing Jenny's assistance.

Burke smiled when the men came in to eat. "I see you're up and about, Paquette. You gave us all quite a scare when you didn't come home last night. What happened out there?"

"'Appen? Where?" She looked about as if he meant someone else.

Burke shot Jenny a questioning look. Jenny shook her head. He turned back to Paquette, who examined a spoon as if she had never seen one before.

As they ate, the men tried to engage Paquette in conversation, but she either didn't hear them or acted surprised that they should address her.

Burke waited until the meal was over. "Can I speak to you outside?" he murmured to Jenny.

"Of course." She glanced toward Meggie.

"I'll watch her," Mac offered.

"Thank you," Jenny and Burke said at the same time. Jenny giggled. *Great minds think alike.*

They crossed the veranda and walked toward the corrals. Ebony whinnied a greeting but Burke steered her away from that particular pen. "He's dangerous. Stay away from him."

She thought it wise to omit telling him she visited him every day and had some very interesting discussions with the animal who proved to be an excellent listener.

They wandered to what she would always think of as their favorite place—the end of the trail that ran alongside the corrals until it disappeared into the open prairie.

He didn't mention the subject she knew was uppermost in both their minds until they came to a halt staring out at the blue-gray land under an endless, cloudless cornflower sky. "I'm worried about Paquette. If only there was a doctor nearby."

"I'm sure she'll be fine in a few hours."

He studied her, a slow smile lifting his lips. "Hoping is not the same as being sure."

She lifted one shoulder. "How can I be sure?"

"Have you prayed?"

"No."

"I thought you would have. This is surely one of those times when God needs to intervene."

"Of course." To her shame she hadn't prayed because she knew she had to stay as long as Paquette was so confused. It was a selfish, unchristian attitude. "I certainly will pray for her to get better."

He squeezed her hand. "Me, too."

A great ache engulfed her. His confession connected her to him in a way she didn't want to acknowledge but couldn't deny. If only she could stay here in this very spot and ignore the realities of her life. She couldn't. Right now Meggie needed her, the kitchen needed cleaning— all excuses allowing her to ignore the silent cries of her heart. She wished for a reason to make it impossible to ever leave.

"I better get back." She should pull her hand from his but when he started back, still holding it tight, she made no effort to slip from his grasp. After all, they were both worried about Paquette.

What harm was there in letting herself enjoy comfort and encouragement from his touch?

Chapter Ten

Burke reluctantly, determinedly, released Jenny's hand as they reached the house. He had to make arrangements for her to leave. Somehow they would manage without her. They must. For her sake. "I'm sending Dug to town for supplies. Is there anything you need?"

"I have letters to post. Paquette needed a few things. I'll make a list."

This was an opportune time. For a heartbeat he thought of telling her to prepare to accompany Dug. It was on his mind to say the words but something entirely different came from his mouth. "Do you mind staying until Paquette is better?" He couldn't deny himself this reprieve. Besides, the truth was Paquette could not care for Meggie in her present condition.

Her eyes flared with what he supposed was surprise. "Of course I will. Someone must care for Meggie." She held his gaze.

He felt her searching deep inside his thoughts, though he couldn't guess what she hoped to find.

Then, even though she didn't move, she withdrew.

Disappointment seared his lungs, making his breath burn his lips in passing. It served to remind him of his intention—not to persuade her to stay but to see she left as soon as possible.

Over the next few days he watched Paquette closely. Often he caught her sitting at the table doing nothing, or perched on a chair on the veranda staring blankly into the distance. What happened out there to change her? Was her state permanent?

He closed his eyes against the treacherous note of gladness that until Paquette was better, Jenny had agreed to stay. It was wrong thinking on his part. He knew it. And his guilt drove him to Paquette's side where she sat on the veranda. "Paquette, how are you?"

"Fine." A bowl of beads sat in her lap, and she sifted them through her fingers.

He turned so he could look in her eyes. Did he catch a flicker of sanity before she ducked away?

She scooped up a handful of beads and let them trickle to the bowl. "Pretty."

Meggie ran outside. She noticed the bowl of beads and leaned over Paquette's knee. "Pretty."

Burke studied the pair. Was he suddenly responsible for two people unable to care for themselves? So long as Jenny was here it wasn't a problem. But Jenny didn't intend to stay.

He didn't intend to let her.

As if his thoughts had beckoned her, she stepped outside and, seeing the three of them together, smiled. "What's so interesting over there?"

"Beads."

"Ah. Paquette enjoys her beads, don't you, Paquette?" She joined them and stroked Paquette's head.

Again, Burke wondered if he detected a flash of something alert in Paquette's eyes, and then she leaned over and mumbled some unfamiliar-sounding words.

Meggie picked a bead from the bowl and popped it into her mouth.

Jenny jerked forward. "No, Meggie. Spit it out." She held out her palm and waited for Meggie to obey. As she straightened, she met Burke's eyes. Paquette should have stopped Meg from putting a bead in her mouth.

Burke gave an acknowledging tilt of his head. Paquette could not be left in charge of Meggie unless she got better…until she got better.

That evening, they took their usual walk. Meggie scampered ahead, pausing often to examine a bug, a tiny flower or her footsteps in the dust.

Burke followed contentedly at a sedate pace, Jenny at his side. This was his favorite part of the day—sharing his love of the prairies with someone who seemed of like mind, enjoying his niece. More and more his love for her grew. He would do what he must in order to provide her with the best. Except send her away. They had only each other and he would not let her be taken elsewhere to be raised. Somehow they would manage. Surely Paquette would soon be back to her normal self.

He thought of those flashes in her eyes and wondered if Jenny had noticed anything. "Do you see any improvement in Paquette?"

She hesitated. "Sometimes I think she is getting better but then I think I've imagined it."

"I get the same feeling. I suppose that's a good sign."

She shrugged. "I have no idea."

"It's times like this I wonder where God is. Why He doesn't do something."

"You mean like make her better?"

"Of course." Why couldn't things be different out here? Not so challenging? Of course, it took the brave and strong to settle new lands. "Maybe I should sell the ranch. Go east. Move into a town. Not back to the cities but someplace civilized."

She spun around so fast that dust engulfed them. "Now why would you do that? I can't imagine you in a town, let alone a city." She glanced about. "I can't imagine you leaving all this. Why would you even consider it?"

"For Meggie." For Jenny. He couldn't ask her to live in the wilds. He snorted. Not that there was any point in asking her anything. She was set to marry the man her pa had chosen for her. Didn't matter where he lived, she wouldn't give him a second consideration. "Lena would want her raised to be a lady."

"So teach her how to be a lady at the same time as you teach her to live like a pioneer. The two aren't mutually exclusive."

He didn't answer. How could he? Yet he didn't want to live in town. Especially when it would make no difference to whether or not Jenny might consider him as a suitor.

"Besides, what would you do with Paquette? Leave her here to manage on her own?"

"I'd take her."

"Can you honestly see her in town? She'd go out of her mind."

"One night on the prairie seems to have done that to her already."

"So you're going to give up on her. Why not send her to the asylum?" Her eyes flashed with anger and something harder, more challenging.

She was calling him a quitter. Blaming him for sending Flora away. "I didn't put Flora in the asylum. The authorities did. For her own protection. Her parents signed the papers."

She relented so fast the air rushed from her lungs. "I'm sorry. I had no right to say that. But it seems you expect all females to crack out here. It's a demeaning attitude, don't you think?"

He wanted to believe it could be otherwise. "If this land can destroy Paquette, do you think anyone can survive it?"

She crossed her arms and gave him a noble expression. "I certainly do. Women have pioneered alongside their men for centuries. Why is this situation any different?"

"It's the land." He waved to indicate the space around them. "It's lonely. Godforsaken, many say."

"And yet I feel like God is closer here than anywhere I've been. It's as if I have only to lift my hand heavenward to connect with Him."

Her voice sounded so content, so happy. Her eyes sparkled. When she realized he watched her, she laughed. "Sorry. I didn't mean to sound so full of fancy."

"It isn't like you plan to stay."

She stared out at the prairie for a long time, silent and still. He wondered if she even breathed. Then she jerked in air. "No, you're right. I am going back home as soon as Paquette is better."

"So this whole discussion is simply…what?" It didn't matter if she could survive the prairie or not. It didn't matter if he wanted her to stay or was convinced she must go. None of it mattered as much as the dust at his feet that would blow away overnight.

She flicked a glance at him. "I just don't want you making a mistake because you judge Meggie too weak to handle the challenges of this life."

"So you think leaving the ranch would be a mistake?"

"If you do it for the wrong reason."

He studied her. She kept her gaze on the horizon, though he knew from the way her lashes fluttered she was aware of his look. "Guess you'd know about doing things for the wrong reason."

That brought her full attention to him in a hurry. "Are you accusing me of having faulty motives?"

"Don't you? Aren't your reasons for letting your father choose your mate based on fear instead of trust? Wouldn't you consider that the wrong reason for doing anything?"

She tore her gaze from him, leaving him burning with regrets.

"I'm sorry. It's none of my business. Except—" He wouldn't say he cared. Because it was too weak a statement for the way he felt. Not that it mattered one hair. She meant to go home. And he would let her. Without a word of protest, knowing it was for her good.

"Come, Meggie. It's time to go back." She took the child by the hand and hurried them home, pausing only long enough for a curt good-night before she left him standing on the veranda.

Paquette had gone indoors, too. Burke had nothing to make him stay. Except his own wayward wishes.

Which he would deny with every breath he drew.

Jenny managed to ignore her thoughts as she prepared Meggie for bed and checked on Paquette. Then she couldn't avoid them. *So you think leaving the ranch would be a mistake?* He'd meant for him. But the words twisted through her like a scouring brush, erasing all her excuses and reasons for going home. Never before had a place made her feel so alive and—as she said to Burke—so close to God. To her shame, she'd never felt for any man the things she felt for Burke—as if their thoughts completed each other's, as if their hearts beat to the same rhythm.

Oh Father God, forgive me for such traitorous thoughts. You saved me from myself once before. Do so

*again, I beg. Don't let me ruin my life by following my
heart. Please, God, help me. Strengthen me.*

She prayed for a long time until finally her spirit was
submissive.

Yet when she rose the next morning she felt relief,
tinged with sorrow, that Paquette continued to be so confused. And she realized she hadn't even prayed for the
woman's healing. *Oh God, forgive me. I don't even realize how selfish I am. Please help Paquette get better.*

Comforted by her faith, she hurried to make breakfast. She loved the challenge of coping with her limited
supplies, the sheer bulk of food the men consumed and
their enjoyment of everything she cooked. Thankfully
she had observed Paquette at work and had insisted on
helping despite the woman's initial protests, so she knew
how to deal with the limitations.

She prepared the food and rang the bell. She wished
she could avoid Burke but he crossed the yard with the
others. Pushing her resolve into place, she vowed she
would not meet his glance. But she couldn't resist and
was disappointed when he had his face turned away from
her. She stole looks several times during the meal. Each
time he looked another direction. As if he didn't want to
look at her. Couldn't bear to see her.

She couldn't blame him. He thought her weak because she intended to accept Ted's offer of marriage.
Better safe than sorry. Only would she rather be safe?
And where or what was safe? Pa seemed to think it lay
in letting him guide her along paths of his choosing. Not
that she for an instant thought he had anything but her
best interests in mind.

Burke seemed to think safe meant living in a sheltered, settled, developed place and yet choosing a man
on her own.

And her? What meant safety for her? Did she even know?

"I'll be sending someone to town for supplies after breakfast." Burke's reminder pulled her from trying to answer her own questions. "Anything you need?"

Happy for a chance to add a few things to the pantry, she said, "I'll make the list."

Burke nodded and left before she'd even started the list. Mac returned for it a few minutes later.

Of course, she wasn't disappointed Burke had sent someone else. Why should she be? They both knew this was temporary.

It was late afternoon before Mac returned. He brought in the supplies she ordered and two letters from home. She set them aside to read after she'd put the things away. But knowing they awaited her, she hurried through the task.

Meggie played contentedly at her feet, pushing her rag doll into a pot and covering it with a lid, then laughing when she pulled the lid away and the doll popped upright.

Jenny laughed at the little girl's play then turned her attention to the letters. She read the date on the postmarks and opened the earlier one first, reading notes from Ma, Pa and Sarah. Nothing but things she'd heard reiterated many times before she left. *Guard your tongue, but even more, guard your thoughts.* She'd tried. Perhaps not hard enough because she knew if Ma and Pa could read her thoughts, see how her heart responded when she was with Burke, they would be dismayed.

But she'd tried. Moreover, she intended to follow through on her promise to return and marry Ted. She'd adjust to her role in life.

Sighing, she opened the second letter. Her dismay grew with each line she read. It was as if Pa could see what she did even hundreds of miles away—proof he knew her better than she knew herself. A convincing reason to follow his guidance.

Daughter, he wrote. *Reading between the lines, I see evidence that your bold spirit has raised its head again. Your boldness is good but must be moderated with wisdom and submission. I don't mean submission to us, as your parents, but to God. You must use your God-given wisdom to discern wise choices from those that seem more alluring, more exciting. I think I need not tell you how important this is. Here is what I think you must do. You must make arrangements to return home posthaste. If you aren't satisfied Mr. Douglas's housekeeper can provide adequate care for Meggie at this time, consider alternatives. There are many, as I'm sure you're aware. Arranging for a nanny comes to my mind. But do whatever is necessary to complete your task. Do not let the temptation of new places divert you from what is best for you.*

He closed as her loving father.

His words blazed through her heart like a hot coal, burning away her pretense, exposing her foolish wishes… wants, really.

Pa was right. She had been using Paquette's illness as an excuse to stay when there were other avenues to explore.

She would write an advertisement for a nanny and send it for Pa to place in the paper back home. Why, there must be lots of young women seeking a way to head west. She thought of Burke and the possibilities with a young woman in residence. Well, perhaps there were some not-so-young ones looking for a chance to relocate, too.

There she went thinking only of herself again. Of course, the best thing for Meggie—and Burke—would be for him to marry. No reason her lungs should stiffen with protest.

She carefully considered the words then penned them on a separate sheet of paper before she wrote a reply to her parents.

If Dug meant to go to town again tomorrow, she would send the letter with him.

With no church in town, she had started having her own worship service. At first she had stayed in her bedroom and read the Bible and prayed while Meggie slept, but too soon she would be leaving this wonderful, free land. She would miss it. She couldn't think of a better place to worship God than outdoors. She didn't want to leave Meggie with Paquette so she took the child. "We're going for a walk," she told the older woman, though she wondered if Paquette, lost in her own world, would even notice her departure. Or wonder if they never returned.

Jenny walked a distance until she felt alone, away from observation from anyone back at the ranch, and rejoiced to see a few trees that promised a bit of shade. She made her way to them. "Meggie, you play here." She gathered some twigs that might interest the child then leaned against the trunk of a tree and opened her Bible. But she wasn't ready to read yet. Her thoughts twisted and turned.

It had been two weeks since she'd sent the letter to Ma and Pa. She hadn't told Burke her plans. Once she had some suitable applicants for him to consider, he would see the benefit of hiring a nanny. He would accept this was the best way. She couldn't stay, and Meggie needed more care than anyone here could provide.

But try as she did, she couldn't prevent a blast of regret

from sweeping through her. Someone else would take her place in caring for Meggie. And in caring for Burke.

Why must her heart be always so willful? Wanting things that were wrong, forbidden, dangerous?

Father God, forgive me for being so weak. Give me strength to face the future. To obey You through obeying my parents.

She clung to her faith, knowing God would strengthen and uphold her. Slowly, peace and resolve filled her soul. As Meggie sang a wordless tune, Jenny turned to her Bible. It opened to Isaiah chapter forty-three. She began to read. The words leapt from the page straight to her heart. "But now thus saith the Lord that created thee—"

Oh yes, God had made her. He understood her better than anyone.

She read on. "When thou passest through the waters, I will be with thee; and through the rivers, they shall not overflow thee; when thou walkest through the fire, thou shalt not be burned; neither shall the flame kindle upon thee."

Yes, Father God. I fear I am about to walk through the waters and the fire when I have to leave here. Only by Your strength can I do what I know is right.

On and on she read, finding strength and comfort.

Burke watched Jenny and Meggie head out into the prairie. What were they doing? He thought of following them but for several days Jenny had gone out of her way to avoid him. He was at a loss to explain why. Apart from having told her she was returning to her parents and their plans for all the wrong reasons and accusing her of being afraid to act on her own behalf, he'd said and done nothing to make her pull back.

He chuckled. That was more than enough, especially

for Jenny. She didn't take kindly to being called a coward in any terms.

She'd proven herself capable of running his house as Paquette continued to wander in her mind. Occasionally he caught a flash of his housekeeper's old self—sharp eyes, quick wit—but it seemed to fade as soon as it came. Lucky reported seeing her leave the ranch a few times. Burke wondered if Lucky imagined it. He'd never seen Paquette leave the veranda.

He bent over the harness he cleaned. A nice Sunday afternoon task. Until Jenny came, the ranch had paid little attention to the Sabbath. Perhaps worked a little slower as Dug and Mac rose late and bleary-eyed.

Things had shifted over the past weeks. Burke couldn't say how or when. Only that it had something to do with Jenny. And perhaps a tiny bit to do with his prayer for help to find Paquette. Seemed to be no way he could deny God guided him that night. And if that were so, did God care about all the details of his life? He couldn't quite get his head around the idea yet but, bit by bit, he had begun to allow God into his life.

He prayed more often. Especially for Paquette's healing. For wisdom in being Meggie's guardian. And for Jenny? Every time he tried to pray for her, he came smack hard against raging conflict. He wanted her to stay. Knew she couldn't. Wouldn't. She was set on returning to this Ted fellow. But even more than that, he wouldn't ask her. If this country could destroy Paquette, what would it eventually do to Jenny? His thoughts circled endlessly on that dreadful question. He must deny his feelings for her. For her sake. Even if she were to give him any encouragement, any indication she might have changed her mind about Ted. Which she never had.

Head down, he rubbed at the leather with the saddle

soap. Tried to keep his mind focused on the task. But his thoughts insisted on racing after Jenny. She'd been gone a long time. Had she gotten turned around? Lost? If it could happen to Paquette—

Shoot. He wouldn't be able to breathe easy until he was certain of her safety.

"Hey, Lucky," he called to the man lounging in the open door of the barn. "I'm going for a walk."

Lucky chuckled. "Saw Miss Jenny headed out. Wondered how long it would take for you to go after her."

"I'm not—I didn't plan—" He waved one arm dismissively. "Just want to make sure she's safe."

"Yeah, boss. You go do that."

Lucky's chortling humor followed him down the path. He walked to the end of the trail and looked around. Saw no sign of them. Glanced at the ground. Little footprints led to the right. He jogged that direction. Climbed a slight rise. In the distance he saw a bit of white. Meggie at play close to some trees. He strained, glimpsed Jenny against one tree, sitting still. Was she hurt?

He shuddered, remembering how Flora had run into the prairie. His memory echoed with her mad screams, sending prickles up and down his spine.

It took every ounce of his will to drive the picture away. But he couldn't edge away the alarm and broke into a full-out run, crossing the prairie in great strides, gulping in dusty air.

Jenny turned at his approach. Sprang to her feet at his urgent haste.

"What's wrong? Is it Paquette?"

He reached her side, gasping air for his starved lungs. "Are you…okay?"

She knotted her eyebrows. "I'm fine. Why?"

He leaned over his knees, sucking hard to ease his

breathing. As soon as he could talk without panting, he faced her. "What are you doing out here? Have you any idea how easy it is to get lost? And to bring Meggie with you? That's the height of stupidity." His anger drove from his mouth words he knew were wrong, offensive.

Her eyes narrowed. Her mouth pursed. She tucked in her chin and looked ready to fight. Then she blinked and her expression shifted. A warm acknowledging of something sweet and precious filled her eyes.

She'd read his worry. Perhaps guessed it went further than simple concern for her safety, or Meggie's. He sucked back his feelings, pulling his impossible love behind a fortress. But she had managed to breech the walls, break down the thick logs erected to protect his heart. He should consider her intrusion a defeat. He could not. No more than he could welcome it. Nothing had changed. It could not be.

She again read his shift of thought and her eyes grew wary. "I'm not exactly a fool. I take note of my surroundings. The ranch is right over there. In fact, you can see our footsteps in the grass."

He didn't need to look to see the evidence in the way the grass bent at each step.

"And over there is a big grove of trees. You can't see them but I see the birds rising from the branches. And Buffalo Hollow is that way. If I look really hard I can see the top of the water tower."

He forced his gaze away from her lest she read his surprise. How many noticed such tiny details? Only those born on the prairie or having spent many seasons learning such things. Amazing she should be so quick to take note.

But why torment himself with such things? Nothing had changed. She was going back east because no matter now astute she was about her bearings, the prairies could destroy anyone. The words echoed through his insides like the wail of a prairie storm.

He would not meet her eyes again. Instead, he sat by Meggie. "Hello, Meg peg. Whatcha doing?"

She waved a handful of twigs and chattered nonstop for two full minutes.

He chuckled softly. "I didn't understand one word."

She nodded, seemingly content with his response.

He picked her up, tossing her in the air until she giggled. Then sat and plunked her in his lap facing him.

Her eyes sparkled with mischief. "Ticco ticco." She dug her little fingers into his ribs and giggled.

"You little tease." He wrapped his arms around her and shook her until she squealed with laughter. They tumbled to the ground and rolled around tickling and laughing.

Finally spent, he sat up and pulled Meggie to his lap, holding her with her back pressed to his chest. Not ready to quit, she squirmed, trying to dig into his ribs again. When she realized he wasn't going to let her, she settled on his knees, resting her head beneath his chin.

He loved her, could pour all his love into her life. No need for anyone else to share with.

Sadness, reluctance and resignation weaved in and out of his thoughts, pulling them together so he couldn't separate one from the other.

"Are you ready to go home?" He spoke to the air in front of him, not wanting to directly address Jenny. Besides, he reminded himself sharply, the ranch wasn't her home.

"We're ready."

At least she didn't correct him.

They returned to the ranch. He left them at the veranda and escaped to the corrals where he could be alone with his useless wishes and regrets.

Chapter Eleven

Over the next few days, Burke found plenty of excuses to be away from the ranch. He rode the entire countryside, checking on his cows and the few neighbors they had. He filled his saddlebags to stay away for several days. At least that was his plan. Seems he couldn't keep away more than one night. Told himself he needed to check on Paquette, spend time with Meggie. He'd taken to putting her to bed when he was around. He enjoyed it immensely, recalling lullabies and nursery rhymes from his childhood.

But as he returned to the ranch, it was neither Meggie nor Paquette's face he ached to see before his lungs remembered their job was to fill with air.

It wasn't until Jenny glanced up, a quick flash of awareness—that she just as quickly masked—lighting her eyes, did he feel he had come home.

How would he survive when she left? And leave she must. Just as soon as Paquette was better. He denied he felt relief that the poor housekeeper showed very little improvement.

His plan had been to spend tonight camping out far from the ranch, but here he was riding back, anticipating the supper Jenny had prepared, Jenny sitting at his left as he ate—

Enough. He couldn't force himself to stay away, but he could refuse to let thoughts of her color every moment.

As he neared home, a buggy approached the ranch. Who could possibly be visiting? He reined in at the end of the corrals to watch.

The buggy drove up to the house, and Mr. Zach jumped down to assist someone descending—a woman in a gray traveling dress, her hair hidden by a bonnet. She paused at the steps and waited for Zach to lift down two cases. Two cases? Who was this woman? And why was she planning to park here long enough to require two cases?

He urged his mount into action and rode toward the house. Lucky stood gaping at the corral as Burke dropped to the ground. "Take my horse."

"Yes, boss. Company?"

"'Pears so."

"You invite someone?"

"Nope." And seeing he was boss, no one else had the right.

The woman disappeared into the kitchen, Zach at her heels with the two bags.

Burke's jaw muscles clenched as he watched those two bags disappear inside.

"Best go see who it is," Lucky said, sounding as if it surely meant bad news.

Burke supposed he was thinking how it had been when Flora descended on them with her whining and complaining, her snobbish ways. Jenny had been a breath of blessed relief after that disastrous visit.

He didn't expect this unannounced, uninvited visitor to be from the same refreshing breeze.

"We'll soon see what this is all about." He strode across the yard, ignoring the steps as he jumped to the veranda and thudded around to the kitchen.

Over the shoulder of the visitor, Jenny's gaze jerked to him. Her face flooded with guilt. Whoever this was, Jenny had something to do with her presence. And he wanted an explanation.

"Burke, I'd like to introduce Miss Smythe."

The woman turned. "Pleased to meet you, sir." She lowered her eyes and gave a little curtsy, then gave him a look that made his mouth want to pucker.

He could hardly guess the woman's age. Her face was young, her eyes and mouth old, as if life had worn her out. The skin around her eyes seemed too tight. Likely because her hair had been pulled back so severely.

"That's Smythe with a y. I'm pleased to meet my charge's guardian."

Paquette sat at the table. She started to mumble rapidly at the woman's brash announcement.

He didn't spare Paquette a glance. "Your charge?" He would not sputter. He shifted to study Jenny. "You know anything about this?"

"I do. Yes."

Miss Smythe with a y cleared her throat. "I was given to understand—"

He grabbed Jenny's elbow and dragged her toward the door. "I think you better explain. In private."

"Sir, if I may inquire—" He left poor Miss Smythe protesting to the door as it slapped shut behind Jenny. He knew a nasty sense of satisfaction when she yelped and jumped to avoid getting slammed in the back.

He didn't release her until they were ten feet from the veranda, then he faced her squarely. "Explain."

"I didn't expect someone to just turn up."

"That doesn't explain anything. Who is this woman and what is she doing here? With two large bags."

"Her name is Miss Smythe. With a *y*." Jenny flashed him a glance full of caution and pleading.

He wasn't about to let her off and made a warning noise. "Don't repeat what I already know. Why is she here?"

Jenny sighed. "It was Pa's idea." She paused as if hoping that would be explanation enough.

He crossed his arms, signifying he wasn't satisfied.

She waggled her hands. "I don't know where to start."

"Why is she here?"

"Pa thought I was taking too long to return so he suggested I arrange for a nanny. So I asked him to put an ad—"

"You what?"

"I arranged—" She said it so meekly he hardly recognized her voice.

"That's what I thought you said. A nanny. What do I want with a nanny?"

Her look scorched him. "I don't know what *you* want with one, but Meggie needs someone to care for her."

Shock at her presumption gave way to a long deep ache reaching to the horizon and back. He'd been lulled into thinking she would stay until Paquette was better. Even thought she enjoyed the time at the ranch, but seems she couldn't wait to get away. "So you did this behind my back?"

"Burke." Her voice sounded strained, as if it hurt to admit her underhanded, sneaky behavior.

As well it should.

"I didn't expect someone to just show up. I thought I'd get some letters and I'd show them to you and discuss it."

"You had it all figured out."

"Except Pa chose the one he thought most suitable and sent her." She waved a letter to indicate her father's communication on the matter.

Most suitable? Likely the only one Jenny's father could persuade to come out here. "How long do you figure she'll stay? One night of coyotes howling, one wind storm screaming around the house and—"

"I described the situation and the setting. I'm certain Pa would have checked the woman out."

"I don't want another woman here." The words came out sharp and bitter. "I suppose you picked someone you thought would be a suitable wife for me."

"Pa picked her out. Not me."

They stared hard at each other, her look pleading and regretful, his likely as accusing and angry as he felt. His heart seemed to have developed a pocket for carrying a ten-pound weight. It lay low in his chest—heavy and unresponsive. She obviously couldn't wait to leave.

He had to drag a reminder from some dark distant corner of his mind that he wanted her to go. Would insist on it, in fact. This country was not for women.

"She won't stay."

"If she'd only stay long enough for Paquette to get better and until Meggie is a little older and doesn't need so much supervision." Her voice echoed his doubt that either of those things would happen.

"You've overstepped your rights in doing this, but perhaps it's for the best. You need to get back to your Pa's plans for your life." He failed to keep the unreasonable bitterness from his words. He didn't want Jenny to stay. Perhaps if he kept saying it he would eventually believe it.

He had nothing more to give. It would likely take the rest of his life for his heart to relearn how to beat solidly.

* * *

Jenny forced herself to smile as she explained again how to wash Meggie's clothes.

Miss Smythe—who said she preferred to be called such and refused to reveal her Christian name—scowled deeply. Jenny was convinced the woman had long ago lost the use of the muscles allowing her to smile.

She made herself stop. Knew her criticism was unfair. It was only because she envied the woman this opportunity.

If only she could stay.

Stop. Stop wishing for things that don't belong to you. She couldn't stay. So why did it hurt to see someone who made it possible for her to leave?

Because she was—as always—given to wild, rash actions. Only this time she would not allow herself to follow her wayward heart.

Miss Smythe proved to be kind and gentle with Meggie. To her credit, after some initial shock, she had agreed to help with meal preparation until Paquette could manage on her own.

Paquette glowered constantly at this intruder—the only word she used in addressing Miss Smythe.

"She's not been well," Jenny explained. "Once she's feeling better…" Paquette had improved enough that she often insisted on doing some of the cooking. But she spent the rest of her time in some kind of vague fog.

Miss Smythe had been on the ranch four days. Four tense days as Burke alternated between sitting at the table, glumly watching Miss Smythe try to learn the intricacies of the primitive aspects of the ranch, or gulping his meals, giving Jenny a dark look then rushing out the door like he couldn't bear to be in the same room.

Meggie had just wakened from her nap and played

cheerfully with Miss Smythe. "Mith," her name for the woman, "see beads." She silently appealed to Paquette to be allowed to share her beads.

Paquette shook her head. "No beads. Mine."

"Look at your dolly." Miss Smythe wisely diverted Meggie's attention by making the rag doll dance and sing.

It was a good time to leave them alone to see how Miss Smythe managed. And Jenny longed to wander the prairie and pack as many memories as possible into her soul. "Do you mind if I go for a walk?"

Miss Smythe looked up and grimaced. "You're going out in this wind?"

Jenny laughed. "I like it." They'd had this conversation before. Miss Smythe refused to venture outside when the wind blew. Jenny warned her it meant she'd spend most of her days indoors.

Miss Smythe shuddered. "I don't mind."

Jenny refrained from asking how it would affect Meggie. The child loved being outside. Burke would have to sort out the situation without her interference.

"I'll be back in an hour or so." The wind hit her a few feet from the shelter of the house. It pushed her skirts around her legs, tugged her hair from the pins that bound it. She laughed and let it carry her along until she was a mile from the ranch. There she stood, her face to the sky, her eyes closed, and let the wind rage around her and sweep through her.

Father God, cleanse me from my wayward, sinful thoughts. Help me keep my eyes set on the path before me. Help me graciously accept the loving guidance of my parents.

She stood that way a long time seeking peace and strength. Then, her resolve firmly in place, she drank in the scenery around her, trying to memorize each detail—

the way the horizon turned gray and misty, rising and falling ever so subtly, the endless sky that at first glance appeared all one color, but with closer study shifted through a range of blues. She found a grassy spot and sat down, breathing deeply of the scents—sage, something sweet and spicy—the source of which she'd never been able to locate—and teases of scented flowers. She sneezed at the pungent aroma of nearby yarrow. The minute details of the place fascinated her. Each blade of grass so unique. Tiny flowers hiding amongst the grass. God surely had created a marvelous world. Never had she been so aware of His hand.

If God so clothe the grass of the field...

He would surely give her all she needed, too. Satisfaction with her life, peace with her surroundings.

I am ready to do Your will, O my God.

She remained there a long time, soaking her senses in the beauty and allure of the prairie and finding rest in obedience to a God she loved and trusted.

Finally, reluctantly, she pushed to her feet. It was time to return. If Miss Smythe were agreeable, Jenny would leave by the end of the week. She could not deny a great ache at the thought, but she was at peace with what she must do.

The wind buffeted her on her way, forcing her to lean into the blast. She laughed and a gust stole her breath and carried the laugh across the prairie.

Oh how she would miss this bold, powerful land.

I am ready to do Your will, O God.

She reached the yard and paused at the wail the wind carried. A different sound than the usual one it made around the house. She pushed on. Suddenly she recognized the sound—Meggie screaming in terror. Jenny picked up her skirts and ran into the wind. A few feet from the house she heard another voice—Miss Smythe's, pleading and panicked.

Jenny fought her way against the wind until—gasping—she reached the shelter of the veranda. She flung open the door and took in the scene.

Meggie sat on the floor, surrounded by Paquette's beads, shuddering with her screams.

Across the room, Paquette held a mop aloft, threatening Miss Smythe who had backed into the corner, her arms over her head.

Jenny kicked the beads away from Meggie to keep her from putting one in her mouth. "Shh, Meggie, sweetie. You're fine." She'd tend the baby as soon as she dealt with Paquette.

She approached the older woman. "Paquette, what are you doing?"

Paquette made a low guttural sound, like a wild animal growling.

"You don't want to hurt anyone." She calmly plucked the mop from Paquette's hands and dropped it to the floor, then pulled the woman into her arms. "Oh, Paquette, what's wrong with you? What's going on in that head of yours?" She rocked until Paquette sighed and relaxed.

"Boss," Lucky called into the barn. Burke was repairing a hole in the wall where Ebony had kicked in protest when Burke tried to saddle him. Crazy horse. Yet he'd seen Jenny stroking the horse and talking to it more than once when she was unaware of him watching. "Awful racket from the house."

"Yeah?"

"Think you might like to check."

Burke knew that tone of voice. Lucky meant Burke

should check *now* so he put down his tools and headed out. As soon as he stepped from the barn, he heard the noise and knew why Lucky was concerned. "It's Meggie." She screamed with terror. He vaulted the fence and galloped for the house, the skin over his spine crawling at the way she cried. If someone had hurt that little girl—

He thudded across the veranda and through the open door. Meggie sat on the floor, crying her heart out. Jenny wrapped Paquette in her arms, murmuring calmly. Miss Smythe huddled in a corner. She couldn't seem to take her eyes from a mop on the floor in front of her. He took it all in with a glance. What was going on? Had Paquette attacked the woman? Had she totally lost her mind? It happened too often. Sorrow laced with acceptance tore through his insides like a flood tearing up roots of hope and flickers of dreams, dragging them away in a rush of dirty raging water.

Yes, he'd allowed himself to hope—he couldn't even say what he'd hoped for. But seeing Paquette like this made it impossible to hope—or dream—or even wish.

This country was no place for Jenny.

He scooped Meggie from the floor and wrapped her to his chest. She sobbed against his shoulder, clinging to him fiercely. He would protect this sweet child from any danger.

Would she be able to survive this harsh land?

He would teach her how. She'd grow with it.

Like Paquette had?

If he had to, he would send Meggie away. If that's what it took to keep her whole and well. A silent groan gripped his throat. His knees melted beneath him and he sank to the bench.

Jenny turned as if checking on Meggie. She noticed him, her eyes widening as they met his.

In that moment of truth something shifted inside him. His fear collided with his dreams and exploded into a thousand flashing fragments nipping at his thoughts. It took several seconds to gather up all the pieces and stuff them back behind the log wall he'd so carefully constructed. "What's going on here?"

Miss Smythe shook her skirts and smoothed her hair. "That woman is out of her mind. She should be locked up."

His gut tightened. His thoughts skittered a protest. Not in the asylum. Not like Flora. Paquette would wither and die in such a place.

Paquette pulled from Jenny's arms and sank to a chair. "Not crazy. My beads. Not touch 'em, her."

"She attacked me. She's dangerous."

Burke had seen it before, how the land, the loneliness, the sound of the wind drove normally calm people into demented rages. Sometimes locking them up was the only way to keep them and others safe—but must everyone in his life end up there?

"Paquette would never hurt anyone. She was only warning you not to touch her beads. They're her most prized possession. We all understand that."

Miss Smythe sniffed loudly and disdainfully. "She's out of her mind. No normal person acts like that."

Paquette peered up at Miss Smythe. "Paquette not crazy." She jabbed a finger at Miss Smythe. "You not stay 'ere. Not belong, you." She turned to Jenny and jabbed her bony finger at her. "You stay. Not her."

Miss Smythe nodded. "I agree. I absolutely will not stay here. It's not safe. The rest of you will be murdered in your beds." She steamed down the hall to the bedroom.

Jenny's eyes were pleading when she looked at Burke.

"She isn't crazy. I know it. She wouldn't hurt anyone. You must not send her away."

Burke understood she meant Paquette. "I don't want to but—" He couldn't put Jenny and Meggie at risk.

Another problem bucked into his mind. "Miss Smythe is leaving. Paquette's...ill. Who will care for Meggie?"

"I can stay until you make other arrangements."

"I can't expect you to do that." Any more than he could continually fight the way his wants warred against the knowledge Jenny must leave. Not only was she set on going, he was now even more set on seeing her leave before she suffered the same fate as Paquette and Flora and so many others.

Yes, it seems some women could survive the prairies. But they were few and far between. And he would not stand by and wait to see who would be next to find the country intolerable.

He stared at Paquette, still unable to believe one bred and born on the prairie had fallen victim to its subtle dangers.

She met his gaze unblinkingly. She was trying to tell him something. But what? Slowly it became clear she showed no sign of confusion, no terror, no anger. Only certainty, as if he would understand her silent message.

He shook his head. "Paquette—?"

She ducked away.

Miss Smythe returned, dragging her bag and looking a bit ruffled, as if she'd hurried to pack everything. "I insist on a ride to town immediately. I can't abide this endless wind."

Burke's gaze rested on Paquette's head. There was more going on here than he understood. "I'll get Lucky to take you." He wouldn't leave Meggie and Jenny with Paquette until he figured out what it was.

Lucky bemoaned having to interrupt his work to make this trip. "Not that I'm sorry to see her go. She ain't our kind of lady. Not like Jenny."

Burke sighed. "Jenny ain't staying."

"You tried asking her?"

"She's got a fellow back home."

"Huh. Don't see no wedding ring. Seems to me that leaves lots of possibilities."

"It's not that simple."

"Boss, nothing is, but did that keep you from starting a ranch in the middle of nothing but grass and sky?"

"That's different."

"How?"

"'Cause grass and sky didn't have anything to say about me being here."

Lucky snorted a laugh. "Seems they have something to say every minute of the day. Some people listen— like Flora. Others—like you and Miss Jenny—just sing along."

He stared at the man. "I perceive you're a dreamer."

Lucky shifted and refused to meet Burke's gaze. "Nope. Just saying it the way I see it. And the way I see it is you're running from the chance every woman might be like Flora. Running from what's right in front of your nose. Boss, maybe it's time you stopped running."

"It's you who don't see what's right in front of all of us."

"Yeah?"

"Jenny intends to go back east. I intend to let her. Just as soon as Paquette is well enough to watch Meggie."

"Yeah, boss." Lucky hitched up the wagon and drove to the house.

A few minutes later, Miss Smythe departed, sitting regally at Lucky's side.

Burke stared after them a long time. He had no re-grets at seeing the back of Miss Smythe with a y, but the reprieve provided only more torment. Because nothing had changed.

Jenny intended to leave.

He intended to see she did.

Jenny knew it was wrong. This gladness that she must stay a bit longer. Ma and Pa would surely warn her to put an end to her foolish behavior. But they weren't here. And she could hardly leave Meggie with only some busy men and Paquette to watch her. Even Pa would under-stand that argument.

Burke still stood on the veranda watching Miss Smythe disappear down the trail. What was he think-ing? Likely that he might never get rid of Jenny.

How ironic that Miss Smythe, who had nothing to re-turn to, couldn't wait to leave while Jenny, who had iron-solid reasons to return, found her heart shriveling like a drought-stricken plant at the knowledge she couldn't stay. Not only did she love the land but—forbidden as it was—she had grown exceptionally fond of the ranch owner.

Burke turned suddenly, catching her staring at him, her heart in her eyes. A gamut of emotions crossed his eyes—sadness perhaps at losing the nanny, though he hadn't ever shown anything but long-suffering tolerance for her so perhaps it was sadness over Paquette's behav-ior. Then his eyes widened as he took in her naked car-ing and regret. At that moment, they were more honest with each other than at any time since she'd landed on his doorstep. Silently they acknowledged a common want—she wanted to stay, he wanted her to.

Guilt burned up her neck and pooled in her eyes, causing them to sting. She ducked away. Would she never learn to temper her desires with reason and submission?

Burke's breath huffed out.

She understood her inappropriateness left him surprised and likely a little puzzled. After all, she'd made it plain from the beginning she wouldn't stay.

Paquette pushed past her. "Make supper, me."

Her words effectively ended Jenny's mental wrangling. She blinked at Paquette. The woman sounded strong and focused. Not at all like she'd been since her night on the prairie. "Paquette?"

"I fine, me." She pulled out pots and handed a pan to Jenny. "Get potatoes, you."

Jenny shot a questioning look at Burke. Was she imagining this sudden change in Paquette? She knew from the way Burke looked at the older woman he was as startled by her behavior as she.

Slowly he met her eyes and gave a slight lift of his shoulders. For a moment they considered each other, silently assessing this new development.

Paquette saw Jenny with the still empty basin and grunted. "Need potatoes."

Jenny hurried to get them from the bin.

Burke shifted Meggie to his other arm as he crossed the room to face Paquette. "Are you all right?"

Paquette giggled. "I fine."

"Did something happen out on the prairie? Were you hurt?"

She giggled again. "Not hurt."

Jenny stared at the woman, a suspicion creeping through her mind. "Paquette, were you pretending?"

Another giggle before Paquette turned to rearrange the pots as if they required all her attention.

"Why would you do that?"

Paquette turned, her black eyes flashing. "Show everybody you need to stay. You belong here, you."

Jenny gasped. Heat stung her cheeks. No doubt Paquette had seen the way Jenny watched Burke and read—misread—what it meant. It meant nothing but normal curiosity and interest. Oh, if only she believed it. But she could ignore it…or try. "Paquette, I can't stay. You know that." She told the woman about Ted.

Paquette snorted. "Die like grass in winter back there."

Jenny couldn't face either of them, certain her longing and pain would reveal itself so she gave her complete and undivided attention to preparing the potatoes. "I'll be just fine."

She told herself the same thing about a thousand times an hour over the next few days. She'd notified Pa Miss Smythe had left. Knew he'd interview other young ladies for the post. But until then she could stay.

Once she got back home, she assured herself constantly, she would remember all the lessons Ma had taught her on proper behavior. She'd remember and she'd apply them and God would surely give her the peace she longed for.

In the meantime, she intended to enjoy her reprieve and hoard up memories to last a lifetime so she took long walks, sometimes alone, often with Meggie and rarely with Burke. She missed his company, sensed he pulled back as if he couldn't wait for her to leave.

She returned to the ranch after a pleasant hour of wandering around, expecting to be there when Meggie wakened. A tail of dust barreled down the trail toward the ranch.

No doubt the new nanny.

She pulled to a halt beside the corrals.

Burke sauntered over and leaned on the top rail. "Let's

hope she's better than Miss Smythe. Preferably someone a little more seasoned. Tough yet kind."

A little thrill bubbled through her at his desire for an older woman. "You should be looking for a wife."

"I don't need a wife. Don't want one." His vehemence tore a bloody strip from her heart and left her gasping. He couldn't be much clearer than that.

There would never be a place for Jenny out here. He only wanted someone to get Meggie big enough to ride with him.

The buggy pulled to the house. The dust wrapped around it, momentarily obscuring it from view. Then the tail of dust drifted on and revealed a man and woman. She didn't recognize the woman whom she assumed would be the new nanny, but the man was familiar.

Jenny blinked. "Pa?"

Chapter Twelve

Her pa? He'd come? Burke immediately straightened and stepped back from the fence, wondering if the man had seen how he leaned close to Jenny, wanting to breathe the scent of wild grasses and prairie wind she carried with her like she'd found a way to bottle them into a perfume. "What's he doing here?"

"I can't imagine. He must have left Ted in charge of the store."

Ah, the elusive Ted. Perhaps he'd asked Mr. Archibald to check on Jenny. Only one way to find out. "You going to introduce us?" He headed toward the pair as Mr. Zach lifted down bags. More bags. He hated seeing them land on the veranda. It meant more upset, and even worse, facing the inevitable—a nanny so Jenny could leave.

It's what he wanted. So he told himself time after time but Lucky's words had built a sturdy home in his heart and would not be ignored. "She sings with the prairie."

As if she was part of it. So long as a person didn't fight the land, they might survive.

Not that any of this made a difference. They'd both chosen a path diverging from this point.

Jenny fell in at his side.

Her father saw them and jogged over to hug Jenny. "Daughter, you are looking well." He examined her closely, no doubt to assure himself she was well in every way.

She hugged him back then turned to Burke. "Pa, this is Meggie's guardian, Burke Edwards."

Mr. Archibald shook his hand and gave him a hard, direct look.

Burke met the man's gaze without flinching. He had nothing to hide, nothing to be ashamed of. But he guarded his heart lest the man guess at his true feelings for his daughter. "Welcome. Come in."

Mr. Archibald waved toward the waiting woman. "Miss Morgan has agreed to come as your nanny. With your approval, of course."

Burke instantly didn't approve. The woman was older, which was good, but she looked as if life carried a dreadful odor. He couldn't imagine letting someone with such a sour expression care for Meggie. How soon before his little niece developed the same attitude? "Let's go inside and talk." He held the door and ushered them in.

Paquette sat on her chair, her arms across her chest, glowering at them. She'd been most cheerful these past few days despite Jenny's insistence she could not stay as Paquette wanted.

"Could we have tea?" he asked Paquette.

She only scowled deeper.

"I'll make it," Jenny said.

He wanted to refuse but Paquette in such a mood would not be reasoned with. He asked about the trip and listened to the comments while a whirlwind of protests filled his mind. He didn't want another nanny.

"Mr. Edwards—" Jenny's father addressed him.

"Please, call me Burke."

"I hope you find Miss Morgan satisfactory because I have come to take my daughter home."

Pain ripped through him. He pushed it away and nodded, his tongue as useless as a hunk of wood. Was this not what he wanted? Had wanted from the first time he set eyes on her? For her to go back to the safety and security of the east?

No. His heart cried. No. No. A thousand times no.

He could not look at Jenny. Could not let her see how he felt.

"I'm sure if you've checked her out, she'll be more than satisfactory." He directed his words to Jenny's father.

Paquette began to mumble and sway.

The tension in the room grew. Burke suspected it was exactly what Paquette hoped would happen. Despite his resolve, he glanced at Jenny. His heart lurched at the hunger he saw. Then she glanced at Paquette, and when her gaze returned to him he saw only concern for Paquette and knew he'd been mistaken in thinking there had been anything more.

The kettle whistled, and she hurried to the stove to pour the water. She cut each of them a piece of cake she'd made earlier and served it on individual plates then poured tea, all the while ignoring Paquette's dark looks.

Meg fussed in the other room.

"I'll get her."

Burke could practically feel her relief as she slipped away, leaving him to listen to a litany of Miss Morgan's qualifications. He could certainly find no fault with her experience. But she lacked the joy of life Jenny revealed.

How would he ever get used to its absence?

Jenny scooped Meggie into her arms and held her close. Meggie, only half awake, didn't mind and snuffled against her chest.

"Oh, Meggie, what am I going to do? I don't want to leave you with a stranger." She shuddered back a sob. "I don't want to leave you at all." Any more than she wanted to leave this place. Or the man who owned it. She wanted to be part of this great adventure of building a home and a future in this raw, new land.

Meggie squirmed.

"You're ready to be up, aren't you? Well, let's go. We have company." She returned to the kitchen. Meggie saw the strangers and ducked her head against Jenny's shoulder. "This shy young lady is Meggie. Meggie, can you say hello to Miss Morgan and my father?"

Meggie turned her head enough to peak out at them. "'Lo." She saw Burke and reached for him. She sat proudly on his lap and stole glances at the two strangers. She'd met Pa a few times but had obviously forgotten him.

Jenny hovered in the background, not wanting to sit at the table. Somehow sharing tea with Pa and the new nanny made the woman's presence far too real.

And the reality of Jenny's situation far too final.

Pa agreed Meggie should have a few days to get used to Miss Morgan. Some very uncharitable corner of Jenny's mind hoped there would be a serious flaw in Miss Morgan's character or references or even her presence, like perhaps a bad smell or an impossible accent that would make it unsuitable for her to stay. She laughed at an accent being a problem, seeing as Paquette's speech was often a challenge to understand, especially when she was riled about something and since Miss Morgan's arrival, she'd been plenty riled. Jenny acknowledged another uncharitable thought. It felt good to have Paquette defensive on her behalf.

But Miss Morgan was the epitome of an ideal nanny. She established a routine, spent time playing games with Meggie and taught her better table manners than most of the others at the ranch exhibited. Jenny hid her amusement at the way the men sat up straighter and used their utensils better when Miss Morgan joined them. Often she chose to feed Meggie before the men came in because it better suited her schedule. Once Paquette realized this, she made certain most of the meals were delayed until after Meggie and Miss Morgan had eaten.

But it must end soon. Pa could not be away long. Jenny had shown him some of her favorite places. He spent much time with Burke and the other men, had even gone away on a three-day trip to check on the cattle.

But she still had things she longed to show him. "Pa, would you like to go for a walk?"

"Love to, daughter." He'd been working on an unfinished window frame. "Trying to make myself useful while I'm here." He put his tools aside.

She glanced around. No longer did she notice all the things that needed completing—the rails on the veranda that Miss Morgan had commented on: "T'would be much safer for Meggie if they were put up." But seeing the place through Pa's eyes, she grew aware of its defects. "Burke lost interest when his marriage fell through."

She'd told Pa in a letter about poor Flora.

"Where to this sunny afternoon?" He pulled his hat down more firmly against the wind.

"Let's just walk." She'd caught up on family news and events around Center City. She'd heard all about Ted's wonderful forward-thinking suggestions for the store. Today she just wanted to enjoy the prairie. They walked two or three miles from the ranch. "This is such beautiful country, don't you think?"

He smiled his gentle smile. "Seems a lonely place."

"Pa, it's teeming with life. Look." She knelt to part a few blades of grass and revealed tiny white phlox. "You just have to learn to look."

Pa squatted beside her. "I guess you've learned where to look."

She heard something in his voice, perhaps a suggestion of admiration, and turned to study his face. But he lifted his face to glance toward the horizon. "It's a big land."

The wind caught his hat and tossed it to the ground, bowling it along. Jenny laughed and chased after it. She caught it and handed it back.

"Windy, too," Pa said.

"I know. Doesn't it make you want to become a kite and sail in the wind?"

Pa chuckled and pulled her against his side. "I have to admit it doesn't."

She turned away to pretend interest in something in the distance. Of course Pa didn't understand. He would think her enthusiasm for a place she must leave behind inappropriate. Another sign of her wayward wildness.

"Come, I have something else to show you." She led him toward the corrals.

"Is it a surprise or can you tell me where you're taking me?"

"I want to show you my special friend."

"Oh."

She knew without looking his eyebrows would have almost disappeared under his hat and she laughed. "It's a horse. See." She pointed toward Ebony's pen. "You stay here until I make sure he'll let you close. Everyone else thinks he's wild."

"Jenny, are you being foolhardy here?"

"No, Pa. I'm not. Ebony is my friend." She stepped

closer, murmuring to the horse who eyed Pa a moment, then decided he was harmless and trotted over to greet Jenny. She stroked his muzzle and scratched his ears. "I'm going to miss you, big guy. I hoped I'd be here long enough to persuade you to let the men ride you."

Ebony snorted and Jenny realized Pa had moved closer.

"He's a beauty, for sure. Is he broke?"

"Not yet. He won't let anyone but me get close to him. Though he isn't too nervous with you this close." But as she spoke, Ebony snorted and raced away, bucking and acting like he meant to destroy every man-made object he could reach.

"I'm surprised Burke let you near him. He's wild."

She reluctantly turned from the horse to face Pa. "He didn't know I was coming out here until it was too late to say anything."

"Jenny, you're bound to get yourself into trouble with your disregard for caution."

"Pa, I know. I try and guard my thoughts and actions. But Ebony was an honest mistake. I had no idea he was so wild. He isn't around me."

"Sometimes horses have been mistreated by men and will let a woman handle them."

"I suppose that might be the reason." So many questions and doubts filled her mind. "Pa, why do I find submission so difficult? Sometimes I think God must have made a mistake when He created me. I should have been born a man so I could do something like build a ranch in this new land or…" She couldn't finish. Didn't even know what she wanted to say. Except the life she would return to seemed constricting. Rules were fine. She knew they served a good purpose. But she craved so much more than being a proper lady. She'd found it here on the ranch, in the midst of the raw prairie, but it would be denied her.

Pa gripped her shoulder. "Daughter, God makes no mistakes. He certainly didn't make one when He created you. 'You are fearfully and wonderfully made,' as it says in Psalm one hundred and thirty-nine, verse fourteen."

She waggled her head. She couldn't argue with what God's word said, yet so often it felt like she didn't belong in her life.

"Jenny, you must learn to accept God's will in your life. Once you do, you will find peace and contentment."

"I know." She would obey her parents, and thus obey God, only she didn't find peace and contentment, she just found emptiness. "I know." Pcacc would surely come once she was back home actually doing what she had promised.

Burke stood back, unnoticed as Jenny led her father toward Ebony's pen. He'd tried to get near the critter. He'd seen the men at various times venture close. But only Jenny had been able to gentle the gelding.

Lucky sidled up to him. "If she can tame Ebony, is there any doubt she could tame the land or at least become a part of it?"

"Sing with it, you mean?"

"Something like that."

"I don't know. And it doesn't matter. Her pa has plans for her."

"The man seems reasonable enough. Might be willing to change those plans if he saw something better for her." Lucky sauntered away, leaving Burke struggling with his dreams—dreams he'd buried when Flora ended up in the asylum, but dreams that hadn't died. They'd been part of his plans from the beginning—a family to carry on what he carved out of this land, a woman to share the journey.

Would they ever die?

Did they need to?

He turned into the interior of the barn and perched on the edge of the empty manger. Did God care about what he wanted? Did He take any interest in helping a man find his dream? Win the heart of a woman?

He shook his head. Seemed like such a petty thing to bother God with. After all, He must be busy with more important things like running the universe and helping seriously ill people.

He had no doubt God had a hand in helping him find Paquette. Several times since then he'd made little requests, almost fearfully. God had not sent angels or done anything spectacular, but always Burke had found the answer after he prayed. Was it coincidence? Or the result of asking?

Jenny fully believed God was concerned with the details of a person's life. He half believed it. Wanted to believe it fully.

But if he did, what would stop him from asking God to allow Jenny to decide to stay? His heart tightened as if squeezed by a miserly fist. Mama cat rubbed against him and he stroked her mindlessly.

He couldn't ask because he feared the answer. Acknowledging love carried an inherent risk. Always there was a danger of losing the loved one. Not necessarily the same way Flora had been lost. But he'd lost his parents. He'd lost Lena. Life carried a risk.

Yes, life carried a risk. And he didn't intend to avoid life because of that. In fact, he welcomed the challenges and risks. It made life worth living.

Why should love be any different? Certainly it was worth whatever risks it came with.

He loved Jenny. With a love as high as the Dakota sky, as wide as the Dakota horizon and as deep as the soil beneath his feet. He had never loved anyone more. Certainly the emotion he felt for Flora was more convenience than this passion wrapping about his heart and binding it with bands of steel.

But what was he to do about it?

Lucky said he thought Mr. Archibald seemed a reasonable man. But would he consider a request from Burke for Jenny's hand a reasonable thing?

His heart overflowing with hope and love, he bowed his head. "Lord God, You are so big, so powerful that it boggles my mind that You would bother with my little problems."

Mama cat meowed and pushed against him, perhaps thinking Burke talked to her. He gently nudged her aside.

"But it seems You're big enough, powerful enough to have time for each of us. So I come to You with one request. Help me find favor with Jenny's pa. Help him see that she belongs out here with me."

That evening after everyone had gone to bed, Jenny pulled out her Bible and looked up the verse Pa had quoted. She read the Psalm. The last two verses seemed to grab her by the chin and pull her attention to them.

"Search me, O God; and know my heart: try me, and know my thoughts: And see if there be any wicked way in me, and lead me in the way everlasting."

The words went round and round in her head until they settled down solidly, forcing her to acknowledge them.

Her love of the prairie did not come from wickedness in her heart. Nor did her love for Burke. Perhaps, if God had made no mistakes in creating her with a heart that sought adventure and new things, He had done so for the express purpose of preparing her to share in such a life as this.

But would Burke withdraw the interest he could not hide if he knew the whole truth about her?

She must find out. She would tell Burke everything, then if he didn't turn away in disgust, she would tell Pa she couldn't honestly marry Ted with her heart yearning after Burke.

She prayed a long time before she fell asleep, asking for guidance and direction in her plan.

Chapter Thirteen

Jenny's heart beat erratically throughout breakfast the next morning as she considered her plan. She'd never confessed the results of her foolhardiness to anyone. Ma and Pa knew, of course. But not even her sisters knew the events of that dreadful day.

She silently prayed throughout the meal and afterwards as she helped clean the kitchen. *Lord, give me strength to be honest.*

Pa returned to fixing things around the house. Miss Morgan sat at the table playing with Meggie. Paquette disappeared to her room. Jenny had no excuse for delay. Didn't want one. She wanted to get it over with and live with the consequences. If Burke turned away in disgust...

During the long night of soul searching she had come to several conclusions. Although certain of her decisions, she did not anticipate her parents' reactions and she grabbed at her stomach as if she could stop the feeling that her entire insides dropped out the bottom. If Burke rejected her after her story, she would have no choice but to return with Pa. Though she would not marry Ted. She would tell Pa she'd sooner be a spinster than marry out of duty. Surely Pa would understand.

Her hope was a fervent plea. Pa would expect her to obey. But she could not. Her heart would never belong to Ted.

"I'm stepping out for a few minutes," she informed Miss Morgan.

"Me come." Meggie started to scramble from the bench.

Miss Morgan caught her but before she could say anything, Jenny bent over and touched Meggie's chin. "Not this time, sweetie. You stay here and play." This was not a time for little girls to be present.

Gathering together her courage, her faith and determination, she stepped outdoors and glanced around wondering where she could find Burke. She'd kept close watch to see if he rode out of the yard and had not seen him but perhaps he'd escaped her notice. She chuckled. He'd have to be invisible for her to miss him. She hadn't taken her gaze from the window for more than a fleeting second or two since he walked out the door after breakfast.

Burke had gone into the barn, left again with Mama cat meowing at his heels. She'd smiled as he bent and petted the cat. She saw his mouth moving and knew he talked to the animal. Burke was a man strong enough, determined and tough enough to challenge this new land—a land he confessed was unfriendly to most, yet gentle enough to pay an old cat attention and to hold a sad little girl close.

And perhaps to forgive a young woman for her sinfulness.

She bound that hope about her heart and stood listening for anything to indicate his presence. A sound drew her attention and she smiled. Burke whistling as he worked. She headed toward the sound and found him leaning against the handle of a pitchfork, staring into the distance like a man studying his world, planning how to conquer it.

He turned at her approach and smiled, a tentativeness

about his eyes. "Hi." Perhaps he expected her to announce she and Pa were leaving to return to their plans…plans that included Ted.

She faltered. What would his response be when she informed him Ted was no longer a part of her plans? Her heart headed for the bottom again at the thought of what else she must tell him.

"Did you need something?"

"Can we talk?"

He hesitated. Caution filled his eyes and then he masked all expression. "Certainly. Want to sit?" He waved toward the wall of the barn and waited for her to arrange herself on the grassy area, her back pressed to the rough boards, then he sat next to her, his legs stretched out before him. He took off his hat, laid it in his lap and tipped his head against the barn.

For a moment neither of them spoke.

She closed her eyes and let the sun warm her. Prayed for guidance and strength.

"What can I do for you?" he prodded.

She sucked in the warm air, filling her lungs endlessly. Still she felt breathless. "You've accused me of letting my father plan my life."

"It's none of my business."

She hoped he'd change his mind about that. "You were right. I—" She'd rehearsed this speech but now couldn't think how to start it. "I thought I had to. Not only because I thought I should obey my parents but because going my own way led me into a pack of trouble."

He shifted slightly, turning so he could watch her as she spoke. Unable to face him, she ducked her head.

"I can see you getting yourself into predicaments." The amusement in his voice caused her to jerk her gaze to his face. She clung to the way his eyes softened as he smiled. "Seems to me you've been heedless of the dangers a few times in our short acquaintance."

"I have not."

"Ebony?"

"I didn't know that was a danger."

"Never crossed your mind. That's what I mean. You don't even acknowledge risks." He said it like it was something she should be proud of.

"That's why I try to always think what Ma or Pa would advise before I act. You see…" She tightened her fists and forced herself to go on. "I learned a very difficult lesson about the folly of not listening."

He nodded, his gaze intent, demanding, waiting.

She ducked her head again and tried to remember how she planned to tell this sordid tale. "I was fifteen when I learned the hard way why I should heed my parents in all things." Almost four years ago and still she fought to make the lesson stick. "I want to tell you about it." To see if he could stand to look at her after her story. "The circus had come to town. Ma and Pa promised to take us the next day but I wanted to see the animals unloaded, the tents put up. I wanted to experience the excitement." Her voice fell to a whisper and for the life of her, she couldn't make it any stronger. "Pa warned me to stay away. Said it was a rough place." She cleared her throat and forced herself to go on. "I disobeyed him and went with some of my classmates."

It had seemed so exciting. They'd laughed as they met away from their homes. The boys pushed each other and roughhoused. She and the other girl giggled and raced after them.

"At first it was fun. To see the tents staked into place and then lifted. They used an elephant to help raise the big top." She'd stared open-mouthed at the lumbering grace of the huge animal and the way it responded to the handler. "We toured the place. Saw the caged lions. Listened to the funny way the people spoke to each other. They seemed to have a language all their own. We watched the booths being set up. It was so exciting." She shuddered.

He touched her hands. She didn't realize how she twisted them until he claimed them and stilled them. "But it didn't end up exciting? Is that what you're telling me?"

"I'm trying to, yes. You see I was so fascinated with the elephant. I said I wanted to see it again. I marched back thinking everyone followed me. The animal was standing with a chain around one leg and munching on hay. Did you know they pick up their food with their trunk and then tuck it into their mouths?"

He squeezed her hands. "Never thought much about it."

"I couldn't tear myself away. I wanted so bad to touch the animal but I didn't dare." She tried to swallow but her throat wouldn't work. She opened her mouth and sucked hard at the still, waiting air. "The handler noticed my interest. 'Want to touch me beastie?' He was a big man with a red beard, and eyes that seemed to see right through me. I knew I should say no but I could not. My foolish desire to experience everything, you know. I giggled and said I would. 'Give me your hand and stay close to me.' I only hesitated a moment. Then I let him pull me forward. 'Sheba, meet a new friend,' he crooned and the elephant lifted its trunk and reached for me. It was like touching a snake. Only warm." She gasped for air and forced herself to calm down.

"I looked back to tell my friends and that's when I realized I was alone. They hadn't followed. And that's when the man jerked me around and—" She tried to keep her voice steady. "He pulled me against him and touched

me—" Her cheeks felt about to melt off her face at her re-
vulsion at the way he had touched forbidden places. "He
said he could show me things a lot more exciting than
an old elephant. I tried to pull away but he laughed—an
awful sound."

She clamped her hands over her ears as if she could
somehow block the memory from her mind.

"He forced me into a little tent. I tried to get away."
The words came out in hot gasps. "He only laughed
again. Wouldn't stop laughing. He—" She clutched at
the material of her dress at her neck and twisted. "He
grabbed my dress and tore it."

She wrapped her arms across her chest. "He touched me."

Her skin felt cold and clammy. He'd pushed her backward. "He had a cot in the corner." The cold metal of the
frame had pressed into her calves. Hard, unforgiving, icy
like winter iron. Press your tongue to it and stick. She
couldn't get away. His huge body blocked her escape. His
hands were everywhere. She couldn't get warm and vibrated with the chill that burrowed into the marrow of her
bones and encased her heart. Her lungs cried for air but
there was none. Only a contrast of hot and cold, fear and
coarse laughter. She tried to squirm away. Fought like a cor-
nered animal. Scratched. He caught her hands and laughed.

Trapped her.

Her teeth rattled as fear and loathing and remembrance
sucked at her until she felt nothing else.

"Jenny?" He touched her shoulder. Gentle.

She shrank back.

"Jenny. I won't hurt you. Ever."

Not the growling sneer of the man. Burke. His voice
soft, kind.

"Jenny. It's okay. Whatever happened, it's okay." He
edged closer and took her hand.

Her fingers remained stiff and unyielding in his grasp. She couldn't respond to his touch. But she couldn't pull away either. God help her but she needed to feel a connection with him. For years she had shut her heart to feeling anything but determination to obey.

"I haven't finished my story." Her words shook as badly as she did.

"You don't need to."

"I do." He must hear it all and then decide for himself who she was.

"He had to release me to reach for his trousers. It was all I needed. I escaped and raced for the flap and right into Pa's arms. He had come looking for me. He took off his jacket and wrapped it around me and made me wait outside. I don't know what he said. All I know is the sheriff arrested the man and he was sent to jail."

"And you ended up afraid of doing anything risky. Afraid to make a decision apart from your parents."

She nodded. It was true. She feared her own thoughts and actions.

He slipped his arm across her shoulders and pressed her close. She didn't realize how badly she shook until he held her against him, catching the vibrations of her body in his grasp and calming them.

Burke fought an urge to stand up and bellow an angry protest. He hoped the man suffered his just deserts in some rotten jail cell. Only her quick thinking had prevented her from being violated in the worst possible way. The disgusting actions of the man had nevertheless violated her in other ways. Filled her with shame. Quenched her bold spirit. Made her see it as a bad thing.

He held her close, careful not to do anything that

would make her feel threatened, absorbing her shudders into his own body.

"So you see why I have felt I should let Pa decide my future."

Actually, he didn't but how was he to explain that to her? Her trauma was real, as were her fears about making another mistake. "You were a foolish child. You are now a responsible, wiser adult. Even so, foolish child or not, you were not responsible for how that man acted. Don't you think it's time to stop blaming yourself?"

She grew still as if considering his words.

This was one time he needed God's help. And felt sure he could ask for and receive it. *Lord God, you see her injured spirit. Heal it. And if I can say anything to help, please give me the words.*

"What I see is a child of fifteen, excited, naturally enough, about a circus, and an evil man who did wrong. And now I see a young woman who is adventuresome and eager, trying to deny those God-given attributes."

"God-given? Do you really think so?"

He chuckled. "Are you not the one who taught me God is interested in the details of our lives? That He not only sees the big things but the little? Now I'm not saying you're unimportant, but if small details and big events are equal in His scheme of things, would you not then accept that He who made the world and everything in it and declared it good, does not think the same about you? Does He not declare His work good?"

She shifted so she could look into his face without leaving his embrace. "Burke, you really believe that?"

He smiled down at her, loving her like he never thought possible. "Don't you?" *Thank you God for giving me words that help.*

"For everyone else. Not for me. Though I am getting

closer. Yesterday I finally acknowledged that perhaps God made no mistake in how He made me."

She met his eyes openly as if inviting him to see her wholly, completely, with no secrets between them. He searched past the places he'd been before, wondering what this meant.

She pushed away, slipped from under his arm and shifted around to face him squarely.

He ached a protest, feeling more than her physical withdrawal.

"What do you think of Miss Morgan as a nanny?"

Her question caught him by surprise. When had anything about their discussion been about a nanny? "She'll do. Why? Do you have some concerns?"

"No. She seems adequate."

"But?"

She pulled in air hard enough to flutter his hair. "It's just…" She ducked her head and didn't finish.

He caught her chin and lifted her head. For a moment she kept her eyelids lowered, then realizing his patient waiting, slowly opened her eyes and met his gaze. His heart leapt for his throat at the hungry longing he saw. "It's just what?"

"Well—" She lowered her gaze then jerked it up and watched him with a demanding expression. "I wondered if I might reconsider and ask for the position of nanny." Her words came out in a rush and she stared, eager and excited as she waited for his response.

He dropped his finger, sat back against the barn wall.

She looked disappointed. "Of course, if that doesn't suit you…."

It didn't suit. He didn't want her as a nanny. He wanted more. So much more. But first he must talk to her father. "Have you mentioned this to your pa?"

"Not yet. I thought I'd see what you thought first."

"Seems he's rather set on you returning with him."

"I know." She sounded so disheartened. "I guess you can understand his concern."

His insides rebelled at the defeat in his voice. "No, I'm afraid I don't. What does he have to be concerned about?" He leaned close, wanting to make this very clear. "Jenny, you are a strong young woman. One of the few I feel with certainty who could face this rough land and survive." She soaked up his words, drank of the assurance he offered. He leaned closer and gently kissed her. Rejoiced when she didn't jerk away in fright. He lingered only a second, despite the demands of his heart. "I'll speak to your pa."

"I'll speak to him, too."

He wanted to linger, enjoy this quiet connection they had so recently reached, but someone called from the barn and her pa answered. It was time to get on with the pressing issues of life.

Jenny crossed the yard. Her heart felt scrubbed inside and out. Burke hadn't shrunk away from her. He'd pulled her close and held her. Always she had felt a little dirty, soiled by what happened. Her parents had forbidden it to be mentioned. Not that she ever wanted to talk about it. But telling Burke had left her feeling cleansed and whole. *Thank you, God.*

Pa sat on the veranda watching her approach.

Her steps slowed at the way he looked. Had she done something wrong? Besides disobey his instruction not to speak of the incident.

"You have that look in your eyes," he said.

She faltered as if she'd been caught doing something

inappropriate. She realized she always felt like she was being accused—not Pa's fault but by her guilty reaction.

She plunked down beside him. "I told Burke about going to the circus."

"Why would you do that?" His words were soft but faintly accusing.

She couldn't say the real reason—that she hoped he would say it made no difference. That he found her acceptable as a nanny. Perhaps more. Oh, how she longed for more. "He was always mocking me for letting you choose my future husband. I wanted him to understand why I did."

"I see. And what was his response?"

"He didn't call me a fallen woman or anything."

"Has anyone else?" A faint hurt tone came to his voice.

"Pa, I've always felt dirty. Defiled."

"I hope you don't think that's how your ma and I felt. We blamed ourselves for not warning you about such men. We only wanted to shelter you."

She understood that. "It was my own fault for letting my curiosity and wildness control my actions." She sucked in air, wanting to explain more. "I've always felt anything that excited me or filled me with joy was wrong and would lead to something bad."

Pa hung his head. "I never meant to make you afraid. And certainly never wanted to quench your spirit. Only guide it into a safe channel."

"I know, Pa. But there is something you must understand. Something I've learned about myself out here. You assured me God doesn't make mistakes when He creates us. 'We are fearfully and wonderfully made.' For a long time I've wondered if I was the exception."

"No, daughter—"

"Let me finish. Last night I took a good hard look at what I was becoming. And I didn't think it was what

God meant me to be. Burke says it takes a special kind of person to be a pioneer. Women, especially, find it hard because they miss the comforts of home and find the prairie lonely and empty. I don't. I love the challenge." She faced her father squarely. "Pa, I believe God has uniquely equipped me to be one of those who conquers this land." She grabbed his wrists as if she could communicate her urgency through her touch. "I don't want to go back with you. I can't marry Ted."

He looked as if she'd stabbed him.

"Pa, it isn't anything to do with you and Ma. I feel whole here. I am excited about the challenges this land presents. I love the wind and the wide-open spaces. Pa...." Her voice fell to an agonized whisper. "I want you to release me from my promise to marry Ted. I want your blessing to stay here."

"But you agreed." Pa paused as if considering his words. "I fear you are letting your heart rule your head."

"Not rule it, Pa. I've finally learned to be happy with who I am. Can't you see that and allow it?" she spoke gently, not wanting to disappoint her father but knowing she much be all she was created to be.

Pa sighed heavily and pushed to his feet. "I need to consider your request. I think I'll take a little walk and seek God's guidance."

She watched him go. It hurt to disappoint him but she could no longer be content to be a meek shadow of herself, hiding behind her father's wishes. She prayed God would intervene. That she could begin to rejoice in the woman she was created to be.

Her heart cracked open and bled a bit. She would stay as a nanny but she wanted so much more. She wanted to share every aspect of Burke's life as his wife and helpmate.

Chapter Fourteen

As Jenny crossed the yard to speak to her father, Burke prayed the man would set her free to be all she was meant to be. From the corner of the barn he watched them talking.

When the man walked away on his own, he prayed some more and waited. He tried to busy himself so Lucky wouldn't offer any comments, but there was little he could do without fear of missing Mr. Archibald's return to the yard.

"Little lady got your ropes in a knot?" Lucky said.

"Nope." He rearranged the reins and harnesses hanging near the door and kept his head down while glancing in the direction Jenny's pa had gone.

"Won't be getting unknotted until you admit what's right in front of your nose."

"Maybe I already have."

"Huh. How's that?" The man abandoned all pretense of work and came to hover at Burke's side.

"I'm waiting for her pa to come back so I can talk to him."

Lucky grabbed his hat and slapped it against his thigh. "Yahoo!" His yell sent the pigeons in the loft into a flurry.

"Boss, the boys and I figured you were going to let a good thing go just because of what happened to Flora." He clapped Burke on the back. "Nice to see you come to your senses."

Burke rolled his eyes. "Nice of you and the boys to be so concerned about my affairs."

Lucky chortled. "We prefer to work for a happy man." And still chortling, he sauntered away.

"There's been nothing decided yet. I have to talk to her pa."

Lucky turned to face him. "The man looks to be reasonable. And what's more, he cares about his daughter's happiness." He waved and headed for the bunkhouse.

Nice to realize he had the support of the men.

Mr. Archibald appeared on the trail. Now to face the man who had a say in Jenny's future. *Lord God, help me find the right words.*

He waited a few more minutes then strode out to meet Jenny's father. "Sir, I would like to talk to you."

"Go ahead."

"I know you have plans for your daughter."

"I only want her to be happy."

Exactly the opening he needed. "Will she be, back East? Her heart seeks adventure."

Mr. Archibald stopped and faced him squarely, his eyes boring into Burke, demanding nothing but honesty. "Will she be happy here?"

Burke faltered, remembering Flora. He swallowed hard. "I would do my best to make her so, but I have to be honest and tell you I failed in the past."

Mr. Archibald's eyes narrowed. "Perhaps you should tell me about it before I render a decision."

"I'm sure Jenny has told you I sent for Flora Larson intending to marry her. I knew her before I came west and we corresponded for several years. However—" He went on to confess he'd expected too much of her. "I blame myself for her current condition." His voice revealed the degree of his pain. "As do her parents."

Jenny's pa squeezed Burke's shoulder. "Son, I expect your guilt is misplaced. From what I've heard at the store, I understand that even before Flora came out here she had spent some time convalescing."

Burke knew he meant because of her mental condition.

Mr. Archibald seemed to consider his next words. "I don't normally like to repeat things I overhear, but in this case I think I should. I believe her parents hoped the change of scenery would help her. Unfortunately, it didn't. But they have no right to blame you. Her aunt and grandmother are in asylums as well."

It wasn't his fault. Flora had been weak in her mind before she came west. Seems there was a weakness in the family. A great burden of guilt slipped from his shoulders. "Thank you for telling me. I've blamed myself, wondered if any woman could live this life."

Jenny's pa laughed. "I expect you've had cause to change your mind on that score."

Burke grinned widely, his insides bubbling with pleasure at the memories crowding his mind. "Jenny has challenged my opinion more than once."

The man studied him long and hard. "Are you asking for her hand in marriage?"

"With your permission, sir. I understand I don't live up to your expectations of what you want for Jenny's future, but I love her and we seem…" He struggled to explain how he felt as if she pulled up beside him and cheered him on the way, bent her shoulder to the challenges. "She would be a great encouragement to me. And I would do my best to see her life is full of joy." He glanced past the man to the rolling grassland. "I haven't mentioned this to her yet. I wanted your permission first."

"Son, you have my permission and blessing." Mr. Archibald held out his hand and Burke shook it firmly.

Jenny watched the men talking, saw them shake hands. "Oh Lord, let Pa agree to let me stay." She waited for Pa to return to the house.

"Jenny, my dear, I wanted only to protect you, assure your happiness but I see you are ready to determine what that requires on your own."

She realized she'd forgotten to breathe and sucked in air. "You aren't holding me to my promise to return home and marry Ted?"

"Doesn't seem to me it would be quite fair to Ted." He chuckled. "Now go see your young man and talk to him."

She stretched up and kissed Pa on the cheek. "Thank you, Pa. I love you."

Pa hugged her quickly. "I love you, too, Pepper." He released her.

She spun from his arms and rushed toward Burke, who waited on the path. It took all her rigid self-control not to fling herself into his arms. Was he going to ask her to stay as a nanny or— she faltered a step—share his life completely and wholly?

His eyes invited her. Suddenly she felt wooden. Her steps slowed as he took off his hat and pushed a hand through his hair.

His lovely shiny black hair. She'd admired it from the beginning. It had grown some since then, which only made him more handsome. She drank in every detail. His lean strength, the way he stood as if he owned the land and dared anyone to challenge him about it. The way his muscles strained at his shirtsleeves as he crossed his arms. She would never get tired of looking at him. She scrubbed her lips together, surprised at how numb they were. Without words she prayed for God's blessing on her love for Burke.

Of their own accord her feet moved forward until she had only to lift her hand to touch him.

Love made her ache to do so.

Uncertainty stifled her reaction. She didn't know what his plans were.

He took her hand and pulled it through his arm, patting her fingers to the warm strength of his forearm and keeping his palm on top of her hand. "Shall we walk?"

She nodded, unable to speak past the expectant lump in her throat.

He turned them toward the corrals. They passed Ebony's pen. He whinnied at Jenny then snorted and reared at her escort.

She chuckled. "It's only pretend."

"He figures he belongs to you and he's not willing to share."

The regretful note in his voice sent her nerves into eager anticipation.

They skirted the barn and returned to the spot they had shared a few hours earlier. Once they were out of sight of the house and bunkhouse, he stopped and turned toward her, his hands gentle on her upper arms.

Slowly, her heart crowding her ribs so she had trouble breathing, she lifted her face to him.

A smile lifted his mouth and creased his eyes. He studied her slowly as if memorizing every detail of her features.

Her skin warmed as his gaze checked her eyebrows, admired her cheeks, lingered on her lips until she ached for him to end this misery of waiting, and kiss her.

Then slowly, almost reluctantly, he brought his gaze to her eyes. She floated in his look.

"Your Pa has given me his blessing to ask you to stay."

Stay? That's all. "As a nanny?"

He blinked, surprised, then chuckled softly, a sound that played harp strings along her nerves. "I hope much more than that. Jenny—" He caught her chin in his fingers, his touch making music in every corner of her heart. "I knew you were different the first time I laid eyes on you."

Remembering his dire warning that day and his insistence for days after her arrival that she didn't belong here, she found the ability to quirk her brows. "Sure could have fooled me."

He lifted one shoulder and looked sheepish, making her want to stroke his cheek and assure him she understood.

"I tried to convince us both, but I'm so grateful you didn't pay me any heed because I can't imagine life without you." He swallowed hard and she perceived his nervousness, his uncertainty.

She touched his shoulder. The twitch of his muscles as he reacted to her touch thrilled her. He was a man who would stand strong through the fiercest storm. Her touch seemed to drive away his hesitation.

"Jenny, I love you. I want to marry you and spend the rest of my life with you."

Her heart exploded inside her chest with such force she couldn't speak, couldn't breathe, couldn't move.

"Jenny, will you marry me?"

Blood flowed again, warm and vibrant, just as her life would be. "Burke Edwards, I love you heart and soul and mind. Of course I will marry you."

His face filled with such joy she almost couldn't look

at him. To know and share such love the rest of her life....
It was more than she could believe possible.

"Jenny," he whispered, his words round with awe. "I
am the happiest man alive."

And then he finally kissed her, his lips warm and
promising. She wrapped her arms about him and gave
herself freely to the kiss, silently vowing to honor and
cherish him the rest of her life.

Finally, he pulled back. "I love you so much."

She stroked his cheek then.

He turned his face and pressed his lips to her palm.

"I have loved you since I saw you on the train, even
though I feared it was wrong." Her words sang from her
lips.

"Nothing about our love has ever been wrong or ever
will be. Not with God as our partner."

He drew her to the spot where they'd sat before, and
they sat side by side. He draped his arm over her shoulder and pulled her close. She snuggled against his chest,
feeling the rise and fall of each breath and hearing the
beat of his heart beneath her ear.

She had found a safe place.

They talked of their hopes and plans and dreams. She
loved him before, but as they opened their hearts to one
another something eternal and precious grew between
them, making them one in spirit.

They talked until the sun came round and blasted them
in the face.

"Can you believe we've been here all afternoon?"
Burke said.

"We'll enjoy many more times like this, sharing our
joys...and no doubt some sorrows." Her heart rejoiced
to know that whatever came, they would find strength
through being together.

He kissed her nose and cheeks then claimed her mouth for several seconds before he pulled her to her feet. Hand in hand they wandered back to the house.

Ebony repeated his performance of acting spooky. He stopped as soon as they passed and hurried to the fence, whinnying for Jenny to stop and pet him. She laughed. "He's determined to be friends with no one but me."

"He's yours."

She drew to a halt. "You're giving him to me?"

"Might as well." He tweaked her chin. "He thinks he belongs to you already."

"Can I ride him?"

Burke grinned. "Do you know how to ride?"

"No, but I can learn."

His eyes flashed with amusement. "Maybe you could start on something more gentle and if you prove yourself a capable horsewoman—"

She didn't let him finish. "Not if—when—I prove my ability."

"You will always face a challenge with the idea of conquering whatever obstacle lies in your way, won't you?" He pulled her to his side as they resumed their journey to the house.

She didn't respond right away as she sorted her thoughts. "God made me this way and I am learning to be grateful for the strengths He gave me."

He hugged her and paused to kiss her upturned mouth. "I will spend the rest of my life being grateful."

Epilogue

Pa's one stipulation had been they go back to Center City to marry, allowing Ma to meet Jenny's future husband, so they boarded the train heading east, Miss Morgan accompanying them as she also returned home.

Paquette had miraculously recovered all her faculties and would cook for the men while Burke and Jenny were away. Paquette had shuffled up to Jenny one evening before their departure. "I leave after you back, me?"

Jenny heard the doubt and fear in the older woman's voice. She hugged the tiny woman. "I hope you won't. I want you to stay. I need you to teach me everything I need to know about living on the prairie. Besides, don't you think we work well as a team?"

Paquette beamed with joy. "We good, us. I stay."

Pa had wired Ma warning her of their arrival, suggesting she prepare for a wedding as quickly as possible.

Ma met them at the station. Jenny flew into her arms. "Ma, it's good to see you."

Ma hugged her hard. "Am I to lose you to a wild man from the west?"

"'Fraid so, Ma. But I think you'll like him." She signaled Burke forward. "Ma, here he is. The man from the west."

Burke took Ma's hand in both his. "Mrs. Archibald, I want to thank you for raising such a beautiful, sweet woman."

Ma beamed and darted a look at Jenny that said she approved.

A week later she stood at Burke's side in the manse and faced the preacher. Her sister, Mary, and her husband stood up with them. The week had been packed with visiting family and showing Burke the store. Jenny smiled as she recalled their first visit. Ted stood behind the counter, his head high, his nose tilted slightly upward. Jenny hated to face him. She'd never spoken a word of promise to him, but she knew Pa had discussed the future and Ted had reason to think she might be at his side.

Burke, sensing her hesitation, strode forward. "You're the efficient young man I've heard so much about."

Ted's nose lowered and he smiled. He liked to be recognized as efficient and forward thinking. After that, the meeting went easily and Ted hid any disappointment at her upcoming marriage. Jenny hoped he'd find someone who touched his heart as much as Burke did hers.

She smiled up at Burke, knowing her heart filled her eyes and revealed the depths of her love. She still found it difficult to contain. She could hardly wait to get back to the ranch where she could run into the prairie and shout her joy without causing people to turn and stare.

Burke met her smile with dark, calm steadiness. Her eyes watered at the look he gave her, full of promise and tenderness.

Then the preacher spoke words that bound them together until death. "I now pronounce you man and wife. You may kiss your bride."

Burke did so, his hunger and love matched by her own.

"From this day forth," he murmured against her ear as they ended the kiss, aware of their audience.

Her eyes overflowed with joy. "Our great adventure is about to begin."

He laughed. "I thought it already had. You've led me on a merry chase already."

"No more than you've led me." She hugged his arm and pressed close to him. She would never stop being grateful for his quiet acceptance of what she'd always thought was the worst moment of her life. It no longer controlled her thoughts and actions. She felt free and fulfilled. A feeling that would no doubt multiply over and over as she shared her life with Burke.

Ma had insisted on preparing tea for them. Only family and a few friends attended as Burke was insistent they leave on the next train.

Sadness mingled with her joy as she kissed her family good-bye. Burke held Meggie in his arms and waited, patient and understanding of her tears.

Pa took them to the station. Here was her last and hardest good-bye. He held her tight. "Be happy, Pepper."

He shook Burke's hand. "I expect she'll make your life interesting."

Burke chuckled. "I'm counting on it."

Pa reached under the seat, pulled out a long package and handed it to Jenny. "A good-bye gift. Open it on the train."

Jenny's throat grew so tight she could hardly speak. "Thank you for everything, Pa."

"All aboard!"

They hurried into the car and found seats where they could see Pa and wave to him until he was out of sight.

Burke caught her hand.

"You'll be back often for visits. I promise."

She faced her husband. "Thank you, but I expect I'll hate to be away from the ranch very much. I might miss out on something." Meggie, exhausted, fell asleep in Burke's arms.

"Aren't you going to open the parcel?" Burke nodded toward the package Pa had given her.

She undid the string and folded back the paper. At first she didn't know what it was—red silk and sticks. Then she laughed. "It's a kite." A note lay on top and she opened it. "Go and fly like you were meant to."

"I once told Pa the prairie wind made me want to be a kite and fly free." Her voice thickened with emotion.

His eyes grew troubled. "I hope you won't find marriage clips your wings."

She laughed. "Sharing my life with you will be the biggest adventure ever. I feel like I am flying every time you kiss me."

"Me, too. And it's a wonderful sensation." He pulled her close and kissed her briefly. "I'll do it well and thoroughly when we get home."

Home. The nicest word in the world, Jenny decided.

Burke tucked her head against his shoulder. "Did I tell you how I thank God every day for bringing you to me? You taught me He cares about every detail of my life."

He had told her but she would never get tired of hearing it. "You have given me so much. Besides your love, the greatest gift you've given me is the assurance that I can be who I am without fear of criticism."

He kissed her again, briefly, gently. "I wouldn't want you to be anything else."

* * * * *

SPECIAL EXCERPT FROM

Love Inspired.
SUSPENSE

*An Amish widow and a lawman in disguise
team up to take down a crime ring.*

Read on for a sneak preview of
Amish Covert Operation *by Meghan Carver,
available July 2019 from Love Inspired Suspense.*

The steady rhythm of the bicycle did little to calm her nerves. Ominous dark blue clouds propelled Katie Schwartz forward.

A slight breeze ruffled the leaves, sending a few skittering across the road. But then it died, leaving an unnatural stillness in the hush of the oncoming storm. Beads of perspiration dotted her forehead.

Should she call out? Announce herself?

Gingerly, she got off her bicycle and stepped up to a window, clutching her skirt in one hand and the window trim in the other. Through her shoes, her toes gripped the edge of the rickety crate. Desperation to stay upright and not teeter off sent a surge of adrenaline coursing through her as she swiped a hand across the grimy window of the hunter's shack. The crate dipped, and Katie grasped the frame of the window again.

"Timothy?" she whispered to herself. "Where are you?"

With the crate stabilized, she swiped over the glass again and squinted inside. But all that stared back at her was more grime. The crate tipped again, and she grabbed at the window trim before she could tumble off.

Movement inside snagged her attention, although she couldn't make out figures. Voices filtered through the window, one louder than the other. What was going on in there? And was Timothy involved?

Her nose touched the glass in her effort to see inside. A face suddenly appeared in the window. It was distorted by the cracks in the glass, but it appeared to be her *bruder*. A moment later, the face disappeared.

She jumped from the crate and headed toward the corner of the cabin. Now that he had seen her, he had to come out and explain himself and return with her, stopping whatever this clandestine meeting was all about.

A man dressed in plain clothing stepped out through the door.

"Timothy!" But the wild look in his eyes stopped her from speaking further.

And then she saw it. A gun was pressed into his back.

"Katie! Run! Go!"

Don't miss
Amish Covert Operation *by Meghan Carver,*
available July 2019 wherever
Love Inspired® *Suspense books and ebooks are sold.*

www.LoveInspired.com

WE HOPE YOU
ENJOYED THIS

LOVE INSPIRED® SUSPENSE BOOK.

Discover more **heart-pounding** romances of **danger** and **faith** from the Love Inspired Suspense series.

Be sure to look for all six Love Inspired Suspense books every month.

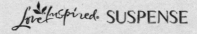 SUSPENSE

www.LoveInspired.com

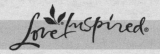
*What happens when the nanny harbors a secret that
could change everything?*

Read on for a sneak preview of
The Nanny's Secret Baby,
*the next book in Lee Tobin McClain's
Redemption Ranch miniseries.*

Any day she could see Sammy was a good day. But she was pretty
sure Jack was about to turn down her nanny offer. And then she'd
have to tell Penny she couldn't take the apartment, and leave.

The thought of being away from her son after spending precious
time with him made her chest ache, and she blinked away unexpected
tears as she approached Jack and Sammy.

Sammy didn't look up at her. He was holding up one finger near
his own face, moving it back and forth.

Jack caught his hand. "Say hi, Sammy! Here's Aunt Arianna."

Sammy tugged his hand away and continued to move his finger
in front of his face.

"Sammy, come on."

Sammy turned slightly away from his father and refocused on
his fingers.

"It's okay," Arianna said, because she could see the beginnings of
a meltdown. "He doesn't need to greet me. What's up?"

"Look," he said, "I've been thinking about what you said." He
rubbed a hand over the back of his neck, clearly uncomfortable.

Sammy's hand moved faster, and he started humming a wordless
tune. It was almost as if he could sense the tension between Arianna
and Jack.

"It's okay, Jack," she said. "I get it. My being your nanny was
a foolish idea." Foolish, but oh so appealing. She ached to pick

Sammy up and hold him, to know that she could spend more time with him, help him learn, get him support for his special needs.

But it wasn't her right.

"Actually," he said, "that's what I wanted to talk about. It does seem sort of foolish, but…I think I'd like to offer you the job."

She stared at him, her eyes filling. "Oh, Jack," she said, her voice coming out in a whisper. Had he really just said she could have the job?

Behind her, the rumble and snap of tables being folded and chairs being stacked, the cheerful conversation of parishioners and community people, faded to an indistinguishable murmur.

She was going to be able to be with her son. Every day. She reached out and stroked Sammy's soft hair, and even though he ignored her touch, her heart nearly melted with the joy of being close to him.

Jack's brow wrinkled. "On a trial basis," he said. "Just for the rest of the summer, say."

Of course. She pulled her hand away from Sammy and drew in a deep breath. She needed to calm down and take things one step at a time. Yes, leaving him at the end of the summer would break her heart ten times more. But even a few weeks with her son was more time than she deserved.

With God all things are possible. The pastor had said it, and she'd just witnessed its truth. She was being given a job, the care of her son and a place to live.

It was a blessing, a huge one. But it came at a cost: she was going to need to conceal the truth from Jack on a daily basis. And given the way her heart was jumping around in her chest, she wondered if she was going to be able to survive this much of God's blessing.

Don't miss
The Nanny's Secret Baby *by Lee Tobin McClain,*
available August 2019 wherever
Love Inspired® books and ebooks are sold.

www.LoveInspired.com